The Incunabulum

Part Two: MALEDICTIONS

Steven Christopher

The Incunabulum Part Two: MALEDICTIONS
Copyright © 2018 by Steven Christopher

Library of Congress Control Number:	2018909935
ISBN-13: Paperback:	978-1-64398-258-8

Printed in the United States of America

 LitFire
PUBLISHING

LitFire LLC
1-800-511-9787
www.litfirepublishing.com
order@litfirepublishing.com

SYNOPSIS

This is the second book in the tetralogy collectively called The Incunabulum.

The first book, **The Incunabulum** part one: *Portents*, told how 15-year old Nathan Christian, in taking a short cut home through the neglected old cemetery bordering his house, happened to notice that the doors to one of the decaying mausoleums were open. Unable to resist exploring the interior of the tomb, Nathan slipped inside only to encounter there the very beautiful and mysterious Phebe, a girl who (unbeknownst to Nathan) is a vampire. And despite Phebe's rather peculiar habits of sequestering herself (by day) inside a mausoleum and reposing in one of its unoccupied crypts, Nathan all but instantly fell in love with the girl. To further augment the mystery surrounding her, Phebe revealed to Nathan that (inexplicably) she already knew his name; the street on which he lives; even his date of birth. Aware also about the cruelty he regularly suffers at the hands of his abusive aunt, Amelia Christian, in whose home the boy lives, Phebe prevailed upon Nathan to allow her to kill Amelia for him.

But while Nathan was concealed in his aunt's bedroom closet, after having opened one of the bedroom windows for Phebe to enter in by, he watched in helpless terror as some monstrous creature slipped into the room and slaughtered his aunt in her bed. Waking from the swoon into which he had fallen, Nathan was introduced by Phebe to her two "traveling companions": the one, a six-foot tall, cadaverous-looking man by the name of Antal Vrancic; and the other, a pale, cruel-faced child by the name of Candy, who revealed itself to Nathan as being neither male nor female, but a "hermaphrodite". And while Phebe continued to repose (during the daylight hours) in the old mausoleum, her two companions,

Vrancic and Candy, dwelt in the house with Nathan, who was sternly warned by Vrancic never to go down into the basement as he was now using that region of the house as his lodgings.

A day or two later, however, Nathan stole down into the basement only to discover the gruesome doings to which Vrancic had been up to down there. Then, on a night following a strange yet amorous encounter in the shower with Phebe, Nathan woke in his bed to the hermaphrodite child, Candy, bending over him and breathing into his face. The odd experience caused a curious change in Nathan, for Candy had (temporarily) breathed into the boy the alluring nature and sexual appetite of the vampire. Feelings of sensuality and amorous desires began to course through Nathan; and, without realizing where he was going, he made his way to the house of Lori Carbone, a classmate of his with whom he'd long been infatuated and the sister of roughneck biker, Marty Carbone. Having stolen into the backyard, Nathan seemed to beguile Lori with his words and mere glance: and once he had drawn her into the garage, his passion for the girl rapidly intensified into an outright macabre lust. Unable to resist the urge to taste Lori's blood, Nathan sank his teeth into her neck. But at the sound of the girl's terrified screams, Nathan was finally roused from the weird enchantment to which he'd succumbed, and, in cutting through the cemetery on his homeward flight, he collapsed in a deep stupor on one of the graves.

This second book, **The Incunabulum** part two: *MALEDICTIONS*, now tells of Marty Carbone's coming to Nathan's house seeking revenge for what Nathan did to his sister, Lori, and the curse which is placed upon him by Candy for his trespass. It also recounts Nathan's discovery of Phebe's vampiric nature; her revealing to him how she received such an accursed existence; and her disclosure regarding an ancient book – an incunabulum, in fact – in whose pages is preserved a spell that can remove her curse: there is only one catch, the spell (Nathan is told) requires the blood of a particular mortal – in this case, his. Moreover, it tells of Nathan's neighbor, old Mr Schiller's growing suspicions regarding the "mysterious" disappearance of the boy's aunt, Amelia, and his persistent spying on Nathan's nightly excursions into the ruined old cemetery. Ultimately, his intractable curiosity and prying lead him to the old mausoleum, and there Phebe herself condemns Mr Schiller to an evil fate by way of a most ghoulish curse.

The third book of The Incunabulum tells of Mr Schiller's gradual (and hideous) transformation as the moon waxes toward the full, and his wife's suspicions and eventual discovery of his horrific deeds in the neighborhood cemeteries; while the fourth and last book recounts Nathan and Phebe's mission to obtain the ancient incunabulum and use the spell preserved within its pages to remove Phebe's vampiric curse.

Contents

Chapter 1   "...I warn you he is clean out of his mind; and...in his wit they could not bring him again, nor to know himself...for I saw and heard by his countenance that he is mad forever..."
—Le Morte D'Arthur..1

Chapter 2   ...Macduff. 0 horror, horror, horror! Tongue nor heart cannot conceive nor name thee!
Macbeth and Lennox. What's the matter?
Macduff. Confusion now hath made his masterpiece. ...Approach the chamber, and destroy your sight... Do not bid me speak;
See, and then... let us meet
And question this most bloody piece of work, to know it further..."
—Macbeth 39

Chapter 3   "...Then in a few short hours a dire woe was visited upon them... for he dealt out fierce and deadly wounds, slaying now this, now that one. Many a one, having fallen in his blood, he did to death..."
—The Nibelungenlied

"...They made a horrible groaning as he shattered their skulls, and the ground seethed with their blood... All were lying in the dust and weltering in their blood: like so many fish netted out of the sea..."
—The Odyssey 77

Chapter 4   "... She sprang... at my wound, which she began to suck with an air of inexpressible delight. She sipped the blood slowly and carefully... then she again pressed the wound with her lips so as to draw out a few more red drops... 'Drink, and let my life enter your body with my blood'..."
—La morte amoureuse 113

Chapter 5   "... sleeping
Soft in the bed,
Empty of sorrow
... She awoke
With all pleasure gone,
Swimming in blood..."
—The Elder Edda

" ... nothing but evil can come if I tell you this secret. For the
mercy of God do not require it of me. If you but knew, you would
withdraw yourself from my love, and I should be lost indeed..."
—The Lays of Marie de France.. 142

Chapter 6   "...Youth: You're an empusa—a hideous Vampire!—covered all over
in blood and gobbets of gore...
—Ecclesiazusae 180

Chapter 7   "...Dreadful is the woe you bid me recall,
For it renews the sad remembrance of my fate:
All that I saw, and part of which I was
...But if your longing is so great to know
how calamity befell me,
Though my spirit shudders at the remembrance
and recoils in pain,
I will tell you of that fatal night..."
—The Aeneid... 229

Chapter 8   "...Once this face was bright, this brow clear...
And I possessed great wealth...
A manor, with gardens... and many riches...
Now, far from kith and kin, misery is my lot...
It is all but agonizing to tell you of my torments.
I do so that you might understand,
And, upon this, consider well,
You are in grave danger:
If you wish to avoid such woes,
Then learn from my fate..."
—The Awntyrs off Arthure 285

Chapter 9   "…You have displayed great zeal… in seeking me out, and it will not seem surprising if you don't gain a great deal of good fortune from your encounter with me… I also lay this curse upon you that these eyes of mine will be always before your sight… and this will bring you to your death…"
—The Saga of Grettir the Strong

"…It's my will now that… you have only anguish from me. And it will come to pass, I assure you. Moreover, all the miseries that have happened here were my doing, I'll no longer hide it from you. I'm to blame. On you, though, I now fix this curse: that my spell causes you unspeakable woe… Indeed, before all is over, every person will see and know it…"
—Eyrbyggia Saga 328

CHAPTER ONE

*"...I warn you he is clean out of his mind; and...in his wit
they could not bring him again, nor to know himself...for I
saw and heard by his countenance that he is mad forever..."*

—*Le Morte D'Arthur*

Scarcely ten minutes after Nathan had wandered off, dazed and
horribly weary, from the premises of Lori Carbone's home, Scott
Webler and his younger brother, Terence, together with Kerry Stark
and Todd Bauer, arrived at its front door and rang the bell. The
door never opened, however, and not even so much as a whisper
sounded from within the house.

Having waited more than half a minute before ringing the
doorbell two or three more times, and still receiving no answer,
Scott Webler decided to knock at the back door, and so, led the
others round back into the yard. After knocking several times
on the back door, and calling out, between each knock, first Lori
Carbone's name, then Marty's, Kerry Stark said: "Come on, let's go;
there's obviously no one here."

"I don't get it," said Scott Webler. "Lori sent me a text message
only a half hour ago: she said she'd be home."

Todd Bauer, glancing round the yard, suddenly noted Lori
Carbone's sunglasses and flip-flops, as well as her cell phone and
a pack of Parliament cigarettes, over by the pool; he was about to
point them out to the others when all at once it seemed to him that
some faint noise had caught his attention. He stood listening for
a moment or two. Presently it sounded again. The others heard it
too, for they stood now with their brows creased and exchanging,

1

each with the other, one or two puzzled and questioning glances. And through the long interval of silence that followed, Scott Webler asked, "You guys hear something?" His brother Terence drew closer to him and looked uneasily round the yard. "Yeah," said Todd Bauer, "I did."

Kerry Stark was nodding his head. "Me, too;" he said, his voice sinking a little; "it kind of sounded like someone crying."

Just then they heard it again—this time less faint, and more sustained—low soft whimpering and sobbing.

For several moments they all stood listening and looking around. Then, "Over there," whispered Todd Bauer, pointing in the direction from which it seemed to him that the moans and sobs were coming. And together the four of them slowly, cautiously edged their way over to the garage. Bending down a little, each then peered inquisitively in under the half-raised door, and saw Lori Carbone huddled low against the rear wall of the garage in a dark and narrow space between her brother's Mustang and his old Panhead motorcycle. She was crouched on the bare, dusty concrete of the garage floor without a stitch of clothing on. Her knees were drawn up under her chin, her arms were wrapped round her legs, and she was shaking and shuddering and weeping bitterly.

Shocked and astonished, Scott Webler and the others continued to peer into the garage at her with their mouths agape and their eyes, round and wide, unblinkingly fixed. After several moments, Scott Webler softly called her name, and asked her once or twice, in timid and doubtful tones, "What happened?"

But Lori Carbone appeared to be utterly oblivious to his words, of his presence, the stunned expressions of the others, and the four pairs of eyes that remained fastened upon her in amazement and disbelief. She merely went on shuddering and sniveling at the rear of the garage, and the one or two things she did moan and gurgle between her sobbing didn't seem to make any sense to either Scott Webler or to any of the others.

At last then, the four boys ventured cautiously into the garage, drew near, and stooped over Lori Carbone, regarding her curiously. They noted bruises on her arms and legs, and saw what looked like impressions in the skin about her shoulders and forearms, impressions that, for all the world, resembled the bite marks of teeth.

Scott Webler bent his head low to look into Lori Carbone's tear-filled eyes. "You alright?" he whispered, not knowing what else to say to her, and half afraid to say anything at all.

As tears gushed down her dirt-grimed cheeks, she rolled her eyes. Then, choking back her sobs, she said: "Do I look alright, asshole!"

"But what happened?" asked Kerry Stark.

In the pause that followed a fit of sobs, she replied, "I was raped!"

A stunned and longish silence succeeded this staggering revelation, until, finding his voice once more, Scott Webler managed to ask, "By who?"

At first only a gush of tears and blubbering whimpers follow-ed his question; then, "By that fucking psycho, Nathan!" said Lori Carbone, and, for the next few moments, she hid her face in her hands, and groaned and swore. Meanwhile, Scott Webler and the others were struck dumb; and after regarding her in silence for a moment or two longer, they stood there speechlessly exchanging shocked and incredulous looks among themselves.

"Wait," began Scott Webler in absolute disbelief; "you're saying *Nathan*—Nathan Christian—*raped* you?"

But suddenly Lori Carbone became utterly still; she silenced her sobbing and sniveling, and, removing her hands from before her face, gazed with fixed, frightened eyes past Scott Webler and the other boys. Then, in a low, trembling voice, "Is he still out there?" she asked them.

"There's no one out there," answered Scott Webler; then, after a brief pause, he said, "Lori, what happened?" He reached his hand out to touch her, but Lori Carbone shrank away, cursing and weeping. "Leave me alone!" she screamed. "Don't touch me! Just get the hell away from me!" And, snatching up her bloodstained body wrap that was lying on the floor next to her, she rose, holding it draped in front of her, edged her way whimpering past the boys, and crept cautiously out of the garage. Having dashed over to the back door, she immediately broke into a fit of terrific shuddering sobs as she quickly drew it open and slipped into the house.

Once inside, Lori Carbone's initial thought was to run upstairs to the safety and seclusion of her room. But she rejected this intention almost instantly; for the thought of confining, sequestering herself within the restricted space of its four walls filled her with loathing. Moreover, the ugly notion of Nathan suddenly returning and stealing up the stairs and into her room terrified her. And so she chose instead to remain on the ground floor of the house and wait there for her brother Marty to come home.

Sobbing inconsolably, Lori Carbone began to pace frantically up and down the floor of the living room. Still too frightened to run upstairs to her bedroom and get some clothes from one of her dresser drawers, she merely continued to clutch desperately at her dust-grimed, bloodstained body wrap with both hands, pressing it firmly to her bosom so that it hung down in front of her to cover her nakedness. At one point, with phone in hand, she even made the serious effort of dialing 911 to report what had happened to her to the police; but having got only as far as the first two digits, a miserable feeling of shame, doubt, and pointlessness swept suddenly over her aching heart, and, groaning aloud, she let the handset slip from her trembling fingers, and dropped down onto the sofa in anguish and despair. And there, for the next several minutes, she sat gently rocking her body back and forth, weeping and moaning hysterically.

When, however, her tears had ceased for a brief interval to flow, Lori Carbone continued to sit there on the sofa, silently rocking to and fro, with her under-lip quivering, and her anxious glance the while roving in misery and confusion round about the room. For a moment it fixed itself on the coat and hat stand by the foyer door. Hanging on it, among a number of other garments, she noticed her brother's navy-blue hoodie. She glanced down then at the bloodstained body wrap she still gripped with both lean hands in front of her and, with a low sob and whimper, she rose, went over to the hat stand, let her body wrap fall, and quickly snatched down Marty's hoodie. Before slipping into it, however, she glanced once more at her shoulders and arms to survey for a moment or two the scratches, bite marks, and bruises Nathan had left upon her skin; pressed tenderly for an instant with the tips of her fingers at the painful abrasion inflicted by Nathan's teeth to the side of her neck; and, in an agonizing gush of despondency, her tears flowed anew, streaming down her cheeks and gurgling in her throat. Then, huddling herself into Marty Carbone's rather oversized hoodie, she sat herself down again in utter wretchedness on the sofa to wait for her brother's return.

Meanwhile, outside, Todd Bauer, Kerry Stark, Scott Webler and young Terence, continued to dither in the yard of Lori Carbone's home, glancing every now and again over at the back door, and discussing softly among themselves what they should do.

"Hey, maybe we better call the police," suggested Kerry Stark.

Scott Webler made a sour face. "Yeah, right!" he jeered. "And tell them what? That some faggot named Nathan raped Lori."

"So you don't believe her?" asked Todd Bauer.

"That Nathan raped her? Come on!" said Scott Webler.

But Kerry Stark was quick to counter: "Well, *something* obviously happened to her."

Just then they heard the thick blatting of the V-twin engine of a Harley Davidson as it came roaring up the street. And they knew at once that Marty Carbone had returned. They heard him pull up in front of the house and kill the engine. The sound of the sidestand going down could then be heard on the quieting street, and the boys dashed down the alleyway to confront Marty Carbone as he was advancing up the walkway to the front door of his house.

Scott Webler quickly informed him how they had discovered Lori Carbone in the garage, the awful state she was in, and everything she had said to them.

Marty Carbone rushed inside, while Scott and Terence Webler, together with Kerry Stark and Todd Bauer, lingered in the walkway at the foot of the front porch steps.

Lori Carbone was still seated on the sofa, rocking her body to and fro with her face hidden in her hands, when her brother came striding into the room. He bent down beside her and asked, "What the hell happened?"

Lori raised her face, smoothed back her hair and, with tears gushing down her blotched cheeks, she told her brother in a low, sob-choked voice that she had been raped in the garage by Nathan.

"Who's Nathan?" asked Marty Carbone. "Have I seen him before?"

Lori Carbone wiped her eyes a moment, then in a trembling voice, "Don't you remember?" she said. "About a week ago! The guy who you yelled at in my room because he pushed me down!"

"That little fuck—again!" bellowed Marty Carbone. "You know where this kid lives?"

Lori Carbone continued to sob and snivel miserably. "I don't know," she whimpered. "I think it's that house by the cemetery, down the block from where you cut the hole in the fence."

Marty Carbone exhaled menacingly through his nostrils and stood up. Then his eyes narrowed and his face darkened with rage, as he adjusted the friction-fit leather sheath that was hanging from his belt. In it he carried a large hunting-knife, a Buck's Zipper, in fact, with a 7 inch guthook, drop-point blade forged of ATS-34 stainless steel that featured a razor-sharp 'zipper' on its edge; and it was a well known fact among those who knew Marty Carbone (whether as a friend or a foe) that whenever he drew that blade it never went back into its sheath without its edge having first tasted someone's blood.

As Marty Carbone came stalking out of the house and down the front steps, Scott Webler and his brother Terence quickly drew to one side, while Kerry Stark and Todd Bauer drew to the other to let him pass. They watched in silence as he strode over to his motorcycle, climbed onto it with a swing of his leg and gave it a ferocious kick. And the instant the Harley's V-twin engine roared to life all four boys came running eagerly over. But Marty Carbone never even so much as glanced at them. As though oblivious of their very existence, he sat glaring straight before him, lit a cigarette, pulled his long black hair back into a ponytail and, with a curious, crab-like movement, he first wheeled his bike backwards, then, throttling up, he shifted into gear and rode off in a thunderous rumble down the street, the tip of his cigarette glowing fiercely like the lit fuse to a firecracker.

Scott Webler turned gleefully to the others and said, "Bet he's going over to Nathan's house!"

"Alright!" said Todd Bauer.

Kerry Stark grinned and said: "Well, let's go!"

"Wait!" said Scott Webler, and, producing his cell phone, he immediately began texting.

"What are you doing?" asked Kerry Stark.

"Telling Neil Keddy to hurry over to Nathan's house," said Scott Webler. "That Marty just went over there to bust his little skull"; he paused a moment to glance up from his phone and smirk at Kerry and Todd; then said, "You two start texting some of the other guys. Tell them to meet us over at Nathan's house; that Marty Carbone's already on his way there to kick Nathan's bony little ass."

In no time at all both Todd Bauer and Kerry Stark had their cell phones out, and no sooner had they finished sending their texts than the two of them went racing down the street with Scott and Terence Webler, on their way to Nathan's house, all four of them excitedly anticipating the brutal beating which they were virtually certain Nathan was about to receive from a dangerously enraged Marty Carbone.

Now, by the time they had turned down Nathan's block, they could see Marty Carbone's motorcycle already parked in the street just in front of Nathan's house. It was leaning silently next to the curb, at a typically cool, jaunty slant, on its kickstand. The boys glanced at it as they drew near; then, without a word, all four walked up to the brick steps of the front porch and paused there to stare at the cheerless exterior of the house, with its blind-drawn front windows, and its fast-shut front door.

Todd Bauer suggested that they all go inside, but no on advanced up the steps. "Let's wait for Neil and the others first," said Scott Webler; and so they remained, one and all, loitering yet a while at the bottommost step of the porch.

After a minute or two, Kerry Stark said: "What do you guys think Marty's gonna do in there to Nathan?"

"Probably rip him a new asshole, that's what," said Scott Webler.

Todd Bauer suddenly stopped texting and, looking up from his phone, said: "Yeah, but, what if Marty winds up killing Nathan; you know, like, beating him to death?" Scott Webler slipped his cell phone into his back pocket and grinned. "Then that's one less faggot in the world," he quipped, and they all broke into laughter and sneers.

As for Marty Carbone, when he pulled up on his Harley in front of Nathan's house, he parked it next to the curb, climbed off, took one last drag on his cigarette before flicking it into the street, and then marched up the steps of the front porch. He yanked the screen door open, and, after having hammered with fist and foot half a dozen times on the heavy storm door, he tried turning the knob. It yielded with a faint click instantly, and the door itself easily opened, swinging an inch or two slightly inward—apparently it had been left unlocked!

Marty Carbone wrapped his fingers around the rubberized non-slip grip of his hunting knife and drew it from its sheath; he then pushed the door open, stepped across its threshold, and paused for a moment or two to gaze straight before him from the foyer area (in which he now stood and whose door was ajar to its fullest gape) into the living room just beyond it. As he stood there, he heard the heavy storm door swing slowly to again behind him with a protracted and eerie creaking of its hinges. And almost the very instant after the door had shut and the squeaking of its hinges had ceased, another sound made itself heard: the ominous clicking of its lock and dead bolt.

Marty Carbone turned round at once and glared at the door for several moments. Somehow it had been securely fastened. His face distorted into a fierce scowl at the notion of some practical joker lurking somewhere hereabouts, and, tightening his grip on the haft of his knife, he turned once more, took one or two steps forward to the foyer's threshold, and swept the living room with his eyes.

Almost instantly, with a single glance round the room, Marty Carbone was aware of neglect and a curtailing or utter suspension of the cheering human influences in its silent and seemingly forsaken premises. Its curtained windows, the thin veil of dust on floor and furnishings, the mournful hush of the grandfather clock in the corner, whose black serpentine hands never stirred past the raised brass Arabic numerals over which they had come to a standstill, all pointed to this conclusion.

And suddenly, with a slight but curious uneasiness, Marty Carbone caught himself (only for a moment) hankering to get back outside, back into the sunlight. But all at once he muttered a curse under his breath at such foolish notions, advanced quickly into the living room and, halting in the very center of its unswept floor, he called out in a deep bellowing voice: "Nathan! It's Marty, Marty Carbone, you little prick!" But the words, as soon as they left his lips, seemed to have been smothered away, as though he had shouted them into a heavy curtain, so deep was the stillness that reigned throughout the house.

For a moment or two, Marty Carbone constrained himself to breathe very softly as he listened intently, but nothing stirred: there wasn't a sound or sign of life anywhere in the house. And yet, and yet, a very definite, a very potent feeling grew steadily within him, an awareness, really, that behind the deep silence of the house, round some hidden corner of one of its sunless rooms, there was something untoward, a faint, stealthy activity just within the veiling edges of the room's stillness: as though some cunning furtive observer was secretly waiting, listening, taking him in with a sneering pair of merciless, penetrating eyes.

And all of a sudden, as by some irresistible impulse, Marty Carbone found himself glancing uneasily round the room. After a moment or two, he gave a loud snort, frowned heavily, and shouted,"Hey! Nathan! It's no use hiding, scumbag! I'll find you sooner or later! So you might as well get your ass over here now!" But even as he said the words, the curtain of silence only seemed to gather all the more thickly about him, muffling up the very sound of his voice.

By now, curious feelings, to which Marty Carbone was thoroughly unaccustomed, began to steal slowly, steadily through his heart—feelings of disquiet, anxiety, perhaps even a shade of *fear*. He strove fiercely, intensely to oppose them, but they persisted, and grew apace within him just the same, refusing to be dispelled. Indeed the airlessness of the room, the artificial twilight produced by its curtained windows, and that peculiar deathly quiet which continued to prevail throughout the house seemed only to add to, and magnify, those acute feelings of discomfort in him. And in a final effort to banish them altogether from his heart, Marty Carbone opened his mouth to demand all the more loudly that Nathan come out now and face him, when a lump of considerable size came suddenly up into his throat, nearly choking him; and only after mastering it with great difficulty was he able at last to bawl out: "You hear me, Nathan, you little shit! You and me, we've got a score to settle!"

But despite the volume of, and the bluster in, his voice, his growing uneasiness remained. For once again the menacing stillness of the house seemed to swallow up his words, and only a deeper, more forbidding silence to follow them.

For a space of some seconds Marty Carbone held his breath, listening intently for any rumor or sign of an occupant moving about in any of the rooms either on this floor or on the one above. All, however, was still—too still. But then, even as Marty Carbone looked first to this side of the room, then to that, licked his parched lips, and passed his hunting knife from the clammy palm of his one hand into that of the other, a sound as of odd hushed whispering reached his ears.

Keeping perfectly still, Marty Carbone continued to listen. Under his breath, he said, "What the fu —" But his mouth shut with a snap, for in the same instant, he became convinced that someone had laughed. He waited; a second or two later he knew he was right. It had not been his imagination. For once again he caught a sound as of faint, child-like laughter coming from one of the rooms.

And even as that low, soft tittering went steadily on, Marty Carbone continued to glance rapidly about himself with furrowed brow, not only uncertain as to the room or vicinity from which the laughter was now emanating, but altogether baffled as to the line of direction along which it was traveling. For it seemed to come to him from everywhere, at once—behind, in front, on either hand, even from overhead; and as it continued to sound on for several seconds more, before finally ending in a subdued yet distinct *"tee-hee"*, Marty Carbone was sure he had discerned a note of unmistakable mockery in it.

Then, through the dense curtain of silence that, having once more descended, seemed presently to thicken all about him, Marty Carbone again raised his voice, "That you, Nathan? You think this is funny, shit-head?" And with several rapid strides forward, he advanced into the dining room. He paused a moment or two to look around, and once again became uneasily conscious of that same menacing silence within its gloomy blind-drawn space. For a fraction of an instant the stillness affected his nerves acutely, but he was quick to dismiss the sharp desire to turn and run—run for his very life—out the front door again. Instead he remarked (or, at the very least, *hoped* to persuade, convince himself that), "This is bullshit!"; and, after having snarled a string of curses under his breath at the deep, uncomfortable silence of the house, he bawled out, at the top of his voice, "Hey! Nathan! You here, asshole?"

And without either keeping still to listen, or pausing a moment or two to wait for a challenge to this extremely uncivil inquiry, Marty Carbone pressed on through the dining room. Oddly enough, however, he caught himself striding more softly, almost cautiously, forward into the kitchen area as though he were wary of encountering... *who?* he asked, becoming suddenly annoyed with himself. Nathan? Some fifteen year-old little punk?

Coming to a standstill over by the kitchen sink, Marty Carbone spat upon the tiled floor as a gesture of his contempt for such thoughts, and, "Bah!" he scoffed—almost scoffed aloud -"That'll be the day!" And as his eyes began to search eagerly for any sign of Nathan in this dim and uninviting room of the house, there came again, for several seconds, that same phantom-like sound as of muted giggling, only this time it was accompanied by the hurried pit-a-pat of light footsteps proceeding from somewhere inside one of the rooms through which he had just passed.

Marty Carbone instantly turned and stood gazing from the doorway of the kitchen through the area of the dining room, into the living room. He was sure he had glimpsed someone's shadow glide rapidly across the boards of its floor.

"I'm warning you, Nathan!" growled Marty Carbone. "If you think this is a game, you little douche-bag, you're wrong—*dead wrong!*" But even as those menacing words went rumbling off his tongue, he could not help but notice that the voice pronouncing them was (inexplicably) neither so harsh nor so loud this time. Moreover, there was a distinct note of doubt, of timidity—even a tinge of apprehension—in it.

For the space of nearly one full minute, Marty Carbone stood motionless in the kitchen, peering intently from its doorway into the other rooms. Then, across the profound hush, he heard another sound. Some of the floorboards in the living room had faintly creaked, as under the stealthy, quiet tread of small, nimble feet. Someone was moving around in there.

Cursing savagely under his breath, Marty Carbone rushed through the doorway, crossed the floor of the dining room in three long strides, and halted again in the middle of the living room floor, only to find the room—*empty!* And presently, while gazing round its sunless premises—all oddly screened from the daylight—he became undeniably convinced of the strange disquieting impression that there was definitely something about the room, its very *atmosphere,* that was not quite right. In addition to this, an ominous sense or feeling reached him, touching his nerves as with a warning, cautioning finger (and this time far more acutely than before) that somewhere in the house someone or something—intensely aware of his intrusion—was steadily regarding him in a cruelly gloating, malevolent way.

Of course, Marty Carbone's less-than perspicuous brains were scarcely able to articulate (even to himself) precisely what he was now experiencing in such clear terminology and phrasing; both his limited intellect and meager vocabulary (not including vulgar slang) made it impossible for him to express either his thoughts or emotions in such concise language. He merely knew, or understood—instinctively, intuitively—that, quite simply, something *in,* or about, the room in which he now stood was beginning to make him feel deathly afraid.

Turning now first to this side, then to that, Marty Carbone anxiously scanned the room, striving desperately to glimpse the unseen watcher whose stirless gaze he continued to feel so resentfully fixed upon himself. But there was neither sign nor sound now of anyone in the room. Only this brooding awful menace that seemed to pervade the very air between its walls. And all at once Marty Carbone was faced with the discomfiting impression that he was standing in the midst of a hostile crowd instead of an empty room; for its entire mood, or character, had become increasingly threatening, sinister, malicious; and seemed to foster and instill—*dread.* What's more, distressing feelings of panic were fast beginning to flood his heart, reducing him, moment by moment, to a terrified child.

Now and again, too, as his glance shifted uneasily from one article of furniture to another, he thought he actually did catch, with the tail of his eye, a fleeting glimpse of a face or head—though whether real or the product of his jumpy nerves he could not say—now come peering out at him for an instant from behind the grandfather clock, now duck down its head again behind the back of the sofa. And for a single instant he even thought he felt the icy fingers of a hand faintly brush the very skin of his arm, as though someone had been standing close beside him.

With a sharp gasp, Marty Carbone recoiled and, shuddering irrepressibly, struck out to right or left with his knife in the perceived direction of his invisible neighbor. The blade's razor-sharp edge, however, cut through little more than thin air. Apparently whatever had touched him and been in his proximity but moments before was not there now (at least nothing of a *physical* nature).

Marty Carbone's glance, meanwhile, continued to course its way fearfully over the room's drab shadowy walls and furnishings. All self-confidence had long since forsaken him; and with it, currently, had withered away all his courage, arrogance, and masterful nature. The fingers that now clutched the haft of his Buck's Zipper hunting knife were trembling uncontrollably. At the same time, confusing and contradictory impulses kept racing through his frightened mind; for one moment, a fierce desire to escape, either by door or window, would suddenly flood the recesses of his pounding heart, while the next, he felt himself overcome by an almost irresistible urge to cringe and cower and hide himself away in some darkened corner of the room—but from *what*?

Once again Marty Carbone swept the premises with his eyes, eyes now round and wide and filled with an absolute terror. He felt as if the blood in his veins, having ceased to flow, had suddenly congealed to ice; and his entire body began to violently tremble. By now his heart was no more dauntless than that of a frightened little child's, a child who, utterly afraid of the dark, had been locked inside a room with all the lights out. He was breathing heavily now, virtually panting, gasping. He kept turning fretfully now this way, now that, glancing frantically into every corner of the room as though in desperate search of someone or some*thing*, and yet terrified of who or *what* he might at last discover. The sweat was pouring down his face and from his limbs. Now and again, too, without his realizing it, his thick under-lip would quiver, and a soft, low blubbering sound would suddenly escape his gaping mouth.

And all in a moment, Marty Carbone—the once intrepid, macho bruiser of Middle Village—found himself more or less beginning to whimper hysterically and on the verge of bursting into tears. But then, at the faint sound of stealthy footsteps behind him, he caught his breath, spun round on his heels, and his bulging frightened eyes fixed themselves on the tall, spare, black-clad figure of Antal Vrancic, standing only a few paces distant from him in the middle of the dining room floor, coldly regarding him.

At first, Marty Carbone could only gape with great staring eyes at the shape of this strange, silent apparition, whose forbidding stature was more than a head above his own. For in the dim and drowsing dream-like twilight of the curtained room Marty Carbone found it rather difficult to tell whether the figure now confronting him was in fact real or merely some delusion, a phantom conjured by his frightened mind. Motionless in his black suit, with dark-ringed eyes fixed steadfastly, unblinkingly on those of Marty Carbone's, he appeared more like a cadaver either recently come from the mortician's embalming room or destined for its coffin in some mortuary's viewing-room.

But as to his being a mere phantom of the senses, of that curious impression Marty Carbone was quickly undeceived. For quite suddenly Vrancic's lips faintly curled into a half-sly grin or sneer, while the speck-like pupils of his eyes shifted for an instant from Marty Carbone's face to rest intently on the hunting knife clenched in his hand. Otherwise he remained perfectly still, as though from top to toe rigor mortis had stiffened every joint and muscle in his body rendering him rigid as a pole.

Once more Marty Carbone's wildly bulging eyes stole anxiously over the drab walls and furnishings of the room; and then, still speechless, he fixed his gaze on Vrancic again. At length, "You Nathan's ol' man?" he managed to ask, unable, however, to suppress the slight tremor in his voice.

Yet again Vrancic's luminous black eyes refastened themselves unswervingly on Marty Carbone's face. "I think," came the sharp retort after a longish silence, "the more pertinent question would be, what do you want here?"

Marty Carbone mopped his brow with a thick hairy forearm and, trying to regain some modicum of his courage, he said, "Nathan! That's what!" And brandishing the blade of his knife at Vrancic, he added, "He raped my sister!"

A faint gleam of interest, almost amusement, stole into Vrancic's eyes. "I see," remarked Vrancic all but cheerfully. "And you've come to avenge her honor by using that knife on him; is that it?" Steadily grinning, he paused for a moment or two, and into the luminous blackness of his eyes had come a wicked ray of scorn. "Well, then," he went on, the sinister grin on his face suddenly expanding into a positive leer of triumph, "far be it from me to stand in your way." And raising his voice, as though addressing another occupant in the room whose mysterious presence remained undetectable by Marty Carbone's watchful eyes, Vrancic began to utter a series of words in a language wholly unintelligible to his crude and unsophisticated intruder. What Marty Carbone, however, did understand was that the language he was now listening to sounded not only harsh and unpleasant to his ears, but to all intents and purposes like the grinding together of so many stones, or the low guttural snarling of a pack of beasts.

Having uttered, then, the last syllable, Vrancic glanced eagerly past Marty Carbone, at the doors to the sun-room; but only for a moment; then immediately resettled his cold intent stare on the face of his unsuspecting visitor.

Then, from somewhere behind him, Marty Carbone heard a faint noise as of the wards of a lock being stealthily unfastened. He quickly wheeled round and saw at once the handle of the doors to the sun-room slowly turning. Next, the sharp click of the door latch being released sounded through the profound hush of the room like the cracking of a whip; and, with a dreadfully protracted, almost sly, furtive motion, the doors began to open outward: at first no more than a mere crack, then, softly, steadily, wider, wider, wider.

Meanwhile, Marty Carbone stood there, watching the exasperating slowness of their movement as though spellbound. He wanted to shout out, sound off a string of curse words, or rush over to the doors themselves and slam them to again, but before he could make a sound or move so much as a finger, he suddenly realized that, after what had seemed a matter of hours, they now stood open to their fullest gape. He noted, too, that, beyond them, the sun-room's interior was nearly as dark as a cavern, and that, presently, from out of its dense gloom, into the living room's thin shadowy dusk, had stepped, without a sound, what appeared to be, in face and form, a very lean, deathly pale child of ten or eleven.

For nearly a full minute Marty Carbone's gaze traveled uneasily over the curious figure of this peculiar child: from its rather long, flaxen-colored locks, to its narrow, bony shoulders, along the spindly calfless legs, down to its bare, narrow little feet—but whether it was male or female he was scarcely able to decide, its gender seemed to utterly mystify him. Further compounding this uncertainty in regard to the ambiguity of its sex was the fact that while the child exhibited some very definite masculine characteristics, it was unquestionably attired in feminine clothing, having on its slim, agile frame a pink cold-shoulder tee-shirt and belted twill shorts.

Meanwhile, mute and still as the very shadows around it, the child continued to stand there, hardly a dozen paces away, peering straight across at Marty Carbone intently. Then, the pale, thin, coldly-grinning lips of the child seemed to breathe across at Marty Carbone, in sweet, almost wheedling tones, "Give to me that which I crave; offer to me that which I want; surrender to me that which I need!"

And edging one or two rapid steps forward across the boards of the floor towards Marty Carbone, the child abruptly stopped a few paces away—and stood with its head slightly leaning sidelong. And as the piercingly sharp, bright blue eyes in the ghastly pallor of its face steadily continued to look at Marty Carbone, the child stooped its head forward a little not only to gaze all the more eagerly, almost *hungrily*, at Marty Carbone, but to sniff long and steadily at him, like a wild beast, with wide quivering nostrils, as though it were savoring, relishing whatever odor it now appeared to scent about him.

But as Marty Carbone gazed steadily back at the strange, androgynous face and figure of this child, instead of there stirring in him a touch of amusement or annoyance—for he knew at once that it was *not* Nathan he was now looking at—he felt himself involuntarily wince and shudder; and, like a man struck dumb, simply continue to stand there and stare. For with the force of a shock, Marty Carbone all at once felt, surmised, *knew* that the being which now stood before him at half his own height and in the deceitfully innocuous guise of a child was something more than human—much more.

Yet again that weird, gynandromorphic adolescent moved a step or two nearer, and yet again abruptly stayed its steps. And its gaze fixed itself on the face of Marty Carbone with such a devouring intensity that this time Marty Carbone actually quailed before it; for the pin-prick pupils in its brilliant blue eyes suddenly shone with a cold inhuman malice and cruelty.

Then, all at once, as if breathed against (or into) his very ear, the soft, seductive words of an eerily bewitching voice seemed to come to Marty Carbone without his being able to determine precisely where they were emanating *from*—coaxing, compelling, commanding him to "sink now onto your knees before your master and willingly offer him, as a libation, to drink of your life's blood."

But as Marty Carbone continued to stand where he was and gaze on in silent astonishment at the child, never venturing even for a moment to remove his eyes from that sinister, bloodless face, the expression in its features suddenly sharpened into unspeakable hatred, and a palpable horror seemed to gather with an icy coldness over Marty Carbone's skin and move all about him. He was shaking now from head to toe, as yet again, like a vast, towering ineluctable wave, the sense or knowledge swept in upon him that he was now in the presence of a terrible, dangerous, deadly being. Almost in the very same instant, he realized, too, that in the lissom, seemingly youthful body of this weird, uncanny child there dwelt indeed something as lethal as it was ancient, and as evil-intentioned as it was eldritch. And a man such as Marty Carbone who, up until that day, had never before known trembling fear or a quailing dread, suddenly began to quake, shudder, and blench in an anguish of harrowing fright.

In less than an instant all the color had drained out of Marty Carbone's cheeks, leaving them almost as pale and bloodless as the face of the child's just opposite his own. "Y-You're not N-N-Nathan," he managed to stammer. And into the fiercely bright eyes that continued to steadily peer out at him across the space that was between them had come a smile half-venomous, half-gloating. "No; I am not," came the child's sneering reply. "Although it would have been better for your sake if I were." Then, with its eyes fixed full in a hideous smile, the child broke into a soft, low protracted laugh that was both grand and malevolent. The sound, once heard, was not soon forgotten, and left Marty Carbone feeling not only appalled, but very nearly petrified.

For a moment or two he gazed on at the child in tongue-tied awe; then, gulping back the sizeable lump that had come up into his throat, "Who are you?" he asked in an almost breathless whisper. And from out of the dead hush of the room somewhere behind him, he heard the sharp unpleasant voice of Antal Vrancic—whose presence in the room he had all but forgotten about—disdainfully provide the answer to his question. "His name is Candidianus."

And all at once Candy's pallid face was transformed, and became inconceivably malignant, while out of it his eyes began to regard Marty Carbone with an acutely fiendish concentration. "Down through an unhastening span of centuries without light," he said, the tone of his voice now thoroughly chilling to the ear, "legion are the names that men have bestowed upon me. But there is one above and beyond all others that best describes me. It is the one which none have lived long enough to breathe aloud, but which all have come to acknowledge as they lay slowly dying at my feet. For those who have the ill fortune to cross my path quickly discover that—to put it quite simply—I am also known as"—and pausing an instant, the features of his face convulsed together into so baleful, so menacing an expression that Marty Carbone felt the knife nearly slip from his trembling fingers, as Candy then softly breathed the word—*"Death!"*

And, as the thin bloodless lips of Candy's mouth slowly curled back in a most horrid bestial grin, revealing a row of large acuate teeth that were fang-like in every way, a terror far more shattering than the kind Marty Carbone had experienced but moments before suddenly invaded the very remotest corners of his being.

Then, in a deep and absolute horror, Marty Carbone watched as Candy spread out his arms and, without so much as the slightest motion of either legs or feet, began to glide steadily across the floor towards him. And the curious rushing movement of the child's whole body rapidly floating across the room in his direction was so startling, so nightmarish that it terrified him beyond belief. Involuntarily his eyes for a moment shut of themselves, and he staggered back a step or two, shouting out in fright. And at the very same time that his arm instinctively swept out, and the blade of his hunting knife slashed downward, he realized that its razor-sharp edge had struck against something, a substance that seemed both soft and yielding, cutting deeply into it. And when once more his eyes had opened, he saw, like an appalling incident in some nightmare-vision, that Candy was already standing close up against him, with eyes glaring malevolently, lips grinning fiendishly, and a huge gaping wound running slantwise across the bluish-white skin of his face from the forehead on its one side to the lower jaw on its other.

But even as Marty Carbone continued to stare at that long hideous gash—from which, oddly enough, not the slightest discharge or secretion of blood so much as trickled—its pallid edges drew rapidly together again, and, with a revolting squelching sound, fused instantly, seamlessly each with the other, leaving no visible trace of either lesion or scar whatsoever. The wound had simply *vanished*!

For a moment or two, Marty Carbone's goggling eyes met those of Candy's in amazement; and in the same instant that the prudent yet all too belated thought stole across his mind to turn and run for his life, the child's hand shot out and its narrow bony fingers fastened themselves round Marty Carbone's wrist, crushing it as in a vice of steel.

With a howl of excruciating pain, Marty Carbone sank to the floor onto his knees; and almost instantly, from shoulder to finger tips, he experienced an utterly horrific numbness in the limb which Candy had seized. Then, as he continued to stoop there on his knees, blubbering and whimpering like a lost and frightened little child, he never once felt, even for the breath of an instant, the haft of his knife slip from the quivering fingers of his bloodless hand which lay so helplessly caught in Candy's iron grasp. He knew at once, however, that it was gone, for he heard it fall to the floor with a loud and ominous clatter. His eyes, half blind with his own tears, even glanced mournfully down at it for a moment, and the fingers of his free hand made a futile groping attempt to retrieve the weapon. But another desperate glance showed him that Candy had already reached down, snatched the Buck's Zipper hunting knife up from the floor, and was now clutching it in *his* lean hand.

All in a flash, then, Marty Carbone realized that the child was no longer standing in front of him, but that it had dashed swiftly round behind him, bounded abruptly onto him and, with its thin spindly legs wrapped securely around his waist, was presently clinging, insect-like, to his back. There was then a brief passage of multiple acute stabbing pains which Marty Carbone experienced in his shoulders, back, and neck, followed each time by the repulsive sensation of something cold and wet and slimy adhering to his flesh, accompanied invariably by that same nauseating slurping noise.

It was not, however, until the initial shock and arrest of his faculties had finally subsided that Marty Carbone was able to truly grasp the full horror of what was now being done to him. And by then he was only too well aware that from the moment Candy had clambered up onto his back, he had been violently inflicting, again and again with the point of the hunting knife,numerous deep cuts to the flesh of the upper part of his body, then quickly attaching his slavering lips, like a suction device, to each stab-wound and hungrily supping up the emission of blood.

In thorough agony and an unmitigated terror for his life, his soul, his very *being*—Marty Carbone began to scream and squeal and call out for help. But Candy immediately reached around with his knifeless hand and clapped its lean, narrow, icy-cold palm and claw-like fingers over his mouth with terrible smothering force, abruptly stifling his outcries.

What ensued next for the hapless and pitiable Marty Carbone was nothing short of a Herculean struggle, a frightfully desperate endeavor to get up and save himself from a most gruesome and agonizing death. For he knew beyond question that if he did not rise to his feet again within the next few seconds, he would scarcely be strong enough to draw so much as another breath. He must try—now! And as Candy continued to clasp himself fiercely to Marty Carbone's back, and viciously pierce him with the knife and fasten his slobbering mouth to the bleeding wound, now at his shoulders, then at his back, and again at his neck—pausing ever and again in this bloodletting orgy to throw back his head, as though in sheer ecstasy, draw a long shuddering breath, noisily smack his blood-smeared lips, then quickly reattach them to a freshly opened wound—Marty Carbone strove and strained in an anguish of terror to get to his feet. And after several doubtful and horrifying moments, the wretched man managed at last to do just that.

In the meantime, Vrancic very calmly and leisurely made his way across the floor of the living room, being quite careful the while to give a wide berth to Marty Carbone and the sanguinary attacker with whom he was now so impotently grappling, and halted before the threshold of the sun-room. Cheerfully whistling, he softly drew the French doors to again and remained standing with his back to them, gleefully watching Marty Carbone's futile attempts to extricate himself from the deadly crushing embrace and dreadful siphoning kisses of his bloodthirsty assailant.

More than once, as he gloatingly gazed on at this most fool-hardy and ill-fated intruder, the thought stole exuberantly across his mind that Candy's latest victim would soon provide him with a substantial amount of meat for his empty pots and idle pans down in the basement. And once or twice he even laughed out loud, thoroughly amused, at the sound of Marty Carbone's panting breaths and wheezing sobs, at the sight of the bulging eyes rolling fearfully in his head, and, most of all, at his clumsy, almost comical efforts to dislodge Candy from his back. But then, his attention was suddenly drawn away by a faint yet steadily swelling noise coming from outside—a low, confused hum, or murmur, as it were, of voices babbling and chuckling together.

Vrancic hastened over to the front door in the foyer. And even as he stooped his head low and furtively approached it, he heard the doorknob being rattled, and the muffled sound of a youthful voice on the other side saying, "I tried it, but it won't open. It's locked." Vrancic laid the thick palms of his hands flat against the surface of the door and cautiously, anxiously peered through its peep-hole. He observed the figure of a boy (Kerry Stark) in the process of turning away and descending the porch steps to rejoin a motley group of a dozen or more teenage boys who were assembled at their bottom.

As for Marty Carbone—who was now standing unsteadily on his feet and lurching one or two paces now to this, now to that side of the room—he kept wildly flailing his arms and writhing frantically about to loosen the hold of his frightful adversary, and so topple him from his back. And only after several wrenching twists and convulsive jerks of his body was he able at last to somehow finally catch hold of Candy's arms by their bony wrists and, half-sobbing, half-bellowing in anguish, wrest himself free of the child's entwining limbs. Then, clutching the child with one hand by its throat, and the other by its thigh, he hurled the vile little brute from him as hard as he could.

The slim, lissom body went sailing through the air, spinning round and round with its arms and legs outspread like a cat. And for a split second Marty Carbone actually felt a slight flicker of satisfaction, of triumph as, gasping and leaning half-bent with his hands on his knees, he watched the child slam with a dull, heavy thud against the living room wall.

But suddenly, as with a shock of icy needles pricking his flesh all over, a crestfallen, horrified expression drew over Marty Carbone's face, and, with his jaw sagging open, he continued to stare, astonished and aghast at something which he knew was simply not humanly possible. For the instant that Candy had crashed into the wall, his body seemed to oddly flatten and spread itself out, and there it remained—never even for a moment slipping down or dropping to the floor beneath. But rather, like a hideous and oversized tarantula, with arms and legs splayed wide, he appeared to cling or adhere to the surface of the wall exactly where he had landed. And once more those coldly glaring eyes fixed themselves on the face of Marty Carbone, who suddenly noted, as the blood-slathered lips of Candy's mouth twisted into that same cruelly petrifying grin, that the blade of his hunting knife was now clenched between the child's large fanged teeth.

The only thought in Marty Carbone's head at this point in time was to run, flee—*escape*! He made the instantaneous choice to do so by way of the back door of the house; for he had glimpsed the tall gangling figure of Vrancic just then stepping across the threshold of the door to the foyer and advancing once more into the living room. And so, turning abruptly, he bolted precipitately across the living room floor, into the dining room, expecting to make his way in no time at all across the threshold of the kitchen, dash over to the back door, tear it open, and dart safely outside.

But what Marty Carbone did not know, or anticipate, was that from the moment he had sped off on this desperate (and ultimately *hopeless*) endeavor to escape, was that Candy, clinging yet to the surface of the wall, in defiance of the laws of gravity, some four feet or more off the floor, had all the while been keeping pace with him. On hands and knees, he went scurrying along the wall of the living room, then across that of the dining room, hooting and hallooing the entire way, as if it were to him a horrible game or amusement. And before Marty Carbone was able to cross the threshold of the kitchen, as he had hoped, the child was already crouching in its doorway. Snarling and hissing like some carnivorous beast ready to lunge at its prey, it prevented any approach or access to the premises of the room beyond—thereby hindering Marty Carbone from any further progress toward the back door and utterly foiling his intended objective to flee.

In despair and wretchedness, Marty Carbone staggered back, lost his balance as he tried to turn, and fell crashing to the floor onto his side. Gasping for breath, he quickly rolled onto his stomach and, sobbing and whimpering uncontrollably, began to crawl, on his hands and knees, away from Candy. But before he had traveled half way across the dining room floor, Candy had rushed over to him and jumped onto his back, sitting astride him as though he were mounted on a horse. And like an equestrian rider clutching onto the reins of his steed, Candy would ever and again pull and tug roughly with his one hand at Marty Carbone's ponytail, while with the other he would hold aloft the Buck's Zipper hunting knife and brandish its blade in the air overhead. Then, sadistically kicking Marty Carbone in his sides with the heels of his feet, Candy would repeatedly sneer down at him, "Giddy-up, you worthless old jade! Faster, faster!"; and each time stab Marty Carbone violently between the shoulders with the tip of the knife blade, then stoop his face low to greedily sup at the oozing blood as it pooled from the puncture wound.

After one or two minutes more of this brutal diversion of torture, Marty Carbone, wheezing, sobbing, and on the verge of exhaustion, collapsed at last, like a foundered steed, in the middle of the living room floor and, with heaving sides, lay sprawled on his face, open-mouthed and gasping like a fish.

For nearly half a minute longer Candy remained clinging to Marty Carbone's back, his lips, like those of an insatiable leech, yet fastened at the most recent wound between the shoulder blades of his prey, repulsively sucking and slurping up the blood. At length, he slowly sat up and, tossing back his head, he drew a long, deep breath and ran his tongue, again and again, euphorically, over his bloodstained lips, emitting the while a long drawn-out, "Mmmmmm." Then, for the next few moments, he continued to squat there on Marty Carbone and leisurely primp and clean himself; for the entire lower part of his face was soiled with blood, which he rubbed and swabbed away with his hands, then licked and tongued noisily from his fingers. At last he indolently climbed off his worn-out victim, and, staring remorselessly down at its spent form, began to slowly circle it, like a lion poised and ready for the kill.

Candy had presently thrust the blade of the hunting knife into the belt of his twill shorts and, as he continued to pace round and round Marty Carbone's prostrate, panting body, he repeatedly curled his fingers into a fist, then swiftly opened and spread them, like a beast savagely retracting then extending its claws. Curling back his lips, then, Candy made a snarling sound with his mouth; came to a standstill at Marty Carbone's head; and let his eyes course half-disdainfully, half-gloatingly over his prostrate figure. Now and again Candy roughly poked and prodded at him with his toes, and Marty Carbone's limbs would feebly jerk and stir, and his voice would faintly mewl, "No more... please, no more." The entire back of his black tee-shirt was in tatters, with large, gaping rents in it, as though the cloth had been violently scraped, again and again, with the sharp prongs of a rake or garden hand-weeder, completely shredding it from its collar and shoulders to its frayed and ragged hem. And through these slits and tears could be seen streaks and stains of clotting blood on the skin of his back, shoulders, and lower neck, where the flesh and its underlying tissue had been pierced and punctured in more than a dozen places. Moreover, encircling each wound was an annular bruise or hickey-like discoloration of the skin, marking the place where Candy's mouth had been hungrily feeding.

Meanwhile, Marty Carbone had raised his trembling head and, groveling, strained his lips again and again to Candy's toes. He was sobbing and weeping, and, in a quavering voice choked by tears, kept pleading and imploring for his life: "Please... please, let me... live.., don't kill me... please." But then his voice seemed to fail him, and, incapable of any further effort, it trailed off into senseless sniveling. Presently, shaking with terrific sobs, he struggled to his feet, toddled feebly a moment or two, then fell plump onto his knees: and there he remained, slumped on them in front of Candy, gibbering and weeping, with his head bowed and his shoulders sagging.

In a flash Candy had suddenly moved behind Marty Carbone, and his bony, claw-like fingers were fixed in the man's shoulders. Then, he lifted his upper lip, showing a row of large, fang-like teeth, and his mouth, in the act of setting upon its victim, gaped wide open. Before, however, those serrated teeth had fastened themselves in Marty Carbone's flesh, Vrancic had come striding up quickly across the floor and called on Candy to stop.

With his mouth only inches away from Marty Carbone's throat, the child paused, and the eyes blazed in its distorted face. Vrancic leaned his head low towards Candy's. "You mustn't kill him," he said, speaking slowly yet impressively into the child's ear. "Did you hear me, Candidianus?" He paused a moment as Candy turned his head with a snarl and encountered his gaze. "I have been looking through the peep-hole in the front door"—went on Vrancic—"he has a number of friends outside—a group of young boys! They must have accompanied him here. They'll be expecting his reappearance. If you don't let him return to them it will rouse suspicions; possibly attract unwelcome visitors—the *police*. You'll jeopardize everything we've come here to accomplish. You must permit him to leave here *alive*. Now—Candidianus. Do you understand me?"

There was a long silence, during which Candy's eyes, still gazing unflinchingly into Vrancic's, seemed to ponder, reflect. Then, turning upon Marty Carbone a long, slow sneering glance, he said, "As it was Fortune's whim to deliver him into my power, so let Fortune's whim determine his fate." And moving round to pause once again in front of a broken and vanquished Marty Carbone, Candy stood eyeing him stonily for a moment or two, as the man remained slouched there helplessly on his knees, blubbering and gibbering, with his face all flushed and puckered and wet with tears.

At length, the thin lips of Candy's mouth stirred into a faint, sly grin as he thrust out a lean hand at Marty Carbone, who suddenly felt the tips of those bony, bloodless fingers brush with a swift, light stroke down the length of his face, from his forehead to his chin. At the brief, unpleasant contact a shuddering sigh shook him from head to toe, as a piercing cold went rushing through his veins. And in the very instant that a horrible vertigo seemed to overcome his senses, he suddenly found himself powerless to stir: there had come a strange terrifying arrest over every bone, joint, and muscle in his entire body. He wanted to rise to his feet and make another mad dash for the back door; he actually made one or two violent efforts to do so; he even strove to fall forward onto his hands, and so attempt on all fours to crawl away. But, as in the nets and snares of some hideous nightmare from which he could not awake, Marty Carbone found that any and all movement for him was utterly impossible.

For a moment or two Candy watched Marty Carbone with a cruel, stealthy gleam in his eyes; then, after some little fumbling with his fingers in the pocket of his shorts, he fetched out what appeared to be a thick golden coin. "Do you know what this is?" said Candy, holding the coin in his outstretched hand before Marty Carbone's eyes. But the image and lettering stamped upon its obverse had been worn so very faint, that all Marty Carbone could discern about the coin was that it looked very old, appeared comparable in size to an American silver half dollar, and had an edge on one side which was slightly warped or crooked.

"This is an aureus;" went on Candy; "a gold coin of the Roman empire, which at one time, long ago, was worth twenty-five silver denarii—but on this day, for you, at this very moment in time, it shall have a far, far greater value; for with it I shall purchase for you either your life or your death!" He paused a moment, and, with his gaze still resting intently on Marty Carbone's face, he thrust the ancient coin yet closer under his wide, staring eyes. Then, "See the faded image the coin still bears on its worn face?" Candy began again, his voice smooth and scornful. "It is that of two crossed swords beneath the head of a once mighty ruler of the Roman empire, a noble Caesar of Rome, the Augusti Galerius. And in an age long before your own, it was to this Roman emperor that this coin once belonged. From my time to yours, for nearly two millennia of accursed nights without number, I have carried this coin with me that I might always look on it and remember the face of the man whom I have hated—and still hate!—beyond all others who have been, are, and shall be in the world. For it was with a whimsical toss of this very coin of his that he determined and sealed my fate, thereby condemning me to a life of eternal shadows and everlasting bloodlust, instead of granting me a merciful death. I will now use this same coin on you to decide your doom—whether to let you live or die."

Once more Candy had paused; then, slowly closing his fingers over the golden coin, his eyes seemed to fix themselves a shade more maliciously on the face of Marty Carbone. "Should I catch the coin, after tossing it into the air," he slowly continued, the cruel expression in his features deepening into a horrid leer of triumph, "and view the image of the emperor Galerius on its face—your life shall be forfeit, and I shall exact the price and the penalty by way of your very blood, which I will then drain from your body to the last drop. But should I view the image on the reverse, which is the representation of dame Fortune depicted as a woman seated like queen on her throne under a gated arch, then you will live, even as I was permitted to live on, so to speak, in the world."

Unable to do anything other than listen, Marty Carbone remained mutely staring, the round, bulging eyes in his head rolling this way and that—apparently the only part of him that was able to stir. In anguish and despair they then followed the coin as it left Candy's hand and went twirling upward. For a single horrifying moment it seemed to dangle, motionless, two or three feet above their heads—the side of the coin stamped with the image of a Roman emperor and crossed swords showing so unmistakably clear, that Marty Carbone literally felt his skin crawl and a cold sweat break out all over his trembling body. Then, with a movement that his swelling eyes could scarcely hope to keep pace with, Candy thrust out a small lean hand and, in an instant, his fingers closed again on the ancient Roman coin in mid-air. Holding tight the disc of gold in his one hand, he then clapped it onto the palm of his other, and the long, thin-boned fingers quickly latched themselves over it.

Eyeing Marty Carbone's face craftily for a moment or two, he then leisurely unclenched his fingers; and, with head stooping, and eyes looking down, stood gazing a while in silence at the ancient coin on his narrow, faintly seamed palm.

"The image of Fortune," he breathed, slowly raising his face again. And out of eyes bright and cold and profoundly cruel, he looked long and scornfully on Marty Carbone. "Your life is spared," he said, holding the aureus up between finger and thumb to exhibit its reverse to Marty Carbone. "And, as promised, you will be permitted to leave here with it, but not, I think, quite the same man as you came. For from this day forth yours will be a life accursed."

Candy stooped his face close to Marty Carbone's, and the eyes in that cruelly inhuman visage peered with such peculiar, corkscrew-like intensity into his, that Marty Carbone felt his senses literally reel for an instant, and a death-like chill spread throughout his entire body. "Who are you?" came Candy's voice in a soft, slow hiss like that of a serpent. "Where do you reside?"

At first Marty Carbone refused to answer. For something seemed to caution him not to reveal these things to the malevolent being who now held his gaze so masterfully with its own; moreover, he somehow perceived that if he did, then something awful, indeed *horrifying*, must only come of it. And yet, against his will, he knew his lips had slowly parted; he felt his tongue begin to stir; and suddenly he heard his own voice, for it seemed to be forcibly drawn out of him, mutter, "My name is Marty...Marty Carbone... I live at 66-04 71st Street..."

Candy's lips curled with hideous satisfaction for a breath, and presently he began to pace leisurely round and round Marty Carbone, coldly, intently regarding him. Then, "No;" he said; "you are not Marty Carbone; that is *not* your name: for Marty Carbone does not exist. He never *has* existed." For a moment or two Candy paused, and, with eyes fixed on Marty Carbone, gazed steadily, piercingly into his. Unable to repel, even for an instant, the persuading power of that infernal glance, nor avert his own even so much as a fraction of an inch, Marty Carbone began to feel—only gradually at first, but then quite rapidly—his very identity growing vague and elusive as a dream.

"Do you understand?" went on Candy. "There is no Marty Carbone. And you are *not* he. As of this moment you have no past."

"Yes... I understand;" said Marty Carbone, the words slipping off his tongue as though he were talking in his sleep; "there is no Marty Carbone... I have no past." Then, slowly, helplessly, irretrievably, Marty Carbone felt his character, his persona, his very psyche growing fainter and fainter; until, all in a moment, he could no longer remember who he was. His memory—and with it his very wits—had now fled beyond recall; and all remembrance of his previous life, from his earliest recollection of events to the most recent, became an utter blank. His face, too, became suddenly blank, and, out of eyes glassily empty and deprived of all speculation, he stared before him, like a sleepwalker, in a dazed and absent way, oblivious to everything around him.

Meanwhile, Vrancic stood in the background attentively observing everything, and grinning his silent approval, as once more Candy resumed his slow, sauntering pace round the motionless form of Marty Carbone, slumped on its knees. Then, "You are someone else," he breathed out softly, scornfully at Marty Carbone, his light eyes the while cruelly regarding him. "Hmmmm; who shall you be? Who should I compel you to become?"

Once more Candy had paused in front of Marty Carbone and, after studying his face for several moments, his pondering eyes drifted down to the floor. But then, quite suddenly, some wicked notion or suggestion seemed to narrow and darken them, and the small wan cheeks puckered up into a sly grin. And the face he now raised to Marty Carbone's had all at once assumed the expression of a cold and diabolic purpose.

"Ahhh, I have it," he said, almost gleefully. "You shall become an old pupil and acolyte of mine; a French nobleman by the name of Gilles de Rais who I once befriended in the fifteenth century, and whom I tutored and instructed in the ways of my kind. I arrived at his castle one winter night in 1432 and, as recompense for his hospitality I discovered to him who and *what* I am. He was instantly attracted to, and excited by, my nature and condition; gave me to drink freely of his blood; willingly allowed me to indulge my appetite in all manner of foul sexual acts upon the flesh of his mortal body. And in return I conferred upon him a Vampire's thirst for blood, instilling him with blood-madness. Through this gift I enabled him to engage without conscience, without the least remorse, in acts of monstrous lust and boundless violence which no man has rivaled before or since that time.

"For eight years of blood-filled night upon blood-filled night, I urged monsieur de Rais on to abominable crimes against the children of the surrounding villages, which he and his servants during the daylight hours had lured within the walls of his baronial castle. Jubilantly I would watch him sodomize, torture, and mutilate one hapless young victim after another. Without fail I made him aware of my preferences this, then that night for the manner in which each child should die, whether it be by decapitation, dismemberment, or disembowelment—a matter in which the Baron-Marshal was more than pleased to accommodate me. For nothing gave my dear chevalier de Rais greater pleasure than to watch his youthful victims die slowly, and in absolute agony. In fact, he would often increase their suffering merely to intensify his own ecstasy."

For a space of some seconds Candy was silent, and into the intense brightness of his cruel, cold eyes had come a remote glint of devilish mirth; for an instant this fiendish glee very nearly mastered him, and he all but laughed out in Marty Carbone's impassive face.

Then, "Some nights," resumed Candy, "simply to gain my approval and esteem, my good Baron de Rais would heighten the torture of his young victims; other times, in the hopes of attaining some word of praise from me, he would glut himself on their blood as their bodies, languishing in death, still twitched; still others, to impress and please me the more, he would violate their bodies only after they had died, and then perform upon their corpses, for my personal amusement, the most unspeakable perversities. Child upon nameless child—to a sum that exceeded eight hundred—was savagely slaughtered at his hands within his castles and chateaux: some by having their throats slit; some, their heads and limbs hacked off; some, their skulls shattered with a mallet; and others, torn open, while still alive, that he might macerate their entrails with his bare hands and drench his face and beard in their blood."

Once again there was a short pause, as Candy's eyes, out of the deathly pallor of his face, continued to gaze on steadily, gloatingly at Marty Carbone. Then, "And all these traits, habits, passions and characteristics of my dear Baron de Rais Gilles de Laval, shall now be your own," continued Candy, leering into Marty Carbone's vacuous eyes. "For you are he, and he is you. And as Gilles de Rais is now thy name, so, too, darkness be now thy day; blood be now thy passion; agony thy pleasure; iniquity thy good; and killing thy supreme joy!" And, stooping his face still nearer to Marty Carbone's, Candy breathed upon him, and a faint vapor, or exhalation, proceeded from his mouth into Marty Carbone's nostrils. An instant later, something happened. Over the expressionless face of Marty Carbone there suddenly stole an oddly sinister cast, or air; and the eyes, glazed, absent, and without speculation but moments ago, were now occupied with what seemed a presence other than his own.

Candy, meanwhile, continued to steadily smile and gaze on at Marty Carbone. "Tell me now your name;" he said, after a long pause; "reveal to me who you are."

Marty Carbone's eyes rested firmly on Candy's, and, "Gilles de Laval, Baron-Marshal de Rais," came the low, clear, unfaltering response.

Candy's eyes glittered malevolently. "Welcome back, my old friend," he laughed softly. "It is I, your master, tutor, lover, and friend who greets you now, le Enfant saunce Pite." And a pair of sinister eyes—certainly not Marty Carbone's, yet nonetheless within his own—peered back at Candy in salutation and acknowledgement. Again his lips parted, and this time a stony, dreadful voice broke out in slow, far-away tones, "Dominus, salve! magister!" And from out of Marty Carbone's face, as though faintly seen through a grimy pane of glass, there steadily peered another, a visage that was cruel, unclean, and seamed with all manner of wickedness and brutality.

Candy extended a lean, bony hand to him, and Marty Carbone stooped his face low over it and pressed his lips to the icy fingers. Then, slowly raising his head again, he met once more the brilliant eyes in that death-pale face which continued to dwell on his in amusement and satisfaction.

"Now take this knife," said Candy, drawing the Buck's Zipper hunting knife from the belt of his twill shorts, "and with it," he went on, placing its haft in the hand of Marty Carbone, "return to the Carbone residence on 71st Street at 66-04, and that which you came here to do to Nathan, do now to the first person you encounter beneath its roof."

Then, the moment Marty Carbone was commanded to rise to his feet, he felt that abominable numbing sensation, that thought-drugging lethargy (or whatever it truly *was*) which all the while had kept him powerless to stir so much as a finger, suddenly withdraw itself from out of his limbs, his muscles, and the very marrow of his bones. His limbs stirred at once, and, like a man whose fettering chains and restricting shackles had been abruptly, magically removed, he gave a sudden lurch forward and rose unsteadily to his feet. In that curiously dazed way of a man walking in his sleep, he turned, and, in a voice that was no longer his own he seemed to be repeating, in slow, soft, monotonous tones, the same words, again and again, as if at the will and dictation of another: "Heu insanio... Furore consumor!"

Vrancic was standing beside him now and, for a moment or two, looked at him closely. He muttered something to Candy and laughed. Then, Marty Carbone heard the smooth, scornful voice of

Candy speaking to him: "Adieu monsieur de Rais, mon ami Gilles de Laval"; and again, after a short pause, he heard Candy sneeringly add: "Adieu, cuer dous, mon redoubte seigneur de Mort!"; words in a tongue utterly strange to his ears, but which he somehow nonetheless sensed, knew, understood (perfectly well) signified, "Farewell, sweet heart, my dreaded lord of Death!"

And, with Candy's lean cold hand clutched firmly in his own, he was drawn steadily forward by the child across the floor of the living room into the foyer. There, Vrancic, who had been silently awaiting them, began to softly undo the locks to the front door. Having turned its knob, he paused a moment to cast one last sneering glance at Marty Carbone's expressionless face, then, positioning himself behind the door, he soundlessly drew it open. And the moment Marty Carbone had stepped outside, across its threshold, Vrancic quickly pushed the door to again and bolted it behind him. Then, stooping his head a little and peering with his eye through the peep-hole, he watched Marty Carbone slowly descend the porch steps.

Never once did Marty Carbone's glazed and tranceful eyes meet those of the assembled teenage boys who suddenly rushed forward with excited and expectant faces to confront him at the bottommost step, but over their heads and away into the distance they continued to glassily stare. And as he strode slowly through their parting ranks with an odd, lumbering gait, as if the use of his legs had grown unfamiliar to him, he kept muttering in a weird far-away voice, again and again, the same words, "Heu insanio... Furore consumor!"

In dumb amazement the press of teenage boys gazed at the huge rents and tears in the back of Marty Carbone's blood-stained tee-shirt; and when they glimpsed, through these slits, all the wounds and clotting gore covering the skin of his back, an audible gasp went up from their young crowding faces as they stared awestruck and agape. Without either speaking or stirring they watched Marty Carbone get on his motorcycle, throttle it up, and go rumbling up the street toward Metropolitan Avenue; and not until he had turned the corner and passed out of sight did they glance among themselves again in speechless wonder.

As if at a signal, then, they all burst into a clamor of debate, asking one another: "What could've happened in there?"; "Why was Marty Carbone's shirt all torn like that?"; "Do you think Nathan did that to Marty?"; "But what do you suppose Marty did to Nathan in there?". And so it continued, on and on, for at least the next five minutes before some of the older boys (such as Scott Webler, Neil Keddy, and Glen Rubino), after grumbling and groaning that it had all been 'a waste', and 'what a rip-off', and 'this sucks', began at last to drift slowly, reluctantly, by twos and threes, away from Nathan's house and up the street. A few of the younger boys, however, while utterly disappointed like the rest, continued to loiter at the foot of the porch steps and glance up every now and again at the front door, as though half-expecting to see it open and emit the badly bruised and heavily bleeding figure of Nathan. But after several more tedious and uneventful minutes, in which no such hoped-for appearance was made by Nathan, the boys began at last to disperse and wander glumly up the street.

Now, about the same time that Marty Carbone had collapsed on the floor of Nathan's living room, where he lay groveling for his very life under Candy's hostile regard, his sister, Lori Carbone, had risen from the sofa in the living room of their house and resumed the anxious pacing of its floor in her bare feet. Occasionally she burst into a fresh fit of scalding tears and shuddering sobs as the anguish, the horror of what she had endured in the garage under Nathan's violent embraces renewed itself in her thoughts.

At length, half dazed and exhausted, she sank down upon the sofa again and tried to control her misery and fears. But it was in vain. She kept shivering fitfully, and tears continued to prick her aching eyes and drop senselessly down her cheeks as the one chilling thought steadily haunting her was, "What if Nathan is still out there, hiding in the garage, waiting for me?" And feelings of terror, like a numbing coldness, struck through her thumping heart at this awful yet unrelenting fancy.

Eventually, though, this fearful notion (and her constant weeping) wore her out, and Lori Carbone stretched out on her side upon the sofa, gathered a pillow or two under her head, and shut her eyes. For some minutes she had even faintly dozed: and after a while, through a thinning veil of elusive dreams, she heard the thundering roar of the V-twin engine in her brother's Harley Davidson as it came bellowing up the street: slowed, softened, and then, in front of her home, was suddenly hushed. Even in her shallow sleep, while a part of her mind dreamed on, the rest was curiously aware that her brother, having returned from his errand at Nathan's house, was now fumbling at the locks and knob of the front door. The lids to her eyes stirred, softly opened and, heaving a trembling sigh, Lori Carbone slowly, wearily sat up.

And presently, from behind her, through the stillness of the house, Lori Carbone heard the front door, as it was opened, swing inward on its hinges. After a profound, almost stealthy silence, she caught the sound of slow, heavy footsteps (her brother's, she naturally assumed) advancing across the floor of the room towards her. She bound her hair back, rose to her feet and, on the verge of tears again, her voice already quavering, said, "So what happened? Did you see Nathan there?"

A dreadful voice, however, that was certainly not her brother's, replied, "Furore consumor... heu insanio!" And turning round, Lori Carbone's eyes, a glint of terror springing suddenly into their pupils, encountered for a solitary instant those of her brother's. Fixed intently, murderously on her, they blazed furiously in his head, as he lifted high the hunting knife clutched in his hand and savagely plunged its blade again and again into her neck, chest, shoulders and arms, all the while repeating, in that same dreadful voice, "Furore consumor! Furore consumor! Heu insanio!"

With her hands half outstretched in a futile attempt to fend off each brutal stabbing thrust, Lori Carbone staggered back and, under the agonizing pain and shock of several more knife wounds to her chest, she collapsed on the floor, and lay choking and spluttering on her back. The hoodie she wore had fallen open, exposing her wound-riddled bosom, and her mouth jerked open again and again to scream, but, with the blood jetting over her lips and tongue from the ghastly punctures in her neck, all she was able to emit were hideous gurgling gasps.

Presently, Marty Carbone strode round his sister's quivering body and paused beside her head, standing perfectly still in the long blood-dyed locks of her loosened hair as they lay outspread across the floor. He stared silently, remorselessly down at her, as if contemplating the feeble convulsions of her next-to naked frame. Then, as the twitching of her limbs subsided with one last shuddering spasm and her body lay unstirring in the final languor of death, Lori Carbone exhaled a faint and final gurgling sigh in the same instant that the deep and mellow Big Ben tone of the grandfather clock's chimes, from a corner of the room, broke out with a slow liquid peal and were stilled.

For several moments Marty Carbone's attention was drawn from his sister's corpse to the chiming clock. He gazed at it with glazed and wildly glittering eyes. Through the beveled glass of the hinged door on the clock's pinched waist, he could see the steady swaying of the brass finished bob to its pendulum, before which hung three heavy weights in their cylinder weight shells of polished brass.

And as a very hideous notion began to shape itself in his mind, Marty Carbone thrust his knife into the sheath on his belt and walked over to the clock. He drew open its waist door, removed the middle weight from the chain from which it depended and, carrying this heavy cylindrical weight in his hand, he returned to where his sister lay. After bestriding her still and lifeless body, he paused once more to stare coldly down at her face. Her unseeing eyes remained wide open and glassily still,the sallow cheeks having already grown cold.

Then, grinding his teeth, "Heu insanio... heu insanio... furore consumor," growled Marty Carbone; and hauling up the brass weight with both hands, he brought it down, again and again, with all his might onto his sister's face and head in an ecstasy of violence, shattering every bone in her skull. Spent and breathless at last, he cast the weight aside and stooped panting over Lori

Carbone's mutilated corpse, his face, hands and chest dripping with her spattered blood and brains.

Upon recovering his breath, Marty Carbone then set about leisurely dismembering the already hideously mangled corpse of his sister, hacking off first her arms, then her legs with his Buck's Zipper hunting knife, snarling all the while through the entire grisly undertaking, "Furore consumor; furore consumor! Heu insanio!" And the moment he had completed this gruesome business, the abhorrent presence that had so irreversibly stolen into his psyche and taken absolute possession of his persona, led him on still further to yet one more horrific atrocity.

For all at once a monstrous impulse to violate the limbless trunk swept like an electrical current through every atom of Marty Carbone's being, causing his hands to shake uncontrollably, his mouth to twist and writhe hideously, and the very blood in his veins to smolder and boil, until, unable to resist a moment longer, he hurled himself savagely upon his sister's butchered carcass, bellowing over and over, "What angel in heaven, what demon in hell, what mortal on earth dares to sin as I now sin! Furore consumor! Furore consumor! Heu insanio!"

CHAPTER TWO

*"...Macduff. O horror, horror, horror! Tongue
nor heart cannot conceive nor name thee!*

Macbeth and Lennox. What's the matter?

*Macduff. Confusion now hath made his
masterpiece. ...Approach the chamber, and
destroy your sight... Do not bid me speak;*

See, and then... let us meet

*And question this most bloody piece
of work, to know it further..."*

—Macbeth

Softly, languidly the hours had slipped away, and the day began to wane. The western sky, abrim now with the splendor of a steadily declining sun, had been transformed into a shoreless lake of dazzling gold. And although, for some while now, all had been utter darkness and confusion for Nathan, there were times when the confusion seemed to dwindle and recede a little, and then, one by one, faces, pale and faint as the moon's rays, came floating up before him out of the enfolding darkness and, as softly and as suddenly, faded away again.

Wraith-like and half-seen, Nathan first glimpsed his mother's face, and his father's; then, for a moment or two, he thought he saw old Mr Lieberman's face, followed by the dour visage of Aunt Amelia scowling at him. But almost at once Nathan knew that none of this could be real, because all of these people were now—*dead,* and had *been* dead (as was the case with his mother and father) for some time now. But then, out of the vast black gulf and vacancy in which he now seemed to hang motionless, one more face swam up before his eyes. At first Nathan thought it was Phebe's face he was now seeing; but, no—either he had mistaken it for hers, or it had suddenly, almost imperceptibly melted away into that of another's—one which he instantly recognized as Lori Carbone's.

And as Nathan gazed on at this phantom countenance of Lori's, with its skin all faintly luminous as by some inward light of its own, he noted, too, that its narrow under-lip was quivering, and the brow was all puckered, and the cheeks all flushed and tear-stained. And all in a moment Nathan had a vague, indefinite sense of something truly awful having happened to her, accompanied by the curious impression (however hazy and unclear) that this "truly awful" incident somehow involved himself *and* her; but he couldn't remember what it was. And whenever he did try to recollect, that hideous confusion, like the chill waters of a slow, heavy wave, would once more sweep in upon him, and the intervening darkness would swiftly spread itself in a veiling mist over his senses.

But then, like one coming coldly, abruptly out of a sleep that had been horribly troubled with crowding dreams, Nathan drew one or two long trembling breaths into his body and was suddenly broad awake. For some while he lay very still, with furrowed brow and restless eyes, wondering in vain where he was. But as his mind began to clear, he found first that he was lying on his back among the tufted sun-warmed weeds and grass of a neglected grave inside the old All Faiths cemetery, with his face upturned to the sky, and next, that faintly, out of the sweltering windless summer air, he could hear some odd, puzzling clamor. He listened to it half-dreamily: a protracted crackling, or popping noise, as if, in the dim far-away of some neighborhood street, on the other side of the cemetery, a dozen or more firecrackers were being set off, one after another— pop, pop, pop, on and on and on. And for some moments he could think of nothing else but that it must be getting very near to the Fourth of July.

Without stirring so much as a finger, Nathan continued to stare up into the cloudless evening sky, and the sun's rays, slanting from out of the west, swept down upon him bright and hot. Then, all at once, he realized that that distant crackling, as of fireworks, had ceased, and the only sound now audible to his ears was the faint, steady chirring of crickets.

Still a little confused and slightly aching, Nathan began to softly stir, turning his head first this way, then that, to let his gaze range from the dense foliage interlacing the cemetery fence on his right, to the evenly spaced rows of huddled tombstones on his left, all the while wondering to himself what in the world he was doing here.

And as his gaze lingered, half-absently, on the darkening monuments and headstones nearest to him, he noted that one and all, in the flocking beams of the declining sun, were casting lengthening shadows across the frowzy grass of the graves. Wearily Nathan lurched onto his elbow, then sat up; and, for an instant or two, the entire cemetery, along with the sky overhead, seemed to pitch and roll and spin horribly round him, before settling and coming right again. And when it had, he caught once more that far-off 'popping' sound, as of firecrackers going off, only this time it was not as prolonged as before. For seconds later the silence had very suddenly closed over it again; and as Nathan sat on, deep in thought, listening intently and staring downward at the parched grass, he realized all at once that the month of July was long past, that it was now August—late in the month, too!—and that whoever at this time was setting off fireworks (if indeed they were fireworks), it was certainly not in celebration of any Fourth of July holiday weekend.

Now once this initial confusion of his had finally passed away, Nathan's mind returned more fully to the mystery of (a) what he was doing inside the old All Faiths cemetery; (b) how he had even come to be here; and (c) why, presently, under an early evening sky, he was just waking up on one of its sunken graves.

But try as he would, he could remember nothing of the day's *unusual* events and all that he had been through since waking that morning. For the unremitting strain of the experiences he had undergone were by now beginning to tell upon him both mentally and physically. And suddenly, to his utter bewilderment, he felt a dreadful lassitude yet again stealing irresistibly over his senses, so that he could hardly keep his heavy eyelids from drooping, or his body from sinking back once more into the grass and weeds of the grave on which he was now seated.

Notwithstanding this, Nathan rose to his feet and, in a desperate effort to get himself back inside his home again before he should yield to this unendurable fatigue, he began to make his way toward the secret hole in the cemetery fence. And just as he was about to part the foliage curtaining the hidden aperture, and slip through its narrow opening, he suddenly paused, for he had heard slow footsteps and a murmur of soft voices approaching. Not daring to make the least sound or stir, Nathan waited, listening; for two persons were talking together just on the other side of the fence where he was now standing. One of the voices was that of a woman's, the other, a man's; and Nathan stiffened when he heard the woman say: "Oh, Erwin, please; you should only listen to yourself! What nonsense you're talking."

With his ears fastened intently on the retort of Mr Erwin Schiller, Nathan kept himself perfectly still. "Alright, then, Muriel, you tell me why, for more than a week now, neither of us have seen Amelia Christian."

At the mention of his aunt's name, Nathan felt his heart begin to knock rapidly against his side, and, for a moment or two, he caught and held his breath as he thought to himself that Mr Schiller's suspicions in regard to the continued absenteeism of Aunt Amelia were evidently growing, deepening, intensifying.

"The last time I saw her," went on Mr Schiller, "was on Friday, August 11th; she was returning home from work; I waved to her from across the street, she smiled, went into her house and hasn't come out since!" There was a short pause; then, "Well, don't you find it strange, Muriel?"

Nathan listened eagerly for Mrs Schiller's response. "But, Erwin," he heard her say, "you yourself said you spoke to some relative of hers—a cousin visiting from Florida —who's staying with her in the house. He told you she isn't feeling well."

"Lies, Muriel! Nothing but lies!" said Mr Schiller. "If that fellow I spoke with is a relative of Amelia's, then I'm Hitler and you're Mussolini!" The two of them moved slowly on, and Nathan kept pace with them on his side of the fence, concealed by the matted vines interwoven in its chain-link mesh, every now and then catching glimpses of them through some chink in the shaggy growth. He could see Mr Schiller holding a leash, at the end of which their little Maltese, Blitzen, was shuffling along. Nathan continued to listen attentively.

"Several times now, Muriel, the man has taken Amelia's car, I've seen him—he drives off in it, and he doesn't return for hours."

"And what's wrong with that, Erwin?"

"So where does he go, Muriel? What keeps him away for such long periods of time? Aren't you in the least curious?"

"No, I'm not, Erwin;" said Mrs Schiller; "and you shouldn't be either."

Mr Schiller was silent a while. Then, "Some nights, lying in bed," he began again, "I can hear the car pulling into the driveway at two, sometimes three, in the morning—always some ungodly hour of the night, Muriel; I've been watching the man."

Nathan opened his eyes wide and felt his heart suddenly jerk and skip as he wondered to himself whether his own nighttime comings and goings into the cemetery to visit with Phebe in the old mausoleum were being as closely observed by Mr Schiller as those of Vrancic's nocturnal errands. "And what," continued Mr Schiller, "do you suppose he's been up to, Muriel: what has been done by him, away all those hours of the night. More importantly, what is he up to in Amelia Christian's house, and what do you suppose has been done by him to that poor, innocent woman?"

"Now, really, Erwin;" said Mrs Schiller; "who says he's done anything to Amelia? You sound as though you're starting to obsess over nothing but a bunch of silly notions."

"Notions they may be," said Mr Schiller, "but they are far from silly, Muriel. Twice now I've seen the man crack open the front door and, keeping himself well hidden behind it, as if he's reluctant to show himself or be seen by anyone, he stretches his arm out to the mailbox on the wall, lifts its lid, takes out the letters and what have you, then slips his arm back inside and quickly shuts the door again. It's all very strange, and very suspicious, Muriel."

When Nathan heard this, he thought to himself, so that's what's been happening to the mail. For the past few days he had been wondering why, each time he checked the mailbox, there were never any letters in it. Apparently Vrancic had been collecting the mail; but what, Nathan asked himself, was he doing with it. Had he taken it all down into the basement? Was he going through the mail himself? Destroying it all? Or simply discarding it? And what about any bills, such as the gas, electric, and water—had Vrancic been paying *those*? Or was he merely secreting them somewhere, dumping all bills and letters down into that grave-like pit he had excavated in the basement floor, so as to avoid rousing any suspicions by having the mail accumulate? If so, thought Nathan, then Vrancic had not been completely successful in this objective of his, at least not where old Mr Schiller was concerned—for not only had *his* suspicions been roused, they had been virtually ignited.

And once more Nathan turned his attention to what Mr Erwin Schiller was telling his wife. "Don't you remember me telling you, Muriel, how I met Nathan the day before yesterday, and questioned him about this so-called relative of Amelia's? Well, I could see by the expression on the boy's face that every answer he gave me was a complete lie! And when Nathan mentioned the state Amelia's alleged relative claims to be visiting *from*, instead of Florida—as the man himself had said!—Nathan told me California!"

Nathan felt his cheeks burn at the vivid memory of the encounter, and the discomfit and embarrassment he had felt under Mr Schiller's all-too heedful eyes.

"So?" Nathan heard Mrs Schiller remark.

"So don't you see, Muriel?—his own lies tripped him up."

"Oh, Erwin, please! All it means, as far as I can see, is that the boy forgot or made a mistake about the actual state the man is visiting from, that's all!"

Mr Schiller's reply followed a long, almost infinite sigh. "You know, Muriel," he said, "sometimes talking to you is about as stimulating as talking to a tree-stump!" They paused again, and Nathan with them, as Blitzen stood snuffling at some savory odor in the dirt only two or three paces from the fence. "And you, Erwin," said Mrs Schiller, "have a very bad habit of jumping to conclusions and thinking the worst about people."

"Alright, Muriel, then explain this to me," said Mr Schiller. "Yesterday, I decided to go to the Take-a-Break diner on Fresh Pond Road, the place where Amelia works as a waitress; and when I spoke with some of the other employees, they told me she quit her job there. And when I had a quiet word with the owner, a Mr Kapur Rajnish, he informed me that on Saturday, August 12th, he received a call from Amelia's nephew, Nathan, who told him over the phone that his aunt wouldn't be coming to work there anymore, that she found employment somewhere else."

Nathan felt his heart stand still for a moment, and an intense chill spread itself through his mind at the notion that Mr Schiller had been looking into things. It made him terribly uneasy; and he could not help but wonder, what else might the man come to discover if he persisted in all this prying and probing.

"Now if Amelia has found another job," continued Mr Schiller, "why haven't either you or I seen her traveling to and from this alleged 'new job', eh? Tell me that, Muriel." They had moved on again, and Nathan followed, listening with fast-beating heart to Mr Schiller venting all his suspicions to his wife; and suddenly, he began to think to himself, what if Mr Schiller were to start venting these same suspicions to the police?

"Well, I suppose," answered Mrs Schiller, "it's like her relative told you, Erwin, when you spoke with him at the back door: Amelia isn't feeling well enough to leave the house, and therefore she hasn't been able to go to work." The netted foliage clambering about the cemetery fence was thinner here, and Nathan could see Mr Schiller, his wife, and Blitzen quite clearly through the tangled leaves and twisting stems.

"Ahh! You're too gullible, too naive, Muriel," grumbled Mr Schiller.

"And you're too suspicious, Erwin."

"And you should be, too!"

At this point, Nathan had arrived at that part in the cemetery fence where part of his house and its backyard projected slightly into the cemetery itself, and here, the Schillers, for a brief space, passed out of hearing as they walked past the front of Nathan's home, while he himself had to dash along the fence to circumvent its backward parts. After a few moments he came round to where the fence again followed the line of the street, and, still hidden by the knitted growth covering its loose mesh, Nathan glimpsed through a veil of leaves and stems Mr and Mrs Schiller as they walked their dog just on the opposite side. He continued to walk with them, listening eagerly, intently to their voices. And when once more he had caught up the thread of their conversation, Mrs Schiller was asking her husband, "Alright, Erwin, then what do you think has happened to Amelia?" And Nathan listened now with held breath, waiting anxiously, almost fearfully for Mr Schiller's theory on the mystery of his aunt's fate.

"No doubt," said Mr Schiller, "she has come to the same unfortunate end as Irene Silverman." Nathan heard Mrs Schiller repeat the name, as if to herself, then ask, "And who on earth is that, Erwin?"

"She *was* a gentle, honest soul," said Mr Schiller, "much the same as you or I, Muriel, who lived in Manhattan on the Upper East Side, in a townhouse, I think. I'm going back now ten or fifteen years, Muriel—perhaps even longer, I can't be sure; but, at some point, this monstrous pair of grifters, a mother and son, named Sante and Kenneth Kimes, I believe, happened to cross her path and attach themselves to the unsuspecting woman. After first winning her confidence, they soon wormed their way into her home and, before you knew it, no one ever saw Irene Silverman again. To this day her fate remains a mystery. The police suspect the Kimes's killed her and disposed of her remains."

"And you think that's what happened to Amelia Christian? Oh, Erwin!"

"Don't you be so quick to scoff at what I'm telling you, Muriel," said Mr Schiller. "It happens more often than you think! If ever I saw a grifter and a scoundrel, it's that fellow who I spoke with at the back door of Amelia's house."

As he listened to all of this, Nathan felt his heart turn heavy as lead and drop within him, for Mr Schiller did not merely suspect, he thought to himself, he somehow *knew*... And Nathan had to choke back the impulse to shout through the fence at old Mr Schiller, It's true, it's all true—all that's left of her are her hands and her head in the basement refrigerator! He's eaten the rest! But suddenly Nathan heard his own name mentioned, as Mrs Schiller said, "And what about Amelia's nephew, Nathan? You're not going to tell me he's part of all this?"

"Yes, Muriel!" answered Mr Schiller, almost heatedly. "The boy knows all about the underhanded business going on in that house! I knew something had happened to Amelia. The signs were all there—first the flock of ravens settling all over her house, and then the horde of rats that went swarming up and down its exterior in the middle of the night! They were harbingers, evil omens, just as I told you, that the death of someone in that household was drawing near. Now it's only too clear, Muriel, that they were tragic portents of poor Amelia Christian's impending fate."

"Oh, really Erwin!" said Mrs Schiller. "You should only hear yourself! I really do believe that all those fables and fairy stories you insist on reading in all those books of yours have finally begun to affect your brain!"

"For the last time, Muriel, they're not 'fairy stories'!" said Mr Schiller, raising his voice. "The books and reference works which I frequently consult are learned and scholarly editions on the myths, legends, and folklore of the world's diverse cultures."

"Well, whatever you call them," said Mrs Schiller, "you really need to stop reading all that nonsense—it's making you fantasize far too much."

"Call it what you will, Muriel, but I can tell you this much," said Mr Schiller, "from this point on, I'm going to keep an eye on

that house—and on Nathan, to see what the boy is up to. He goes
into the cemetery far too often, I've noticed. What's in there, eh,
Muriel, that causes the boy to make these frequent visitations?
You mark my words, there's something—" But Nathan had to stop
here, discontinue his eavesdropping, and allow the Schillers to
pass out of earshot and continue on their way down the street with
Blitzen toward the railroad tracks, for at this point the cemetery
fence ceased to be matted with the thick embowering growth of
either vine or ivy; and to venture so much as an inch beyond their
curtaining foliage would be to utterly expose himself to Mr and
Mrs Schiller. Besides, he was more than a little relieved to finally
part with them; for listening to all of Mr Schiller's suspicions and
shrewd guesses and all-too accurate conjectures had been a very
unsettling experience. And the aftermath of it all left Nathan's mind
in a commotion of fears and forebodings that Mr Schiller was not
going to stop searching, investigating, enquiring into his aunt's—
he couldn't exactly say 'disappearance', but rather her—'ongoing
non-appearance' in the neighborhood, until he finally uncovered
the truth regarding her actual (and horrible) fate. And what then,
wondered Nathan.

But suddenly, out of the far-away, there broke in upon his
thoughts the muted peal of St Margaret's church-bells, faint with
the intervening distance between where he himself now stood
inside the old All Faiths cemetery and the location of that esteemed
house of worship on 79th Place.

One by one, in the quieting hush, the bells rang out, tolling the
evening hour of the Divine Office. And as Nathan stood perfectly
still, half-listening to those pealing bells, he fell into a faint, dream-
like reverie through which stalked the face and form of Phebe in all
her solemn, mysterious beauty. And it was not until long after their
dim, echo-like chiming had thinned away, then ceased altogether,
that Nathan came once more to himself and, glancing up at the sky,
in the stillness that followed, fully realized that the church bells had
been ringing the six o' clock hour of Vespers. And Nathan thought
to himself that there was only another hour or two of daylight; for
he could see that the sun was more than halfway on his way to

setting; it would soon be dark; and then.... He caught his breath a moment, and casting an anxious glance in the direction of the old mausoleum, "Phebe," he breathed.

Without another moment's delay Nathan hurried back to the hole in the fence and plunged through its hidden opening. He then covered the distance between it and his home in a swift but cautious sprint, keeping close to the ivy-matted fence the entire length of the way. And by the time Nathan had stolen up the porch steps, opened the front door to his house, and slipped inside, the Schillers had reached the railroad tracks at the far end of the block and turned. Presently they were coming slowly back up the street, with poor Blitzen being carried in his master's arms, just like a baby, for the walk in such heat and glaring sunlight had been more than the little beast could comfortably manage, and his tongue was dangling out of his head.

Now, once safely inside his home again, Nathan rushed into the kitchen, seized by a sudden, torturing thirst; for like Blitzen, he, too, was now feeling faint and torpid with the day's stifling heat. In fact, his entire body felt as though it had been parched through and through by the sun's fierce rays which had long been blazing down upon it all the while he had lain unconscious among the grass and weeds of one of the cemetery's graves. And it was not until after Nathan had dashed over to the kitchen sink, filled a tall glass with water from the faucet, and greedily gulped down its contents (only to refill and empty it three more times), that he noticed something on the floor: something which he had not seen when he first entered the room.

With the half-empty glass of water (his fourth) still raised to his moistened lips, Nathan had suddenly paused, and his whole attention became centered on the thing on the floor. It appeared to be a small puddle, or stain, of some kind, equal in size and shape to a small dish, lying between the front and rear legs of the outermost chair that was drawn up close to the kitchen table. For nearly half a minute Nathan continued to stare at it stupidly, before finally setting his glass down and going over to it for closer inspection. And almost instantly he knew what that stain or puddle actually was—vomit from his cat Ichabod. And in its very center, as Nathan stooped over it for a moment or two, he suddenly noted a fleshy lump or pulpy mass, which—although Nathan did not want to hazard a guess at—looked for all the world like the lower part of a human ear.

After cleaning up and disposing of this repugnant mess of spew, Nathan heard a loud miaou and, turning, saw the four-legged culprit himself come sauntering very casually into the kitchen. Nathan stood by the sink, gazing on at Ichabod for some seconds in silence, loathing the very sight of him now, ever since he had caught the little beast banqueting on Aunt Amelia's severed nose in the basement. In fact, he felt nothing but revulsion for the animal from the moment he had learned that Vrancic, over the past few days, had been battening him on human flesh.

Presently, Ichabod sat down by the back door and began to miaou again and again, in an effort to indicate to Nathan its desire to go outside. In utter disgust, Nathan glanced down at Ichabod, went over to the back door, opened it, and let the cat out, hoping that it would never return.

Then, having pushed the back door to again, and locked it, the next thing Nathan experienced, in addition to his burning thirst, was a ferocious hunger, almost painful in its extremity. Hardly able to move fast enough, to gratify this terrible craving, Nathan quickly made himself a couple of Bologna sandwiches, which he then devoured in extraordinary haste and with immense fervor. But as he was still not satisfied, and this curious gnawing hunger persisted in the pit of his stomach, he then gobbled up, with equal gusto, liberal amounts of peanut butter and grape jam, direct from their jars with a large spoon.

Ignoring, then, the low, muffled rumblings which continued to emanate from his belly, Nathan rose from the table and discovered, upon going into the bathroom to urinate (which, like his intake of food, was excessive), that smears and splotches of dried blood stained the front of the inside of his underwear, as well as the skin all around his private area.

Quite naturally, Nathan assumed that the blood was his own, and was immediately shocked and afraid, for his initial thought was that he had somehow cut himself somewhere down—*there,* and had all the while been bleeding.

But after examining himself carefully and closely, and finding no wound on any part of his body, he could not for the life of him understand where the blood had come *from!* For having no memory whatsoever of his encounter with Lori Carbone and what had happened between the two of them in her garage, he never once, even for an instant, suspected that the blood with which his skin and underwear were now soiled was actually from Lori Carbone's menstrual discharge.

Completely mystified by it all, Nathan quickly undressed himself, got into the shower, and washed Lori Carbone's menses from his body. He then changed into a fresh pair of underwear and jeans, and dropped the soiled ones into the hamper, which was now quite full of dirty laundry, as Nathan was no longer able to use the washing machine, since it was down in the basement. To go down there again was to risk a second encounter with his cannibalistic house-guest, Antal Vrancic, or, worse still perhaps, catch yet another unsightly glimpse of Aunt Amelia's severed head. And Nathan shuddered violently at the thought that if it was indeed still down there, it must by now be in a most hideous state of decomposition.

And so, unable to obtain access to either the washer or the drier, the pile of dirty clothes continued, day by day, to steadily accumulate.

Nathan, meanwhile, had left the bathroom and returned wearily to the solitude of his own room. For minutes together, in a dull and empty stillness, he stood before the open window, looking out over the clustering headstones of the cemetery. Dreamily his eyes gazed off into the distance towards the old mausoleum, while his every thought revolved around the longed-for one slumbering, in all her beauty and mystery, in one of its crypts.

But then, as a sudden wave of horrible drowsiness swept irresistibly over Nathan's senses, he crept, thoroughly exhausted, into his bed, and, just as he was, in his sneakers and jeans, drifted instantly away into a deep and dream-riddled slumber.

Between four and five o'clock that same afternoon—more than an hour after Candy had sent Marty Carbone back to his home with the Buck's Zipper hunting knife and the firm instructions of what to do with it once he got there—first one, then a second NYPD police cruiser, with turret lights flashing and sirens wailing, turned up 71st Street. Shattering the dreamy tranquility and early evening hush of the quiet residential block, they pulled up, screeching, in front of the Carbone residence.

The emergency call regarding the brutal homicide of Lori Carbone had been made from within the home at the crime scene itself to the 911 operator just seven minutes prior to the two area cars being dispatched to the location. And the first pair of uniformed NYPD cops to arrive in front of the house and climb out of their radio car were officers Miguel Alonso and George Reese. Both entered the home with their hands on the butt of their holstered guns; followed seconds later by a second pair of uniformed officers.

Neighboring residents began to peer inquisitively from windows and stand dithering in the open doorways of their homes, anxiously gawking; while the more curious were already beginning to drift down toward the scene and, in spectator-like fashion, line up along the curb.

Minutes later, two more police squad cars appeared on the scene; followed soon after by a Crime Scene unit, whose technicians began stringing up yellow police tape round the home. And within half an hour of the first NYPD cops on the scene, police barricades had been set up in front of the home to hold back the press of people, in the street and on the sidewalk, whose numbers continued to swell and multiply as details of Lori Carbone's horrific murder rapidly spread through the neighborhood.

Then, around 4:40 p.m. yet another car drove up and parked on the sidewalk in front of the Carbone residence: a dark-blue unmarked four-door law enforcement vehicle, from which two plainclothes detectives on the homicide unit of the 104th Precinct (in Ridgewood, Queens) emerged.

The slimmer, and slightly shorter of the two detectives was Dennis Stavola. Aged about forty, he was clean-shaven, and very smartly dressed in a dark, double-breasted suit. The nails of his fingers were buffed and well manicured, and on the pinky of his left hand was a thick gold ring with a sapphire (his birthstone) in its bezel. His light blond hair was slicked back, and his eyes, which at the moment were hidden by a pair of dark sunglasses, were blue as the birthstone in his ring.

His partner, Frank Burns, who was neither so stylishly dressed nor so well-shaven, wore dark baggy slacks, a rumpled grey jacket, and a garishly striped tie. And although he appeared to be his partner's senior by at least ten years, due in part to his greying hair, expansive paunch, and deeply lined face—made all the more pronounced by his excessive smoking (and drinking)—he was, in fact, the younger of the two men, being several years shy of forty.

Detective Dennis Stavola, an only child, had lived in Middle Village all his life, and, having never known his father, an FDNY firefighter—who died shortly after his son's first birthday—he was brought up (by a very stern, overly-pious mother) to be a devout Roman Catholic with an unwavering allegiance to the Pontiff in Rome. As a youngster he had attended St Margaret's Catholic school, where he had been baptized, received his first Holy Communion, served for several years as an altar boy, and made his Confirmation. And it was among the best kept secrets of his adult life that, before any notion of joining the ranks of law enforcement ever crossed his mind, he had answered, at the age of nineteen, a unique calling (which he himself at the time felt to be genuine) to enter the priesthood—even graduating at the age of twenty-three from the seminary of Cathedral College in Douglaston, Queens.

In the academic years he spent studying there, Dennis Stavola had read a great deal about the world's other religions, in particular, Islam, which, according to his own theories, was little more than a pretend religion, compounded (so he'd read) of early Arabian and Sabaean beliefs, as well as Judaism and the creeds of several heretical Christian sects. And this adverse opinion of his, with regard to

Islam, seemed to him all the more valid following the September 11th terrorist attacks. Both he and his partner, Frank Burns, were then only two or three years out of the police academy, working as two patrol officers in a squad car in Queens. It was a job which neither of them found particularly exciting or interesting; and before long the slow, dull hours of their duty in an area car began to bore them—that is until the first anniversary of 9/11. That day was to be a turning point in their careers.

For in the days leading up to the anniversary, numerous threats from an anonymous caller had come in to One Police Plaza against a number of mosques in and around the five boroughs. The Mayor of New York and the Police Commissioner were taking these threats very seriously; for which reason NYPD officers in their cruisers were dispatched to the locations of those mosques specifically mentioned by name as potential targets. Officers Dennis Stavola and Frank Burns had been assigned to the Albanean American Islamic Center of Queens on Myrtle Avenue in Glendale.

Double-parked on that busy thoroughfare just across the street from the mosque, the two rookie officers had been keeping vigilant watch from their radio car for more than a week. It proved to be a very tedious assignment which (to them) grew more and more boring with each passing day. But on the morning of the first anniversary of September 11th, as the two men were yawning and fidgeting in the front seat of their police cruiser, they decided to pass the dull, dragging hours by resuming their ongoing debate (which they'd begun in the early days of the academy) regarding which was the better pistol carried by law enforcement officers: the revolver, or the semi-automatic.

Detective Dennis Stavola was partial to the revolver—not that he was completely against semi-automatic pistols; he carried one himself (a PT 24/7 9mm) as a back-up gun, and a reliable semi-auto pistol it was. Still and all, his primary weapon of choice was (and always would be) his Smith and Wesson M642 revolver, pointing out to Frank Burns, through their numerous discussions over the past two years, that the revolver was simple, compact, and more reliable; having (as was the case with the M642) no exposed hammer to cock, and no safety to remember should things get chaotic in a crisis—just aim and fire it.

But as his partner, Frank Burns, was in the middle of giving his side of the argument in defense of the semi-automatic's advantages over the revolver—particularly the Glock Standard G17, which he himself carried—what should they see striding down Myrtle Avenue toward the mosque the two of them were assigned to protect, but the burly figure of a man wearing military fatigues and carrying a 9mm semi-automatic rifle.

Officer Stavola instantly surmised the man's intention and destination: being what day it was; the attacks that had taken place one year ago on that very day; and the threats that had come in to the department over the past couple of weeks. And despite the pain and bitterness he felt on that day, or the negative view he had of the Islamic faith, he was not about to let some psycho go into a mosque and start a massacre of innocent people. Moreover, not only had he sworn, the day he graduated from the academy, to uphold the law and protect civilian life, but, being a religious man, who proudly carried a crucifix on a gold chain round his neck, he knew it was his solemn duty as a practicing Christian to prevent that madman from taking innocent lives. And so, laying his hand on the butt of his revolver, he turned to his partner who was sitting behind the wheel.

The thoughts of officer Frank Burns were in every way the same as his partner's that morning. He, too, had been brought up as a devout Catholic, but having lost his enthusiasm for the church with the failure of his first marriage, he ceased to attend Mass. And by the time he had gone through a bitter divorce from his second wife, he had lost his faith altogether. Like his partner, Dennis Stavola, he, too, had a low opinion of the Moslem world, the fanaticism of its people, and their zeal for terrorism. But on the morning of that 9/11 anniversary, when officer Frank Burns had seen a man briskly advancing down Myrtle Avenue carrying a semi-automatic rifle, he also suspected who he was and what he intended to do.

Simultaneously, the two rookie officers climbed out of their cruiser with guns drawn. At one and the same instant the man opened fire on them, hitting Frank Burns in the left arm. Officer Dennis Stavola then gave chase, shooting and killing the gunman on the steps of the mosque. Frank Burns was rushed to the nearest hospital, where he made a speedy recovery from the superficial gun wound he'd suffered, and upon his release, both he and Dennis Stavola received the personal thanks from Hizzoner, the Mayor himself, on the steps of City Hall before a sea of journalists, photographers, and TV reporters with camera crews for the television networks. For their foresight, bravery, and quick-thinking they were given commendations from the police commissioner, and, soon after, officially upgraded to the rank of detective.

Now, when detectives Dennis Stavola and Frank Burns had made their way past the police sawhorses in front of the Carbone residence, they both paused a few moments to look at, and admire, Marty Carbone's Harley Davidson which was parked at a cool tilt on its kickstand in the driveway.

Frank Burns stood there with his hands deep in his trouser pockets, eyeing the bike with eyebrows arched high on his puckered forehead. "*Nice* Two Wheeler," he said, pursing his lips and emitting a long drawn whistle. "Maybe it's Elvis's long-lost Harley;" he quipped, turning to his partner; "or the one Marlon Brando rode, you know, in that movie 'The Wild One'."

Dennis Stavola lifted his sunglasses a little and gazed at the bike from under their rims. "It's neither," he said, setting his shades once more on the bridge of his nose. "Brando's bike was a Triumph Thunderbird; and the King's long-lost bike is a Harley Davidson Big Twin, which, according to rumor, was inscribed under the rear fender by James Dean, who gave it to Elvis as a gift. This one here," said detective Stavola, indicating Marty Carbone's bike with his chin, "is a customized 'Moo-Glide', as they're called."

Detective Frank Burns eyed his partner quizzically a moment, then grinned. "Well, well, well, whaddaya know—a Harley Davidson aficionado," he laughed.

Faintly smiling, detective Dennis Stavola said, "Something like that"; and together, he and his partner advanced up the walkway. Mounting the front steps of the house, a uniformed NYPD officer appeared in the doorway and raised the waist-high yellow police tape for the two detectives to slip the more easily underneath it. And the moment they stepped across the threshold and into the foyer they were nearly overpowered by the charnel smell of blood and death, which even at the front door hung heavy and noisome. In fact, it permeated the very air throughout the entire first floor of the home, whose every room reeked with the taint of a slaughterhouse.

By degrees the two detectives became acclimated to that foul stench, and were presently standing in the middle of the living room, glancing round. There were several uniformed NYPD officers standing about the room, while a police photographer was snapping a few shots from different angles of the victim—or what was left of her.

For some seconds the two detectives, unable to either move or speak, stared in shock and horror, their eyes fixed on the decapitated and limbless trunk of Lori Carbone lying on the floor in front of the sofa. Then, "Holy Jesus," breathed Frank Burns, in utter disbelief, as Dennis Stavola made the sign of the cross. The two detectives then raised their eyes and fixed their gaze on the wall of the room behind the sofa, where several words had been scrawled, apparently in blood—the victim's, no doubt, thought Dennis Stavola to himself. He removed his sunglasses and stared at the words; for a moment or two his eyes narrowed and his brow creased. Then, "Heu insanio... furore consumer," he muttered, scarcely above a whisper.

Frank Burns's gaze fixed itself obliquely for an instant on his partner's face, then returned to the words on the wall. "Looks, and sounds, to me like mumbo jumbo," he said.

Dennis Stavola's eyes continued to scan the writing. "Actually, it's Latin," he remarked; and, removing a pen and notepad from the breast pocket of his jacket, he copied the words onto a blank page in the pad. Restoring the pen and pad to his pocket, Dennis Stavola went over to the victim's mutilated trunk, and Frank Burns followed him. Overcoming his revulsion, detective Stavola squatted down by it as near as he could, for the blood that had leaked and jetted from the butchered carcass had spread itself round in a pool of clotting gore. He stared down at the body for some while, his eyes to and froing over the gaping stab wounds with which the chest area of the victim had been sadistically riddled.

Frank Burns, meanwhile, stood there beside his partner feeling his stomach—which, until that moment, he'd always considered to be 'cast-iron', as he called it—literally tumble and turn within him. He had been assigned to view his fair share of grisly homicides, but the ferocity, the brutality of this one was beyond anything he'd ever seen before, it was virtually ghoulish, diabolic. And through the next few moments of awkward silence, he deliberately shifted his repelled and restless gaze first to the dour-faced medical examiner who was standing nearby jotting down a series of notes onto a clipboard, and then to the crime scene investigators who were collecting evidence with swabs and tweezers from various parts of the room, before finally returning, almost reluctantly, to the victim's remains.

Unable to bear the silence a moment longer, Frank Burns heaved a long, tired breath, and, in an effort to appear unaffected and, at the same time, suppress the growing queasiness of his stomach, he quipped, "It's my guess that we're dealing with a guy who must've just graduated from the Charlie Manson University for Deranged Killers, with a master's degree no doubt in the slicing and dicing of his fellow man—and woman."

The M.E. glanced up from his clipboard a moment and gravely shook his head, but otherwise remained silent. Dennis Stavola stood up and, with his eyes still mournfully fastened on the body, remarked, "This guy's work would probably make Jack the Ripper blush."

Frank Burns took a pack of Marlboros from the breast pocket of his shirt and abstracted a cigarette. "Okay," he said, "here's part of our victim"—and pausing a moment to first sniff the cigarette, then slip it behind his left ear—"so what happened to the rest of her;" he continued; "you know, arms, legs, head?"

The medical examiner paused in his writing and pointed with his pen across the room. The two detectives turned their eyes in the direction indicated and, on the far side of the room, under one of the windows next to the grandfather clock, they noted a blood-soaked sheet, underneath which bulged its grisly contents. Two assistants of the M.E. were standing there with a stretcher, already preparing to bag, load, and remove what was concealed beneath that stained sheet.

Together Dennis Stavola and Frank Burns crossed the room and bent down next to it. Dennis Stavola did the honors of lifting the sheet aside, and he and Frank Burns peered beneath it.

First gulping back their breath, then breathing out one or two low exclamations of horror, the two detectives in shock and revulsion quickly jerked their faces aside. For the victim's severed head had been reduced to a horrid shell-like husk round which a tangled mass of blond and gore-clotted locks spread themselves out: while embedded deep in the midst of what remained of the pulpy flesh and shattered bones of her mangled face was one of the cylindrical brass weights from the grandfather clock. As for the victim's limbs, evidently they had been placed in deliberate conjunction with the smashed head, so as to form a truly ghastly representation of a skull-and-crossbones configuration.

Dennis Stavola let the sheet fall from his fingers and, in an effort to refrain from vomiting, covered his nose and mouth a moment or two with the lapel of his jacket while holding his breath. Then, without saying a word, the two men again stood up and their eyes, for the next few moments, slowly, intently swept the room, from its floor, to its walls, to its ceiling, as though in diligent search of something—*anything* to replace the gruesome images of what they had just now seen under that sheet.

Still in that same deep, musing silence, their wandering gaze presently drifted at one and the same time across the living room's threshold into the dining area where they observed an NYPD officer interviewing a grey-haired man seated in a high-backed chair before the dining room table. The man's black attire and white clerical collar clearly identified him as a priest; and the uniformed cop who was holding a notepad and writing in it with a pen, was evidently taking down statements.

Dennis Stavola instantly recognized the officer as Miguel Alonso, a second generation cop, in his late thirties, who, glancing up from his pad for a moment, caught detective Stavola's eye and nodded to him solemnly.

Frank Burns nudged his partner, and said, "Hey, it's our old amigo from the academy—soon to be a kinsman of yours."

Officer Alonso greeted the two detectives as he advanced into the living room. He and Dennis Stavola had formed a close bond while in the academy together, during which time it had become almost a ritualistic amusement between the two men to jokingly bust each other's chops: Stavola about Alonso's eyebrows, which (then) met together in the middle of his forehead to form a distinct 'unibrow'—and Alonso about Stavola's unruly hair. For back then officer Dennis Stavola had a projecting tuft of hair on the top of his head, like that of the freckled kid, Alfalfa, from the Little Rascals, for which some of his peers in the academy bestowed on him that very designation as a nickname. But on the recommendation of Miguel Alonso, officer Dennis (Alfalfa) Stavola went to see Alonso's cousin, Elena Melendez, owner of the Pastel Pagoda hair salon in Middle Village, who cut and styled his hair, slicked it back, and so rid him forever of the Alfalfa-like 'cowlick' he had sported since high school. And at the same time that he lost his cowlick, he gained a girlfriend, for the attraction between himself and Elena Melendez was instant, and they continued to see each other exclusively from their first movie- and dinner-date till now. In fact, only a week ago, Dennis Stavola had placed the engagement ring on Elena Melendez's finger and officially agreed on a wedding date of June 2018: something which detective Stavola looked forward to, since he was tired of his bachelorhood. Even though his partner, Frank Burns—a veteran of two failed marriages (with his third already heading for the rocks)—kept warning him that 'marriage ain't all you'd think it's cracked up to be'; cautioning him to stay a 'free man', and not to 'sign up for a life sentence'. But despite his partner's ominous (and unsolicited) counsel, Dennis Stavola had his sights set on becoming not only a 'loving and faithful' husband, but the 'prospective' father of at least two kids, a boy and a girl—so he hoped. Give him that, and he'd have all he ever wanted out of life.

As for Frank Burns, he thought his partner was 'nuts'. He himself had three kids from his first marriage, and two from his second: and by the time he'd married his third wife, he'd gone to the local clinic and had a vasectomy, as a preventive measure to any further procreating. 'You cease to live when you have kids,' he warned Dennis Stavola. 'The minute they're born, everything you do is for them. A pain in the ass from day one. But don't take my word for it. Go ahead; have all the kids you want. You'll see what I mean—like they say, there's no substitute for experience.' And detective Stavola intended to do just that, and 'go ahead' indeed; for the wedding date was set, and his fiancee, Elena Melendez, was on board with having their first child within a year or two of saying 'I do' at the altar.

Officer Miguel Alonso shook hands with the two detectives in the living room, and, after a brief exchange of small talk, Frank Burns, with a glance toward the priest sitting in the dining area, asked, "So who's our padre, and what's he doing here?"

Over the squelching of his radio, officer Miguel Alonso said, "His name's Father Matthews. He's our eyewitness. Parish priest at St Margaret's church."

Dennis Stavola's eyebrows arched. "Father Gregory Matthews?" he asked, his eyes looking past officer Alonso into the dining area where the priest was seated. Frank Burns turned to eye his partner quizzically. "You know him?"

Dennis Stavola continued to stare into the dining room at the priest. "Quite well," he replied; then, to Alonso, "But if you hadn't said his name just now, I would've never recognized him. Last time I saw him—which was more than fifteen years ago—he was about seventy pounds heavier; his hair was all black; and he had a beard and moustache." There was a moment's silence. Then, "So what's his story?" detective Burns asked Alonso.

"Walked in on our perp," answered officer Alonso, "as he was smearing blood all over the wall there—writing whatever the hell that says"—for an instant he indicated with the tip of his pen the words *Heu insanio*—"He says the victim's mother, a Valerie Carbone, is a close friend of his. Right now she's away—upstate, according to Father Matthews—with her boyfriend, a Dominic Bradden. She asked Father Matthews to check in on her kids whenever he could. Father Matthews gave us her cell number and the number to Bradden's home upstate. We're trying to contact them right now."

"And where's our victim's father?" asked Dennis Stavola. Alonso said: "According to Father Matthews, Hector Carbone died six years ago. Heart attack."

Frank Burns glanced across the room at the M.E.'s two assistants who were now bagging and loading Lori Carbone's remains onto the stretcher. "So what's our victim's name?" he asked. After giving the name to the two detectives, officer Miguel Alonso took a framed photo of Valerie Carbone with her two children from the shelf of a wall unit and handed it to Dennis Stavola. "That's our victim in better days," he said, pointing out Lori Carbone in the photo, "with her arm around her mother; and that's her brother in the background." He paused a moment, shook his head, and added: "She's just a kid, really. Only turned sixteen a couple of weeks ago according to Father Matthews."

The two detectives scanned the photo in silence. Then, "And our perp? Do we have a name? A description?" asked Dennis Stavola.

"You're looking at him. He's right there in the photo," said Miguel Alonso. For a moment the two detectives lifted their eyes from the photo and stood facing the NYPD officer in stunned silence. "Father Matthews," he went on, "ID'd our perp as the victim's own brother."

Frank Burns drew a long, heavy breath and, frowning, exhaled it loudly and wearily. Dennis Stavola stood a while in thought, his eyes fixed on Marty Carbone's face in the photo's background. "Not a very good picture," he said, squinting his eyes a little. Then, glancing over at the wall unit shelves for a better photo, he happened to note, on the coffee table, a large family photo album. He handed the framed photo back to officer Alonso, flipped through the photo album, and extracted three close-ups of Marty Carbone, one of which he handed to his partner.

"So this is our psycho-butcher," Frank Burns remarked. Silently, attentively Dennis Stavola continued to scan the two photos he himself was holding. Then, "So what the hell set this guy off?" His question was followed by a perplexed, intent look. "I mean, what makes a guy," he went on, "kill his own sibling in such a brutal, inhuman way?" The three men exchanged looks, but not one of them said a word, for all plausible, all rational suggestions seemed impossible.

Officer Alonso clicked his pen and, in answer to the next question asked him by Frank Burns, he replied: "Perp's name is Martin Vergil Carbone."

Faintly smirking, Frank Burns glanced at his partner. "Vergil —now isn't that cute?"

"He's a member of a small-time punk bike-gang here in Middle Village," went on Alonso. "You know, Hell's Angels wannabes. Got a rap sheet longer than your arm. In Queens and Brooklyn he's been charged with misdemeanor assault, menacing and harassment, drunk and disorderly, resisting arrest, a couple of drug-related offenses—the list goes on."

Frank Burns's eyebrows arched as he took the cigarette that was nestling behind his ear and lit it. "Hmm; well, it seems," he grunted, after taking a long drag and exhaling the smoke, "now ol' Martin Vergil can add homicide to that list."

Dennis Stavola asked, "Do we know where he is?"

"No; according to Father Matthews, who placed the call to 911," said Alonso, "our perp fled the scene on foot carrying a large knife—presumably the murder weapon." He paused to flip over a page or two of his notepad, then said, "Perp's description, as provided by Father Matthews, is as follows: black tee-shirt, denim blue jeans, dark boots; long hair—pulled back in a pony tail. Oh, yeah; something else. Father Matthews says the back of his tee-shirt was in tatters, and his back was covered in blood. Looked like he had some nasty cuts himself all over his back."

Dennis Stavola asked, "Scratches? Stab wounds?"

"Father Matthews said—to him—they looked more like stab wounds."

There was a long silence. Then, Dennis Stavola spoke. "So what the hell are we saying here? That the victim and her brother got into some kind of quarrel which then escalated into the two of them attacking each other with knives? If so, where's the victim's weapon?"

"No knife has been found on the premises," said officer Alonso. "Father Matthews did say he saw Carbone fleeing the scene with what looked like a large hunting knife."

Frank Burns scratched his head. "Maybe the victim had the knife first," he suggested. "She attacked Carbone with it; he got it from her, and then went to work on her with it." Another long silence followed. For some seconds Frank Burns watched his partner's pensive face. At length, Dennis Stavola spoke. "How long's it been since Carbone fled the scene?"

"I'd say not more than ten or fifteen minutes before the first squad cars pulled up," replied Miguel Alonso.

Dennis Stavola said: "Then it's a good chance that he's still somewhere nearby in the area." He breathed a long, heavy breath. "Okay. We'll put out a BOLO on him," he went on, "and we'll circulate these photos and use them to track him."

"I think we should also have the other members of that bike gang Carbone's in, brought in for questioning," said Frank Burns. "They might know where he's hiding; or maybe he's even gone to one or two of them for help."

Detective Stavola nodded his head. "Good. In the meantime, we'll have a few plainclothes canvass the area, knock on some doors, and talk to some of the residents," he said. "Who knows, maybe there's someone out there who's recently spotted our perp on the streets, or in an alley, or some neighbor's backyard. If so, hopefully we'll pick up our Jerk the Ripper and have him off the streets within the next hour or two."

Dennis Stavola handed the photos of Marty Carbone to officer Miguel Alonso and advanced into the dining room. Another uniformed NYPD cop (Alonso's partner, George Reese), who was coming from the kitchen, nodded to them as the two detectives walked past him and continued on toward the dining room table where Father Gregory Matthews was seated. He was a smallish man, aged somewhere between sixty-five and seventy, with large, dark, deep-set eyes that, when the two detectives stepped quietly over to him, peered up at them with a far-away, almost startled look in their depths. But when they fixed themselves on the face of Dennis Stavola, a look of recognition all at once entered into them, and he continued to steadily regard the detective as if he were seeing a ghost.

Dennis Stavola quietly returned his stare, while Frank Burns exhibited his gold shield to the priest and gave his name and his partner's. Father Matthews's eyebrows rose. "Detective," he echoed, a tinge of sarcasm in his voice, and for the fraction of an instant, with his eyes still fixed on Dennis Stavola's face, his mouth stirred in a faint sneer.

"Father," said Frank Burns, after he'd stubbed out his cigarette in an ash tray on the table, "I know this has been a day like no other for you; and I'm sure the last thing you need now in the middle of this traumatic experience is some cop asking you a lot of questions. But if you're up to talking, we'd sure appreciate you helping us sort through what you witnessed here, so that hopefully we can make some sense of it." Father Matthews withdrew his stony gaze from Dennis Stavola and nodded his head. Then, "We're told you knew Lori Carbone," said Frank Burns. "Is that right?"

"Yes," said Father Matthews. "A sweet girl. I baptized her, and assisted the bishop at her Confirmation, as well as her brother's. I still can't believe this has happened. An absolute tragedy."

Frank Burns nodded his head. "Yes; no doubt of that, Father," he remarked; and, after a short pause, he asked, "Are you a close friend of Lori's mother?"

"Yes," said Father Matthews. "Valerie and her boyfriend, Dominic, for the past few summers now, have gone upstate to Oneonta where Dominic owns several acres of land and a summer home. They stay there sometimes a couple of weeks to a month, during which Valerie has asked me if I would periodically check in on her son, Marty, and her daughter, Lori. I've been doing this now for the past four years. My mother lives in the apartment above the stationary store on Metropolitan Avenue just around the corner; and so, I now and again drop in on Lori and Marty when I stop and see my mother."

"So, Father," said Frank Burns, "before stopping here to check in on Valerie Carbone's children, you were coming from—where?"

The priest glanced for an instant at Dennis Stavola, who was standing beside his partner in silence, listening attentively, with his hands clasped behind his back. "I stopped to visit with my mother in her apartment," answered Father Matthews. "I made her some tea and we talked for a while. Then, a little after four o' clock, I left and, before returning to the church, I decided to look in on Marty and Lori here at their home. I knocked on the door several times, but no one answered. Then, after ringing the bell, and still getting no answer, I tried the door. It opened; and when I stepped inside I found Marty in the living room covered in blood. He was standing behind the sofa, holding a knife in one hand, and writing on the wall with his other blood-soaked hand the words there. He turned then, and looked at me, but on his face there was no expression of any kind whatsoever—no recognition; no remorse; nothing. It was as if he was unaware of my presence, or in no way concerned that I was there." Father Matthews was silent for a little; and then, slowly signing himself with the cross, he began again, in a low hesitating voice: "And yet, when our eyes met, there was a look in his unlike anything I'd ever seen before—it was absolutely inhuman. I felt as though I'd stared into an abyss; it froze my blood. Then he quietly turned and, after he had calmly walked out of the house, I immediately called the police."

Frank Burns asked: "Did he say anything to you, Father; or you to him?"

'I said, 'Oh, my God', and then I called his name, twice, I think," said Father Matthews. "And, as he continued to stare into the distance with that horrid look in his eyes, I heard him say, 'Marty Carbone doesn't exist; Marty Carbone never has existed; my name is Gilles de Rais, marshal of Retz'." A look almost of astonishment came into Dennis Stavola's eyes when he heard the name. Frank Burns noticed it and, for a moment or two, eyed his partner curiously, before asking Father Matthews, "About the words on the wall,

Father, which you say you witnessed Marty Carbone writing—is it fair to say you know what they are?"

"If by that you mean, what language they're in;" said Father Matthews; "yes: it's Latin. But how in the world Marty Carbone would know Latin, I can't say."

"Do you know the meaning of those words, Father?" asked Frank Burns.

Father Matthews said: "Yes; and so does your partner, detective Stavola. Why don't you ask him?" And pausing a moment to coldly regard Dennis Stavola's silent face, Father Matthews added, almost snidely, "I'm sure he could give you a very accurate translation: he studied Latin for several years here *and* in Rome!"

For a moment or two, with a half-quizzical look, detective Frank Burns eyed the face of his partner, who stooped his head a little and slightly blushed. Then, after an interval of awkward silence, Father Matthews stood up and said: "May I leave now, detectives, if you have no further questions?"

Frank Burns nodded his head. "Sure, Father," he said. "Just one more thing. We'd better take down a number so we can reach you in case there's anything else we need to ask you about." And after Father Matthews, having given his cell number, had walked away, Frank Burns turned to his partner with a half-amused, half-incredulous look, and said: "*You* studied Latin—in *Rome*, no less?"

Dennis Stavola met his partner's eye for a moment with a wry, embarrassed grin, and nodded his head. "So you know what that stuff in there says?" Frank Burns asked him.

"'Heu insanio'," said detective Stavola, "means, 'Ah, woe! I am mad!'; and,'Furore consumor', 'I am devoured by frenzy!' They're the words of the French nobleman, Gilles de Laval, Baron de Rais—the last ones he spoke as he was led out to be hanged at the gallows on a high patch of ground just on the outskirts of Nantes. According to the record of his execution, he is said to have shouted those words over and over again as he stood under the gibbet and the noose was placed around his neck. Executed along with him were his two servants, Griart and Poitu, for aiding and abetting their master in the pursuit of his abominations."

Frank Burns rolled his eyes. "Well, that's terrific," he said, sardonically; "but you wanna tell me just who the hell this Gilles de what's-his-name is!"

"A serial killer of the fifteenth century," said Dennis Stavola, "best described by today's psychologists as a cruel and sadistic necrophilist who suffered from what is medically termed hematomania, a mad thirst for the taste and consumption of human blood. He is said to have confessed at his trial that he could only attain sexual pleasure by first seeing, tasting, and drinking blood. According to court records of the time, he admitted to having killed some eight hundred children over a period of eight years: some by decapitating; others by dismembering; and still others by disemboweling. He was tried by the Church in France in 1439 for his inhuman crimes. During his trial his two servants gave detailed testimony concerning their master's perverse and heinous outrages, the most notorious of which were inventing his own ghoulish version of ninepins by using the severed heads of several children as bowling balls, and drinking the blood of a living child while seating himself comfortably in the boy's bowels. Toward the end of his trial, Gilles himself claimed to have been led on in these atrocities and sadistic excesses of blood and violence by a mysterious person whom he identified as le Enfant saunce Pite, 'the Child without Mercy'; and whom he described as a ten or eleven year-old blond-haired hermaphrodite whom he swore was none other than a Vampire who had been wandering across Europe since the time of the late Roman empire."

Frank Burns whistled, and said: "And I thought our modern day society had the monopoly on all the kooks and crazies in the world."

"You wouldn't think that way again," said Dennis Stavola, "if I was to tell you about Elizabeth Bathory, Sergeant Bertrand, and an Austrian beggar from the village of Polomyja, named Swiatek."

Frank Burns stood thinking as he rubbed his stubbly chin. Then, "Okay," he said, "so you're gonna tell me that our perp, Marty Carbone, knows all about this Gilles de who's-it, and how to speak and write in Latin?" He paused and, with a skeptical grin, viewed his partner steadily; then, before Dennis Stavola could reply, he said, "Better yet, you wanna tell me how you know Latin—and how the hell this Father Matthews knows you studied it in Rome of all places?"

Dennis Stavola shook his head and, half-frowning, half-smirking, said, "I guess I might as well make a full confession here"—and heaving a long, tired breath—"Years ago," he went on, "I studied in Rome to become a priest. I met Father Matthews when I was still in the seminary at Cathedral College in Douglaston. He had been ordained then for some ten years when I entered the college. He took a liking to me; sponsored me; and sent me to Rome at his expense."

"So what happened with that?" asked Frank Burns.

Dennis Stavola sighed, and said: "I'll give you the abridged version. I met a girl. She got pregnant, and the Church hushed it up. I was then packed off back to Queens, and Father Matthews and I became—estranged. We haven't spoken since. This is the first time I've seen him since all of that happened."

Frank Burns stared at his partner in silence. Then, "And you became a cop. Unbelievable."

"You want to know the best part?" said Dennis Stavola. "Before Father Matthews entered the priesthood—*he* was a cop."

"You're shittin' me."

"No; I'm dead serious," said Dennis Stavola. "He told me that long before he thought of becoming a priest, it had always been his childhood dream to be an NYPD cop, like his father."

Frank Burns said: "So what the hell happened with that?"

"He was a rookie," said Dennis Stavola, "on the force no more than a year when a kid in the Bronx pulls a gun on him. Father Matthews—then, NYPD officer Matthews—fires first; the kid's killed; and the gun turns out to be a toy. His dream of being a cop died that day along with the kid, he told me. I guess becoming a priest was for him some form of penance, a way to gain absolution for what he considers the sin of murder."

"Whew! Tough break for the poor guy," said Frank Burns. "That's a shitload of guilt to be carrying around." Detective Dennis Stavola remained silent. He and his partner lingered about the crime scene a while longer, then went outside.

As they reached the end of the walkway to the house, a group of young teenage boys, leaning on the police sawhorses, attracted their attention. Barricades had been set up in the street along the curb and across the pavement on either side of the house to keep the growing crowds back. Behind one of the police sawhorses in the street, a dozen or more boys—among whom were Scott Webler and his brother Terence, Todd Bauer, Kerry Stark, Rodney Martello, Freddy Scalone, and one half of the now defunct heavy metal garage band, The Gore-Men (namely Glen Rubino and Kevin Hansen)—had been waving and gesturing to the two detectives.

Dennis Stavola paused a moment to glance over at the boys, and instead of continuing to advance toward their unmarked car, as his partner Frank Burns did, detective Stavola, upon hearing one of the boys (Scott Webler) shout that they knew something, suddenly changed direction and, in the hopes that a talk with the boys might yield some useful information, he went over to them.

Frank Burns, after standing a minute or two idly by the car waiting for his partner, soon joined him over by the police sawhorse where he was talking with the boys. As Frank Burns came sauntering over he heard the tall boy (Scott Webler) telling his partner about Lori Carbone. "She was a mess," he was saying, "and it looked like she had blood on her."

"And it was *inside* the garage that you found her like that?" asked detective Stavola.

Scott Webler said: "Yeah; and she was real upset: 'cause we could see she was crying."

"And she looked really scared, too," Kerry Stark added.

Detective Stavola watched the boys' faces as he said: "Then something must have happened to her; is that it?" Todd Bauer and Kerry Stark began to nod their heads eagerly, but before they could say anything, "I guess so; I mean, yeah," said Scott Webler, "something must've."

"Did Lori tell you what it was?" asked Dennis Stavola.

"Well, yeah," said Scott Webler, "she said she'd been raped—by Nathan."

Detective Stavola regarded the boy's face a moment. "Raped;" he echoed; "by Nathan." And with a meaning look he glanced sidelong at his partner.

"Yeah, Nathan Christian," said Scott Webler. "He lives in the house by the cemetery on the other side of Metropolitan Avenue. He goes to the same school as we do."

Dennis Stavola produced pen and notepad from his breast pocket and again repeated the name to himself. Then, to the boys, "So he's around your own age?" he asked. The boys all nodded. "He's a weird guy," said Todd Bauer. "Hangs out in the cemetery a lot; mostly by himself."

"And what cemetery is that?" asked Dennis Stavola.

Scott Webler said: "The one behind his house on 73rd Place."

"He goes and visits his parents' grave there," said Kerry Stark. "Me and Todd went there with him one time, a while ago, just for a few laughs. Nathan told us it's in Row J, Section 9, I think."

Dennis Stavola began to write all of this information down. It was his peculiar habit to jot down rapid notes into his pad by means sometimes of abbreviating every word and name; other times by way of writing only the initial letter of a name or word; and yet again, with the vowels left out altogether and only the consonants of a word appearing. Frank Burns, one day glancing through his partner's notepad, couldn't understand how Dennis Stavola was able to decipher such "meaningless scribble" (as he called it), and which he then declared, after having strained both his eyes and his patience, to have all the hallmarks of some kind of Japanese imperial code. In fact, to the uninitiated eye, detective Stavola's notes looked less like a form of private shorthand, and more like the enciphered message to a cryptogram.

Consequently, in taking down the information supplied him by Scott Webler and Kerry Stark, he wrote the initials NC (for Nathan Christian); then a sequence of letters and numbers HA73P (indicating 'home address, 73rd Place'); followed by the consonants

CMTRY (signifying 'cemetery') and RJ/S9 (for 'Row J, Section 9: the location of the grave of Nathan's parents).

Detective Stavola then looked at the boys, after he'd finished writing, and said: "So, about Lori Carbone: after she told you Nathan had raped her, did she say anything else?"

"She wanted to know if Nathan was still outside, you know, in the backyard," said Scott Webler. "But there was no one around. No Nathan—nothing. We didn't believe her anyway—about Nathan raping her." And the other boys all nodded their heads in agreement.

Dennis Stavola looked at their faces keenly. "Why not?" he asked them. "What made you doubt her story."

Scott Webler leaned on the barricade and grinned. "'Cause Nathan's like, well, he's like gay," he said, and the other boys started to smirk and laugh. "He hardly even talks to girls," went on Scott Webler, while the others continued to giggle and jeer. "Probably never even kissed one before."

"Yeah, and he's never even been laid before," said Kerry Stark (to sneers and loud guffaws). "He's definitely still a virgin; so how could he just go and rape Lori like that. It just doesn't make sense." To which most of the other boys wholeheartedly agreed, some by way of murmuring a low "yeah", others with an approving nod of the head.

The only one to differ with them on this point, however, was Freddy Scalone. "Nathan can't be gay," he argued. "If he's gay, why's he got a girlfriend?"

Dennis Stavola said: "Girlfriend? And what's her name?" "No one knows," said Scott Webler. "We only saw her once." Dennis Stavola asked: "Do any of you know where she lives?" "Inside the old mausoleum," said Freddy Scalone, "not far from where Nathan's parents are buried."

Detective Stavola arched his eyebrows and looked at the boys wryly. Behind him he could hear Frank Burns chuckling. "It's true," a few of the boys asserted; then, Scott Webler said: "Yeah; we saw her in the cemetery that night, just as it got dark; she came out of the old mausoleum—the one that's all covered in vines and plants and stuff. She beat the crap out of Russ Gorman. Broke his baseball bat with her bare hands; snapped it in half like it was a twig. Then she picked Russ up by his neck like he was a stuffed doll or something: she almost killed him."

"Yeah; Russell's so scared now," said Rodney Martello, "he won't even come outside anymore. He just stays in his house all day and all night."

Dennis Stavola asked: "Why is that?"

"We asked him," said Todd Bauer, "and Russ said, 'cause the girl promised him—not in words (he said) but with her eyes—that in seven nights she'd see him again, and then she would take him, or have him, or something like that; and then he told us she showed him what she looks like—really looks like."

Perplexed in the extreme by the boy's words, detective Stavola stared at him a moment or two quizzically, with puckered brow. "What did he mean by that?" he asked; to which Freddy Scalone simply grimaced and shrugged his narrow shoulders. Then, after a short silence, Kerry Stark said: "All we know is that she was strong, like, like she was a robot or somethin'."

"Nathan told me and Brian," said Freddy Scalone,"that she only comes out when it's dark."

Glen Rubino, with a broad smirk, said: "That's 'cause Nathan's kinda screwy in his head."

"So's that girl," said Kevin Hansen.

Rodney Martello shook his head. "Yeah; she ain't normal," he muttered, "that's for damn sure."

"Russ Gorman told us she even grew fangs," said Freddy Scalone. Detective Stavola, meanwhile, had been listening to all of this attentively; and notwithstanding his partner's smirking mouth and shaking head, for some inexplicable reason, Dennis Stavola could not help but believe every word the boys were telling him. Certainly it all left him feeling rather bewildered and somewhat troubled, yet he had the distinct impression (a gut feeling, really) that what was now being related to him by these boys was indeed a factual account regarding something very unusual (extraordinary perhaps), which all of them had witnessed occur inside the cemetery. And the detective very rapidly wrote down in his notepad, in his own personal cipher-like shorthand, the following sequence of consonants: STRNG G-F (for 'strange girlfriend'), then, TOM, signifying 'the old mausoleum'. And he thought to himself that it might be worth having a talk with this odd and rather unpopular boy, Nathan Christian, who lived by the cemetery, just to hear his side of the story, if only on the slim but not altogether unlikely chance that it might yield a few more details with regard to Lori Carbone and her brother—perhaps even one or two hints at a motive as to why Marty Carbone would kill his own sister. But as for this mysterious girl, with superhuman strength, who came out of some old mausoleum—he didn't know what *precisely* to make of all that.

Detective Stavola then said to the boys: "So what happened then to Lori Carbone after she told you that Nathan had raped her?"

"She ran inside her house," said Scott Webler. "And a little while later we heard Marty come home on his motorcycle. So we told him how we found Lori in the garage, and what she said about Nathan, and he rode over to Nathan's house."

"Which," said Dennis Stavola, consulting his notes for a moment, "is on 73rd Place."

"Right," said Scott Webler. "It's the only house on the same side as the cemetery." And detective Stavola quickly jotted into his pad, 'cem-home-side'; then, "Okay. So Marty goes to Nathan's— then what?"

"Well, it was weird," said Scott Webler. "I mean, Marty went into Nathan's house—but, when he came out again, his shirt was all ripped up in the back, and he had blood all over him, and, like, cuts all over his back."

Dennis Stavola turned to his partner, and long, slow looks passed between the two detectives. Then, looking at the boys again, Dennis Stavola said, "You mean, when Marty entered Nathan's home he was fine—"

But Kerry Stark quickly broke in, saying, "Well, we didn't see him go in—when we got there, he was already inside."

Dennis Stavola slowly nodded his head. "Okay; so you're saying," he suggested, "that when Marty Carbone drove off to confront Nathan, he had no cuts on him—no rips or tears in his shirt, is that it?"

"Yeah," said Scott Webler. "But then he came out of Nathan's house, and walked right past us, funny-like, like he didn't know us or even see us standing there; and that's when we saw his shirt all torn, and cuts on his back."

Detective Stavola faintly nodded his head and, pursing his lips, again exchanged looks with his partner. Then, giving the boys a thumbs-up, he said, "Thanks guys"; and together, he and Frank Burns, turning away from the police sawhorses, walked over to their car. Once inside, the two detectives sat for a while quietly thinking. Frank Burns, with one hand on the steering wheel, slipped the key into the ignition and said, "So what do you think?"

Dennis Stavola, with a somewhat puzzled look on his face, shook his head. "I don't know," he said. "Something's missing. It just doesn't add up. Let's say this Nathan kid did rape Marty's sister, like the kids there claim Lori Carbone told them; and Marty goes over to Nathan's to confront the kid."

Frank Burns nodded his head. "Okay."

"So what happened in there that gave him all those cuts on his back?" said Dennis Stavola. "Do we just assume this Nathan Christian, a fifteen year-old kid with a popularity problem, cut up a street-punk bruiser like Carbone and then sent him packing?"

Frank Burns said: "Maybe there was someone else in the house with Nathan; someone who stood up for the kid."

"Okay; let's assume there was," said Dennis Stavola. "Let's say this other individual put the cuts on Marty Carbone's back. It still doesn't explain why Carbone would then come walking out of this Nathan-kid's house, climb onto his bike, ride home and then decapitate and dismember his sister. Something had to set him off—make him snap. But what?"

For nearly a full minute the two detectives sat on in silent thought; then, Frank Burns turned to his partner, and said, "So whadda you want to do?"

Dennis Stavola said: "I think we should go see this kid Nathan; maybe he can tell us something that'll make sense of it all."

Frank Burns turned the key in the ignition and started the car. With his foot still on the brake pedal, he put the car in gear, and said, "Where'd they say the kid lives again—73rd..." Dennis Stavola glanced into his notepad and said: "73rd Place—it's the house that's on the same side as the cemetery." Then, hitting the siren a couple of times, Dennis Stavola signed to two uniformed NYPD cops over by the barricades, who removed one of the police sawhorses and directed the crowd to move back so that the detectives' unmarked car could pass through.

Scott Webler, Kerry Stark, and a few of the other boys followed the car a little ways, waving at the two detectives as they pulled slowly away. Then, on the outskirts of the crowd, the boys halted and watched in silence as the law enforcement Chevy turned left at the corner and slipped smoothly into the traffic on Metropolitan Avenue.

CHAPTER THREE

"...Then in a few short hours a dire woe was visited upon them... for he dealt out fierce and deadly wounds, slaying now this, now that one. Many a one, having fallen in his blood, he did to death..."

—*The Nibelungenlied*

"...They made a horrible groaning as he shattered their skulls, and the ground seethed with their blood... All were lying in the dust and weltering in their blood: like so many fish netted out of the sea..."

—*The Odyssey*

Within a matter of minutes detective Frank Burns had turned down 73rd Place, pulled up in front of Nathan's house and, following his partner's lead, who had already opened the passenger door to their unmarked police vehicle, he dragged himself out from behind the wheel of the car. As he followed Dennis Stavola up the walk to the front door of the house, he kept dabbing the glistening beads of sweat from his face and forehead with the wrinkled sleeve of his jacket, for not the least breath of wind tempered the sun's unclouded rays that late afternoon, making the heat feel like a hundred.

And yet, as they ascended the porch steps to the home, both detectives had noted, with a single comprehensive glance, that while the slats to the blinds beyond the rather grimed glass of the front bay window were turned, presumably to screen the interior of the room against the sun's heat, the narrow casements themselves were shut tight.

"Unless they've got plenty of fans going, it must be like the tropics in there," quipped Frank Burns to Dennis Stavola who, like his partner, also found it fairly odd that the windows should be shut fast like that, since the two men had neither detected with their ears the low stertorous droning of an air-conditioner, nor glimpsed with their eyes its box-shaped bulk projecting from some side window or wall of the home.

Detective Stavola had noted, too, that the exterior of the house was very poorly maintained, and therefore dingy-looking in the main, and in need of substantial repair work. And while he was in the midst of these reflections, the front door, not long after Frank Burns had knocked on it several times and rung the bell, was quietly opened an inch or two, and a tall spare man (Antal Vrancic) peered round its edge at them in what appeared to be a singularly distrustful and unfriendly manner.

The two detectives noted it instantly, and the look of suspicion and hostility on Vrancic's face seemed only to deepen all the more the moment the two men showed him their gold badges embossed with the letters NYPD, and introduced themselves as detectives on the homicide unit in the 104th Precinct. Several moments of silence followed; then, "Yes;" said Vrancic, somewhat crossly; "how can I help you?"

"We were told," said Dennis Stavola, replacing his gold shield and NYPD identification in the breast pocket of his jacket, "that this is the home of Nathan Christian."

During the prolonged silence that followed these words, Vrancic peered at the two men mutely, his luminous black eyes shifting rapidly from the face of one detective to the other. "Sir?" said Frank Burns. "Is that right? Does Nathan Christian reside at this address?" Vrancic's regard fixed itself steadily, almost resentfully on the face of detective Burns for several moments; then, "Yes," came the curt, stony reply. Dennis Stavola eyed Vrancic attentively. "And you are?" the detective asked him.

"I'm Nathan's uncle," Vrancic lied. "Arthur Christian. Has anything happened?"

"We'd like a word with Nathan, if you don't mind, Mr Christian," said Dennis Stavola. "Nothing serious; only a couple of questions regarding another neighborhood resident who we were told by several eyewitnesses came here to see your nephew."

Vrancic pretended to ponder the detective's words for a little. Then, "Ah, yes," he said, smiling blandly. "You must mean the young man who came over earlier today on his motorcycle. I believe Nathan said his name is Marty—Marty Carbone."

"Then he did come here?" asked Frank Burns.

"Yes; I think it was a little after two this afternoon," replied Mr Arthur Christian (a.k.a. Antal Vrancic). "He rang the bell, and asked if my nephew, Nathan, was home. I called Nathan, who then came down. They spoke for a little here in the living room, and then Marty left."

There was a moment's silence; then, Dennis Stavola spoke. "Do you happen to know, sir, what the conversation between your nephew and Marty Carbone was about?" The question had been preceded by an intent steady look. Vrancic met the detective's gaze blandly. "I have no idea," he replied. "I was in the kitchen at the time."

Dennis Stavola continued to view the man steadily as he asked, "Is your nephew home now, Mr Christian?"

"Yes, he is," Vrancic answered. "Would you like to speak to him?"

"It would be very helpful if we could," said detective Stavola.

Vrancic's luminous black eyes seemed to glitter coldly, and there was a faint tinge of scorn in his voice and his attitude as he said, "Come in, then. He's napping right now in the sun-room. Come; I'll wake him up."

Turning then, Vrancic paused a moment and, after having cast a single stony glance over his shoulder at the NYPD detectives, he motioned them to follow him. And the moment Dennis Stavola and his partner stepped across the threshold of the foyer, behind the tall, thin, stooping form of their guide, who continued to move forward swiftly and silently in front of them, with great strides over the dusty boards of the living room floor, the two detectives were instantly struck by a curious sense or air of neglect, loneliness, and abandonment which seemed to pervade the entire room—indeed, the house itself!

Having taken only one or two steps into the area of the living room, detective Stavola suddenly paused and, for some seconds, peered half-intently, half-cautiously round himself through the room's artificial twilight. Point to point, over floor, walls, furnishings, and ceiling, his gaze steadily, warily, uneasily traveled: for almost it seemed to him as though all genial human influence in the room had long since ceased to be welcome there; as though such influence in it were no longer even remotely possible now.

Emerging rather abruptly from these somewhat disquieting reflections, Dennis Stavola moved on toward the French doors to the sun-room where he found Vrancic and his partner waiting for him. Once before those doors, he noted immediately how their glass panes were veiled on the inner side by what appeared to be a blanket or quilt. And even as the two detectives were in the act of glancing at one another, Vrancic had tapped softly with the hairy knuckle of a thick finger on one of the door's thin glass panes, and said, "Felebredni! Felebredni, gyermek; a rendorseget van itt!"

Detective Stavola instantly recognized the language as Hungarian, for it was among the several languages which he had studied and mastered many years ago while in Rome. And never once noting the questioning look in Frank Burns's eyes as his partner slowly turned his face towards him, Dennis Stavola continued to stare at the profile of Vrancic's sneering face, having suddenly started at the man's words, not because he had understood that the man had said, "Awake! Awake, child; the police are here"; but rather at the *way* in which the man's voice had *conveyed* those words. For an undercurrent of derision—no! malice—seemed to run through each word, as though every syllable of that sentence had been strung upon a black and ominous thread of secret meaning. Moreover, almost it seemed to detective Stavola that the man had been summoning not so much a child, but rather coaxing some kind of beast to come out from its lair and inspect the dainty morsel that was now being offered to it.

And presently, as detective Stavola continued to stand there alongside his partner, waiting for the French doors to open and admit them into the room beyond, an unreasoning desire to turn and flee, to run back outside to their car and drive off as fast and far away from that house as he could, suddenly took possession of him. For it seemed as if a vague belief, or impression, kept arising in his mind, pricking and prodding at him, like an ominous warning, with regard to something of tremendous dread and peril on the other side of those doors. But the feeling remained elusive, indefinite; and despite every effort he made to deny, ignore, dispel this unaccountable yet nonetheless awful sense of dread, Dennis Stavola found himself suddenly beginning to shiver and tremble.

All at once, then, with his heart full of dark forebodings and a strange heaviness, detective Stavola heard a faint, almost stealthy clicking sound, as of the unoiled wards of a lock being slowly turned by a key; and a tremor of fear instantly swept over him as he saw the blanket on the inner side of those glass doors slowly, steadily furl itself up, like the lifting of a heavy curtain to the stage in a theater. Immediately after this, without a word to, or glance at, the detectives, Vrancic had drawn the French doors wide open and, with a single swift movement, edged to one side to allow the two men to pass on in front of him.

And although Dennis Stavola was still unable to comprehend precisely what was causing him to experience such acute feelings of panic and dismay, or producing one quaking shudder after another to pass over his body from top to toe, he hesitated awkwardly for an instant or two on the threshold of that room before finally (almost reluctantly) following his partner, Frank Burns, through its doorway. But after two or three slow, halting steps into the sun-room, he paused yet again to glance half-ruefully over his shoulder; and, as his eyes encountered those of Vrancic's, just before the man had shut-to the French doors, he observed a cold mocking gleam in their black luminous depths.

Now, from the moment detective Dennis Stavola had stepped across the threshold of that room, a strange and awful torpor, something like sleep and yet of a physically exhausting and oddly mind-numbing quality, began to gather steadily, irresistibly over him. His limbs felt utterly weighed down by it; his very thoughts dulled and adrowse with it; and his senses all but drugged by it. He could scarcely put two thoughts together. And as this mysterious, almost delicious inertia continued to mount over his senses, he began to doubt just about everything in the room which he now either saw with his eyes or heard with his ears. The one thing, however, of which he *was* absolutely certain, was the smell. For the thin, stifling, sunless air in the room seemed heavy with a peculiarly rank smell, an odor of noisome decay, as it were: something, in fact, not unlike the stench from the decomposing remnants of half-eaten prey that pervades the unclean lair of some wild carnivorous beast; a stench at which the two detectives, upon having first inhaled its foulness, sharply caught their breath and nearly choked.

Subsequent to this unpleasant experience, the next two things which Dennis Stavola and his partner noted with regard to the room was its thick gloom and—most curious of all—the rather disagreeable and unnatural chill in its atmosphere; a thing which must be due, no doubt (theorized detective Stavola to himself), to the thoroughness taken in obstructing the sun's heat and rays from penetrating the room. For he and Frank Burns presently observed a heavy quilt, which had been fastened to the wall, hanging down like a makeshift drape or curtain over the front bay window, completely hiding its blind-drawn casements; while over the side window, on their right, they noted a second quilt suspended in the same manner, evidently to perpetuate as much shadow and darkness in the room as was possible. But why all this opposition to the sunlight, thought both detectives to themselves; what did it mean?

And at one and the same time, the two men glanced at one another and, with their eyebrows arched high on their forehead, they exchanged quizzical looks. Frank Burns gave a slight shake of his head, and pointed with his finger at the rows of plant pots along the side window in which the once-green and flourishing snake plants (at one time the pride of Aunt Amelia) had long since withered from neglect to blighted skeletons; and in their pots along the quilt-hung bay window, they noted a number of unwatered and sun-starved Boston ferns, now all rank and rotting as well.

What also struck the two detectives as peculiar was the fact that there was no furniture in the room other than (incongruously enough) a solitary reclining chair; and lounging in that chair, with its feet up, unspeaking, unmoving, but watching them nevertheless very keenly with its eyes, they suddenly perceived the room's sole and unobtrusive occupant: a small, spindly-limbed child who, so far as the detectives were able to judge through the room's dusk-like murk, appeared to be about ten or eleven years of age.

The initial thought of Dennis Stavola was, "Ah, this, then, must be Nathan Christian"; and he opened his mouth, straining his lips, again and again, in an effort to address the child, to produce some sound, a word at least, with his voice. But all at once he felt himself overtaken by yawn after shuddering yawn, and, although his gaze remained fixed on the face of the child, he could barely summon the energy to keep the lids of his glazing eyes from slipping down over their aching orbs. For from the very moment his eyes had encountered those of the child's, that peculiar feeling of sleepiness, which only seconds before had stolen over him, had by now intensified into a torturing physical exhaustion. And detective Stavola kept thinking to himself, "But what the hell is wrong with me? Why am I suddenly so tired... so weak? I've never felt like this in all my life."

He was trembling now uncontrollably from head to foot, and, at the same instant, conscious of this acute sense of malaise and apprehension. This was accompanied soon after by an utter powerlessness to stir his limbs, or to even so much as turn his head and glance over at his partner, who he was all but certain must be undergoing the same frightening experience. Then, very gradually, he became aware, too, that all the while he stood there defenseless as an infant, something like his strength, his vitality, or his physical courage was now being steadily drained, siphoned off from his body.

And yet, strange to say, even amid such feelings of lachrymose helplessness and dreadful hysteria, which were now rapidly increasing in him, detective Dennis Stavola still continued to gaze on, as if spellbound, at the child in the recliner, while at the same time ruminating on the suddenly all-too apparent fact that this certainly was *not* (and could not be) the boy Nathan Christian whom he and his partner had come to see. For he was quite sure now, even though his mind was being overborne by a maddening sensation of wretched dreaminess, that the boys with whom he'd spoken earlier today had described Nathan to him as a boy their own age: some fifteen or sixteen years old—whereas the child here in the recliner looked scarcely more than ten.

And as Dennis Stavola continued to stare at the child he became intensely conscious of something about its face, something *out of the ordinary* that made him feel—*what*? For a moment or two he struggled to define, identify it. But he could not think clearly now from sheer drowsiness. Again and again he strove to rouse himself, to oppose the unpleasant influence of this infernal lassitude. The effort, however, proved utterly futile. And though still unable to stir or turn his head, he was nevertheless able, with the tail of his eye, to catch just a glimpse of his partner standing beside him, unspeaking, unmoving; and once again detective Stavola found himself wondering, half-dreamily, if Frank Burns was also feeling as queer, weak, and fatigued as himself.

Then, once more, the detective's attention reverted to the pale, narrow face of the child. Only dimly could he distinguish its features through the dense, veil-like shadows of the room, and yet, the longer he gazed on at it, the more that curious sense of vague disquiet crept over him. For there was something rather bizarre about the child's face—indeed, about the child itself: a singular ambiguity in both its face and form which seemed to hinder one's ability to determine whether the child was in actuality male or female. And it was the child's peculiar androgynous quality, in addition to its longish blond-hair and seemingly adolescent age, which somehow reminded Dennis Stavola of something—words, perhaps, or a description—he had only recently heard, or read, or spoken himself. But the detective's sleep-numbed mind was unable, at the moment, to make the association. The capacity to think, to call to mind was fast deserting him; and every effort to do so resulted in mental agony for him, as though some opposing will or power, or mastering presence, which he could scarcely hope to resist, were doing its best to thwart and prevent him.

Maugre the excruciating pain it caused him, detective Dennis Stavola's next-to vanquished wits strove ever and again to cogitate and remember. And as his mind groped achingly on, fumbling like a blind man feeling along with trembling hands in the dark, quite suddenly that word '*androgynous*', which he'd used but moments before with regard to the child, seemed to steady and rally the thoughts in the consciousness of his pain-afflicted and heavily drowsy brain. For all in an instant he remembered that the Greek word, *androgyne*, which means, literally, 'man-woman', is but one of two terms in the Greek and Roman languages for *hermaphrodite*; and at the word 'hermaphrodite' the detective violently started, and, at the same time, began to recollect the very words which he himself had spoken earlier today to his partner concerning "le Enfant saunce Pite"—a ten year-old, blond-haired hermaphrodite who, as Gilles de Rais himself had asserted, was a....

Dennis Stavola's eyes dwelt now in horror and fascination on the face of the child before him, who all this while, by the expression on its face, seemed to have been listening carefully to every thought passing in the detective's mind; for all at once the voice of the child faintly obtruded itself into the man's haze-like misery, and said: "Yes... who was a —*vampire!*' And presently, as in the frightful grip of some will-paralyzing nightmare, Dennis Stavola seemed to hear, barely above the faintest whisper, his own half-articulate voice breathe out beyond his trembling lips, "The Child Without Mercy."

And as his eyes continued to dwell with a horrible dread on the child's face and its expression of gloating cruelty, something not human seemed to materialize through its features which instantly reminded the detective of a large monstrous....

Exactly what, Dennis Stavola could not later distinctly recall. All that he could remember was his own freezing terror and intuitive awareness of it as a creature of diabolical power and awful ruthlessness. And then, quite suddenly, across all other thoughts cut the words spoken fairly recently to him over the police barricade in front of Marty Carbone's house by one of the neighborhood boys regarding Nathan's so-called 'girlfriend' from the old mausoleum, how she had shown a friend of theirs what she looked like—*really* looked like...

And all at once Dennis Stavola understood the terrifying implication of those words: for the ghastly visage which the child had presently disclosed to him froze the very blood in his veins and caused the soul within him to faint away with an inconceivable terror.

Evidently that horrid face was no less visible to himself than to his partner, for he faintly caught the sound of Frank Burns' voice issuing now in low gasps and indistinct murmurs from the stiff and straining lips of his half-open mouth. And at one and the same time that Dennis Stavola became acutely, almost unendurably conscious that an awful doom of unimaginable suffering and nightmarish horror now impended, he strove ever and again to reach with his hand for his holstered gun. But his fingers only twitched and quivered ever so slightly in a futile effort to grip the butt of his pistol, while his arm remained uselessly limp and unstirring, as though shackled to his side by unshatterable bonds.

And even as detective Dennis Stavola opened his mouth to cry out with a loud scream, the profound darkness of a heavy sleep closed over his senses, and he knew nothing more for some while.

When consciousness had once again returned to Dennis Stavola, he was instantly and somewhat painfully aware of an intense light whose brilliance was dazzling his aching eyes even through their closed lids. And when at length he ventured to open them—for at first he could barely summon the energy to do so—he found himself sitting bolt upright in the front seat of his law enforcement Chevy, looking nearly straight into the fiery orb of a blazing sun.

Suspended low in the west, its ruddy-golden disk slowly, almost imperceptibly sinking, the sun's next-to level rays came streaming in through the windshield of the car almost full into his squinting eyes. Blinking them again and again, Dennis Stavola slightly stooped his head and, in so doing, became instantly aware that his hands were clenched tightly on the steering wheel; and, after noting the whiteness of his knuckles, he soon realized, too, that for some infernal reason, try as he would, he could not get his fingers to loosen their hold. At one and the same time he was also conscious that the key was in the ignition, and that the car was running, for he could feel the almost soundless pulsation of the engine throbbing with a rhythm as hushed and steady as that of the heart within his own body.

All this detective Stavola realized in brief, successive intervals; but it would be some while yet before he could actually remember precisely what had happened to him. For the time being he could only suppose that while sitting in his car he had (inexplicably) fallen asleep. And as his perplexity continued to steadily increase with regard to this, his glance, anxiously to and froing about himself, came to rest at length upon the conspicuously vacant passenger seat of the car, and he suddenly began to ask himself, what was he doing here—alone; and where was his partner, Frank Burns.

For what little he *did* remember (and that most clearly!) was that he and Frank Burns had driven here together. But where they had come *from*; where they were going *to*; and why they had stopped *here,* he could not for the life of him recall. And all at once a terrifying confusion beset his mind. It was all so mystifying, so dream-like, so *unreal* that the detective expected at any moment to see the glass of the windshield dissolve before his very eyes, and the steering wheel crumble away in his very hands, and then to awake at home in his bed, shivering at the fancies of this strange and unsettling nightmare. Instead, however, his hands only tightened their grip all the more on the steering wheel, and his foot, resting heavily and without feeling on the brake pedal, slightly stirred.

Detective Dennis Stavola wanted to reach down to the key in the ignition and shut the car off, and once or twice he even made a half-motion to do so, but he suddenly realized that he hardly had the energy for the effort. For not only was his body feeling intolerably languid as with some deadly and leaden slumber, but he was all at once aware, too, that he was beginning to feel sick and abominably faint, and that his head was now throbbing with a blinding headache. And yet, try as he would, he could not conceive what had brought him to this wretched condition. It was an absolute mystery. A mystery which Dennis Stavola did his utmost to solve. But the endeavor was a vain one; and in the end he was not only at an utter loss to account for the whereabouts of his partner, Frank Burns, but also what he himself was doing sitting here, alone in the car, parked on this dead end street.

Indeed it would be some while yet before he was able to fill this damnable gap in his consciousness. And so his bewildered mind went on striving, scrabbling, fumbling yet a while in vain to realize what had happened to him. But then—as if a curtain of mist had slowly, soundlessly withdrawn itself from his addled wits, conferring on him a somewhat limited capacity to backtrack his own doings—he began at last to recollect certain things.

His memory of events was still rather blurred and sketchy, but he nonetheless recalled having come from the crime scene of a brutal murder. He remembered having arrived there with Frank Burns and having viewed the victim's body, a young female, whose name he suddenly recalled was Carbone, Lori Carbone. He remembered, too, that he and his partner had left the crime scene some little time ago, and that it was only quite recently that the two of them had arrived here and parked their car on this street—"73rd Place... this is 73rd Place," detective Stavola whispered solemnly to himself. But the reason as to why he had driven here with his partner remained as yet elusive.

Then, slightly turning his head, Dennis Stavola gazed obliquely at the drab, narrow house before which he was parked. He continued for a while steadily staring at its blind-drawn front windows and faded brick exterior, till all at once a kind of recognition ensued, and he heard his own voice softly repeating to himself, "It's the only house on the same side as the cemetery." Somewhere he had heard those words spoken before—but where, and by whom he could not recall.

Very gradually, then, detective Stavola seemed to dimly recollect having gotten out of the car with Frank Burns and gone over to that house. It was all so absurdly vague and indistinct, but he also seemed to remember having spoken to a tall, peculiar-looking man who had opened its front door for them. But his memory as to what had taken place immediately after their conversation was an utter blank.

Then, while continuing to gaze earnestly at that house, with its fast-shut front door and oddly darkened windows, all in an effort to focus his will on the single endeavor of recalling precisely why he and Frank Burns had come here, a preposterous litany of jumbled words, letters, and numbers began to arise piecemeal in his consciousness and sound on, again and again, like some imbecilic gibber: 'insanio... RJS9... T.O.M...'—then, after a long pause—'consumor... HA73P... NC... furore'. And notwithstanding their rather cryptic and inscrutable aspect, Dennis Stavola was certain that this curious sequence of words, letters, and numbers signified something of utmost importance. But what, he asked himself, as his mind went puzzling restlessly on.

Misgiving after misgiving swept up through the detective's heart as he struggled frantically to discover their meaning—a task which, at first, proved quite impossible. But then, after several tedious and disheartening minutes, Dennis Stavola underwent something of an epiphany in connection with that baffling series of letters and numbers. For while their actual meaning continued to elude him, their *source* became unmistakably apparent: they were from his very own notepad! And at the very instant that his groping consciousness came to realize that the words, letters, and numbers were, in fact, abbreviations in his own personal shorthand, the reason as to why he and Frank Burns had driven here flashed suddenly into his mind like the flaring up of a candle's flame. They had come here to question a boy by the name of Nathan Christian, whose very house this was. And all at once a number of other details began to revive: for suddenly Dennis Stavola vaguely recalled having gone inside that house with Frank Burns; and he was also perfectly conscious now that he and his partner had only recently exited the home. But of all that had happened in the interim, either to himself or to Frank Burns, while the two of them were *inside* that house, he still had no memory whatsoever.

Presently, Dennis Stavola shut his eyes and made a determined effort to concentrate his will, and so recall what had taken place inside the home. Several minutes passed, but there was still nothing! And the detective thought to himself how maddening it was that whatever had occurred inside that house should so completely elude him. For he called to mind distinctly enough his trivial impressions while walking up to the front door of the house—noting how odd it was that the front windows were all shut fast and blind-drawn; and the exterior of the home being in need of a fair amount of repair work. Why, then, after the door had opened to them, was all the rest oblivion? What could possibly be the cause of this inability to recollect any further?

Once more detective Stavola turned his face toward the solitary house, and gazed intently at its windows and front door. And as the minutes slipped by, a few imperfect and fragmentary recollections, like images in some drunkard's dream, began to reveal themselves to him: firstly, of exiting the home; then, of descending the worn brick steps of its porch in a somewhat dazed way; and lastly, of advancing together with Frank Burns down the front walk with slow, lumbering steps. But afterward he could remember nothing—only that on the way back to their unmarked car his body felt utterly fatigued and his wits horribly dulled with sleep. He had a vague impression, too, that when he had glanced sidelong at Frank Burns, he could see that in his partner's one hand was his unholstered semi-auto pistol, while in the other he clutched an old faded cloth that was wrapped closely about something. He seemed also to recall that Frank Burns kept repeating, over and over, some nonsense about how he 'must obey'; then something regarding (what he thought was) 'the empusa'; and then a string of garbled mutterings which ended with, 'have to kill them all'.

Of course, at the time, Dennis Stavola could make no coherent sense of what he seemed to hear. But as he began to dwell now with careful deliberation on these blurred and fragmentary memories, very soon, like a violent blow across the face, the truth all at once smote him: and he suddenly realized that somehow both he and Frank Burns, while inside that house, had been put under some strange form of mesmerism or hypnosis.

And almost immediately after, detective Dennis Stavola started to remember a great deal more. He could not recall everything at once, but, bit by bit, amid frequent pauses in which he had to think long and hard, the past began to piece itself together, slowly reconstructing for him what he had seen, heard, and experienced inside that house. He vividly recalled having entered the home. He remembered then that the man at the front door had conducted Frank Burns and himself through the living room to the doors of the sun-room. Through those doors he and his partner had passed; and in the room beyond they had seen a recliner occupied by a young child in whose strangely pale face was a pair of intensely heedful eyes with a chilling, almost menacing gaze. But his memory, at this point, of what actually took place inside that room remained yet a while hopelessly confused and imperfect.

Of this much, however, Dennis Stavola was quite certain: that once he was face to face with the child in the recliner, both he and Frank Burns were hardly able to keep aware of what that peculiar and unpleasant adolescent said or did to them, for its eyes seemed utterly to master and bewitch them.

Indeed, even now, he could only dimly remember encountering the child's piercing gaze with acute sensations of fear, and listening obediently, submissively to the commanding tones of its forbidding and strangely compelling voice. But had he only dreamed, *imagined* all that then followed? For as detective Stavola presently recalled gazing on in cowed speechlessness at the child lounging comfortably in the recliner, peculiar little details began to come back to him, the most curious being a bizarre, almost surreal recollection of the child's sinister eyes peering in gloating cruelty first at himself, then at his partner. He seemed to remember, too, the child's intent, unswerving regard producing in him an unwelcome feeling that was almost hypnotic in effect, but the impression remained hazy at best.

At any rate, bits and pieces of that weird scene inside the sun-room, in the presence of that extraordinary child, grew steadily clearer the longer he dwelt on them. And he was finding it increasingly difficult now to keep from shuddering as distinct and vivid memories in the form of strange and disquieting images began to float up in a succession of quick flashes before his mind's eye. But by reason of the disturbing nature of those images, a sudden panic took possession of him. He felt as though he was very gradually being reduced to a feeble child again, helpless and afraid of night-time bogies.

In an effort, then, to steady himself, detective Stavola quickly shut his eyes and, tightening his grip upon the steering wheel, strove desperately to repress and drive those images away. But it was all in vain. For the more he attempted to exorcise them from his mind now that he started to remember, the more vividly they returned to harass and trouble him; until he began, at last, to fear that he had overworked himself both physically and mentally; that he was now being afflicted by the first symptoms of some mysterious germ; a bad illness (influenza, he supposed) due in part, no doubt, to his physical exhaustion and stress-ridden brain. For which reason his mind (or so he tried to persuade himself) was now being plagued by this awful series of intensely shocking *imaginings*, as he preferred to call them.

But then, quite suddenly, detective Dennis Stavola paused in these "convictions" of his and, for a moment or two, wondered whether those so-called 'imaginings' could in fact be genuine recollections. Very quickly, though, he dismissed such a terrifying notion. No; he told himself; it must be this infernal sickness he was in for, brought on (he kept thinking) by his having overburdened himself on the job, and which now gave form and substance to these nightmare-like fancies; images, he assured himself, that could not be real, could not be *true* recollections of things that had actually transpired in that house, inside the sun-room. And yet, after another flurry of doubt and uncertainty, he paused once more to ask himself: or could they?

And presently, detective Dennis Stavola began very clearly to recall that the eyes of the child in the recliner had regarded, first Frank Burns, then himself, with an intensely hostile scrutiny, but more particularly so, his partner.

Of course, he could only distinguish the child's face dimly for lack of any substantial light in the room, but he remembered now being instantly conscious that the cast and air of its features which he was able to make out—young seemingly as a fresh spring day, yet ancient as the darkness at the roots of the mountains—were altogether cruel, deathly pale, and distinctly inhuman. It was as though something of another age, an oldlier world, a different reality were clinging visibly about the child's face. He could not determine precisely what it was at the time, but now, in retrospect, he realized it was in fact an aura, or atmosphere, of ghastly sin and violence that spanned whole centuries of time.

Very clearly, then, Dennis Stavola recalled that when his eyes had met those of the child's, its gaze, of such intensity and power, seemed to master and encompass him, so that all in a moment he felt abominably weak and helpless. He remembered, then, having heard the child speaking softly out of the darkness in a language of which he himself had no knowledge. He realized, too, that the child was not addressing either Frank Burns or himself, but reciting, as it were, a torrent of meaningless words and phrases to some kind of weird song-like incantation.

Detective Stavola recalled how his thoughts went desperately astray at their sound, and how their cumulative effect – whether spoken words or actual singing, he never could distinguish -seemed to extract and siphon off the strength from every muscle in his body. And he remembered that, at one and the same time as the child's voice had ceased its unpleasant chanting, he suddenly felt a powerful and overmastering inclination to shut his eyes and go to sleep. And all in a moment the detective realized that not only had his will and physical strength been stolen from him in this way, but he was now quite certain that the unaccountable and irksome failure in his memory was also due, in fact, to some devilry by this strange and terrifying child.

Dennis Stavola could not be sure of what happened next, for his memory at this juncture became hopelessly vague again, but he seemed to recall the child speaking at some length to Frank Burns, for he was conscious once more of the child's voice -only this time it was speaking in a tongue which he knew and clearly understood. Unable to rouse himself from that dreadful lethargy, Dennis Stavola remembered standing there in a terrifying helplessness, gazing on stupidly at the child as though caught in the deep folds of a dark and awful dream. He recalled trying desperately to follow what the child was saying, but every now and again the lids would descend over his aching eyes and his thoughts would drift and mingle with irrelevant fancies, so that the child's voice kept sinking away into little more than a senseless droning in his ears. He, therefore, could not now recollect everything the child had said to his partner. But what he did hear distinctly, and could remember with absolute certainty, was that the child kept remarking how Frank Burns bore an uncanny resemblance to someone he once knew. Detective Stavola could not be sure, but he thought he heard the child identify this 'someone' as "Severus", a military tribune, or—as ludicrous and outlandish as it all sounded then to the detective (if not even more so now in retrospect)—a senior Roman officer of the praetorian guard!

The child was crouched now on all fours in the recliner like a beast preparing to spring upon its prey. And detective Stavola recalled how it sniffed audibly, repeatedly at a mute and motionless Frank Burns, not unlike an animal whose curiosity and hunger was being steadily aroused by a certain intoxicating scent, as it went on to say, "*Are* you Severus? *Could* you be Severus? You have his eyes and nose; the same mouth; the same closely cropped greying hair. It's as if I'm staring at the man's rebirth." Then, after a brief pause, Dennis Stavola remembered the child saying to Frank Burns, "If indeed you *are* Severus—incarnate once again—I wonder if you remember having had, in your previous life, a reputation throughout the empire for being among its most bestial pederasts? Do you remember now how it was your single greatest passion in life to have anal intercourse with little boys—some as young as six and seven? Do you recall even now—today, I wonder—how you never tired of having those same small boys stroke and fondle your private parts and, while doing so, speak to you, as a rule, only as Priapus, the name belonging to that foolish Roman deity with the oversized and permanently erect phallus?"

Dennis Stavola recalled that for some while after this, the child remained silent, and seemed to search and study Frank Burns's face closely, intently. Then, he remembered hearing the child say, "Well, whether or not you are truly he, from this point on I shall treat you as if you are, in fact, our long-lost Severus, a ghost from my past returned to me after all these centuries. And now that you've come back to me, Severus, it is only fitting that I return to you what was once yours, and which I have kept and carried with me over a span of many centuries as a memento of our last encounter."

The child then began to address someone else in the room. Dennis Stavola could not now be sure, but, at the time, he thought it must have been the tall, peculiar man who had let Frank Burns and himself into the house. Evidently he had been in the room with them all the while, but the detective now remembered having been completely unaware of his presence until then.

At the child's bidding he remembered the man silently withdrawing from the room. How long he was gone for, Dennis Stavola had no way of knowing; the strange lethargy which seemed to paralyze his physical and mental capabilities made the reckoning of time next to impossible for him. All that he could presently recollect with any degree of certainty was that when the man had returned, he was holding something which he immediately placed in the hands of the child. And Dennis Stavola remembered that, as the child put out its hands to take the thing, he had observed, somewhat hazily, that it appeared to be a small mass or bundle, about whose shapeless contents the tindery folds of some old moth-eaten cloth had been closely wrapped. He remembered also having observed, very clearly, too, that the cloth's once bright scarlet coloring, with which apparently it had been dyed, was all but faded now out of its worn, dirt-grimed folds.

Dennis Stavola's recollection of what was subsequently done or said by the child remained vague and imperfect at best. For he remembered continually dozing one moment and starting awake the next. He did recall, however, hearing the child mention something regarding the Roman Emperor, Galerius, whose wrath and ill-will he (the child) had somehow incurred. Then, very clearly, he remembered the child saying to his partner, "And it was you, poor unfortunate Severus, who eagerly and rashly volunteered yourself—in the hope, no doubt, of gaining honor and profit from our dear benevolent emperor—to undertake the task of leading me beyond the city's confines to the place of my preordained doom."

After that, however, like the lacuna in one of the vellum leaves of some ancient manuscript, there came a significant gap in Dennis Stavola's memory of what the child said next, and what few details he did happen to catch were, unfortunately, rather fuzzy. Notwithstanding this, he seemed to vaguely recall the child describing some towering cliff at whose base was a vast cavern, and then something or other about hordes upon hordes of dreadful bats inhabiting the everlasting gloom of the cave's echoing tunnels. And into its sunless depths, by order of the emperor, the child said something about being confined for three nights and two days.

Dennis Stavola couldn't be certain about what came next, for it was all very dream-like and bizarre, but he seemed to remember the child going on about the constraint of some sort of incantation, or wicked curse, pronounced upon him at the mouth of that cave by a kind of witch, or sorcerer, or necromancer. It was all very difficult, though, to follow, or even make sense of, for the detective had the curious impression that the child's speech kept leaping and switching into different languages, passing quite abruptly from English into Latin, then very suddenly to ancient Greek, shifting yet again into some archaic form of medieval old French, and then back to English.

Quite vividly, though, detective Dennis Stavola recalled the child saying to Frank Burns, "And do you remember, Severus, do you recall how, before carrying out your beloved emperor's cruel edict, you first stripped me of my garments and forced me, again and again, to endure your shameful lusts—mounting me several times, like a stallion his mare—at the entrance to that awful cavern, before your vile passions were finally sated? And then, into the cave, naked, shamed, and weeping bitterly, you roughly drove me, forcing me to remain in the chill darkness of its tomb-like tunnels, with nothing but the leather-winged bats of their depths for my companions. Ahhh, but when I was permitted, after the time prescribed by our darling emperor, to emerge from that cavern, I was, to say the least—*different*.

"And there you still were, too, Severus: waiting to see me, to mock and jeer at me. Your arrogance and curiosity had recklessly goaded you to linger—whereas the others had all wisely fled!—and witness with your own eyes the outcome of my cruel and loathsome fate. But how quickly your gloating faded when you saw my changed nature, and the shape into which that forbidden rite had cast me. Remember how you attempted to flee? But this time it was *my* passions *you* would have to endure; and I caught you before you could so much as stir a finger."

For some little while the child's voice had fallen silent, and Dennis Stavola recalled how its motionless eyes continued to glare with a murderous hatred at the still and silent face of Frank Burns. How long an interval of time before the child then resumed its awful tirade against his partner, detective Stavola was utterly at a loss to recollect, but as to what was said when it had, that, oddly enough, he found himself able to remember quite clearly. For he recalled his heart quickly turning to a lump of ice within him as the child said to Frank Burns: "It is said that a youth never forgets his first love; the same is true of vampires and their first victim! For as I gulped and supped the blood from wound upon wound that I inflicted on your helpless body, my dear Severus, and felt all the vital forces slowly, steadily ebbing from you, I was overpowered by such violent and erotic sensations of intoxicating pleasure that no climax of sexual excitement in the mortal body can even faintly compare. Then, feeling your heart still faintly fluttering beneath its bosom, I unsheathed your sword, and, where you had thrust your private member into me, I then thrust its blade into you—and violently broke it off... After which all that remained in my hand was this—"

Vividly, clearly, Dennis Stavola recalled gazing down, with rigidly bent head, at the child's pale, narrow hands as they slowly, carefully turned back the rotting folds of faded cloth to the closely wrapped bundle in its lap. He remembered, then, how the child had silently laughed as it drew aside the last fold, laying bare what appeared to be the time-worn hilts to a very old sword, a weapon from a long-vanished age of the world. To the best of detective Stavola's recollection, the pommel, cross-guard, and wire binding of the grip all seemed to be of gilded bronze, and he could recall, too, that in places where the gilding had been worn away there were green stains of verdigris. All that remained of the sword's flat, two-edged blade, however, was its shoulders, or the thick end. This remnant on its one side scarcely had an edge, but on the other side a jagged shard projected, some three or four inches, from the hilt's quillons, or cross-guard, like a beast's tooth or fang.

Dennis Stavola then recalled hearing once again the voice of the child speaking out of the shadows, telling his partner, whom he persisted in calling 'Severus', several odd and rather creepy details regarding that sword hilt, such as how he had carried it about with him all these centuries as a sort of 'love-token'; how he'd kept it carefully wrapped about in a piece of the praetorian officer's military cloak, after having torn it from his lifeless body; and how, every now and again, in looking on that hilt, it never failed to remind the child of the agonized expression on poor Severus's face as he (the child) drove the long heavy blade of that sword to its very hilts into the Roman officer's anus till its point protruded from his open mouth.

Over these and several other very disturbing recollections, detective Dennis Stavola seemed to linger for some while yet in a deep abstraction. And only after he had felt the tires of his vehicle jolt roughly over a bump or into a pothole in the road did he suddenly come to realize that at some point, during this protracted absorption of his, he must have put the car in gear, pulled away from the curb to make a U-turn in front of Nathan's house, driven back up 73rd Place, and arrived at its intersection with Metropolitan Avenue.

And presently, even as the detective became fully conscious of what was now happening to him, his foot pressed slowly down onto the gas pedal, his hands rigidly turned the steering wheel, and the car moved smoothly forward, slipping into the steady flow of Metropolitan Avenue's traffic. With a dull shock he realized, too, that what he was now doing, and where he was now going was entirely against his own volition. It was as though he were acting now in accordance with the decrees of another, obeying the authority and overmastering will of someone else.

After having driven for the next few minutes east down Metropolitan Avenue, Dennis Stavola sped smoothly through the intersection with 80th Street, and continued to drive eastward at a steady clip, the Avenue itself bordered now on either side by St John's Cemetery. Less than half a mile further on he came to the intersection with yet another busy thoroughfare, and, as though ruled now by the compulsions and impulses of a madman, he suddenly turned left. Then, in the aftermath of nearly a minute or two of absolute panic and confusion, detective Stavola was suddenly aware that he was now traveling north-east along Woodhaven Boulevard in its innermost lane.

But—*why*, he asked himself, why am I doing this? And almost in the very same instant that that questioning thought had formed itself in his bewildered mind, he *knew* precisely why—because he had been told, instructed—*commanded*—to do as he was now doing, and go where he was now going, some still, faint voice in his conscience seemed to remind him.

Detective Dennis Stavola was about to ask himself, but *who* had given him this command, when all at once he distinctly recalled the strange and terrifying child in the sun-room. A child whom he was now convinced must be none other than 'le Enfant saunce Pite', that cruel, sadistic adolescent of whom Gilles de Rais had spoken some five centuries earlier.

And all at once, floating up into Dennis Stavola's memory —his clearest remembrance yet of those strange and terrifying events in the sun-room of Nathan's home—he saw and heard once more the deadly-pale face and dreadful voice of that monstrous little child as it proceeded to sternly interrogate himself and Frank Burns. And neither he nor his partner, he recalled, had the least ability to do anything other than stand there in a horrifying trance-like anguish and answer the child's every inquiry.

As clearly as though he were seeing it happen all over again, even now, with his wide and wildly staring eyes, Dennis Stavola recalled how Frank Burns was compelled by that beastly child to stoop his face down low over the recliner so that the child could violently strike him, again and again, across the face with its open hand. And with each stinging blow, the child taunted and mocked the man, calling him 'Priapus', 'darling', and 'beloved Severus'.

Then, the child sprang out of the recliner and, standing before them, Dennis Stavola recalled how it demanded that Frank Burns fall down on his knees and worship it. And, very clearly now, he remembered seeing his partner burst into a passion of weeping as he sank, groveling, to the floor and embraced the child's knees in adoration. The child, meanwhile, laughed and gloated, and struck his partner several more times on the head as though it were beating a dog; then, still calling him 'Severus', Dennis Stavola recalled that inhuman little juvenile demanding, with a terrible menace in its voice, to know where the two men had come from. And 'Severus' (alias, Frank Burns), still shaking and snuffling like a frightened boy, with one sob after another, submissively revealed to the child: "From the house of Lori and Marty Carbone."

This seemed only to deepen the child's ire and rouse its suspicions, for a number of questions then followed, the majority of which detective Stavola could not now remember with any certainty. He did, however, recollect, with perfect clarity, the child having asked, "So why have you come *here*? Who sent you to *this* house?" And he remembered Frank Burns being forced to reveal how he and his partner had spoken to a group of boys outside the house of Marty Carbone, who then informed them that Marty had come to this house looking for Nathan.

When the child heard this, its chalk-white face seemed to sharpen with fury, and it repeatedly struck Frank Burns on the head and about the face for the next few instants; then, it suddenly paused as, off to one side, there broke out the harsh tones of another's voice. Dennis Stavola could not at the time see the owner of this unpleasant voice, but now, in retrospect, he could only assume that it must have been the tall, ill-favored man with the partially disfigured face who had let them in. He remembered hearing the voice tell the child that in all likelihood it was the same motley group of boys who had been gathered outside earlier today awaiting their friend's (Marty Carbone's) reappearance.

Dennis Stavola then recalled the horrid little child, after having struck his partner once more in the face, speaking to Frank Burns in a tone of fearful command: "I want them all dead! Do you hear me, Severus? You are to go back to where you spoke with those boys, and you are to kill every one of them with your gun!" And the child reached its hand in past the detective's jacket, fetched the semi-auto Glock pistol from its belt holster and placed it in Frank Burns's right hand. "And then, once you have used your gun on them... this," said the child, forcing the detective to clutch with the fingers of his other hand the ancient sword hilt, the jagged remnant of its iron blade jutting fang-like below the quillons, "this," went on the child, after he had drawn the worn folds of the old military cloak carefully about it again, "this you are to use on yourself;"—and the child's eyes fixed themselves for an instant or two with gloating malice on the closely wrapped bundle in the detective's hand—"do you understand me, Severus?"

And Dennis Stavola recalled it all so vividly, how Frank Burns, standing there like a sleepwalker, nodded his head to the child in a slow, dazed, almost thought-drugged manner. After which he remembered that monstrous adolescent slightly turning its head so as to fix its chilling, sinister gaze steadily on himself. "And now for you," it said, sneering malevolently. "What fate should we devise for you." The child had paused and stood a while in silent thought. Then, "Now, let me see; what is it that you fear more than all things else in the world?" it said, musingly, as, out of its strangely gynandromorphic face, its glittering eyes continued to regard the detective's silent face with a singularly fearsome intensity.

And Dennis Stavola remembered now, how he felt the child somehow probing his thoughts. Rooting, rummaging, searching, with its cruelly piercing gaze, through the most secret places of his memory. It seemed to dip into all the long-buried anxieties, repressed fears, and past nightmares of his adolescence. And one above all the rest stood out and seemed to trouble the detective repeatedly as far back as the teenage years of his early youth. It was a recurrent nightmare in which he was behind the wheel of a speeding vehicle, tearing down what appeared to be the Long Island Expressway at a frightening velocity.

But what made this nightmare truly horrifying for Dennis Stavola was that he was driving on the wrong side of the expressway, and heading full speed toward the cars, trucks, and vans of its oncoming traffic. It was absolutely terrifying to him (then, only a boy of thirteen or fourteen), and he would wake gasping for breath, literally bathed in a cold sweat, with his heart pounding. And it was this fearful nightmare—long-hidden, horrible, and half-forgotten—which the child had somehow been able to divine and dredge up out of the murky well of the detective's subconscious. For Dennis Stavola remembered hearing the child's voice assume a tone of dreadful authority as it said to him, "Go now, go and live out that very nightmare from your youth by getting into your car and driving it exactly as you drove it in your dream!"

Then, detective Stavola remembered the voice of the child, when it spoke to him again, penetrating the dulled sense of his hearing in curiously sleep-compelling and slumber-inducing tones, as it instructed both himself and his partner to leave now. And the two detectives, like obedient slaves eager to carry out the will of their master, silently left the house and returned to their car.

Detective Stavola recalled feeling a frightful drowsiness creep rapidly over him at the time, and being acutely aware that his entire body was numb; that he could not even feel the ground with his feet as he walked back to the car. And as he stepped into the street to get in on the driver's side, Frank Burns had paused on the other side and stood staring at him for a moment or two over the top of the car. He recalled now, noting the deathly pallor of his partner's face, and how its expression was one of blind and awful desolation. He remembered, too, noting how Frank Burns, with tears in his eyes, fixed his own face one last time with a mournful glance, before turning away and walking, with a slow, stumbling gait, up the street, carrying in one hand his Glock G17 semi-automatic pistol, and in the other that shapeless bundle folded about in its faded cloth. As for himself, Dennis Stavola remembered getting into his car, then, and sitting slumped behind its wheel with his whole body utterly empty of any feeling. He recalled somewhat vaguely, after starting the car, just sitting there with his eyes closed and wanting desperately to be allowed to sleep. And his last recollection, before he had fallen asleep behind the steering wheel, was hearing his own faint voice, repeating stupidly to himself, "I must drive... must drive... drive..."

Now, about the same time that Dennis Stavola was regaining consciousness in their unmarked Chevy parked on 73rd Place in front of Nathan's home, Frank Burns, on foot, had already turned the corner off Metropolitan Avenue and was walking in a sort of dazed way in the middle of the road up 71st Street. Slowly, steadily he continued to advance toward the crowd of spectators gathered behind the police sawhorses in front of Marty Carbone's house.

In the middle of the street, on the outward skirts of the crowd, in small groups of twos and threes, were the teenage boys with whom the two detectives had spoken earlier that day, as well as several new arrivals. These included Brian Gorman, who, standing next to Freddy Scalone, was showing off his brand new K2 Shadow Nine Mountain Bike, on which he'd ridden over; Russell Gorman's (ex) girlfriend, Beth Conte, who had come over from Juniper Valley Park with her two closest friends, Doreen McGlynn (her BFF) and Karen Elkner; Pete Marino (Russ Gorman's marijuana dealer); and lastly, the other member of Russell Gorman's cheesy garage-band, former lead singer Neil Keddy, who was telling his former band mates (Kevin Hansen and Glen Rubino) how he was 'gonna write a song about what Marty did to his sister and call it "Brotherly Love".

Scott Webler, upon hearing these snide comments, turned with a grin to remark about them, when, in so doing, he noticed detective Frank Burns coming up the street toward them. He was about to wave to the man, when all at once he noted the detective's maniacal expression, the unholstered pistol in his hand, and his arm extending itself to point the muzzle of that gun in their direction. Without a word to anyone, Scott Webler instantly bolted into the thick of the crowd, dragging his brother, Terence, after him. And even as he reached the police barricade on the other side of that throng of spectators, he heard—bang!—the gunshot ring out, suddenly, sharply, like the cracking of a whip.

At first, a loud collective gasp went up from the crowd; after which, on its farthest skirt, one or two piercing screams broke out. Then, as the sound of more gunshots followed, the crowd took fright; panic spread all in an instant, and the air was immediately filled with unpausing shrieks and yells. The two or three uniformed officers who were outside, swept their guns from their holsters and took cover behind their police cruisers, while the officers inside the Carbone residence rushed to its front windows with their weapons drawn.

Scott Webler, meanwhile, had slipped under the police saw-horse and, with his younger brother in tow, dashed up the alley of Marty Carbone's house and crept in under the half-open door to the garage. There, in the same narrow space in which he and his friends had found Lori Carbone earlier that day, between Marty's 2001 Mustang GT Bullitt and his old Panhead motorcycle, Scott Webler secreted himself and his little brother. For the next few minutes, without either stirring or speaking, he held his brother Terence close, with his fingers clamped tightly over his terrified sibling's mouth to prevent him from screaming, as gunshot after gunshot sounded off amid shrieks and cries of agonized terror. And it was these same shots which Nathan, upon first waking inside the old All Faiths cemetery, mistook for the distant sound of fireworks, while wondering to himself, in his initial confusion, if today was the Fourth of July holiday weekend.

Of course, Nathan had no way of knowing at the time that those far-off crackling sounds had nothing whatsoever to do with pyrotechnics (as he had believed), and it would be some while yet before he would discover that the actual truth behind it all was detective Frank Burns pointing his semi-auto Glock pistol at one youngster after another on 71st Street and squeezing the trigger again and again. "Kill..." snarled the detective, grinding his teeth like a man possessed, "kill them... kill them all..." And with that, detective Burns flicked off the safety, pointed his gun at his first victim, and shot Glen Rubino from behind.

The boy had only just raised a glass bottle of Coca-Cola to his lips and was in the act of swallowing a mouthful of that carbonated beverage when the bullet smashed through the back of his head. After boring through the teenager's brain, the slug exited from his open mouth at the tongue's root, shattering the boy's front teeth along with the glass bottle of soda he had just then tilted to his lips. A split second later Glen Rubino lay sprawled in the street, the delicious taste of Classic Coke on his tongue mingled with the metallic flavor of a 9mm Luger-caliber round.

Frank Burns turned, then, and, pointing his pistol at Todd Bauer, pulled the trigger. The slug passed clean through the boy's tender neck. And as Todd Bauer dropped and lay half-twisted on his side, with the gurgling blood spouting from the bullet hole in his throat, his arms and legs kept jerking and twitching with the senseless stir of a marionette mimicking a living form—till all at once, with one final spasm, the boy's limbs went as still and lifeless as the rest of him.

By now many of the people in the crowd, in their frantic efforts to flee, some this way, some that, began to push and shove their terrified neighbor, while others, too, paralyzed with fear to even move, stood like frightened deer caught in the headlights, simply screaming and cowering in shock and horror.

In the meantime, Frank Burns had fired off two more rounds. The first of these hit Kerry Stark in the upper part of his body. He was sent careening backward with the impact and tumbled to the ground, where he lay unconscious, the slug having mangled his right shoulder, shattering the collarbone. The second shot struck and killed Brian Gorman as he tried to make good his escape by speeding off on his brand new Mountain Bike. The slug, however, hit him between the shoulder blades and then skidded into his heart. Sideways and down he went, still seated on his bicycle. As he lay gasping on the ground, with the blood spurting from his mouth and nostrils, he kicked with one or two quick jerks of his feet at the pedals, as if still attempting to ride away, and then lay without any movement.

When Freddy Scalone saw Frank Burns then point the gun at him, he bent his head low and, screaming, put his hand out as if to fend off the bullet. The gunshot rang out and the slug sheared off three of the boy's slender fingers and the upper part of his hand with them. In agony, with the blood flowing from his mangled hand, Freddy Scalone crumpled to the ground; and detective Burns, marking the boy, quickly squeezed off yet another shot. The boy's head jerked with the impact of the slug as it entered his left temple, killing him instantly.

Without pausing, Frank Burns trained his pistol on his next victim. But before Rodney Martello could either scream or run, there was a sharp click, then an explosion, and the boy was shot point-blank in the head. Without even so much as a twitch, Rodney Martello collapsed in the middle of the street in a contorted heap: a small entry wound over his left eye, and the back of his head blown clean away.

This was the seventh shot; and although the Glock G17 when fully loaded has ten shots ready to fire, Burns's pistol, for whatever reason, was three rounds short of its full capacity that day. And so, having squeezed off its seventh round, he had to pause here to reload, while Kevin Hansen stood watching, frozen with shock, his face on one side smeared with the spattered blood and brains of his friend Rodney Martello. "Please," was all he managed to whimper before Frank Burns pulled the trigger and the bullet smashed through the boy's chest, killing him in the blink of an eye.

The next two rounds detective Burns fired off hit Pete Marino, first in the spine, then in the back of the head as he was fleeing. Seeing this, Neil Keddy, who was standing nearby, instantly realized that flight equaled being gunned down, and so decided, in a desperate and cowardly attempt to protect himself, to seize Beth Conte and hold her in front of him as a human shield. No sooner had he done that, however, than Frank Burns turned the gun on him. And when Beth Conte dropped to the ground, convulsing with a bullet in her throat, Neil Keddy received the next slug between the eyes and immediately sank beside her body just as her limbs made their final convulsions in death. As for Beth Conte's BFF, Doreen McGlynn, and her girlfriend, Karen Elkner, they stood clasped in each other's arms, and, sobbing and screaming, together fell down dead still clinging to one another: both shot point-blank in the head by Frank Burns, as he repeated, "Kill them all... Kill them... Kill! Kill!"

Now although all of this tragic violence seemed to unfold over a period of many minutes, in actual time these horrific executions, carried out by Frank Burns on a dozen local teenagers in Middle Village that Sunday evening of August 20th, took place in little more than thirty seconds. And throughout the entire nightmarish proceedings of that cold-blooded massacre, never once did NYPD officers fire so much as a single round at the gun-wielding madman, the psychotic executioner. Uniformed cops behind the patrol cars with their weapons drawn, as well as those who had stolen out of Marty Carbone's house, either to join their fellow officers behind the police vehicles or take up positions behind one or two nearby trees, were unable to get a clear shot at Frank Burns in the street due to the number of civilians in whose midst he stood as he turned now this way, now that, and gunned down victim after helpless victim. Some of these civilians stood shivering and screaming in each others' arms as they huddled up against the police barricades; while others, crouching and cringing, here and there, in small groups in the middle of the street, too afraid to make a run for it, could do little more than tremble like frightened rabbits.

By the time, however, it had all ended, and a deathly hush in its aftermath had fallen like a black pall over 71st Street, officer Miguel Alonso and his partner George Reese, accompanied by half a dozen other uniformed cops, had cautiously ventured out from behind their cover into the street. There, bent on his knees in the middle of the road, they found Frank Burns, his Glock semi-auto pistol lying next to the curb where he had tossed it. They noted, too, that he knelt there naked to the waist, for he had stripped himself of his jacket and shirt, and, having drawn aside the last fold of worn cloth from the bundle which all the while he'd been clutching in his other hand, he now held its gleaming metallic contents at arms' length high over his head. To the heedful eyes of the slowly advancing police officers it appeared, to all intents and purposes, to be some kind of sharp knife-like instrument; precisely what, however, they could not as yet tell with any certainty.

Halting, then, some eight or ten paces away from detective Frank Burns, officer Miguel Alonso and the other uniformed cops, with their weapons steadily trained on the detective, began to urge him to drop whatever it was he was holding in his hands. But all at once Frank Burns's voice broke out, and he shouted and barked at them fragments of outlandish sentences, which to the ears of the onlooking officers amounted to little more than senseless gibber, about "obeying my Master"; and "the merciless child"; and something about a "Roman officer of the praetorian guard".

The detective kept repeating these startled phrases in dozens of different ways while, with his bulging eyes wildly rolling to and fro, crushing volumes of emotion seemed to course, like an electrical current, through his entire body, causing it to jerk, shudder, and twitch uncontrollably.

And presently, officer Miguel Alonso had edged a step or two cautiously forward, and said: "Frank, it's me, Alonso; Miguel Alonso. Whatever you've got in your hands—please, just drop it!" He paused a moment or two, as Frank Burns began to grind his teeth and laugh like one possessed; then, "You know how this is gonna end if you don't," the officer went on. "Why you wanna do it this way?"

Frank Burns suddenly fixed officer Miguel Alonso with a ferocious look as he snarled: "For the empusa!" And with that, he instantly thrust the ancient sword-hilt's fang-like shard into the lower left-hand side of his body, and, bellowing with pain, he began very slowly and steadily to carve himself open from the left side of his body to the right. And as the blood streamed downward from this ghastly incision, out gushed his warm entrails till they lay in a hideous tumbled pile about his knees. Then, as his head stooped forward, and his chin sank upon his breast, detective Frank Burns died with his glazed, downbent eyes staring blankly at his guts.

Perhaps only a minute or two before Frank Burns had fired off the first shot from his Glock pistol, hitting Glen Rubino in the back of the head, Dennis Stavola, without being in the least conscious of it, had pulled away from the curb in front of Nathan's house and turned onto Metropolitan Avenue. And presently, so deeply, so intently was his mind preoccupied with trying to recollect where his partner had got to and why he was sitting here alone in their unmarked law enforcement Chevy, that not even for a single, solitary moment had his ears caught the faintest rumor of gunshots just then beginning to ring out only a couple of blocks away on 71st Street.

In fact, by the time detective Stavola was able to fully and clearly recall all that had happened to himself and his partner after parking their car and going up to the door of Nathan's home, he was already traveling down Woodhaven Blvd, trying desperately to understand (and resist!) the strange and terrifying impulses now stirring in him.

And even as he remembered the strange, dreadful, androgynous child in the sun-room of Nathan's home commanding him by way of some overmastering authority to climb into his vehicle and live out the horrifying nightmare of his youth, Dennis Stavola knew that he was utterly powerless to defy this cruel and diabolic injunction. For by then he had swung past Eliot Avenue, shot under the trestle supporting the train tracks to the Long Island Railroad and, in a minute or so, had come to a full stop at a traffic light just a few yards south of Queens Boulevard.

Without turning his head even so much as a fraction of an inch to glance at his surroundings, Dennis Stavola knew that on his right was Wetherole Street, while to his left was the sloping one-way road leading off the eastbound side of the Long Island Expressway—the very offramp of that highway in the recurring nightmare of his youth onto which he invariably drove his car like a suicidal maniac against the oncoming flow of traffic.

And suddenly, detective Dennis Stavola, like a petrified child, began to violently tremble; for everything was now unfolding with such terrifying exactness to his nightmare that he felt as though he had somehow passed from the reality of the waking world to the harrowing regions of dream. Moreover, he felt as though he were now being unrelentingly suffocated: his heart was hammering furiously; he was laboring ever and again to catch his breath; and the sweat was now pouring down his face and limbs in streams. For he knew that he was now on the awful verge of entering the full misery and horror of his nightmare.

And even as Dennis Stavola, with a feeling of numbing panic rising in his heart, recalled in his dream suddenly turning the steering wheel—despite the two fire-engine-red signs, bearing in large, white, forbidding letters, "WRONG WAY" and "DO NOT ENTER"—and veering with terrifying speed onto the offramp of the Long Island Expressway, he was all in a moment living out that paralyzing nightmare of his youth, experiencing its appalling terror in actual time and reality!

For all in an instant, Dennis Stavola felt his foot press heavily, firmly down onto the gas pedal; he heard the swelling roar of the engine; and the horrid squeal of the rubber tires, as the car lurched forward through the red light. At the same time he felt his hands and arms become agonizingly numb and rigid; and, as if a power other than his own will controlled them, they very abruptly swung the steering wheel left.

Instantly, with horrific speed, the car shot across the intersection and swerved onto the offramp of the Long Island Expressway. And almost before Dennis Stavola knew what was happening next, he had already accelerated into the mid-most lane of the Expressway, and was presently speeding west on its eastbound side, full against the heavy traffic of cars and trucks coming from Manhattan.

Horns were honking, screaming, whining, as car after car veered left and right to avoid colliding head on into the detective's onrushing vehicle. And it was only by small, agonizingly painful movements that Dennis Stavola himself managed to slightly turn the steering wheel, and so make an effort to veer and swerve his car, barely avoiding the oncoming vehicles which he was, no doubt, meant—just as it always happened in his dream—to crash head-on into.

Again and again Dennis Stavola told himself to remove his foot from the gas pedal; to set it down forcefully on the brake. Repeatedly he tried to do just that; tried with all his might to raise his foot; but his strength and will were less than nothing. From the gas pedal he was unable to so much as stir his foot: it was as though his shoe had become a very part of it. He made one desperate, determined effort after another. And he seemed himself, ever and again, to strive and struggle and rage, but his foot barely quivered as it continued to press down all the more heavily onto the gas pedal.

For a single instant Dennis Stavola sought his own reflected panic-stricken eyes in the glass of the rear-view mirror, as if to plead senselessly, hopelessly with himself for help. Then, the cold, all but bloodless fingers of his right hand, obeying the last resurgent shred and reserve of his enfeebled will, slowly, painfully loosened their hold of the steering wheel and slid blindly along the breast of his shirt. They fumbled in panic with one of the upper buttons.

And the instant he felt it come undone, Dennis Stavola slipped his trembling fingers through the opening where they groped for (and found!) the little crucifix hanging on its gold chain just over his heart. And in the very same instant that he clutched it with his chilled, numb fingers, it was as though some invisible bond, or the link in some constricting chain, had been shattered, and his ability to move was suddenly restored to him.

Continuing to gaze in a misery of terror over the dashboard and steering wheel of his vehicle, detective Stavola suddenly cried out as he saw hurtling head-on toward himself, like some inescapable tsunami on wheels, a Freightliner 40-ton multi-axled concrete mixer, with a 12 cubic meters by 15 cubic yards capacity rotating drum.

The very next instant, and Dennis Stavola had managed to lift his foot off the gas pedal and thrust it down onto the brake. Directly after, he heard the tortured screeching of the tires; the warning thunder of the Freightliner's deafening horn; and then the violent wrenching of twisting metal and shattering glass.

As for detective Dennis Stavola: he felt no painful sensations whatsoever in the wake of the horrific impact. Only a sudden death-still quiet, coupled with an all-pervading coma-like emptiness of mind, body—existence. And all in an instant he ceased to know anything more.

CHAPTER FOUR

"... She sprang... at my wound, which she began to suck with an air of inexpressible delight. She sipped the blood slowly and carefully...then she again pressed the wound with her lips so as to draw out a few more red drops... 'Drink, and let my life enter your body with my blood'..."

—*La morte amoureuse*

A day or two after the horrific events that had taken place on 71st Street, first inside, then outside, of the home of Marty and Lori Carbone—tragic incidents about which Nathan, for some time afterward, remained ignorant and uninformed, living as he did a lonely, friendless, almost reclusive life—a singular change had begun to manifest itself not only in Phebe's disposition, but in her very demeanor. And with the steady approach of Nathan's birthday of August 26th, this curious change in her became more and more evident.

For quite unlike her previous nocturnal visits to Nathan in his room, during which she behaved in ways that (to Nathan) were mysterious, bewitching, seductive, and exhilarating, Phebe's mood now seemed gloomy and distracted; her bearing utterly listless; and the expression of her face pensive and distraught.

And ever and again, while lying in bed with Nathan, face to face, in the candled darkness of his room, Phebe would lapse into long, solemn reveries, during which, with fixed, unswerving gaze, she would stare mournfully, almost tearfully before her. And as Nathan lay upon his side, silent and motionless, his eyes drinking in the unearthly beauty of the pale narrow face slightly drawn into the pillow on which it lay just opposite his own, almost it seemed to him that while Phebe's mind continually slipped into and out of this never-ending anguish of day-dream and disquiet, her heart appeared to fall deeper and deeper into sorrow and dismay. And no matter what Nathan said or did to try and cheer her, or draw her into some kind of pleasant conversation with himself, she remained obstinately morose and reticent.

In fact, when once Nathan happened to remark to Phebe that his birthday was only three days from tomorrow—in the hope that its mention might bring only so much as the shadow of a smile to her pouting lips—he was all but startled when she suddenly fixed on him the most pitiable, almost heartsick glance he had ever seen. And in a voice scarcely above a whisper, as if she were still half in dream, "I know;" she breathed out to him sadly through the hush; "it's my birthday, too"—and, after a prolonged silence, yet more softly, sorrowfully, she added—"in a way..."

Moreover, Nathan observed that whenever Phebe emerged from these long, dismal reveries into which she frequently sank, she would suddenly begin to ask him a number of odd, rather unsettling questions. At first, pressing him about his feelings toward her; then, wanting to know whether or not he truly loved her; and, if so, how deeply; and, yet again, if his love for her was deep as he claimed it to be, would he be willing to prove it by doing *anything* for her—even if that 'anything' meant something 'terrible'. And having asked of Nathan these, and other things still more peculiar and discomfiting, Phebe, while listening to his replies, appeared to watch his face anxiously, heedfully; as if, with each inquiry, she had been in truth secretly *testing* him.

Now, on the third night following Lori Carbone's brutal murder, Nathan happened to discover, quite by chance, after a series of vain efforts to cheer her, that Phebe was immensely fond of reading; and that she never enjoyed a book so much as when she was reading it to someone else. She confessed, too, that 'long ago' (as she put it) she would often spend many happy hours in the company of her 'betrothed' poring together with him over books, and, he and she reading them aloud, one to the other.

And when Nathan, after hearing this, informed Phebe that Aunt Amelia had a number of books in her bedroom that might interest her, the revelation seemed to lessen the heaviness of her mood and, at the same time, pique her curiosity.

But when Phebe had examined the meager selection of books that comprised the sum total of Aunt Amelia's literary treasures, she found that they were, for the most part, of a theological or Biblical character. All had sumptuous bindings with their spines exquisitely worked and gilded, but none more so than a tall, thin volume on the lore and legends of creatures strange and otherworldly. And although the content of this last work would soon prove to be of immense interest and importance to Nathan with regard to Phebe's true nature, Phebe herself expressed a deep aversion and lack of interest for the dull assortment of books in his aunt's room.

A little later, however, in browsing over the titles to the few volumes ranged along the bookshelf in Nathan's room, one in particular, by some curious fortune, seemed to defy Phebe's disinterest and obstinacy. And, having abstracted the volume that had caught her fancy, her lips, as she scanned once more the title on its worn and faded cover, curled in a slow, mysterious smile.

"I think I'd like to read this one," she said, pausing in the silence to gaze across at Nathan out of eyes wide and lustrous and half-merrily, half-mischievously aglint.

Nathan drew near and, glancing down a moment at the old dog's-eared paperback which Phebe now held in her slim, narrow hands, he read to himself the following title, *Three Gothic Novels of the Vampire*. It was one of several books, along with Mary Shelley's "Frankenstein" and Stevenson's "Dr Jekyll and Mr Hyde", which had been given to him not so very long ago by Eric Schiller, a day or two before he moved out of his parents' house. And although it had been in Nathan's possession now for little more than a year or two, occupying its familiar station undisturbed on the narrow wooden shelf in his room, Nathan himself was thoroughly unacquainted with the book's contents. For he had never once opened the volume to either browse through its pages or dip into the strange, supernatural tales bound between its sun-bleached covers. To put it quite simply, Nathan found the horror genre (vampire fiction in particular) completely unappealing.

But as Nathan's eyes gazed steadily across into those of Phebe's, he thought to himself, if such a book was able to keep Phebe from lapsing back into that despondent and doleful mood of hers, he would be only too willing to indulge her in her peculiar literary tastes.

And so, facing one another, they sat down together on the floor and, opening the book, Phebe began at once to read from it to Nathan. But after only the first page or two of John Polidori's *The Vampyre*, Phebe found the story, from its very opening, so exceedingly dull, that she quickly skipped on ahead to the second of that book's trio of "gothic novels", an acknowledged classic in vampire literature by S.J. Lefanu, entitled *Carmilla*.

Nathan sat faintly smirking as Phebe commenced her reading of the work, for the title alone seemed to suggest to him both a dull and unpromising tale. Of this premature notion, however, he was soon undeceived. For he found himself, by its second chapter, listening very intently to every word; in fact, from the very moment Phebe had read to him the opening line of, 'I am now going to tell you something so strange that it will require all your faith in my veracity to believe my story', Nathan felt himself instantly ensnared.

But by the time Phebe had read further on to the following passage in the fourth chapter—"and she would whisper almost in sobs, 'You are mine, you shall be mine, and you and I are one forever'—what but the loveliness of Phebe's face seemed to shape itself out of the imagery and music of its prose in Nathan's mind, casting over his heart and thoughts a strange yet uneaseful enchantment.

And more than once Nathan was shocked upon noting a certain, startling change that came over Phebe's face as she read those particular passages in the story pertaining to the girl Laura's description of the sensations she experienced in her sleep as her blood was being drained from her by the female vampire, Carmilla. The first was with the line, "it was as if warm lips kissed me"; then, "longer and more lovingly as they reached my throat"; and yet again, "there the caress fixed itself". For at each of these lines (and two or three similar ones) a repelling look of greed, amounting to absolute yearning, crept into Phebe's features, and her nostrils and mouth seemed to quiver with excitement. And once, as Nathan encountered a stolen glance out of Phebe's wide shadowy eyes when she lifted them, for a solitary instant, from the page on which they had all the while been so intently fixed, he was quite sure that in their depths he caught a cruel glint of stony, wolfish hunger.

But there was one passage more than any other that had laid hold of Nathan's imagination. It was toward the end of the tale, where Laura's father discovers the vampire, Carmilla, sleeping in her ancient tomb, with her eyes open. "The limbs were perfectly flexible, the flesh elastic; and the leaden coffin floated with blood, in which to a depth of seven inches, the body lay immersed. Here then, were all the admitted signs and proofs of vampirism". And for several days afterward those words sounded on (disagreeably) in Nathan's thoughts, haunting his fancy, and conjuring awful images in his dreams.

Now, as soon as Phebe had finished her reading of Lefanu's vampire story, she immediately, and almost thirstily, embarked upon the third and final tale in that anthology's triad—Bram Stoker's *Dracula*. It was, however, a rather curious edition of the work, for the text had been considerably abridged, and each chapter was followed by a page or two of critical commentaries.

Nathan listened, like one fascinated, bewitched by Phebe's voice as she read on, page after page—the prose weaving its nets and snares over his mind. Now and again though, Phebe would pause to criticize the author for having got something or other 'not quite right' in his narrative, but then, when she felt he had, she'd suddenly cry out, 'Ahhh!'

And once more, as with "Carmilla" before it, one passage in "Dracula", beyond all others, attached itself to Nathan's thoughts with disturbing vividness, and, long after Phebe had closed the book and he himself had gone to sleep, pestered and plagued his imagination. It was the scene in Count Dracula's castle, where Jonathan Harker discovers his vampiric host asleep in his vault. The words seemed to echo on endlessly, uneasily in Nathan's thoughts: "on the lips were gouts of fresh blood, which trickled from the corners of the mouth and ran over the chin and neck. Even the deep, burning eyes seemed set amongst swollen flesh for the lids and pouches underneath were bloated. It seemed as if the whole awful creature were simply gorged with blood". And fearful images conjured by this passage, along with the one from "Carmilla", did not cease to vex and haunt Nathan over the next few nights, chilling his mind and troubling his dreams.

As for Phebe, her face was again strangely, wonderfully transfigured, as when, pausing a moment or two in her reading of *Dracula,* Nathan glanced across at her and saw her peering eyes fixed solemnly, reflectively on his face from over the book. It was long after the passage where Jonathan Harker encounters the Count's three weird women, and becomes enamored of their strange otherworldly beauty. "I could feel the soft, shivering touch of the lips on the super-sensitive skin of my throat, and the hard dents of two sharp teeth, just touching and pausing there". But the most startling passage came at the close of the chapter, in the commentary that was appended to it.

More than once Phebe read the passage aloud to Nathan, telling him, "Now listen, Nathan; listen to this... 'Since blood in all vampire tales symbolizes semen, the one being a metaphor for the other, it therefore follows that the penetration of the throat with the teeth and the sucking of the vital fluid, and the emission of blood from the wound, has the equivalence of a particular sexual act."

Then, for some while after, Phebe sat on very still and silent, and seemed to be lost deep in her own thoughts. And yet again, a few lines further down, upon having read, "the intermingling of one's blood with that of another, whether by means of transfusion or by orally imbibing it, constitutes the sacrament of marriage in the eyes of God", Phebe suddenly paused, and sat once more in silent thought. After a space of some seconds, her eyes, glancing softly up, met those of Nathan's over the book, and a mysterious absorbed expression stole across her face.

But then, upon having once more resumed her reading, she came at length, a little further on, to the passage where Jonathan Harker's wife, Mina, relates to her husband how the Count forced her to drink his blood. Very slowly and very carefully, Phebe read the words aloud, "...his long sharp nails opened a vein in his breast. When the blood began to spurt out, he took my hands in one of his, holding them tight, and with the other seized my neck and pressed my mouth to the wound, so that I must either suffocate or swallow some of the—Oh, my God..."

Raising her eyes suddenly from the page, Phebe pronounced it the finest passage in the entire book; for by this act, she was telling Nathan, the Count makes Mina his bride, or as Dracula himself proclaims, "'flesh of my flesh; blood of my blood.'" Again Phebe had paused and, looking across at Nathan, a curious notion seemed suddenly to deepen the luminous darkness of her eyes and their depths to glitter wonderfully with some definite resolve.

For all at once Phebe laid the book aside and clasping with her cold, lean hand that of Nathan's, she rose together with him. And gazing into his eyes, she said, "Nathan, why don't you and I do as they have done in the story? For if this mingling of blood truly does constitute matrimony, then tonight, by that very act, you will become flesh of *my* flesh, and I, in turn, blood of *your* blood."

And then, in the same manner as Jonathan Harker's encounter with the vampiric women in Dracula's castle, Phebe sat Nathan down on the bedside and told him to lie back. Then, as he gazed at her out of half closed eyes, she unzipped his jeans, and gently drew them down. Going down onto her knees, then, Phebe began to kiss and caress him with her lips. And for a brief spell, Nathan was unable to either move or speak, as suddenly he felt the chill wetness of Phebe's mouth press and fix itself with a very peculiar kind of caress against his skin at a certain place between his navel and his crotch.

The feeling was at once wonderful and terrifying; for, presently, Nathan felt as though he were struggling to catch his breath, which seemed to grow faintlier by the second, as his heart began to jerk and lurch against his ribs. An instant later these frightening and extraordinary sensations were followed by a sharp, sudden stinging pang, or twinge: for Phebe, using her teeth, bit into his flesh. Curiously, however, to Nathan, the bite of her teeth felt more like two sharp prongs of a fork puncturing deeply, coldly into his skin.

But then, all at once, he felt her trembling lips and the sharpness of her teeth withdraw themselves from his flesh; and, with her slim, narrow-boned fingers, cold as ice-water, she squeezed and squeezed at the wound until the blood came spurting out from it upon her cheek, into her open mouth, and over her tongue. She then swallowed the blood and licked it from her fingers. And when Nathan sat up, Phebe hungrily pressed her mouth to his with lips that, while piercingly cold, left burning kisses which nearly exhausted him with the sweetness, the passion of their indescribable caress. And throughout each of these delectable kisses, Phebe breathed out to him, "Now I have swallowed your blood—or, as the book tells us that blood is a metaphor for something else, I have swallowed *that,* too. And I am now flesh of your flesh: your life is inside me."

Then, Phebe removed her clothes, and, climbing into Nathan's bed, she kneeled beside him, where he sat, with her body pressed close up against his. And pricking her breast just below its nipple with the sharp nail of her thumb, she took Nathan's head between her hands and drew his face down to the wound until his lips were pressed against it. And although Nathan wanted to resist, to withdraw his head from her grasp, or at least turn his face aside, the sound of Phebe's soothing voice, like some faintly beguiling childhood lullaby in his ear, persuaded, seduced, prevailed upon Nathan that he, "drink, drink; and become blood of *my* blood". In this way, all his resistance was thwarted, and, at the same time, all his doubt, hesitation, and disinclination instantly became acceptance, desire, and a hungering greed.

And all in a moment Nathan found his lips eagerly sucking at the self-inflicted wound in Phebe's breast, licking, supping greedily with his tongue at the flowing blood. But even as he swallowed it, even as he felt that gelid and unfamiliar fluid passing down his throat, and heard himself choking, his lust, his desire for Phebe became suddenly mingled with an overpowering sense of loathing.

With a sudden bound, then, Nathan recoiled from Phebe to the other side of the bed. And as he stood there, by the bedside, wiping Phebe's blood from his mouth and chin, feelings of revulsion, cold and awful, swelled within his heart as he continued to peer across at her crouching there, motionless on his bed.

Steadily, silently Phebe gazed back at Nathan for several moments through eyes stirlessly fixed and strangely gloating upon him. Then, with slow, languid movements like that of a cat, Phebe came slinking towards him on hands and knees across the bed, her eyes aglint and the lips of her mouth curled in a seductive leer that seemed to intoxicate his senses.

And on having reached Nathan's side of the bed, without once removing her gaze from his face, Phebe laid herself down on her back, her large dark eyes regarding him with the most enticing, alluring of looks. And just as the restless tides of the sea are stirred and drawn by the sorceries of the moon, so was Nathan now drawn, compelled by the witching glamor in Phebe's dark luminous eyes. In the breath of an instant, almost against his will, he found himself stooping low over the pale, slim body of Phebe stretched languorously across the bed.

Then, abruptly, inescapably Nathan felt himself entwined, manacled in the embrace of her strong supple arms, and as suddenly wound about and caught within the constraining grip of her smooth, shapely legs. And all at once Nathan felt as though he was being compressed and clasped by a corpse. For a cold, bemusing thrill, wonderful and peculiar, seemed to pass from Phebe's naked flesh and the limbs with which she enveloped him, into his very bones and blood, freezing him.

And as the burning caresses of Phebe's bloodless lips seemed to travel in a devouring storm—everywhere, at once—over Nathan's entire body, sensations of an awful mental and physical fatigue soon beset him. What's more, as the beating of his heart dangerously slowed, and a terrifying breathlessness, that could only be likened to suffocation, swiftly ensued, Nathan began to be mortally afraid. This horrifying experience seemed to last interminably, until all at once a profound drowsiness overcame his senses, and he lost consciousness.

When Nathan woke the next day—two days now before the eve of his and Phebe's birthday—an interesting thought suddenly occurred to him late that morning, as he was quietly sitting alone in the kitchen over his breakfast. Since he and Phebe were 'sort of going steady now', he told himself, and he had more than once suggested to her that the two of them should celebrate their "birthdays" together this Saturday night, how thoughtless and inconsiderate it would be of him if he didn't have some little gift or trinket to give to her.

In fact, the longer Nathan sat there musing on the matter, the more steadily resolved he grew in trying to conceive of something to give to Phebe as a birthday present—something that was special, *unique;* something, he was intent on, which would greatly please and delight her.

Initially, Nathan considered going to one of the gift shops on Metropolitan Avenue to purchase something for Phebe by using some of the money that remained from the thousand dollars she had given him. But then it occurred to him that that would be like Phebe buying herself a gift with her own money. As an alternative to this, however, Nathan came up with the idea (after having thought it all over very long and carefully for the next few minutes) of resorting to Aunt Amelia's bedroom in the hopes of discovering there some precious bauble among her things that he might hand to Phebe on the night of their birthday.

And so, for the first time in many days, Nathan drew open the door to his aunt's bedroom, stepped soundlessly in across its threshold, and stood peering round the room's vacant and shadowy dimensions; and although there was nothing extraordinary or peculiar in the room's calm and empty quiet, the unbroken silence in it lay so intensely deep that at first it made him feel somewhat uncomfortable, even a little apprehensive. But after a minute or two, as Nathan grew accustomed to the room's curiously 'disagreeable' hush, he noiselessly crossed the floor, and, without a second thought, went over to the large cherry wood armoire that stood opposite the foot of Aunt Amelia's bed.

Confident that he would find in it at least some kind of trinket or piece of jewelry to give to Phebe from among whatever hoarded possessions of his aunt's might be stockpiled away there, Nathan began to open, one by one, the dovetail drawers in the lower portion of that antique cupboard. After, however, a hurried and profitless search among the folded garments of each drawer, from which the mingled odor of cedar and mothballs floated up to Nathan's nostrils, he drew open the narrow doors to the armoire's upper portion and, with eager fingers, began to explore its interior.

At first, these preliminary efforts of his went unrewarded, and, after having inspected one item after another that had been carefully stored away by his aunt on its three broad shelves, Nathan began to feel less and less optimistic that he was going to discover much of anything, either of interest or of value, among the armoire's paltry cache of bibelots and curios.

But upon sounding, in a perfunctory and dispirited way, the space underneath the armoire's lower shelf, Nathan carefully drew from its place, in a corner at the very back, a small lidded ceramic receptacle resembling a two-handled jar or vase. As he looked it over very curiously, Nathan saw at once that the jar itself was quite plain, having neither mark nor ornament of any kind other than a small, thin lozenge-shaped plate of bronze which appeared on its rounded belly. And engraved on this narrow plaquette, in a very beautiful style of lettering, Nathan read the following inscription:

Jozsef Szekler 1934 - 1999

For some reason or other, the name sounded familiar to Nathan. He had heard it before somewhere; and as he continued to gaze on at the letters, and, once or twice under his breath, mutter the name to himself, he suddenly came to realize that this was the name of Aunt Amelia's husband. And all at once Nathan knew that the dates on the jar's cartouche-like panel—1934 - 1999—apparently signified poor Mr Jozsef Szekler's birth and (untimely) death.

Moreover, Nathan soon became conscious of the fact that the receptacle he was now holding was no ordinary jar, but more accurately termed an urn—Mr Jozsef Szekler's urn!—and contained, no doubt, all that now remained of what had once been *him*—no more now than a pile of ashes!

With an almost queer fascination, Nathan ran his eye inquisitively over the urn, astonished and somewhat disconcerted at the rather unsettling thought that this small jar-like vessel which he now held in his less-than steady hands contained what had once been a living, breathing man.

Nathan himself had no memory of ever having made the acquaintance of Mr Jozsef Szekler before: he would have been only two years old at the time of the man's premature demise. But the longer he stared at the urn, the more he felt an almost irrepressible urge to look inside and view its contents, and so finally 'acquaint' himself with poor Mr Szekler, or (more properly) what was left of him.

For yet a while longer, Nathan continued to stand there dithering, uncertain as to whether or not he should remove the urn's lid. But after giving the urn a slight shake while inclining his ear to its side, and having distinctly heard—and felt!—something within softly rattle about, Nathan, as if by some irresistible impulse, at last drew off the urn's covering and, without the least excuse or reservation, peered in at Mr Jozsef Szekler's earthly remains. In so doing, Nathan instantly observed that, other than a substance which for all the world appeared exactly like the ordinary ashes left in an ash-tray from dozens of cigarettes, there was also some article of creased or folded paper that had been stuffed deep into Mr Szekler's ashes.

Intent on discovering precisely what that paper was, Nathan quickly set the urn down next to where he had already placed its lid, and very gingerly reached his hand down into the vessel's narrow mouth. A moment later, between the extreme tips of his finger and thumb, he had drawn out, by one of its bent corners, the heavily creased and discolored object.

After having gently and carefully unfolded the thing, Nathan came to realize almost instantly that it had once been a very pretty and expensive greeting card (a Hallmark, in fact, which someone— for whatever reason—had felt the necessity to crumple up and then deposit into the urn among the cremated remains of Mr Jozsef Szekler!). At one and the same time, his whole attention became centered on the small stoppered glass bottle around which, much to his astonishment, that greeting card had been so closely wrung and twisted.

Nathan saw at once that the bottle's finely gilded cross-shaped stopple was in the form of the Jerusalem Cross, while the shape of the bottle itself was not unlike the kind used on a table for holding vinegar or oil.

For the next few moments Nathan stood there without stirring, as if, in the mere contemplation of the thing, he had softly and suddenly slipped away into the dreamy stillness of some deep reverie. And while his keen eyes continued to dwell, almost vacantly, on this new-found and unexpected prize, he suddenly noticed that it was nearly filled to its stopper with a perfectly clear fluid.

And as Nathan stood there with his head slightly bent, and his eyes looking down in the hushed dimness of the room, he became slowly, steadily conscious of a sort of undeniable *churchliness*, as it were, in the very cast and aspect of the glass vessel and its liquid contents. In fact, its cross-shaped stopple seemed to lend to it an air of unquestionable sanctity and piousness. And presently, at the back of his mind, Nathan realized why that was: for it had suddenly dawned on him that this kind of bottle was more properly termed a 'cruet', and the pellucid liquid contained within it was nothing other than *holy water*.

Furthermore, Nathan observed that round about this small bottle of holy water, from its tapered neck nearly to its rounded middle, had been firmly wound what at first he took to be merely a very curious and beautiful string of beads. But from the very moment Nathan had unwound this circlet of beads from round the cruet, he recognized it at once for a rosary—a rosary unlike any he had ever heard of or seen before.

Now, after standing fixed and motionless for several moments, staring, first at the rosary, then at the cruet of holy water, Nathan began to feel a faint, unreasoning covetousness towards them. No more, perhaps, than a fancy to keep the two items yet a while longer in his possession; even the curious impression that it would be 'just plain wrong' (maybe even *disrespectful)* for him to simply surrender them by dropping them, along with the greeting card, back into poor Mr Szekler's ashes.

And so with his heart and his mind in a flurry of doubt and compunction over what should ultimately be done with the two curious items and the greeting card, Nathan suddenly set them down on Aunt Amelia's bed. He carefully replaced the lid onto the ceramic urn, and then, as though without being in the least aware of what he was doing, he hastily restored the urn itself, with its contents of Mr Jozsef Szekler's cinerary remains, to its columbarium-like niche under one of the armoire's three broad shelves.

What prompted Nathan's next impulse, even he could not conceive. But, as by some unreasoning and intractable caprice of the moment, he slipped the cruet of holy water into a pocket of his jeans. Then, clutching once more in his lean hands the rosary and the crumpled greeting card, he drew awkwardly back from the armoire as though half-expecting at any moment to hear the faint, muffled voice of Mr Szekler issuing from the urn demanding that Nathan return those three items to their place in the dust of his lonely ashes. But as no disembodied voice broke the stillness of the room, Nathan calmly stooped forward into the faint light that was wanly filtering in from between the chinks of one of the window's blinds, and began very curiously to examine both the card and the rosary he had brought to light.

Opening the greeting card, Nathan saw at once that it was actually a 'birthday card', and that a large portion of its inner side was scrawled over with a hand written note, or message. In addition to this, he observed, in the card's upper left-hand corner, a date, *1987*, followed by the words: *To my dearest Amelia happy 28th birthday*. And Nathan saw that underneath the card's three or four lines of printed verse appeared the signature of the well-wisher himself: *Love Jozsef, ever your faithful and loving husband*.

Only once in the seven long miserable years that Nathan lived under his aunt's roof had he heard her mention the name of her deceased husband. It had been as recent as last summer, in the kitchen, he remembered, during one of her after-dinner drunken binges. She was just finishing a bottle of whisky, and, preceded and followed by a string of vulgarities and ill-wishes, Nathan had heard her growl out Mr Szekler's name in a long, snarl-like slur over her half-empty glass.

And at one and the same time as Nathan was in the very midst of recalling this less-than pleasant incident regarding his aunt, out of his wide brown eyes he was gazing closely and inquisitively at the unusual chaplet of beads. For he suddenly noted that the rosary's groups of ten spheres were neither of wood, glass, plastic or stone, but rather of some other substance, a material which Nathan was unable to put a name to. Moreover, they seemed to have about them a peculiarly pleasant fragrance that was in some way reminiscent of flowers. In fact, the longer Nathan stood there scenting the perfume of that string of beads, the more it seemed faintly suggestive to him of once-real roses; as if instead of being confined for over a decade, along with Mr Jozsef Szekler's ashes, to the inside of an urn, the rosary had lain for summers without end in the middle of a garden thick with roses.

Nathan noticed, too, that the solitary larger beads, separating each of those rose-haunted decades, were certainly of some kind of unusual mineral, as was the singular crucifix dangling at the end of the rosary's pendant of five beads. But since their unfamiliar variety was beyond his limited knowledge and ability to identify, Nathan once again turned his attention to his aunt's birthday card. For occupying the space of the card opposite its printed poem or message, was that long handwritten note (in pencil) from Mr Jozsef Szekler to Aunt Amelia, his wife. And sitting down on the edge of his aunt's bed, Nathan began to read to himself the following words:

> 'My dearest Amelia, on this your 28th birthday, I want to give you something exceptional, something you will find truly special. Which is why this rosary and this little phial of holy water are now yours. You know that I am Hungarian by birth, born in the small town of Nagyleta, just a few miles west of the Romanian border. And there, much of my adolescence was spent; but when I was very young, my father often took me

to stay with his mother's relations in Romania, on a large tract of farmland, at Ecsed, in Transylvania, a very beautiful and mysterious region of the world. In the Romanian tongue it is called Ardeal, and in the Hungarian, or Magyar, it is Erdely.

'There as a young boy I came to learn the language of my grandmother's people, and it was she who gave to me, on my eleventh birthday, this special rosary and cruet of holy water, and which I now want you to have. In the Romanian, the rosary is called *matanie;* and here is why the Romanian rosaries, or *matanie,* are unlike those fashioned anywhere else in the world: the sets of ten beads are composed of the compressed petals of wild roses, and each sphere, if held near the nose, gives off that flower's wonderful fragrance.

Nathan paused a moment to glance over at the rosary he still clutched in his other hand, and inhaled once more the rose-scented fragrance of its groups of ten small beads before continuing to read on:

'And it was my grandmother's wholehearted belief, poor superstitious woman, that the Romanians use this flower's petals specifically because its mere fragrance is a bane to witches, werewolves, and vampires. She once told me the mere odor of the rose repels these creatures of darkness, and that the slightest contact with a rose or its petals burns them like the flame of a fire. What's more, the larger beads which divide each of the rosary's decades is a very peculiar variety of crystal called staurolite, from the Greek for 'cross', as the mineral is formed naturally of two wedges—one crossing the other at right angles, and appearing exactly like miniature crosses. This interesting crystal was sometimes known as the baptismal-stone whenever it was used as an amulet at baptisms. And my grandmother could not resist

from informing me that these crystals, known from
of old as 'lapis-crucifer', or 'cross-stone', are still worn
by Romanians throughout Transylvania as charms to
ward off vampires.'

Again Nathan paused, for the once-dark, penciled handwriting on
the time-foxed paper of the card became somewhat faint at this
point, and he had to strain his eyes in order to decipher the blurred
and half-faded words that followed. Still, he was able to make them
out, and once more read slowly on:

> 'And one more thing you must know, my dear: the
> Crucifix on the rosary's pendant is of a variety of
> jasper known as the bloodstone, and is a singularly
> appropriate stone, since the red specks on it are
> regarded as having a mystical significance, symbolical
> of the drops of blood that flowed from the wounds of
> Our Lord. It is believed, yet again, by the superstitious
> populace of the Transylvanian forests to be injurious
> to revenants, evil spirits and, of course, the dreaded
> Undead of their childish fears.'

Nathan raised his eyes, and held up before them the rosary. For
nearly a full minute he gazed on at the red-speckled crucifix dangling
from its pendant, whose limbs broadened outward at the ends,
indicative of the Maltese cross. This was the cross which, of all the
various types represented in the Christian faith, Nathan admired
most. Once more, then, he resumed his reading:

> 'But even more remarkable about the rosary and
> holy water, my dear Amelia, is the very popular and
> strangely Gothic legend surrounding the two. For my
> grandmother once told me both the holy water and
> the rosary come from a small village in Transylvania
> called Rozeta, which means "'rosette", and which is
> said to have been founded in the 12th century shortly

after a young Cistercian monk came to the region from the west. But prior to the coming of this pious youth, the once desolate and depopulated region had, according to local tradition—or superstition—an older, darker history, and was called "Blestemat", which my grandmother told me is Romanian, for "accursed, or lying under a curse"; for the region was believed to have been the haunt of numerous vampires, who used its caves and woodland grottoes for their lairs by day.

'Now, the religious zeal of this young Cistercian monk induced him to make the journey to this unclean district armed with no more than a garland of roses which he'd taken from a statue of the Blessed Virgin in the parish church, and a cross fashioned of aspen wood, to expel the evil revenants. He is said to have destroyed a great many of these blood-drinking creatures of darkness, but was ultimately overcome by his enemies just before dawn. His faith and his sacrifice, however, became the occasion of a miracle, for it is told that from a rock, which the cross of aspen wood struck when the monk fell, there gushed a spring of purest water; and where the garland of roses, that had fallen from round the monk's neck, touched the ground, countless roses multiplied, until the body of the monk and the encompassing waste were overgrown with the blooms and dense foliage of roses of supernatural beauty and fragrance. Indeed, roses sprouted up in such profusion throughout the region that the vampires fled shrieking before them, and to its wooded hills and glens they have never dared return.'

Again in his reading of the card, Nathan had paused, for he saw that the point of the pencil used by Mr Szekler must at this point have broken while he was writing, for there was a slight puncture mark with a faint smear. Then, the following words:

> The legend goes on to say that with the land thus cleansed, people returned, built a church near the spring, and round this church, amid the dense rose-bushes, the village of Rozeta grew up. And from that very spring near the Transylvanian church in Rozeta comes the holy water in this cruet; just as it is from the compressed petals of countless roses in that fabulous region that the beads of this unique rosary have been fashioned. The local villagers in this quaint hamlet of Rozeta still celebrate the young monk's sacrifice with torch-light gatherings at his tomb, and many wonders and miracles are alleged to have occurred there. And so, my dearest Amelia, I now bestow on you, with all my love, these two wonderful heirlooms of my grandmother's people—the holy water and the rosary, with all their curious lore, on this your 28th birthday.'

Nathan ceased to read any further. And yet his eyes remained fixed in an abstracted way on the card's penciled writing. For quite suddenly it had occurred to him that it was Aunt Amelia herself who, by way of expressing her contempt for poor Mr Jozsef Szekler, had thrust the card, along with the rosary and cruet of holy water, into the urn with her husband's cinerary remains.

And Nathan could just picture to himself the towering rage his aunt must have been in to learn, upon her husband's death, that while the bulk of his fortune had gone to his beloved church, the effects bequeathed to her amounted to little more than this triad of bottled water, ashes, and a string of beads. And doubtless, thought Nathan, here—relegated to the very back part of the armoire's lower shelf—the three had remained undisturbed from 1999, the date of Mr Szekler's demise, until this very moment.

Meanwhile, Nathan's glance, after having vaguely wandered once more over the greeting card's penciled writing, strayed on almost stealthily to his other hand which was holding the chaplet of beads with its crucifix of bloodstone. And as he continued to gaze on at it, he suddenly thought to himself this extraordinary rosary would be the perfect gift for Phebe on this *her* sixteenth birthday! For just as she had given to him this wonderful ring (and Nathan raised his hand to glance at the bright ruby hololith band that encircled the finger on which Phebe herself had placed it) as well as its little box, the ring-treasury, and had told him all those wonderful things about them, he now had something in turn to give to her. A gift possessing a strange and fabulous lore all its own, which he (by reading those parts written by Mr Szekler on his aunt's birthday card) could now inform *her* all about. Moreover, Nathan was all but certain that Phebe had nothing like this unusual rosary among her hoard of curios.

And with a sudden thrill of excitement rushing through his veins, Nathan got up and hurried out of his aunt's bedroom, carrying away with him the spoils of his fruitful search, both the card and the rosary tightly clenched in either hand.

Now, that same night, long after the sun was set and the skies had narrowed and darkened, slowly ascending its eastern slope could be seen the thin crescent of a waxing moon. And at the same time as its horns cleared the horizon, and Nathan finished his supper, there came noises from his bedroom upstairs, a sound as of someone closing his bedroom window, followed by the soft, light tread of that someone's dainty feet crossing the floor.

All in an instant Nathan caught his breath and, for a moment or two, sitting perfectly still, he listened. Then, as the name of the longed-for one flashed across his mind, his eyes opened round and wide, and from off his tongue, faint as the faintest breath, slipped the words, "She's here". Straight away, with a furious jerk, his heart began to flutter with unspeakable excitement and expectation. He rushed out of the kitchen, darted up the stairs to his room and, opening its door, there, just as he had hoped, was Phebe, already inside, waiting for him.

Fingers and thumb still clutching the doorknob, Nathan paused for some seconds on the threshold of his room to gaze across at her as she lay, like some wonderful vision seen only in dream, stretched across his bed, her dark, dwelling eyes peering at him seductively out of the loveliness and pallor of her face. She was lying there on her side, without a stitch of clothing on: her one hand lying along the rondure of her hip, while her head was propped upon the other.

The blind hung down over the window to its last slat, and several wax candles in brass candlestick-holders were brightly burning on the dresser. Phebe sat up at once as Nathan came over to her, and, laughing sweetly, she helped him out of his clothes and drew him eagerly into the bed with her. For ever since the weird blood-sharing ritual of the night before, she seemed again like her old, beguiling, exuberant, provocative self.

Nathan kept smiling as his head, on the pillow with Phebe's, stirred now and again, and he could feel, as her large dark eyes shone tranquilly close to his, the tip of her lean icy forefinger gently tracing the letters of his name on his bosom. But suddenly over his heart it paused, and her eyes dwelt in a fixed and protracted stare on Nathan's. And as he continued to meet her unstirring gaze, with his thoughts the whole time so hotly bent on the curious gift he had gotten for her, Phebe seemed suddenly to decipher it in Nathan's glance. Even more so, she seemed to divine it in the very rhythm of his fluttering heart, which Nathan did not doubt she could easily detect, such was the hush and stillness that prevailed so deeply throughout the house. Aside from that though, such was the close interrelation now of her thoughts with Nathan's, that almost it seemed to him that Phebe was silently aware not only of everything that was secretly passing through his mind, but everything he was feeling in the inmost recess of his heart as well.

And all at once Phebe's lips broke into the most beautiful smile. "You have something for me," she laughed. "Don't you, Nathan? What is it?"

Nathan could not refrain from laughing, too, as he said, "A birthday present."

Phebe's eyes widened, and a faint glint awoke in the depths of their intense darkness. "Give it to me;" she said; "I want it now"; and laughed again.

Nathan slipped out of bed, and stooping low over his jeans which lay on the floor where Phebe had tossed them, he drew out of its front pocket the matanie, or rosary, he had discovered inside his aunt's armoire. Holding it in his clenched fist behind his back, he turned then to Phebe, who was kneeling in bed near its edge, smiling, and gazing at him expectantly. With a guileless grin on his lips, Nathan told Phebe to first hold out her hands, and shut her eyes.

For an instant, Phebe's dark eyes met his: then, shutting them, she laughingly extended both pale tiny hands towards him and waited.

Very gently then, into those two small, lean-fingered hands, as pale and cold as December snow, Nathan placed that strange and wonderful rosary. And no sooner had the chaplet's pendant, with its five beads of compressed rose-petals and crucifix of bloodstone, come into contact with the skin of Phebe's narrow palms than tiny fronds of shadowy smoke went up from her flesh, accompanied by a horrid stench and a hissing noise as of something being singed. In the same instant, from Phebe's lips there broke out a blood-curdling shriek and howl of pain; and with queer, stiff, rapidly jerking movements that were horrible to see, Phebe recoiled backwards on hands and knees away from Nathan across the bed.

Nathan stood frozen in shock and confusion, and stared with wide, frightened eyes across the bed at Phebe, who now stood crouching on its opposite side. She was snarling like a wild beast at the rosary's crucifix which, to Nathan's astonishment, seemed to glow or burn with an angry ruddiness as the red heart of a fire.

And while Phebe, out of blazing eyes, continued to glare fiercely at the crucifix, the loveliness and beauty of her features seemed to slowly, steadily drain away out of her face, and with it, much, too, even of her very humanity. And in its place, oddly enough, was faintly disclosed the physiognomy of something else, something fearsome, bestial, ghastly.

It was singularly odd, too, that at that moment Nathan did not realize or associate the resemblance of this "something else" with a certain leathery-winged nocturnal creature. He did, however, observe (much to his horror) that the two small livid, seam-like scars on either of Phebe's hands now appeared inflamed and swollen with blood, as though ready to burst open. Moreover, a number of small, prick-like scars became visible all along her forehead as well, bulging and swelling as though about to break open and bleed.

Meanwhile, Phebe's wildly glaring eyes remained unswervingly fixed on the rosary with its dangling crucifix, which Nathan, in dazed astonishment, still extended to her in his outstretched hand. And not only could he see, but he could actually *feel* the glance of hideous dread, of unspeakable hatred that she cast on it from under her furrowed brows, while screaming at it, again and again, in the tones of some awful, startling voice: "Recede, miser, recede!"

And suddenly averting her face, Phebe collapsed on the floor, and lay there convulsing, as that dreadful voice, so inexplicably like—and yet, in some odd, extraordinary way, far deeper and more imposing than—her own, broke appallingly out once more: "Spes nobis nulla... Confusi sumus... Recede, miser, recede!"

Nathan darted round to the other side of the bed and, still clutching the rosary in his hand, he bent low over Phebe's writhing form. She instantly covered her face with her hands and, letting out a single wail of mortal terror, she began to beg Nathan: "Put it away; put it away; please, Nathan; put it away!"

For several moments, rigid and dumb with astonishment, Nathan stood motionless, staring down at Phebe; then, recovering his wits, he reached down for his jeans on the floor, and thrust the rosary deep into its pocket again.

Very gently, and very anxiously Nathan helped Phebe to her feet. As he did so, he noticed that the little series of scars on her forehead had completely vanished, leaving no trace of themselves; and only faintly now were the scars to the mysterious wounds on her feet and hands once more visible. He noted, too, as he gazed at Phebe's face for some time in silence that its curious pallor had intensified to a corpse-like bluish-white, and that she now looked faint, and frail, and very ill.

For a moment or two, Phebe stood with her head bent low. Then, lifting her eyes, she turned their peering, wistful gaze directly on Nathan, as her voice, soft and low, broke the silence. "I'm sorry you had to see that, Nathan."

But Nathan was suddenly finding it difficult to meet Phebe's eye, and quickly lowered his gaze, as he said, "Yeah; me too."

Phebe sat quietly down on the edge of Nathan's bed. For some while there was silence between herself and Nathan; and, with her head bowed low, her knees pressed tight together, and her slim, lean-fingered hands folded in her lap, she remained quite still. Then, once more, she raised her head and stole a longish, plaintive glance at Nathan's face out of her deep, dark, forlorn eyes. "You're angry with me?" she asked.

Faintly Nathan shook his head and, for a moment, held his breath. Then, with eyes yet averted, he said, "No"; which indeed was true enough, since Phebe's reaction to his intended gift had caused him to feel absolutely nothing in the way of anger, but rather deadly frightened and all but physically sick.

Again Phebe spoke, asking Nathan if he was alright. And with almost sightless eyes fixed on the floor, Nathan silently nodded his head, for try as he would he could not as yet bring himself to look at Phebe; he simply stood there motionless, with his head bent low. Then, having stolen a fleeting, uneasy half-glance at Phebe's face, the question which he could no longer refrain from asking, slipped faintly, anxiously off his tongue, "What happened to you?" And pausing a moment to draw a deep breath, "Why did you act the way you did," he went on, in a hushed, almost whispering voice, "when I put the rosary in your hand—it was like you were in pain."

Awaiting her reply, Nathan slowly raised his head and his eyes encountered those of Phebe's. For a moment or two there came into her pale, narrow face an expression of unspeakable misery, as she said, "Please, Nathan, try and understand that who and what I am does not permit me to touch such religious symbols." For one or two moments more her troubled eyes continued to meet Nathan's, until, looking mournfully away, she added, "And because of this, I am forbidden to even so much as handle a rosary." And Phebe's soft, sweet voice trembled, as if in fear, at that last word.

Nathan stood for some while without speaking, his pondering eyes fixed on Phebe. Then, "So what are you saying: you're, like, not a Christian; is that what you mean?" he asked at length.

Once more Phebe turned her head and fixed Nathan with a gaze still more forlorn, more tragic, as she said, "Like you, I was baptized a—" she began. "But, no;" she broke off suddenly. "Very long ago I renounced my faith; became one of the Un—" she paused a moment or two; seemed to reflect; and then, "—the Unbaptized;" she continued; "and I am now bound by beliefs, as it were, that are very different from yours, Nathan, beliefs which do not allow me to come into contact with the relics or symbols of your faith." The dark, lustrous, large-pupilled eyes regarding him had been withdrawn, and were now downbent, fixed on the pale, slender hands folded in her lap.

Nathan, meanwhile, repeated to himself, slowly and softly, the curious term which Phebe had used. *Unbaptized.* And for a space of some seconds the word echoed on in his brain, rousing all kinds of hints, surmises, suspicions as to the actual meaning Phebe had intended to convey to—or *conceal from*—him by using such an odd, ambiguous term.

In doubt and perplexity, Nathan continued to gaze on at Phebe's face; for, as always, he knew that she was being deliberately vague, or cryptic, with her words; and whatever answers she conveyed to him seemed to be not only evasive, but couched in riddles.

All but lost to his surroundings now, Nathan stood there still and silent. He seemed to be deep in thought, as again and again he stood pondering, considering very carefully to himself what Phebe just now had told him, all the while making every effort to discover the least inkling of any hidden meaning in her words.

But it was all as strange and mystifying to Nathan as if Phebe had said it to him in Greek or Arabic. And all at once he found himself wondering, if Phebe wasn't a Christian, as she herself seemed to be suggesting, and her own 'beliefs' (whatever they were) did not permit her to handle the symbols of another's faith, what then did she mean by *"unbaptized"*? Or, even more so, by the words, *who* and *what* she is? And all at once Nathan's curiosity overcame his fear and astonishment, as he asked, "Are you saying that there's something about you that isn't—" He stopped himself, for he had almost said, *human*; but instead, from off his agile tongue came the words, "that's not *right*?"

Phebe's deep and dark and luminous eyes, fringed by their shadowy lashes, fixed themselves once more on Nathan's face. "Ah, *'not right'*," her sweet, yet tremulous voice had caught up the words. "Yes, Nathan; and as different from you as darkness is to day."

Phebe gazed steadily back at Nathan; and a remote glint had come into her wide, intensely dark eyes. Nathan dropped his gaze a while and tried hard to think. And presently, the strange, mysterious series of words Phebe had uttered, "recede, miser... spes nobis nulla... and, confusi sumus" suddenly came rushing back into his mind, throwing his thoughts into disorder, and impressing themselves upon his memory like the black and white images in some old photograph. And the longer Nathan stood there pondering over Phebe's bizarre reaction to the rosary, and that strange series of words she had recited after coming into contact with its crucifix, and the hazy, cryptic reason she had given for it all, the more he kept asking himself, what was the truth, the *real* truth, behind it all.

And when once more Nathan had raised his eyes to those of Phebe's, he saw that she was on her knees, in a very seductive posture, in the bed, with her slim, narrow-fingered hand stretched out to him. "Come, Nathan;" she said, faintly smiling; "come and lie down in bed next to me, and don't think about it anymore."

But Nathan did not stir; a strange disinclination held him where he stood. Phebe's dark peering eyes continued to intently regard Nathan, and a shade of anxiety came into her face and voice as she asked him, "Are you afraid of me now?" For a moment or two Nathan strove to speak, for a desire had risen up in him to tell, to order, to demand that Phebe get out of his house and never return. But it was his love, his fidelity for Phebe—not his fear—that sealed his lips; and his devotion to her made his tongue powerless to stir. And his mind was suddenly haunted by a misery of guilt as to where Phebe might go and what she might do once he had driven her away.

For some time in silence, Phebe continued to hold Nathan's eyes with her intensely mournful gaze, which all the while seemed to be pleading, entreating, persuading. Then, "If you're not afraid of me, Nathan," Phebe said to him, with her hand still extended towards him, "you'll prove it by taking my hand."

Without hesitating a moment longer, Nathan slowly reached out a trembling hand; and, feeling it clasped firmly in hers, Phebe once more drew him into the bed with her. For some time the two lay in bed on their side, facing one another. Nathan was very quiet and thoughtful as he stared at Phebe, and watched her face; while she, now and again, spoke to him in a low whispering voice, and smiled, gazing full into his eyes, and caressed him, ever and again, with her cold slender hands.

And as the night wore on, and the candles burned low, and the moon sank over the old All Faiths cemetery, Phebe, for the first time since commencing her nightly sojourns with Nathan in his bedroom, exhibited to Nathan on this night a surprising (and unexpected) reluctance to part from him and return, as had been her unvarying habit in the past, to the old mausoleum before day-break. Instead she remained in the bed with Nathan in his room, nestled close up against him.

For some while now neither of them spoke or stirred; but then, for a moment, Phebe slipped softly out of the bed, went over to Nathan's bookshelf, and abstracted one of its grimy old paperbacks. Snuggling next to Nathan in the bed again, she began to read aloud from it.

Nathan recognized the opening line at once, for it was none other than de la Motte Fouque's *Undine*. And as he lay still and silent, listening, with eyes half-shut, to Phebe's sweet, soft voice, his lids began to droop, half open, then droop again. At some point or other, not long after Phebe had stopped reading to him, he must have at last fallen asleep, for after a while, through the strangeness of vague, disjointed dreamings, Nathan began to experience a series of the oddest impressions.

The first was that Phebe had slowly withdrawn her arms from about him, and the next that, softly moving to one side of the bed, she had stealthily risen from it. He also felt or sensed that her prolonged absence from his bed, from the very room itself, had lasted a considerable length of time; for he seemed to be aware in some mysterious, inexplicable way that he was lying alone in his bed (and in his room), bereft of her presence, for a period of at least several hours. Of course, Nathan could not be certain about any of this, for in the time that it all occurred his mind had been in a peculiarly dreamy, half-conscious state.

But some time during this perceived absenteeism of Phebe from his room, perhaps only shortly before he woke, Nathan must have passed into a profound slumber, for all at once he dreamed he was standing in full sunshine, in an open field or meadow of green grass. Nearby stood a tree whose wide-spreading boughs were covered in pale, carnation-like blossoms, and the blue sky overhead was cloudless and bright. A man was standing not very far from him in the distance, with his back to him, so that Nathan could not see his face. He could see, however, that the man was clothed in a robe of snowy whiteness, and that his dark hair hung well past his shoulders, and in his hand he was holding a wooden staff like a shepherd's crook, and all about him grazed and huddled a flock of sheep.

Nathan felt he should somehow know this man; there was something wonderfully familiar in his appearance. Then, the shepherd, or the man—whoever he was—began to stride away, and the sheep to bleat and follow after him. Nathan also felt an odd longing to go with him; it seemed almost urgent that he do so. His fast-beating heart seemed to warn him not to linger or hesitate. And as he began to hurry after him, from somewhere behind, he heard a voice break out, clamoring, calling him back.

Nathan turned and, in the opposite direction to which the man was walking, he saw Phebe standing, with both arms extended towards him. She called his name repeatedly, desperately. Nathan did not know who to run towards. Should he follow the Man with his sheep, or run to Phebe? And nearly at the same time as Nathan stood pondering, debating which course to choose, menacing clouds began to mount and gather over the blue sky, and a cold gloom, cheerless and unsettling, crept into the air. Then, a shadowy mist, like a grey veil, seemed to fall between Nathan and the Man he yearned to follow. The mist swiftly deepened, darkened.

Feeling lost, alone, forsaken, Nathan turned and ran the other way to Phebe. He was hastening along now, muttering almost breathlessly the while to himself a series of curious words, some queer verses that were somehow familiar, and yet, at the same time, dire and strangely foreboding. It sounded to him like the wonderful, silvery language used by Shakespeare in his plays: "Eyes look your last! Arms, take your last embrace! and, lips, O you the doors of breath, seal with a righteous kiss a dateless bargain to engrossing death!"

Where he had got those lines from, Nathan could not now say, nor how or why they had become so clearly imprinted on his memory. Nor did he care, for quite suddenly Phebe was nestling tenderly in his arms with her head against his shoulder. And as he looked down at her face, he could not tell whether she was weeping or laughing, for the mist was now coming between them. He heard her then, after having spoken his name, softly whispering, as if to herself, some verses, too (were they from Shakespeare as well?): "O God, I have an ill-divining soul! Methinks I see thee now, thou art so low, as one dead in the bottom of a tomb. Either my eyesight fails, or thou lookest pale."

And no sooner were these words out of her mouth than everything vanished instantaneously, leaving only darkness and a faint peculiar echo of Phebe's words. Then, with a tremor and a startled movement, Nathan opened his eyes very suddenly, stunned and terrified out of his dream.

CHAPTER FIVE

"... sleeping
Soft in the bed,
Empty of sorrow
... She awoke
With all pleasure gone,
Swimming in blood..."

—*The Elder Edda*

"... nothing but evil can come if I tell you this
secret. For the mercy of God do not require it of
me. If you but knew, you would withdraw yourself
from my love, and I should be lost indeed..."

—*The Lays of Marie de France*

For the first minute or two, as Nathan's heart continued its steady thundering gallop behind the small cage of his ribs, he lay vainly but desperately struggling to recall whatever elusive dream had just now aroused him so suddenly out of his sleep. But the dream's vaguely unsettling imagery had already drained away into an emptiness past all hope of recollection, leaving behind only a thin crust, or film, as it were, of uneasiness and confusion to trouble his thoughts.

Lurching up in bed onto his elbow, then, Nathan saw, after glancing round, that although the wax candles on the dresser top had long since flickered to extinction, a pale uncertain light suffused the room's dimness. This he soon realized was from the bluish-grey light of daybreak which, stealing in round the edges of his window's blind, was just then beginning to faintly dusk his room.

And when once more his heart had resumed its normal pace and rhythm, Nathan suddenly realized two more things. Firstly, that this was the morning of August 24ᵗʰ, the eve of *the eve* before his and Phebe's birthday; and secondly, that Phebe had *not* returned to the old mausoleum, but was still lying next to him in bed in the warm, slowly-paling twilight of his room.

For a full minute and more, Nathan gazed down at the alluring figure of Phebe as it lay, pale as marble, stretched upon the bed. She lay perfectly still, with her two lean, long-fingered hands clasped together and folded over her bosom, which (although Nathan could not be certain, since the room was still too dim and shadowy) seemed never once to rise or fall with even the faintest stir of respiration.

Nathan's eyes then fixed themselves on the lovely impassive features of Phebe's solemn face. Leisurely they coursed their way over the fast-shut eyes with their dark-lashed eyelids, the full lips, the delicately rounded chin, and those long black glossy tresses of her mane-like hair, lying spread about her in thick, heavy coils that flowed from over the pillow, round her neck and shoulders, and down to her shapely hips.

Then, lower, nearer still, Nathan stooped his face to look on that of Phebe's; and all at once the still and stony aspect of its loveliness, the pale and bloodless color of its skin, seemed to remind him less and less of a living person, and all the more of a lifeless waxen image, or the semblance of one who, recently dead, had been freshly embalmed.

And suddenly, as at some vague yet awful misgiving, his heart gave a furious lurch inside his body. For almost it seemed to him (though he could hardly believe it himself) that, gaze on as he would, he was still unable to discern either the least slow, soft measured rise or fall of Phebe's breasts, or so much as a solitary tremulous breath escaping from her stirless lips.

But then, as Nathan's anxious glance strayed once more to Phebe's dark still eyelids—and for a fleeting instant he wondered to himself whether the mind now dreaming behind them was in the least aware of his presence—he suddenly thought that Phebe's eyes appeared to be only half-shut, so that from between their lash-fringed lids showed a thin line of white and a dark lustrous glint of her large, wide irises. And despite the fact that Nathan could plainly see that Phebe was sound asleep, her eyes, nevertheless, very abruptly seemed to shift (as if of their own will) and fasten themselves intently on Nathan's face. The movement was so strange, so sudden, that Nathan visibly started and caught his breath. For almost it seemed to him that Phebe, even while unconscious, was still heedfully watching him. In fact not only could he see her gaze fixed upon himself, he could actually *feel* it: a shrewd, vigilant glance that seemed to follow and regard him piercingly.

Now, just as Nathan leaned his face down low over Phebe's in an effort to catch the faintest whisper of her soundless breathing, he became suddenly conscious of a dark, syrupy fluid beginning to trickle from the corners of her eyes. And as he continued to gaze on, half-doubtfully, he noticed that same viscid fluid begin to trickle first from one of her nostrils, then from the other. And quite suddenly it dawned on him that the fluid he was now seeing leak and seep steadily out of Phebe's eyes and nostrils was—*blood*!

And directly Nathan came to this singularly awful realization, he noted, much to his astonishment and alarm, a thin, slow trickle coming now from the left corner of Phebe's mouth. But even as he stared, with goggling eyes and gaping mouth, a second trickle began to leak from the other corner of her mouth; until, all at once, the lips of Phebe's mouth seemed to stir, curl in a slow, faint grin, then slightly part, as over the lower lip began to ooze a thick, gurgling stream of frothy blood. And in silent horror Nathan watched as it spread down and across Phebe's chin, then flowed steadily down her slender white neck, where it divided into two equal streams, to seep onto the fitted sheet, and so round either of her pale narrow shoulders.

Then, quite suddenly, Nathan felt its cold, sticky wetness spread along the sheet where his chilled fingers lay. At this brief contact Nathan instantly withdrew his hand, and, recoiling to the edge of the mattress, he sprang out of bed with an awful feeling of shuddering revulsion. He stood swaying a moment or two beside the bed, shaking uncontrollably from head to toe, as he continued to stare breathlessly down at Phebe. And only after having striven against the deadly numbing fear that for some seconds had prevented him from either stirring or speaking, Nathan was at last able to utter Pbebe's name aloud two or three times. But as Phebe remained lying in the bed as still and speechless as a block of stone, Nathan fled in a wild and fluttering panic to the other side of his room, felt for, and found, the toggle switch along the wall near his door, and, with something between a gasp and a sob, he flicked it on. Then, by the full flooding radiance of the three light bulbs in the ceiling fixture, Nathan stole warily, stealthily over to the bed once more. For the briefest instant he stood bending over the naked figure of Phebe lying stretched, without the faintest movement, upon the mattress. He could see her face and form quite clearly now, as well as the great dark blood-stain outlining the upper part of her body from her pale narrow shoulders down to her smooth, slim waist.

And with a horrid shock of fright and disbelief, Nathan watched as the blood continued to trickle with a dull, faint burbling sound from under Phebe's eyelids; from over the red grinning lips of her sensuous mouth; and from the slim, still nostrils of her nose. There was even (he presently noticed) a thin, watery trickle issuing from the orifice of her small delicate ear—contributing even more blood to the stain already around her that was slowly, steadily flowing and spreading outward from either side of her slender form along the cloth of the fitted sheet in an ever-widening radius.

Initially, Nathan had thought, in the first terrified instant of his panic, that Phebe had died. That her heart, or some principal artery leading to it, must have burst within her some time during the night, and the internal bleeding (which he presumed had been ongoing for some while now) was at last finding its outflow through any and every convenient orifice in her body.

But in the instant following this assumption, Nathan happened to see the dark, lash-fringed lids of Phebe's eyes tremble, and her blood-smeared lips stir and give out something like a long, inexhaustible gasping breath, or sigh, in which he caught, faint, and slow, and strangely drawn out, the whispered syllables of his name—"Naaathaaan." And he thought to himself, Then Phebe isn't—dead; she's still... alive?

But the longer Nathan stood there, fixed and staring at that deathly pale, utterly motionless form, from which the blood never for an instant ceased to dribble and ooze, the more he wondered, Or is she?

And as he continued to struggle with a frightened and doubtful heart, Nathan suddenly shrank backward, away from the bed, completely unnerved at last, and overwhelmed by a violent sensation of repulsion. For something truly appalling to his soul, dreadful beyond all expression, lay in the nightmarish sight of Phebe lying there, still and pale as a cadaver, in his bed in a pool of blood, hemorrhaging through her nose and eyes, and breathing out his name the while through a froth of blood on her grinning lips.

And even as Nathan came to a sudden halt beside his bedroom window, and his trembling fingers groped out, as by some pointless, unreasoning impulse for the cord to draw up its blind, Phebe's eyelids flickered, moved, then swiftly lifted. And the head, which all the while had been pressed stirlessly into the pillow, instantly swerved to one side, so that her face abruptly turned in Nathan's direction; and the fierce, penetrating gaze of those large, dark lustrous eyes fastened itself so intently on him that almost it seemed to Nathan from out of their depths they were piteously crying across to him in mortal alarm, anxiety—terror!

It was a ghastly look—scarcely human in expression—that made Nathan's heart shudder and then stand still in a cold and awful dread. Then, "No! Nathan—*don't!*" was the deep, stony command barked out at him across the room from those blood-slathered lips.

Half stupefied by the tone and authority of that voice, Nathan found himself, like a small and timid animal, obeying it. For all at once, without the least movement, he stood very still and quiet, watching Phebe, half in wonder, half in fear as, slowly, stiffly, she sat upright in the bed, her hands remaining clasped across her bosom, her pallid face turned full upon his, and her eyes never swerving, even by a hair's breadth, from his own. "Don't pull the blind up;" she went on; "you'll let in the—" Phebe hesitated an instant, and Nathan distinctly noted a faint shudder pass through her as she all but whispered the word, "—*sunlight*."

Nathan stared at Phebe with scared, anxious, questioning eyes, and, after a long pause of silence, he managed to faintly inquire, "So what if I did?" He fell silent, and continued to gaze across at Phebe. Then, "What's wrong with letting the sunlight in the room?" And his eyes continued to meet Phebe's uneasily, doubtfully. "Why are you so afraid of it?"

Phebe met Nathan's look with an anxiety as intense and unmistakable as his own. "It's—it isn't good for me," came the miserable, stammered answer. And through the awful silence that now fell between them, Nathan regarded Phebe warily, mistrustfully. The steadily growing feeling of intense physical revulsion which he was now experiencing toward her was alarming even to himself, as he continued to watch her futile efforts to swab away, with the narrow palms and lean fingers of her hands, the streaks and gouts of blood on her face.

And all the while, as Phebe's eyes steadily continued to dwell on Nathan, he stood there, held fast in a tranced and empty stillness by that heedfully peering gaze of hers. But then, all in a moment, with a cold, curious, quiet apprehension gathering at his heart, he shut his eyes, fearing that they might well betray to her the secret loathing roused in him by the sight of her vain attempts to preen and rid herself of all that blood.

But no matter how fast, or how diligently, Phebe's little hands rubbed and wiped the blood from beneath her eyes; or from her nostrils and the cheeks of her face; or from round her mouth, chin, and neck, Nathan, upon opening his eyes and fixing them once more on Phebe, could still see smears and blotches of it on her pallid features. And as she sprang out of bed and drew the sheet round her body, so as to hide the blood staining her back and sides, she moved forward across the room to where Nathan stood. "It's alright," she said. "I'm not hurt"; and pausing a moment to nestle against Nathan, she added: "Sometimes this happens to me, Nathan. Don't be afraid. It's nothing."

Nathan drew sharply back a step or two from Phebe, and stood looking at her suspiciously for some while without speaking; then, "But there was... blood, Phebe, and it was coming out of you... from... from everywhere," he managed to stammer at last. "Did you cut yourself?" He paused a moment or two, and, barely able to conceal from her his repugnance, he stepped back yet another pace and glanced uneasily into Phebe's eyes. "And all in back of you," he then went on, "you're covered in blood, like you were sleeping in a pool of it." Again he paused; and the anxious dark eyes gazed steadily back at Nathan, as very faintly he added: "Maybe I should call a doctor for you?"

Again Phebe came nestling up against him; and before Nathan could draw away from her, she had put both her arms about his neck and drawn his face close to hers. Very gently, then, on both cheeks, she kissed him twice. Then, drawing her face back a little, her eyes peered anxiously, forlornly into his, as she breathed, "Don't, Nathan; there's no need. I'm not hurt." And all in a moment she had stooped, caught up her lace dress where it lay on the floor at her feet, and, with it, hurried so softly across the hall to the bathroom that Nathan never once heard her steps.

The next moment Nathan had followed Phebe to the bathroom; but she had already shut and locked its door. Nathan made a light rattling at the doorknob; he turned it again and again in vain. Then, tapping on the panel, he said, "Phebe, open the door!" But Phebe made no answer.

Nathan listened a while. He distinctly heard the glass tub-door slide; then, the hushing sound of the water jetting from the showerhead; and he knew that Phebe must be washing the blood from herself. He stooped against the door, tapped sharply at the panel again, and raised his voice so as to be heard above of the noise of the water. "Phebe, I want to know what happened to you. Tell me! Why were you bleeding like that?"

"It's really nothing, Nathan," answered the slightly trembling voice from within the bathroom. "You don't have to feel worried about it." There was a brief pause; and once more Nathan stood waiting, listening. He thought he heard a sob; then, "I wasn't quite myself before;" he heard Phebe continue; "but I'm okay now." And in her voice Nathan thought he caught not only a slight tremor but the faintest hint of tears.

After a while Nathan gave another sharp tap at the door, and said, "But what's going on with you, Phebe? I want you to tell me. A normal person doesn't wake up in a pool of blood like that. And you're telling me it's nothing to worry about! That this *'happens'* sometimes? Why?"

"I can't tell you why—not now," came the muffled, lachrymose tones of Phebe's voice again. "Please, believe me, Nathan. I'm sorry."

With his heart desperately uncertain and afraid, and the thoughts in his mind confused and aimlessly astir, Nathan stood listening at the door a while longer. Then, hesitating one last instant before crossing the hall, he returned in a dull and empty wretchedness to his bedroom.

Pausing at the foot of his bed, Nathan stood perfectly still and quiet. For the first few moments he surveyed impassively the sleigh-like curve to the bed's hardwood-framed headboard, before his wandering gaze came to settle with something like a wince on the large wet oviform bloodstain over the place of the fitted-sheet where Phebe's body had lain.

For a single solitary instant Nathan cast an uneasy glance over his shoulder at the empty doorway of his room. Then, taking a deep breath, he glumly proceeded to strip the bed of its blood-soaked blanket and sheet, only to discover that the mattress beneath was also stained and drenched with blood. The smell was unspeakably foul, like the reek that permeates a slaughter-house.

Holding his breath, so as not to inhale that revolting odor, Nathan pushed the mattress off the bed, then stood it on its edge against the wall to see if the blood had seeped all the way through to its other side. Unfortunately it had: the mattress was utterly ruined.

Nathan then went on to ruefully examine the box-spring. He saw at once that (regrettably) over the upper cloth covering the top of its frame, the blood had seeped through to form a large, dark circular stain. Moreover, upon bending down on hands and knees to look under the bed, he discovered that the blood had filtered down through the box-spring's rows of coil springs. Even now as he gazed under the bed, he saw droplets of blood leaking through the bottom cloth of the box spring onto the floor, where they continued to collect in a steadily widening puddle over the floorboards underneath the bed.

Shaking his head, Nathan very gloomily flung himself down in the old wheel-back chair near his window and, with his chin cupped in his hands and his elbows on his knees, he tried hard to think. His mind, however, continued in a whirl of relentless doubts and nagging suspicions with regard to Phebe and all the bizarre incidents surrounding her over the past few days—an unsettling litany of inexplicable episodes that left Nathan feeling far from comfortable in reflecting on.

At the same time, Nathan's restless gaze had wandered off to the mattress again. Leaning on its edge at a steep tilt against the wall, his eyes fixed themselves on the large smear of blood staining its sturdy fabric. In no time at all he had drifted off into a weird, disquieting reverie in which he seemed to hear a concourse of faint, far-away voices unceasingly arguing, professing, declaring to him out of the deep, unearthly stillness that—There's something wrong with Phebe... She isn't normal... Normal people don't wake up in a pool of blood... Or with blood trickling out of their eyes, nose, ears, and mouth... There's definitely some horrible secret about her that she's hiding, keeping to herself... But what could it be? More importantly, what could Phebe herself... *be*?

On and on, for the next few minutes, Nathan mused and pondered like some lost and frightened child awaiting, expecting, attentively listening for a small, inward, guiding voice to deliver him at last from this maddening riddle that plagued him.

But then, quite suddenly, in the midst of his uncertainty, there came this strange quieting hush over all the vexing thoughts in

Nathan's mind. And very gradually he began to recall having read—
or had it been Phebe who had read it to him?—a truly macabre
passage from some old Gothic tale in which the principal character
(or characters) experienced an extraordinarily similar occurrence
to that which he had just now seen Phebe undergo in his bed. A
passage describing, in hauntingly vivid prose, the title character
as lying asleep in its own blood, while that same viscid substance
continued to ooze out of its eyes and mouth—much the same as
it had from Phebe.

And all at once Nathan realized that it had only been the other
night when Phebe had read to him those disquieting passages first
from *Carmilla,* then from *Dracula*—two Gothic novels whose title
character in either story turned out to be a V—But quite abruptly
Nathan checked himself, and caught his breath. For in the very
same instant, the muffled thumping of his heart had jerked to a
sudden standstill at the dreadful, incomprehensible notion that
Phebe herself, then, just might be a... No; thought Nathan, trying
hard to repress the word and avoid even *thinking* it to himself.

But once again that awful, inconceivable suspicion obtruded
itself that Phebe could very well be a... There was again a sudden
pause, as Nathan shivered and tried to master, curb his thoughts,
only for that singularly chilling surmise, belief, conviction to
resurface, persist, and trouble his thoughts once more that Phebe
must in fact be a V—And yet again Nathan paused, gulped back
that one unutterable word, and held his breath: for a faint shadow
had stolen across the threshold of his room, and, looking up, there,
just within the doorway, as though by some uncanny response to
his groping thoughts, his startled eyes fixed themselves on Phebe.

A striped towel was wrapped closely round her, and the long
black tresses of her hair hung wet and tousled on either side of
her pale narrow face. For a moment or two Phebe stood perfectly
still, watching Nathan very heedfully, so heedfully that Nathan
grew afraid she must be listening to the very thoughts stirring in
his mind. Then, without a word she glided over to where he sat,
dropped upon her knees, and rested the small cold palms of her
hands on his thighs. Again Phebe's large dark eyes dwelt on him.

Then, low and faint, Nathan's voice broke the silence. "Are you alright?" he asked.

With eyes fixed stirlessly on his face, Phebe softly nodded her head and all but whispered, "Are you angry with me?"

Nathan took a deep breath, and quietly met Phebe's dark dwelling eyes. "No," he answered after a long pause.

Gazing at him steadily, Phebe laid her head for a moment or two upon his knee, and Nathan felt her cheek, cold as ice-water, through the fabric of his jeans. Then, lifting her head again, she gazed into his eyes, and, "You're sure you're not angry?" she asked him.

For some time without speaking, Nathan gazed on at her face. Then, barely above a whisper, "Yeah," he breathed; after which a long silence fell between them.

Phebe's intensely dark eyes continued to watch Nathan with unwavering attention, as her cold, lean, slim-fingered hand stole into his and tenderly clasped it. She brushed his fingers with her lips; twice she gently kissed them, all the while gazing out of those forlorn dark eyes at him. At length, Nathan said, "You better get dressed."

Phebe softly withdrew her eyes from Nathan's and, with a faint, sad smile, she stood up and nodded her head. Before leaving the room, she paused in the doorway and turned. "I'm sorry about your bed." She spoke the words very low.

Speechlessly Nathan encountered the keen steady regard of those dark mournful eyes before managing at last to say, "Me too." Then, glancing wistfully over at the bloodstained mattress leaning against the wall, he added, almost as an afterthought: "I guess I'll have to sleep in Aunt Amelia's bed." And when his eyes had strayed from the mattress back to the doorway of his room, Phebe was gone. He heard the door across the hall softly shut, and he knew that she had returned to the bathroom to dress herself.

Nathan sat on yet a while, still and silent, in the chair by the window. And although his eyes had fixed themselves once more on his bloodstained mattress, the acute inward gaze of his mind, meanwhile, had been steadily fastened on the sharply conjured vision of Phebe lying corpse-like in his bed. Once again, in retrospect, he observed thin streamlets of blood oozing from her nose, mouth, and eyes, while the whole upper part of her body lay encompassed by a large elliptical bloodstain.

Like the touch of tiny icy fingers, shudder after irrepressible shudder ran up and down Nathan's spine as the ghastly thought crossed his mind that, had the blood not filtered down through the mattress and box-spring of the bed to the floor beneath, Phebe's body would have been lying in a dark shoreless pool of blood.

And all of a sudden Nathan felt his heart fall cold within him, as up into the awful infinite stillness of his consciousness there surfaced once again those two haunting passages, first from Lefanu's "Carmilla", how the vampire Carmilla's "coffin floated with blood, in which to a depth of seven inches, the body lay immersed"; then, from Stoker's "Dracula", how the blood "trickled from the corners of the mouth and ran over the chin and neck...as if the whole awful creature were simply gorged with blood".

And then, quite without warning, yet another brief passage from "Carmilla" went ringing and clamoring across Nathan's frightened mind like a chilling truth shouted in some vault of boundless echoing stone—"Here then, were all the admitted signs and proofs of vampirism".

Unspeakably weary and miserable, Nathan continued to sit there, listening, in a brooding dream-like hush, to those chilling words echo on and on eerily through his thoughts: "signs and proofs of vampirism... Vampirism... VAMPIRISM..."

Then, as Nathan came softly, breathlessly out of the momentary nowhere of this intensely disquieting daydream, he arose, half-dazed, with cold hands and a thumping heart, and began to walk slowly, almost stealthily down the hall to his aunt's bedroom.

For that strange, solitary, unsettling word—*vampirism*—sounding on now faintly yet inexhaustibly, in Nathan's mind, like vaguely harrowing and dangerous hints in a dark dream, had suddenly recalled to him a certain book in Aunt Amelia's bedroom. He had seen it as recently as two nights ago, when he had brought Phebe into Amelia's room to show her the meager stockpile of books once belonging to his aunt. No more than an instant had his own browsing eyes settled on the volume's thin, leathery spine with its brightly gilded lettering. But he could remember well enough its peculiar and rather intriguing title: "Supernatural Creatures in Legend and Myth". He did not think *then* to open the book and glance into its pages. At the time he had shown next to no interest at all in it, as his main concern was to find something with which to cheer and entertain Phebe.

But now, as that haunting, menacing word, which Nathan found himself again and again scarcely able (or willing) to articulate, broke out once more in low, dreary, appallingly protracted echoes across his mind—vampirrisssmmmm!—Nathan felt an irresistible and overpowering compulsion to consult the contents of that book and browse through its pages.

And presently, ignoring that same curiously potent sense of unease which he had felt only yesterday when he had entered his aunt's room in quest of some bauble to give to Phebe, Nathan slowly, almost cautiously pushed open the door and stepped quietly across its threshold.

Taking one or two uncertain steps further into the room's peculiarly hushed and mournful atmosphere, Nathan's eyes all but instantly came to rest on the large wall curio cabinet, just to the right of the closet, with its three glass sides and intricately carved moldings at the base and top.

This cabinet had always held a singular attraction for Nathan ever since he had first come to live under the roof of his aunt's home. For it was divided into two equal halves, a lower and an upper. And the row of leather-bound books, ranged upon the midmost of its three glass shelves, never ceased to beckon and invite Nathan to them from the moment his eyes first fastened themselves on their gilt-lettered spines, which were tantalizingly visible through the clear glass of the hinged door to the cabinet's top half.

Ever and again, Nathan had wanted to steal into his aunt's room, open the cabinet's door, and remove two or three of those enticing volumes to glance through their pages. But his nerve and daring had always failed him, as it was one of Aunt Amelia's most austere injunctions that Nathan never meddle with the things in her room.

But with Aunt Amelia now dead and—he had almost said 'buried', but suddenly recalled the actual fate to which her remains had come. And so, after a brief pause, thought to himself, the more accurate phrasing (in this case) would be, "with Aunt Amelia now dead and... *gone*", that set of exquisite books, which had always had a peculiar allure for him, as well as the very cabinet encasing them, could now be considered his, to do with and dispose of as he saw fit.

Nathan paused a while to stare at the cabinet. At length he drew a little nearer; paused again before its door and gazed through the glass at the book backs to the dozen or more cloth and leather-bound volumes that amounted to the sum total of Aunt Amelia's meager library. Slowly, eagerly his gaze lagged along the wonderfully lettered titles that gleamed and glittered in lustrous gold down the length of their ornate spines. But then, on the third volume from the last—the one he sought—it came to a sudden halt and there it fixed itself.

Faint as a whispering breath, Nathan read out its title to himself, "Supernatural Creatures of Legend and Myth." And then, for the first time since he had come to live with his aunt, Nathan drew open the door to the curio cabinet, reached his hand in, and ran the tips of his fingers lightly over the hubbed spines of the row of precious, forbidden volumes. Had Aunt Amelia still been alive, and only known, it would have been a most unpardonable transgression, for she had been adamant about no hands touching those books except her own.

With heedful eyes and eager hands, Nathan continued, however, to violate Aunt Amelia's stern directive by stroking and caressing the book backs to those taboo volumes, noting the while that only two or three were actually bound in leather, the others in cloth, and others still in buckram.

Then, having removed the tall, thin volume that he wanted, Nathan paused a moment or two to look it over. He noticed at once that, unlike the other books, it was only quarter-bound in crimson leather, and had sides of black cloth. And the faint yet pleasant odor of the leather with which the book was partially bound, and which he instantly inhaled upon withdrawing the volume from its place on the cabinet's shelf, became mingled with the scent of the printer's ink as he raised the book's cover and began softly turning, one by one, its gilt-edged leaves.

Finding the book's table of contents, Nathan observed that each of its thirteen chapters pertained specifically to some ghoulishly nocturnal being. One after the other he silently read them over, as he steadily drew his finger down the book's listed subject matter, until he came to the chapter-title marked by the number six. Here his finger had abruptly paused, and his eyes, having fixed themselves, intently stared. Then, breathing out a long, slow breath, he managed to blurt out at last the single straddling word that made up the chapter's name... "Vampires": after which a stillness, strange and fathomless, seemed to fall coldly, intensely all around him.

Nathan continued for some seconds to scrutinize that solitary word. Almost it seemed to startle him, make him feel as though he had been caught spying on... on *her*; or worse still, as if Phebe's own voice had piped out the word at him from the awful brink of some thundery abyss.

Yet again Nathan drew a slow, deep breath into his body; then, with a slight tremor in his voice, faintly uttered, as if to another whose presence was unseen, the title to the book's sixth chapter, "Vampires." And all the while his eyes continued uneasily to regard that single ominous word, a cold and dismal feeling began to steal over his heart, and he was suddenly overwhelmed by a strong inclination to shut the book up and hasten from the room.

But then, against the half-heeded misgiving that was now gnawing miserably at the roots of his chilled and fluttering heart, Nathan began gingerly turning over the thick glossy pages of the book until he came to its sixth chapter, whose heading, *VAMPIRES*, sprawled across the top of the page in bold, blood-red lettering.

For what seemed minutes together, Nathan's eyes continued to course their way to and fro over the sinister character of that word, as though within its forbidding sequence of vowels and consonants lay the answer to every secret, every riddle, every mystery surrounding Phebe.

Then, slowly, steadily Nathan drew both his finger and his gaze down the smooth glossy surface of the page, from its rubricated chapter-heading to where its text, printed in double columns of considerable length, commenced. And with an intent, uneasy expression on his face, he began slowly to read (murmuring the words aloud to himself as he did so) the chapter's opening sentence:

'Of all the ghoulish revenants which lurk and dwell in the lightless dark, none is more terrifying, more threatening to mortal-kind than the fearsome, blood-drinking vampire.'

But hardly had Nathan finished reading this sentence when, all at once, he broke off and, with eyes yet fixed on the glossy black ink of the printed text, stood there, perfectly still—waiting, *listening.* For he had become suddenly conscious that a pair of shrewd, penetrating eyes were keenly, steadfastly regarding him; the eyes of *someone* who, in all likelihood, had been, for some time now, standing behind him, still and silent, in the doorway to his aunt's bedroom, looking in on him.

And every muscle in Nathan's body tensed and braced itself as he heard the faint rumor of that 'some one's' light, unhurried footsteps softly approach, then pause. Again they drew near, only to pause once more; and Nathan suddenly caught his breath. For all in an instant (although he found himself unable to withdraw his eyes from that solitary, rubricated word, VAMPIRES, or so much as even slightly turn his head to look) he knew with absolute certainty that standing directly behind him, with her eyes gazing anxiously over his shoulder at the open book in his hands, was—Phebe.

Then, that soft, solemn voice asked, "What are you reading?" And so close behind him was Phebe now standing, that her lips had virtually breathed the words into Nathan's ear.

Holding the book low in his trembling hands, Nathan slowly turned round and, as he did so, softly shut the book up. He was silent a moment, as he encountered Phebe's piercing gaze; then, "Nothing," he breathed faintly, as the peering glance of those dark luminous eyes, which had been intently scanning his face, strayed downward for an instant and rested shrewdly on the book in his hands. "You're sure?" she asked, in a low, almost listless voice as her gaze immediately settled on Nathan's face again.

But as Nathan continued, with startled eyes, to meet that motionless gaze of Phebe's, a curious cold spread along his limbs, and his hands grew clammy, and his voice suddenly failed him. For the dark, lustrous eyes regarding him had grown a shade more intense in their scrutiny of his silent face, as though every expression in his features were even now discovering to her his most secret thoughts. And all at once Nathan quickly lowered his gaze to evade the searching scrutiny of Phebe's dark dwelling eyes. "So what are you doing in here?" she asked him.

Nathan replaced the book on its glass shelf in the curio cabinet as he said, "Just waiting to use the bathroom." Phebe's eyes once more fixed Nathan's face with an intensely penetrating look. Then, after a long pause, "You can—I'm finished in there," she said.

Nathan hesitated; met once more the dark luminous eyes gazing gravely, almost reflectively on at him; then turned away and hastened from the room in dread that Phebe might indeed be eavesdropping on his thoughts.

For a moment Nathan could hardly see out of his eyes, and the very boards of the floor seemed to pitch and undulate beneath him as he scrambled down the hall and into the bathroom. A pace or two just beyond its threshold he paused, and, in a wearisome and heedless misery, his gaze first wandered to the single-handle chrome faucet of the sink which he noticed at once had bloodstains on it from Phebe's hands. Then, almost in stealth, he glanced a moment into the basin of the pedestal sink which was also speckled with tiny droplets of blood. Nathan's eyes then strayed uneasily along the floor, following the faint prints of Phebe's dainty feet daubed in blood on the ceramic tiles and leading, in a curved trail, from the sink to the tub enclosure; while in the tub itself, he noted little pink-hued drippings of fresh blood where the spray of water from the showerhead (apparently) had been unable to reach and wash away.

And suddenly, like the faint, hollow clinking of bones to some hidden skeleton hanging in a closet, that disquieting passage from *Carmilla* broke out once more in Nathan's mind, only this time their words were eerily disjointed and out of sequence—"...vampirism... signs and proofs of... vampirism... admitted signs... vampirism... Here then... proofs of... vampirism..."

Then, with heart numb, cold, and thickly beating, Nathan went over to the small storage cabinet mounted above the sink and, without the least notion of what he was doing, he removed the towel from it which Vrancic had placed there to conceal the plate glass mirrors in the unit's sliding doors.

For nearly a full minute, with eyes fixed in a curious trance-like stillness, Nathan stood quite motionless in front of them. Into the shadowy surface of their dust-veiled glass his eyes half-absently gazed on, scarcely aware of the pale, anxious face that, vaguely reflected there through the film of dust, stared solemnly back at him. And all the while he stared, his ears were intently listening for any rumor of Phebe stealing up behind him, or moving about in his room, or wandering furtively through some other region of the house. But no sound broke in upon the aimless stirrings of his skittish thoughts. In fact, the whole house was so deathly still that Nathan might have been standing, dazed and drowsing, on those mistily far-off marches between what is reality and what is dream.

At length, Nathan turned on the faucet and, stooping over the basin of the sink, he began laving his face and hands with cold water. But then, all at once, he paused, and for a space of some seconds, with wet face and hands, remained quite still. For somewhere in his proximity he had felt—intensely, deeply—the presence of Phebe, and instantly, almost apprehensively, he looked up from the sink.

Not for a single moment did Nathan doubt having heard Phebe's light footsteps sounding behind him as she softly entered the bathroom; nor having listened to the silvery tones of her sweet voice as she inquired if he had showered. But when he had glanced up into the mirror's ice-like stillness, expecting to confront with his eyes the slim figure of her reflection just behind his own, the poky dimensions of the room behind him, its narrow doorway, and part of the hall beyond it, as reflected in the glass, appeared utterly empty, vacant, *unoccupied*—Phebe was nowhere to be seen! And yet, after casting, out of startled eyes, a single, slow, furtive glance over his shoulder, there, just over the threshold of the door, Nathan saw Phebe standing, gazing silently across at him.

Once more Nathan turned his head and peered with anxious, astonished eyes into the mirror's tranquil, silvery deeps, and yet—Phebe's person was still *not* reflected there—everything else *was,* but *she* simply was not! The whole thing roused a horrifying degree of awe in his soul, and sent a chill shivering icily down his spine.

Then, from softly behind him, "Is anything wrong, Nathan?" came the voice of Phebe, a faint yet unmistakable hint of suspicion in its silky tones.

At first Nathan gave no reply, he was literally dumbstruck: for he suddenly felt mortally alarmed, afraid of—*her.* And for several seconds he hesitated between answering her with the truth, or with the cowardice of a lie. Then, slowly, speechlessly, he twisted round and, hovering between dread and amazement, confronted with his own panic-stricken eyes the intensity of Phebe's shrewd, keen, penetrating gaze, as she stood, without movement, before him, only four paces or so of dimly lit air separating the two of them.

With her dark, lustrous eyes stirlessly dwelling on Nathan's silent face, Phebe's voice again broke the silence. "Everything alright?" she asked.

Still utterly tongue-tied, Nathan faintly nodded his dizzy head. Then, fearing lest Phebe should divine the expression of alarm in his eyes, he quickly, instinctively averted his gaze. Notwithstanding this, Phebe's eyes continued their close scrutiny of Nathan's features as she said: "If there *is* something bothering you, Nathan, you can tell me."

Again Nathan's eyes doubtfully encountered those of Phebe's; then, slightly turning a faltering head, he threw a sidled, fleeting glance over his shoulder at the mirror over the sink, before refastening his frightened gaze on herself. Phebe continued to wait, staring at him. And for a single instant, "The mirror," was all he managed to whisper.

Silently, intently Phebe stood regarding him; and as her dark eyes searched his face long and keenly, a hush of such intensity fell between them that Nathan again grew afraid Phebe was playing eavesdropper to his every thought.

At length Phebe withdrew her dark eyes from those of Nathan's; fixed them for an instant a little uneasily on the mirror behind him; then, immediately returned them, almost resentfully, to Nathan's face.

Meanwhile, never so much as stirring, Nathan continued to stand there, with startled eyes and dry, parted lips, watching her. And almost it seemed to him that an intenser silence, so unearthly as to be out of dream, had presently fallen between himself and Phebe—over reality itself—like a dense curtain of cold mist; and that the two of them (he and Phebe) were mere hallucinations, vague fancies that had somehow strayed from across the borders of nightmare.

Then, moving slowly forward, Phebe stood for some moments with her whole body quietly close up against Nathan, her dark, large-pupilled eyes gazing with a curious fixity straight into the depths of his own. And although Nathan sensed rather than saw the forbidding aspect in her face as she continued to steadily regard him; there was no mistaking the austere tone of her voice as, reaching past him with her arm to replace the towel over the mirrors in the sliding doors of the storage unit, she asked, "What *about* the mirror, Nathan?"

And despite his disinclination to answer her, Nathan somehow found the pluck, the daring to blurt out, "You're not"—he paused a moment; gave a faint nod toward the mirror; then said—"*there...* You don't reflect."

Phebe's eyes fixed themselves, with less even than the faintest smile in their depths, somewhat more attentively on Nathan's face, as she said: "I doubt very much whether you would like it if I did."

Mystified by whatever ominous hint (if any) Phebe had meant to convey to him by such a cryptic remark, Nathan's eyes, all the same, opened round and wide; and even as he gazed on at her in silence, for a solitary instant those puzzling words of hers had caused him to all but visibly flinch. And for a space of some seconds, perhaps no more than thirty, yet which seemed to Nathan as immeasurable as infinity, he and Phebe gazed stirlessly, most searchingly into one another's eyes.

But then, all at once, that one question Nathan dreaded asking Phebe, and which until this very moment he had found impossible to articulate, was slowly, softly breathed out, as though prompted by some intractable mood of recklessness: "Are—you—a—" But quite suddenly Nathan paused, as the features of Phebe's pale beautiful face seemed to harden into an awful stare and the intensely dark eyes to pierce him to the marrow.

"Yes, Nathan;" said Phebe, her voice all but sinking to a hushed whisper; "am I a—*what*?"

And all at once that solitary word, of its own accord, slipped faintly past Nathan's unwilling lips, as though he were muttering it in his sleep—"Vampire."

A faint, curious scornful look had crept into Phebe's pale, beautiful face, and a deeper darkness into the dusk of her eyes. At the same time, all friendliness seemed to fade out of the loveliness of her delicate features as, "What if I am?" she said; and, after a long pause in which her dark peering eyes studied Nathan's face intently, she suddenly added: "What would you do?"

Completely taken aback by this unexpected retort of hers, Nathan remained icily still, and simply continued (in a dull, lingering shock) to stand there helplessly meeting Phebe's faintly quizzical, faintly derisive gaze. And whatever strange, incomprehensible meanings were then passing across the air between them from Phebe's eyes into his own, Nathan could not say; of this much, however, he was absolutely certain, Phebe's face suddenly petrified him. For in some astonishing and indescribable way its actual features (for a single instant) had become different—*otherwise*—and some nameless quality seemed to gather about them, and as swiftly, and suddenly, depart.

And then, just as swift, sudden, and strange was Phebe's withdrawal from the room—a next to imperceptible retreat that bordered on *envanishment*. For one moment she was there, and the next, almost it seemed to Nathan, like something in an eerie dream, the very space of the room she had occupied was vacant. That is not to say, of course, that Phebe had *actually* disappeared, but certainly her departure from the room had been nothing short of extraordinary.

For as Nathan stared at Phebe, the nerves transmitting impulses from his eyes to his brain had assuredly observed her—all the while stilly facing him with her deep, dark, luminous eyes fixed unswervingly on his own—begin to glide steadily, soundlessly *backwards.* Her figure one moment appeared to move a pace or two across the floor away from him, and the next, like some image in film that has abruptly skipped further on to several frames ahead, it was already passing silently through the doorway of the room. Another instant, and Nathan was aware that the distance between himself and Phebe had widened still more: for her figure appeared to have slipped, with a weird, ghostlike, almost indiscernible motion, more than halfway down the hall. And then, after the strange, unearthly stillness of a timeless pause, in which Phebe seemed to linger, *wait,* she was quite simply, and quite suddenly—*gone.* In a flash her figure had passed altogether beyond the limits of Nathan's visual perception. How or where *to,* Nathan could scarcely bring himself to imagine, nor did he try.

Anxious and oppressed, Nathan remained where he was, standing, with hands clenched, perfectly stone-like and icily still. In memory he went over all that had happened and been said between himself and Phebe, from their initial encounter inside the old mausoleum, up until this very moment when he woke in bed beside her with blood dribbling from her mouth, nose, eyes, and ears. And most, if not all, of these remarkable incidents with regard to Phebe's peculiar behavior, the odd (sometimes creepy) things she had said and done, even up to this very point in time, seemed to him like some vividly inexplicable, bizarre, and (in many ways) frightening unreality.

And notwithstanding the curious sense of relief Nathan experienced when Phebe had finally withdrawn from the room, a faint yet growing apprehension gathered at his heart as Phebe's very presence seemed still to pervade and haunt the air about him, like a specter. And for some minutes Nathan remained staring blankly before him, as though the pair of imaginary, phantom eyes he was now meeting, so piercing, so intensely keen in their regard, were actually those of Phebe's.

Meanwhile, echoes of the last words to pass between them, before Phebe had retreated so strangely from the room, had stolen with a sharp misgiving into Nathan's mind. And he caught and held his breath, to listen in reverie, almost cautiously, anxiously, as though fearful of being discovered eavesdropping on his own secret thoughts, to the question he had put to her—*Are you a vampire.*

But as Nathan paused to consider Phebe's unnerving reply, he seemed to lose himself for some while in its vaguely fearful insinuations, and was once more alarmed, troubled, caught back by those singular words of hers—*'What if I am'.*

Like tormenting echoes, ceaseless and unfainting, that fearful question of his, along with Phebe's shocking reply, ran on and on through Nathan's thoughts. Inexplicably, though, his agitated and unsettled wits persisted in abbreviating Phebe's answer, eerily curtailing it by altogether removing its first two words of "What if", and repeating only its remaining two words of "I am", over and over and over. So that, uneasily, chillingly, hauntingly across his thoughts, again and again, sounded first his question, "Are you a vampire", and then Phebe's contracted response, "I am".

And over the next minute or two Nathan's fretful mind began to alter the words to both the question and its answer, ultimately modifying and reworking them into, "You're a vampire?... I am..."; then, "a vampire... am I... a vampire... am I"; and finally, "I am... a vampire; I am... a vampire... I'm a vampire!"

Exhausted and shivering, Nathan shut his eyes; for that word, 'vampire', summoned no definite picture to his imagination. And yet, he wondered to himself, what then gave it such a dreadful power to unsettle, appall, and terrify him? For now that he truly considered the word, and the very creature designated by that peculiar term, he suddenly realized that he was for the most part ignorant as to what precisely a vampire is.

But after having vainly ruminated for some moments on the subject, the term, and the creature itself, unexpectedly, the opening words to the sixth chapter of the book in Aunt Amelia's room leaped out from their small niche in Nathan's memory. Like some strangely familiar voice, mistily faint and far away, sounding off from across the corridors of dream, they began to softly vocalize themselves through his strained and listening thoughts:

> 'Of all the ghoulish revenants which lurk and dwell in the lightless dark, none is more terrifying, more threatening to mortal-kind than the fearsome, blood-drinking vampire.'

At that last solitary, sinister word –'*vampire*' – there rose up, impetuously, into Nathan's mind, Phebe's startling reply, 'What if I am... What would you do...' And all in an instant a small, faint voice in Nathan's mind seemed to be saying all that it possibly could to urge, persuade, convince him to return to his aunt's bedroom. To dip once more into the pages of the sixth chapter of that book in the curio cabinet, and discover from its content all that he could with regard to the nature of the vampire, and whether there were any distinguishing traits or signs by which one could recognize and identify a person as such.

Very suddenly, then, Nathan's eyes cleared, and he looked up sharply. He crossed the tiled floor of the bathroom in two or three broad strides, and, as if impelled by a curiosity, an inquisitiveness beyond his control, found himself softly advancing, with slow, cautious steps, down the hall to Aunt Amelia's bedroom. And by the time he had reached its fast-shut door, and paused a moment or two, with the knob clutched firmly in his hand, to listen at the panel, that intractable curiosity had transformed itself into an unshakeable resolve.

At length, Nathan slowly, stealthily pushed open the door, soundlessly stepped across the threshold into the dim and shadowy blind-drawn room, and abruptly paused. He went over to the curio cabinet, paused again, and, while gazing through the cabinet's glass door at the row of book backs on the shelf to its upper half, he saw at once that the volume he had come to consult was—*missing*. Some *one* had removed it from its place on the shelf.

Nathan caught his breath as, stiff and chill, he continued to stare at the narrow empty space on the glass shelf. Then, as if in echo of the infinitesimal voice within that had softly breathed out at him, he faintly gasped in a half-stifled whisper, "It's gone!"

For some seconds, from head to foot, Nathan stood perfectly still. Then, turning first to his left, then to his right, his eye fell on the very book he sought lying sprawled upon the floor, all by itself, at the foot of Aunt Amelia's armoire. Apparently that same 'someone' (for whatever reason) had unceremoniously dumped it there: for it lay open at about the middle, with its pages, verso and recto, flat to the floor, and its ornate spine and finely bound covers facing upward.

Nathan's first thought was that Phebe must have taken it from the shelf after he had gone into the bathroom and dropped it here. But then he paused in some amazement to ask himself, "If so— why?" Certainly there was something of a mystery in the matter.

Nathan stooped and very gently picked up the book. Then, slowly turning over the pages till he had come to that commencing the sixth chapter—at page 105—he felt his heart, after two or three bounding gallops, all at once stand still. At the same time, with a sharp gulp of dismay, he heard himself suddenly draw in his breath, for the chapter's page, with its double-columned printed text, had been grievously slashed from top to bottom, again and again, as by some razor-sharp implement.

The unexpected sight was shocking beyond measure, and all in an instant over Nathan's heart swept a mingled feeling of bewilderment and apprehension. Very quietly, then, he seated himself on the edge of Aunt Amelia's bed and stared down uneasily at the heavily damaged page—wondering all the while what could be the reason, the aim, the purpose behind Phebe's violent treatment of the book. For he was quite certain that she, and she alone, was responsible for the book's present condition. But why (he wondered to himself) intentionally—and so viciously!—spoil its pages? What could be her motive?

Without waiting to concoct a reason, or to try and invent some unconvincing explanation, Nathan began turning over the pages of the book to examine each of them, one by one, from the first leaf to its last. He soon discovered that only those pages to the sixth chapter had been injured and ruined—some slashed and scored straight down; some rent slantwise from the upper right-hand corner of the page to its lower left-hand corner; and others gashed repeatedly straight across, from the book's gutter to the very edge of the page. As for the other chapters, Nathan noticed that the pages to those sections of the book were (inexplicably) untouched, unharmed.

Again Nathan paused in astonishment to wonder why Phebe would do such a thing. But after puzzling over the matter for several minutes, during which he could find no plausible or sensible explanation, he turned the leaves of the book once more to the spoiled pages of its sixth chapter.

For some seconds his light brown eyes strayed vacantly over the slashed text of the chapter's opening page. And of the few rubricated letters to its heading which had not been effaced by the deep rents scoring the page, Nathan could only distinguish the following: 'V-MP—ES'. Then, having recovered somewhat from his initial shock, he very faintly, with a near-breathless murmur, pronounced the dread word signified by those letters—"Vampires." And instantly Nathan shut his eyes, for it was as if that strange, solitary word had drawn him against his will to the brink of some nebulous dreamlike void, from whose swirling, impenetrable glooms Phebe's solemn voice called up to him, "What if I am... What would you do?"

Nathan waited a full minute, stirlessly listening, until that curious, unpleasant thrill roused in him by Phebe's words had at last subsided. Then, with a slight shiver, he once more opened his eyes and fixed those five letters, V-MP—ES, with a gaze still more intense, searching, and anxious. After some moments, however, his downbent eyes began to wander, at first half-absently, over the fragments of the printed text that had escaped damage. Slowly, idly he read their lines to himself. But after a longish pause in which he seemed to gravely reflect, once more Nathan's eyes became fixed and darkened with some unshakeable inward resolve. Again he fastened his attention on the bits and fragments to the first and second column of the page's text that were still legible, and (this time more intently) began slowly to read them over.

Much of the text throughout the first column was in great part unintelligible due to the numerous slits and punctures scoring the page. But with some difficulty, Nathan was able to distinguish the following lines:

> '...vampires, traditionally, will inhabit old cemeteries, neglected tombs, or decaying mausoleums, for although they feed by night on the blood of the living, they must take refuge, by day, with the company of the dead...'

and then:

> '...As ordained by its accursed existence, the vampire must sleep in either a coffin or a crypt, thereby compelling it to endure its severance from the society of the living, and at the same time betokening its everlasting association with the Dead...'

And all in an instant those chilling words brought to the surface of Nathan's mind, Phebe's bizarre insistence on taking shelter inside the old mausoleum, along with her creepy preference for sleeping in one of its unoccupied crypts.

And presently, with his chilled skin turned suddenly to goose-flesh, Nathan's eyes strayed on to the text of the second column which was so heavily scored that he found it next to impossible to decipher. All that he could distinguish from its badly slashed text were the following fragments:

> '...ampire has the ability to defy gravity; ascending and passing through the air as swiftly and silently as the bat...'

and then, a line or two further down, he read:

> '...they have the power to cling to, or clamber up, the
> sheer surface of perpendicular ascents, such as a steep
> rockface, a smooth precipice, or the vertical walls of
> buildings, with all the ease and agility of a spider...'

And Nathan's breath came heavily as that peculiarly vivid recollection abruptly obtruded itself into his consciousness of the night Phebe brought him out to see the Perseid meteor shower. With perfect clarity he called to mind now how she had been able to cling to the brick facade of the crematory, and scramble swiftly up its surface to the building's roof.

In the wake of this perturbing memory came a long, tense, breathless pause, in which Nathan stood utterly still, without the least ability to either think and speak, or feel and stir. Then, taking a deep, shuddering breath, he slowly drew his trembling finger down the remainder of the column's scored text, before turning to the next page.

Unfortunately all but the entire text to the first of its two columns had been obliterated, but a substantial block of print commencing the text to the second column was as follows:

> '...At all costs, the vampire must avoid the sun's
> purifying rays. For nothing is more deadly, more
> irremediably destructive to its existence than sunlight.
> And should a person exhibit a fierce intolerance for
> sunlight entering their abode, or manifest an extreme
> unwillingness to be out in the daylight, it may in fact
> be evidence of their vampiric nature...'

And a profound and sudden chill settled over Nathan's mind as he paused in his reading to recall how, ever since he had met Phebe, the blinds to every window in his home were habitually kept lowered and their curtains tightly drawn. He called to mind, too, how Phebe herself appeared to him only at night: never during the day—claiming (rather evasively) that the sunlight was 'not good' for her. And after having reflected somewhat anxiously a few moments longer on the discomfiting subject, Nathan continued, then, slowly to read on:

> '...And since the moon's light is in fact reflected sunlight, its rays to the vampire (while not lethal, like the full light of day) are in many ways harmful. Indeed, the vampire's supernatural powers are at their acme when the moon is new, waning, or as yet slight in its waxing: or, yet again, still to rise, far upon its setting, or altogether hidden behind clouds. When, however, the moon approaches, or attains, its full, their powers are greatly reduced; and in some cases, when the vampire is exposed to the beams of a fulling moon, senescence has been known to result, and their shape will suddenly appear wizened and frightfully aged...'

And with an uneasiness that deepened by the moment and horribly intensified, Nathan recalled that night in the cemetery with Phebe, how, as they stood holding hands in the full, flooding radiance of the moon, she seemed all at once to appear hideously old and wrinkled and decrepit.

With a slight shudder, then, Nathan quickly turned over the page. The printed text, however, to either of its two columns was so severely damaged that, for all his painstaking efforts, he could scarcely discriminate more than two sentences. But, as Nathan slowly read them over—'unless invited by a resident of the home, the vampire cannot cross its threshold. For just as evil cannot draw near unless accepted, so the vampire is forbidden to enter the home of the living without first being welcomed'—his face turned white as chalk. For all at once there had stolen into memory how Phebe, the night Aunt Amelia had been killed, had all but commanded him to "invite" her into his house by having him say to her, *'You may enter my home'.* And a feeling of intense disquiet that bordered upon actual fright swept through Nathan's entire body with the iciness of an arctic chill.

For some minutes, utterly crestfallen, Nathan sat on and brooded almost ruefully over the hastiness of his words that night to Phebe, now some two weeks ago. Then, after having examined the severely gouged and slashed text to pages 113 and 114, and finding it far too difficult to decipher more than a few oddments of words here, and snippets of sentences there, Nathan turned over the page and read the following passage that was still legible to the text in the second column:

> '...while resting by day in its crypt or coffin, the eyelids to the vampire never quite shut, for its baleful gaze is always shrewdly peering round itself, alert to any and all trespassers to its lair, and vigilantly aware of all who would seek to destroy it...'

And Nathan was instantly reminded of how, only this morning, as he stared down at Phebe—dare he say, *asleep?*—in the bed next to him, he had noted the lids to her eyes only partially closed. Moreover, between them, he had observed the narrow, shadowy film of her lustrous pupils suddenly shift and fix themselves intently on his face: as though, even while she slumbered, she was still somehow keenly watching, regarding him.

And then, fixing his attention once again, almost fearfully, on the page, he read, toward the bottom of the column, the following startling passage:

> '...at times during its nocturnal feeding, the vampire will gorge itself so abundantly on the blood of the living that, in its slumber during the day, the blood will seep out of the gluttonous revenant's nose, mouth, and eyes, giving it the appearance of lying in a pool of its own blood...'

Nathan caught his breath and glanced suddenly up from the page. For almost it seemed to him that the words gripped with icy fingers at the very core of his soul, evoking at the same time the unnerving memory of Phebe lying still as a corpse in his bed this morning, oozing dark streamlets of blood from her mouth, ears, nose, and eyes.

And then, a page or two after this, Nathan was able to make out in the printed text to the first column these four sentences:

> '...from earliest times most cultures have held water as a symbol of life, for which reason the Undead detest it fiercely, especially the kind blessed and made sacred by ministers of the Christian faith. This "holy water" is believed to be endowed with special powers to harm and repel creatures of darkness. None more so than the vampire, to which it is most injurious and lethal. Once the vampire's flesh comes into contact with holy water, it bursts into flames and turns instantly to ash; and an unbroken line of holy water poured across a threshold will render a vampire's crossing it impossible...'

and then, after a few unintelligible lines, Nathan read:

> '...according to occultists the rose is baneful to many evil creatures, most especially, werewolves, witches, and vampires. Its very fragrance repels them, and its petals will sear their flesh. For the rose signifies both the wounds of Christ and the Chalice into which his blood had flowed, and also denotes the Blessed Virgin as the "Mystic Rose". And because the rosary employed by the Romanians in Transylvania has the advantage of its beads being compressed rose petals, and the cross or crucifix to its pendant being composed of bloodstone, a semi-precious stone whose antivampiric properties are well known, the

matanie, or Romanian rosary, can be ranked among the most potent weapons used against vampires...'

And suddenly, Nathan paused upon recalling the small cruet of holy water he had appropriated from Mr Jozsef Szekler's urn, and which he had even now in his pocket. By impulse he fetched it out; glanced at it; slipped it into his pocket again; then, from his other pocket, produced the Romanian rosary. Gazing on at it, almost breathlessly, he began to recollect, very clearly, how a shadowy steam seemed to go up from Phebe's hand when the beads of the rosary's pendant came into contact with the flesh of her palm. And all at once Nathan felt—no! virtually *heard*—the thick, rapid beating of his heart, as yet again that haunting line from Lefanu's *Carmilla* floated softly, coldly up into his thoughts like a specter from its grave: 'signs and proofs of vampirism.., signs and proofs of vampirism... vampirism...'

Then, after replacing the rosary in his pocket, the considerable block of print he was able to distinguish at the head of the second column's text literally froze his blood as he read it to himself. In fact, Nathan was so startled by what he read that, for some moments afterward, he was utterly deprived of the capability to read another word:

'...cross or crucifix is among the most powerful talismans against the vampire: for it is the emblem of Christ, the Savior himself, and symbolizes his passion and Redemption, as well as His crucified body and his sacrificed Blood. And of all the various types of crosses, none is more potent in repelling the Undead than the Maltese Cross with its eight points. For these are said to represent the eight beatitudes: the promises by Christ of specified rewards to those who perform good works. And because the vampire does no good works, only evil, and is eternally denied and doomed never to attain these rewards, the mere sight of this type of Cross causes it to shrink violently away with hideous shrieks. And vampirologists consistently agree in their reports that the vampire cowering before a Maltese Cross will shout in Latin at the holy symbol such terrible phrases as: "Hence, vile one, hence!"; and, "No hope for us!"; and yet again, "We are confounded!"...'

And with chilled and bloodless fingers, Nathan clenched the book's covers ever more tightly, as though should the tall, unwieldy tome slip from his grasp, he too must plunge down with it to the floor and remain there in a dead faint. For Phebe's outlandish words, as she recoiled shrieking from the Maltese-shaped crucifix of the matanie's pendant, swept up with a vivid rush of remembrance into his anxious thoughts as though they had imprinted themselves on his memory like the stark black and white images in a photograph. What's more, the odd certainty that he now knew the precise meaning to those words suddenly dropped, with an icy chill, right into him. And in the breath of a faint and half-swallowed whisper, Nathan's lips began slowly to repeat them to himself: "'Recede, miser, recede!'... 'Hence, vile one; hence!'"; then, after a short pause, "'Spes nobis nulla'... 'No hope for us!'"; and still faintlier, after yet another pause, "'Confusi sumus'... 'We are confounded!'"

But just then, Nathan glanced up from the book with a violent start. For it seemed to him that someone had drawn near to listen; had stolen into the room behind him; or, had stealthily passed across the doorway and, in hurrying by, had looked in on him. Certainly he had felt a presence. And with startled eyes he instantly rose to his feet, turned, and gazed long and steadily at the empty doorway.

But as not even the ghost of a sound betrayed another's presence, Nathan's anxiously peering eyes once more strayed downward to fix themselves intently on the open book. And on the next page, toward the bottom of the first column, after he had read the following fragment—'...among its many supernatural powers, the vampire possesses a physical prowess far superior to that of mortal man...'—the recollection of Phebe wresting the baseball bat from the grip of Russell Gorman pricked its way horribly into his frightened mind. For all in an instant he recalled how Phebe had snapped the bat in two with her bare hands, and then, after seizing Russell Gorman by his throat, she had lifted him with one hand off the ground as if he was a stuffed toy.

And the growing unease produced in Nathan by this vividly awful memory soon increased to dismay, then outright alarm, as the next passage he was able to distinguish in the damaged text of the book, a page or two further on, sent an icy shiver down his spine:

> '...the vampire also possesses transformative powers,
> and is believed to be able to appear in the shape of
> a'— (the word was difficult to make out, but Nathan
> thought it looked like) —"*wolf*".

Catching his breath with a slight start, Nathan began to tremble as the memory of Phebe and himself in the tub suddenly revived in startling detail. And a singular deepening dread brushed his soul upon recalling how her shape seemed to alter and elongate into a ghastly wolf-like aspect.

And then, after one or two more undecipherable pages, Nathan was able to distinguish, more toward the bottom than the middle of the second column's text, the following fragment:

> '...vampires are essentially blood-drinking revenants.
> They are the Non-living, the Undead, accursed to
> linger in the world of the living by consuming the
> blood of humans...'

Once more Nathan had paused, and a violent shudder ran through his entire body as he recalled how Phebe, the night he had his nosebleed in front of her, licked the blood from round his nostrils, saying, '*I thirst, I thirst*'. And instantly, on the heels of this disquieting recollection, there flashed yet another, for Nathan seemed to vaguely remember (although even now he was still not certain if he had only *dreamed* it) Phebe softly fastening her open mouth to the side of his neck.

And all at once, with his heart beating thick and cold, Nathan seated himself once more on the edge of his aunt's bed, and laid the open book down across his knees. Then, with the tips of his fingers, he began gingerly probing and feeling the skin of his neck on either side, half-fearing, half-expecting to discover the wounds of two small puncture-like holes from Phebe's teeth. Much to his relief, however, his neck bore neither mark nor injury, and its skin on both sides was without either scab or abrasion.

Then, once more, Nathan picked up the book and resumed his reading:

> '...never does the vampire feed with a more voracious appetite and gorge itself more abundantly on the blood of the living than on its 'birthnight', that accursed date on which it passed from the society of the living to the abhorred company of the Undead—the night when it died to its mortality and was "born" anew unto death and darkness without end...'

and then this fragment at the foot of the column:

> '...as the vampire is evil, possessing no moral code. Being a creature of darkness and death it has severed all ties to the society of the living, upon whose members it must prey, mercilessly killing and drinking their blood to maintain its own Godless existence. But of all its inhuman and horrific acts, none is more fiendish than that of forcing the victims of its choosing to share its own accursed nature, transforming them into equally monstrous creatures by ingesting their blood and forcing its victim to ingest its own...'

With a loud gasp of dismay, Nathan looked up sharply from the page as a frenzied feeling of alarm, of sudden panic yet again swept over his worried mind. For he suddenly recalled how only the other night, when Phebe had read to him from Bram Stoker's

'Dracula', she had (in "imitation", so she claimed, of a scene in the novel) bitten him and sucked his blood from the wound. But then, from a self-inflicted wound to her breast, she in turn forced him to swallow some of *her* blood! And with a faint, startled breath, Nathan whispered, "Am I now going to become a..." But he suddenly broke off: consciously refraining from pronouncing that one unutterable word to complete both that horrid thought and appalling sentence.

Then, slowly turning over the page, Nathan saw that it and the remaining half-dozen or so pages to the chapter were so heavily rent and slashed that the pages themselves were all but falling to pieces, and their printed text utterly illegible. With some difficulty, however, Nathan was able to make out the following lines on the next to last page of the chapter:

> '...When the vampire is unable to avoid or destroy a mirror, it will hinder its image from being seen by casting no reflection in the glass. For the vampire seldom appears to mortals in its *true* shape, deceiving the optics of the human eye by conjuring a false, yet pleasing aspect. This false, non-existent shape, however, cannot be reflected in the mirror as it is illusory, unreal. And so, rather than reveal its "true" semblance, which the vampire itself is loth to confront, it veils its shape altogether, thus preventing the mirror from reflecting it at all...'

And with that, Nathan's confusion and helplessness were complete, as into his mind there arose, uneasily, the vivid remembrance of Vrancic having covered all the mirrors in the house under the pretext that Phebe suffered from spectrophobia, a fear of one's own reflection. But only this morning, in the mirror in the bathroom—the memory seemed now to haunt Nathan's thoughts—Phebe had cast no reflection at all... "Just like a *vampire*," he heard himself whisper in a faint, drawn-out breath, as there began to stir in him at last the unwelcome, disagreeable realization of what Phebe actually was.

For some while, then, Nathan sat on quite motionless, shrunken and withered it seemed almost to nothing, as that sense of awfulness, that feeling of incredulous horror continued to whelm steadily over him.

Abruptly, then, Nathan stood up, shut the book, and restored it to its place on the glass shelf of the curio cabinet. For several minutes he stood staring blankly at the gilt lettering on the book's hubbed spine, listening the while to a babel of disjointed sentences—'Are you a vampire... What if I am... Recede miser... I thirst, I thirst... You may enter my home'—lisp and siffle their way like a series of dull echoes across the turmoil of his thoughts. But above all the hubbub and confusion of this medley of memoried fragments, that same wraithlike voice, soft as the low, muffled pulsing of his fluttering heart, sounded endlessly on and on: 'signs and proofs of vampirism... vampirism... vampirism...'

Nathan shut his eyes a moment or two and stood there panting a little, as though he were attempting by some convulsive effort of the will to blot out that fearfully dire question now confronting him—"Could it be that Phebe *is* in fact a vampire?"

For even if he made due allowance for any exaggerations on the part of his memory concerning Phebe's bizarre habits and peculiar behavior, there were still things she had said and done that tallied perfectly with all the strange, uncomfortable lore he had just now read in the book's sixth chapter with regard to the character and traits of vampires.

And still, after carefully considering all the details in seriatim, Nathan stood there trying diligently to argue, deny, disbelieve it all. At length, however, he began to lean toward the following conclusions, (a) that Phebe was definitely *not* human; (b) that she possessed 'unique' capabilities vastly superior to mere mortals; (c) that she was a creature of a very old and supernatural order; and (d) that this kind of 'supernatural' being was designated by human society under the name of—"vampire"!

Of course, Nathan was reluctant to be certain about any of this; and yet, he thought to himself, Phebe *must* be a vampire, for only so could she have accomplished the numerous extraordinary feats he had seen her do. Nonetheless, the longer he stood there anxiously ruminating on these convictions, the more he seemed to doubt, question, and contradict them. At any rate, he said to himself, even if Phebe is a—(he hesitated a moment or two, unwilling to say the word; then)—even if she turned out to be—*that!*—would it really change the way I feel about her?

And naturally enough a curious and rapidly growing impulse in Nathan suddenly prevailed, and he decided then and there to find out the truth for himself; to discover beyond all doubt whether it was true; to know with absolute certainty that Phebe was a vampire.

Obstinate now as St Thomas, Nathan persisted in his skepticism and disbelief. And even as that doubting Apostle refused to believe unless he could first see the nail prints and probe the Master's wounds, so too Nathan dismissed all that he had read. Until he had seen with his own eyes Phebe's teeth fixed in a victim's throat, and heard her with his own ears supping the blood from the grisly wound, he simply would *not* accept the notion that she was a vampire!

"I just can't—and won't!—believe it all," Nathan said, all but whispering it across to that tall, thin volume on its shelf. Then, very softly, he shut the glass door to the curio cabinet and, feeling appallingly weak and helpless, he soundlessly withdrew from his aunt's room, listening the while to the multitude of cautioning yet ominous thoughts that seemed to haunt his mind.

CHAPTER SIX

*"...Youth: You're an empusa—a hideous Vampire!—
covered all over in blood and gobbets of gore...*

—Ecclesiazusae

For some while yet, that same morning, the thoughts in Nathan's mind seemed to struggle in a net of doubt and denial as to whether Phebe *was*—or *wasn't*—a 'vampire'. But by the time he had walked away from his breakfast (which, for the most part, he'd left untouched), and crawled wearily back upstairs to his room, there had grown up rapidly in his brain a contemptuous disbelief in all he had read in the sixth chapter of that exquisitely bound book in his aunt's room. He was now of the opinion that it was all pure fantasy, or—as Aunt Amelia herself would say when classifying anything she considered utter nonsense—*flapdoodle!*

"Vampires," murmured a faint (yet reassuring) voice from deep within him, "simply *don't* exist. Get it? That's why the book in which all that strange and fabulous lore regarding them has in its title the words 'myth' and 'legend'—and not, 'fact' and 'reality'! They're *imaginary;* fictional creatures, and nothing more."

And yet, despite the comfort and encouragement these words seemed to impart to Nathan, faint misgivings continued nonetheless to prey upon his nerves through the remaining hours of the morning. When, however, these had finally begun to quiet down, there arose in their place a vague foreboding that companioned him, like a miserable specter, all the rest of that afternoon into the evening. Indeed, almost it seemed to Nathan, as he wandered listlessly from room to room, much like a miserable ghost himself, looking for

Phebe, that his numbly beating heart and overwearied mind were empty as the empty rooms through which he now vainly searched.

Still, for the better part of an hour, as if impelled by some nameless influence, Nathan persisted in this useless, fretting quest of looking for Phebe. At times, all but lost to his surroundings and half-sunken in a cold and cheerless reverie, he continued to range aimlessly from one room to the next. And through it all this small, inward voice, curiously remote yet mournfully bitter, seemed incessantly to mock at his futile efforts, using Phebe's very own words: 'Spes nobis nulla; spes nobis nulla... No hope for us; no hope for us', and 'Recede, miser, recede... Hence, vile one; hence'.

At one point, in complete disregard of Vrancic's stern injunction about the doors to both the basement and the sun-room, Nathan, in his desperate search for Phebe, even found himself knocking repeatedly on them with a light knuckle. And more than once, after having rattled at their knob, he stooped awkwardly against the doors themselves and called out, to unheeding ears, Phebe's name, only to wait on and anxiously listen through all that brooding hush for an answering voice on their other side which never came. But, in all honesty, Nathan expected as much. For he gradually came to recognize that Phebe *had* retired, withdrawn, gone away— *somewhere.* Not far, he fancied; but far enough to keep just out of hearing; and, of course, from being seen.

Notwithstanding this, Nathan waited on, as though in desperate hope of catching even the faintest whisper of a stealthy sound or furtive movement in one of the empty rooms that might betray Phebe's whereabouts. But, wait on as he would, every region of the house remained stubbornly adrowse in its own fathomless quiet.

And then, as Nathan stood idly, vainly, impatiently listening in the doorway to his room, a complete realization, for the first time, was his. Even though, for the past day or two, he had begun to grow vaguely conscious of it, he wasn't fully aware till now that, ever since Phebe had forced him to swallow some of her blood, a new and unfamiliar quality (or, *otherness*, as it were), had added itself to his heart, his reasoning—to the very soul and vital force within him.

For Nathan suddenly remarked that the thoughts of his mind had become curiously astir with a new and heightened sense of existence. That the sight of his eyes had been acutely sharpened: the hearing of his ears unusually enhanced; while the light of the sun's flocking beams had become to the pupils of his eyes less beautiful and almost painfully bright. Moreover, into the gloaming's ethereal shadows had stolen an all but unendurable allurement to his senses; and the promise of night's hueless air and faintly starred solitude was like a manna whose sweetness he had never so much as tasted till now. Something, it seemed, of his former self, his very *mortality*, had passed away to return no more; and Life itself seemed to have become encased in the translucent-like atmosphere of dream. But what did it all mean?

Ruminating long and deeply on this one inscrutable, sphinxian riddle, Nathan frittered away the remaining hours of that strange and rather startling morning. And in Phebe's absence, as the dismal hours of afternoon slowly followed those of morning into eternity, never more to be known, Nathan began to feel more and more like a man accursed, condemned to a desolate solitude he seemed scarcely able to cope with. Consequently, he griped and grumbled at being thus so cruelly forsaken by Phebe, and for the duration of that day's wretched loneliness did his best to keep himself busy.

Still, in spite of the seemingly interminable hours of that day, and the weariness and misery he was compelled to helplessly endure by reason of Phebe's prolonged and mysterious absenteeism, Nathan was never unaware, even for an instant, of the curious impression that Phebe was still lurking in some region of the house. For he was acutely aware of her presence—that strangely wonderful atmosphere of hers which never failed to announce itself to his senses whenever she was nearby.

Besides, it was still broad daylight. And as Nathan felt quite certain that Phebe would never venture from the secrecy and shelter of his home (or risk the return journey to the old mausoleum) while the sun was still up, he concluded that she must still be inside some part of the house. He immediately narrowed it down to one of two places. Either Phebe had retreated to the sun-room to spend the remaining hours of daylight with her sinister young friend, Candy, the hermaphrodite; or, gone—and Nathan shuddered at the notion—down into the basement to fraternize with her so-called 'traveling-companion', Antal Vrancic.

And so, in a kind of faint anxiety and creeping apprehension, Nathan went about occupying his time with a number of things around the house. One of which, having priority over all others, was to clean up the excreta of blood left by Phebe in (and underneath) his bed.

Fetching a mop, sponge, and a bucket of water, Nathan swabbed up the puddle of blood on his bedroom floor, and disposed of the blanket with the bloodstained fitted sheet by tossing them into garbage bags. Over the stained mattress of his bed, where he'd leaned it against one of the walls, he then threw an old moth-eaten comforter; and over its ruined box-spring he placed a frayed and tattered throw-rug to hide the large ovate smear of blood staining its cloth.

Then, from the linen closet, Nathan brought out a clean set of sheets and a fresh quilt, and, as he would now be sleeping in his aunt's room, he set about making up her bed for himself.

And while Nathan was about this task, he found himself, more than once, making an all but supreme effort to choke back the objectionable feelings steadily whelming over his heart at having to sleep in that vast colonial-style bed. For quite suddenly, the mere notion of lying down on the very mattress where Aunt Amelia used to lie—and worse still, where she had been brutally slaughtered!—was an almost insupportable concept, and evoked in him a profound sense of discomfort.

But Nathan had little choice in the matter. He knew he would never get any sleep by improvising a bed on the floor of his own room; and he wouldn't even consider using the sofa in the living room. Not with a cannibal lurking downstairs in his basement, and that weird, unpleasant child (Candy) just on the other side of the doors to the sun-room. That's not to say that his aunt's bed ideally suited him, or that the room itself was without any draw-backs of its own.

To Nathan's mind, both the room and its bed had a peculiarly mournful, off-putting aura. And from the room's quilt-veiled mirror, its ternary of blind-drawn windows—even its less-than comfortable-looking armchair in a corner by the bed—there seemed to emanate a subtle standoffish, almost resentful air whose sole purpose (or so it seemed) was to intimidate any and all visitors.

In addition to this Nathan was extremely conscious that the bedroom walls themselves, despite the cheerful hues and flowery print of their wallpaper, seemed to encompass a trace, a suggestion, a *ghost*, as it were, of the sullen, dour mood of the room's former (and now defunct) occupant. And within the close, stagnant air enclosed by those same drab walls, he was able to faintly scent, with unspeakable loathing, the lingering unsavory odor of Aunt Amelia's distasteful perfume—the bottles of which yet cluttered her dresser-top.

One and all, these intensely disagreeable elements gave Nathan the distinct impression that they were in collusion with one another, conspiring together to make his prospective experience of sleeping in the hushed and strangely brooding atmosphere of that vacant room all but an emotional torture.

Be that as it may, Nathan had his aunt's bed made up in little more than a quarter of an hour, and, by the time the other three quarters of that same hour had elapsed, he had fixed himself and consumed (unenthusiastically) a sparse and tasteless supper. Then, shortly after the last feeble rays of a declining sun had withdrawn from the now cloud-darkened kitchen, Nathan dragged himself back upstairs to his aunt's room, where, in a dulled and exhausted state, he flung himself across its bed just as he was, in his jeans, tee-shirt, and sneakers.

Sleep, however, came neither so promptly, nor so easily to Nathan once he shut his eyes and felt his swiftly beating pulses settle into a more serenely measured rhythm. He had first to struggle through a very tedious series of tossings and turnings; during which, for the better part of an hour, he would one moment sit straight up in bed and, with his skin chilled and clammy with his own sweat, glance uneasily round; and the next, lie down again and, keeping perfectly still, listen intently for even the faintest rumor of any untoward sound.

But through all that frivolous tension and fretting, a poignant, almost agonizing longing for Phebe's company took complete possession of Nathan. And with every passing second, he lay there hoping, yearning, expecting to feel, any moment now, the delicate touch of her long-fingered hands in the empty darkness; to hear the silvery tones of her sweet voice whispering across to him in the quiet of the room's loneliness; and gaze on through its inky shadows into the darker darkness of her eyes as she lay softly pressed against him.

For the flames which Phebe had kindled in Nathan's young heart—though presently sunk to flickering ashes, ruddy and aglint at their core, since awaking that morning to find blood dribbling from her mouth, nose, and eyes—had never, even for a solitary moment, ceased to smolder and burn. And the least thought of her deep, dwelling eyes, of the strange, bewitching tones in the tenderness of her voice, of the curious fragrance about her long shadowy tresses and next-to-bloodless pale skin, instantly fanned those glowing coals to a flaring blaze.

As was the case now. For even as Nathan lay sprawled flat on his stomach across the quilt of his aunt's bed, with the lids of his drowsing eyes heavily drooping, his thoughts, though half in dream, drew solemnly away to Phebe asleep in one of the crypts of the old mausoleum. And all at once he felt as though his heart, like a windswept bonfire, had burst into the swelling flames of an inextinguishable blaze.

But then, the next thing Nathan knew, Phebe's cold slender arms had wound themselves tightly round him in the slow-fading dregs of the room's steadily darkening twilight. And the cool of her breath softly brushed his cheek as her lips, close to his face, whispered, "Guess, Nathan; guess who it is."

And after Nathan had stirred and opened his eyes, and Phebe had shifted a little nearer to him, that sweetly thrilling voice of hers once again breathed out to him, "Guess, Nathan; guess who." Softly, then, across the narrow empty space that yet remained between them on the bed, Phebe squeezed her body closer still to Nathan's, and, clasping him tightly round, she pressed her cheek, cold as a stone at the bottom of a well, against his own.

"Am I forgiven for ruining your bed, Nathan?" she asked; and, without waiting for Nathan's reply, "And I'm sorry," she went on almost hurriedly, "that you had to see me like – *that*, this morning; and that it frightened you."

Nathan drew back his head a little, and his brown worshipful eyes peered straight into the dark lustrous shadowiness of Phebe's for several moments. Then, "It's okay. Just forget it," he said, raising himself on his elbow. "Besides, I'm not afraid; not of you, Phebe, or anything about you. Not anymore. And I don't believe you're what—you know—I asked you; or that there's anything wrong with you. I read all sorts of weird things in that book in my aunt's room about vampires, but I don't believe any of it. It can't be true. I mean, things like that just aren't real—they're myths. Right?"

Nathan's words were followed by a deep and longish silence, during which Phebe watched his face intently, anxiously for some time without speaking. She seemed to reflect a while; then, "But what if they're not myths, Nathan?" she almost whispered. "What if it turned out that vampires are real, and I was one—would you despise me?"

Without even a moment's thought, Nathan shook his head. "No; never," he answered, as he continued unflinchingly to meet Phebe's intensely dwelling eyes.

"Is it because you love me, Nathan; is that it?"

Again, without hesitating, Nathan replied, "Yes"; and he felt his cheeks suddenly burning in the darkness as he half-shyly lowered his gaze.

Phebe stooped her face closer to Nathan's, and softly into his ear, in a little shaky voice, she whispered, "Let me hear you say it, then, Nathan. Let me hear you say you love me."

Nathan raised his eyes again, and, the moment they encountered Phebe's, he heard his own voice, curiously hushed and faint, breathe out to her in the darkness, "It's true. I love you, Phebe." And the next instant he felt Phebe's lips slightly quivering, and more than once on his cheeks the wetness of tears, as she kissed his face and mouth many times.

Then, Phebe put her hands to Nathan's cheeks, and holding his face between her narrow-boned fingers, she said, "O, Nathan, there is no gift, no treasure in this world that you could have given me on my birthday that would have been more precious to me than hearing the words you've just spoken."

"Then tomorrow night," said Nathan, "when we're together on our birthday, I'll say them to you again and again."

But all at once Phebe became strangely silent. Softly from Nathan's face she withdrew her hands; and her gaze, still meeting that of Nathan's, for a space of some seconds, became so remote, so blank, so non-attending that it seemed the 'self', the secret *someone,* within those darker than dark eyes of hers had simply gone elsewhere. And then, shortly after the darkness of those emptily still eyes had become re-occupied, Phebe gazed suddenly out at Nathan with an expression of the most tender sorrow. "Nathan," she said, in a faint, mournful voice, "I can't be with you tomorrow night on our birthday."

"But you promised that we'd spend our birthday together."

"I know. But I realize now it's a promise I can't keep," said Phebe, in a plaintive little voice, as she drew her face away from Nathan's, and slowly sat up. "A promise I shouldn't have made." And as she threw back the long dark tresses of her hair from her narrow shoulders, she stared wistfully down on Nathan.

"But why?" Nathan asked when he had struggled up, too, and had sat for some while gazing at Phebe through the room's shadowed air, seeing her now quite clearly by that odd ghostly glimmer that seemed to emanate, like a thin, milk-pale mist, from the bluish-white pallor of her own skin.

"It's very difficult for me to explain that to you, Nathan," replied Phebe.

And Nathan asked: "Then, where will you be tomorrow night, if not here with me?"

Phebe sat on in silence a moment, with her head bent, as if lost in thought. Then, suddenly she breathed a heavy sigh and, lifting her head, said, "I have to be somewhere else."

"And I can't be there with you?" Nathan managed to whisper after a long pause. Phebe slightly turned her head, and the dark luminous eyes of her shone across at him inkly black as a moonless night of cloud-veiled stars. "No, Nathan," she answered very solemnly. "On any other night, except tomorrow, our birthday, it would be alright for you and I to be together."

For nearly a full minute Nathan sat on, silently pondering Phebe's words, wondering uneasily at their significance. But whatever cryptic meaning was hidden in them, it was beyond his poor wits to try and puzzle it out. Then, "But where will you be spending our birthday, if not here?" he pressed her.

Phebe got up, went over to Nathan's dresser, and, lighting the stub of a wax candle that was on it, she said, "It's better if you didn't know." Then, she turned round and, holding the lit candle, stood for a moment gazing over its pale narrow flame at Nathan; and in the mirror-like stillness of her dark, large-pupilled eyes, twin reflections of the candle's steadily burning flame appeared in perfect miniature.

And it was *at*, not *into*, those two tiny simulated flames shadowed in the Stygian dusk of Phebe's eyes that Nathan suddenly found himself gazing as one entranced. Then, as if out of the strangeness of a dream-filled slumber, and in a voice he scarcely recognized as his own, he breathed across to her, "You'll be in the old mausoleum, won't you?"

Phebe was silent a while; and as she continued to steadily, gravely meet Nathan's eyes, she softly shook her head. Then, without once removing that piercing, stirless gaze of hers from Nathan's silent face, she set the wax candle in its brass holder down on the floor, and seated herself once again on the bedside next to Nathan.

"I don't believe you," said Nathan, after Phebe's eyes, intent in their regard, had suddenly fallen. "And to be sure," continued Nathan, "I'll go to the old mausoleum tomorrow night and see for myself. So you might as well tell me the truth." And through the narrow space of faint candle-lit air between them, Phebe's eyes once again confronted those of Nathan's, only this time with what just for an instant Nathan thought was alarm, or incredulous horror.

"Nathan, don't go *near* the old mausoleum tomorrow night;" Phebe all but pleaded with him; "don't even leave the house. You won't be safe if you do. Please; listen to me. Whatever you may be thinking, your life will be in terrible danger if you go outside tomorrow night and come to the old mausoleum."

"Then that's where you'll be, won't you?"

Phebe seemed to hesitate answering; and for the next few moments the dark eyes anxiously pondered; but then, "Yes," she almost whispered. "But you mustn't come there to see me tomorrow night, Nathan. I won't be—" and suddenly she paused to draw a sharp breath that was more like a sob. "I won't be myself;" she went on hastily; "and in such a condition I could... hurt you... or, do something even worse to you. So promise me, Nathan, promise me that you'll stay indoors tomorrow night, otherwise your life will be in terrible jeopardy. Please, promise me." And Phebe smiled faintly, sadly down on Nathan when, having given her his promise to remain indoors tomorrow night, Nathan shut his eyes and laid softly back down again on the bed. "Sleep now, Nathan;" he then heard Phebe bidding him in a soothing, wonderfully persuading voice; "sleep now, and remember well your promise to me..."

And then, the last thing Nathan was conscious of, before all thought, memory, and sense itself had emptily settled into a warm and welcome drowse, was the dreamlike impression of Phebe's sweet voice calling him seductively away to the dark, peaceful nothingness of a slumber deeper than death.

For a space of some hours, Nathan must have lingered in this inertial and deliciously somnolescent condition, for somewhere between two and three o'clock of the early morning of August 25th, his drowsy brown eyes had once more blinked themselves wide open. Glancing round, he found the room about him in an all but absolute darkness, and the vast bed in which he lay, utterly empty of another occupant. He was unequivocally alone, not only in his aunt's oversized and uncomfortable bed, but in the still, unfriendly dark of the room itself.

Evidently, at some juncture, while Nathan had been fast asleep, two things had taken place. Firstly, the candle which Phebe had left burning in its brass holder on the floor had either been extinguished by someone (Phebe, perhaps?), or gone out by itself. And secondly, Phebe herself had withdrawn from the room, and this time she was nowhere to be seen, heard, or so much as *felt* by Nathan—her whereabouts could not even be vaguely sensed by him.

Quite naturally, Nathan made the assumption that after she had quietly retired from his aunt's bedroom, she must have stolen downstairs, slipped out either the front or back door of the house, and then secretly returned to the old mausoleum in the cemetery. And with regard to this last point, Nathan felt thoroughly convinced. For even as he lay, still as a stone, in his aunt's bed with his every thought in that still, small darkness fixed on Phebe, he was unable to discern so much as the faintest suggestion of her wonderfully sweet presence either in his aunt's room or in any other drowsying region of the house. No; of this he was certain: Phebe had left him alone, abandoned him, and on this, the morning of August 25th, the eve of his (and her) birthday.

But why? wondered Nathan. Why did Phebe insist that she had to be 'somewhere else' (as she put it) on their birthday; why was it so vitally important that they spend that day *apart*; that on their birthday she had to be away from him, inside the old mausoleum by herself? And what did Phebe mean by warning Nathan not to come there to see her on their 'birthday'; that she wouldn't be *herself*; and that she could hurt him—or do something worse to him—'in such a condition'? It was all so mysterious; so puzzling; so—bizarre! Phebe had also warned him that if he did go out to the old mausoleum tomorrow on their 'birthday', that his life would be 'in terrible danger'. But, *how...why ...* and from *what*?

Feeling all but half-stifled and abominably oppressed, Nathan lay yet a while in his aunt's bed blinking at, and listening to, nothing in the empty dark. And for the next several minutes he found himself unable to think of anything but Phebe's face; Phebe's voice—how frightened the former had looked, and how anxious the latter had sounded when she had half-warned, half-pleaded with him not to come looking for her at the old mausoleum on their birthday.

And all at once, Nathan's heavily beating heart grew cold, and his tired and bewildered mind began to ache at the thought of Phebe and himself spending their birthday away from each other. She confined (for no apparent reason) to the mournful solitude of a decaying tomb, while he languished inside a miserably lonely house, banished, expelled to the nothing, the emptiness of—himself.

To Nathan it made no sense at all that the two of them should be apart; and the more he thought about it, the more it baffled him as to why Phebe insisted that it had to be so.

At length, unable to listen on another moment to the ceaseless stir and clamor of his own thoughts, Nathan sprang out of bed. Without the least notion of what he was doing, he heard himself breathe out, in a low, gasp-like whisper, the familiar sound of Phebe's name as he groped his way anxiously over to the windows of the room.

But the less-than cheerful prospect from the windows to Aunt Amelia's bedroom gave out onto the broken pavement, crumbling blacktop, and dingy red-brick warehouses on the dead end street of 73rd Place. And now, more than ever, Nathan preferred, needed, longed for the view from the small, narrow window of his own room, which looked out upon the old All Faiths cemetery with its rows of clustering tombstones, half-sunken graves, and neglected mausoleums—especially *that* one, the one (although distance and a number of intervening monuments hid it from sight) which she had chosen to inhabit.

And so, in a fever of apprehensiveness, Nathan pulled open the door to his aunt's room, hurried down the hall, and ran over to the solitary window in his own bedroom. The sash to the window was still up, and the cooler airs of the pre-dawn dusk flowed in through the dirty screen and from over the paint-chipped sill.

Nathan stooped his head a little, and, through the shadowed air, gazed out across the cemetery's black and featureless distances.

And although he could not *see* the old mausoleum with his eagerly peering eyes, in imagination he was already seated on its dust-veiled floor together with Phebe, in the soft light of a dozen steadily burning candles, near the vine-curtained doors to its entrance.

But all of a sudden, this still, dreamlike abstraction of Nathan's was vaguely troubled by something like a low, protracted droning that seemed to come from somewhere near at hand, and yet, at the same time, as if out of nowhere. And as that faint, steady undertone continued to break in upon Nathan's serene reverie of wandering with Phebe, afloat and phantom-wise, among the cemetery's silent gravestones, he presently stood with his whole attention carefully fixed upon it, blinking and listening in the empty, lightless stillness of his room.

And very gradually, to Nathan's straining ears, that low, incoherent sound began to grow and shape itself, faint and hollow, yet quite distinctly, into that of voices (certainly no less than two in number, Nathan speculated) talking, almost whispering together among themselves.

At first Nathan thought that the sound of those voices, filtering indistinctly through the screen of his open window, was coming from somewhere *inside* the cemetery, just beyond the fence of his backyard. But as he continued to stand at the window of his bedroom, stiff as a post, like a spellbound listener, he soon became aware that the voices were actually those of two persons who were talking in muffled conversation not only *within* the limits of his own backyard, but just below the window of his bedroom.

Little by little, then, as Nathan went on listening, the voices became more and more distinct; and although he could not as yet distinguish any clear words to what they were saying, he was almost certain that one of those voices was Antal Vrancic's.

Nathan pricked up his ears, making every effort now to catch a sentence, a phrase, even so much as a single word, but then, quite abruptly, the talking ceased. Nearly half a minute went by without so much as the tiniest whisper. And Nathan, keeping perfectly still, waited on. At length, growing somewhat impatient, he leaned forward to rest his hands on the window sill, and, scarcely daring to breathe, continued to listen intently. But as all remained utterly still, he was intending to quietly raise the window screen and stoop his head out into the air, when the voices suddenly resumed their talking, and Nathan's heart all but jumped inside his body at the sound, as he caught his breath and drew noiselessly back.

After a few moments, however, when once more his courage had revived, Nathan stooped his head forward a little to the screen of his window, and, ignoring as best he could the muffled thumping of his galloping heart, again stood listening. He was positive by now that one of the two voices *was*—indeed had to *be* Vrancic's; while the other (although Nathan could not satisfy himself as to exactly whose it was) he fancied had to be Candy's, the creepy hermaphrodite child—whose else, Nathan thought to himself; certainly it did not sound anything like Phebe's.

Now, as this muffled conversation between Vrancic and (Nathan supposed) Candy steadily progressed, and Nathan continued to listen to it all very attentively, by degrees the sound of the two voices grew more distinct. And every now and then Nathan began to catch one or two half sentences (which to him conveyed no intelligible meaning), and a few disjointed yet nonetheless tantalizingly mysterious phrases.

And although Nathan could not quite guess at the moment exactly what it was all about, he got the unmistakable impression that he was now engaged in eavesdropping on the deadly plot to an extremely secret and sinister affair. For all of a sudden he heard the voice of Vrancic ask: "Do you have the one to whom she made the promise that in a sennight they would meet again?" The other, whom Nathan was almost certain now must be Candy, informed Vrancic in a cold, gloating voice that he had "summoned" *him* from his bedroom window late last night, and had brought him away into the cemetery.

And Nathan, listening with growing amazement and a creeping sense of horror, then heard Candy go on to explain that whoever they were referring to was now "as helpless as a fly in a web", securely bound and safely stowed away in an old nineteenth century family mausoleum awaiting his fate.

"Good!" grunted Vrancic. "Then I'll bring him and the others to her lair before she wakes so that—" But he and Candy passed just then out of hearing as they sauntered off together some little distance across the yard, and began to stroll back and forth along its fence.

Peering out through the screen of his window, Nathan could just glimpse the top of their heads as they paced slowly to and fro. Now and again, as their voices rose through the shadowed air he began to catch once more their peculiar discussion; but he could distinguish only bits of bizarre phrases and the absurd remarks to several bitten-off sentences: "—her birthnight—she'll be hungrier than on any other—need to feed—must have at least five to satiate her thirst—bring them to her tomorrow precisely at midnight—hour when she was born anew—sleep deep till then—"

Then, a short silence followed, and Nathan held his breath, for even though he could attach no definite meaning to all that he had just heard, he came to realize, with a touch of dismay, that they were talking about *Phebe*.

And presently, Nathan glimpsed and heard the two of them approaching again, coming back toward the house. And just as they halted once more below his window, Candy was saying, "She wants you to take every precaution that Nathan comes to no harm tomorrow." When Nathan heard his own name mentioned, he felt his heart, for a single instant, jerk to a sudden standstill. Then, "Tomorrow night," he heard Vrancic reply, "when he goes to sleep, I'll be sure to lock him in his aunt's room. There'll be no chance of him getting out, or coming into harm's way." Upon hearing these words, Nathan turned cold all over and, with creeping flesh, remained standing at the open window, afraid for the moment to either move or breathe.

Then, Vrancic's voice, answering, it would seem, a question which Candy had asked him, but which Nathan, lost in a series of alarming imaginings, had apparently missed, said, "Because on her birthnight, her feeding will be excessive; and vampires are often incautious then, due to their blood-lust being so potent. In some cases they will leave far too many clues as to what has truly happened. Consequently, the discovery of so many blood-drained victims, whether human or animal, rouses suspicions. You must Remember, there are still some among the society of men who believe that vampires do indeed exist. And among these can be found a number of self-proclaimed vampire *hunters*."

In the brief pause that followed these extraordinary words, Nathan heard a gush of scornful laughter from Candy. Then, "Laugh all you want;" went on Vrancic; "but mark my words: vampires on their birthnight (as you yourself ought to know) will frequently indulge themselves in their feeding all too recklessly. Some, in their greed and imprudence, have drunk and fed until daybreak, and so perished in the rays of the rising sun. They had gorged themselves so long and deeply on the blood of their victims that they had grown heedless of the waning night's fleeting hours. Others glutted themselves so abundantly and with such cavalier disregard, they left a number of their victims lying blatantly about, so that their existence could not be doubted even by the staunchest of skeptics. Thus giving rise to the danger of an organized hunt by vampire-hunters. And others, still more careless during their feeding on their birthnight, have left a trail of clues that led these would-be hunters to the very doorstep of their lair. After which they were either pierced with stakes or consumed in flames when doused with holy water. In order to avoid this happening here, I have decided to provide her with victims to feed on in the solitude and sanctuary of the mausoleum she has chosen as her lair. And when she has drunk her fill, you and I will carefully dispose of the carcasses so that there can be no suspicions, surmises, or allegations of vampire activity by even the shrewdest of those who acknowledge their existence."

A deadly chill had swept over Nathan as he stood listening to all of this; and, for what seemed several minutes, his head swam. Then, when once more he had recovered himself, after one or two whispered words, Nathan heard Vrancic's disagreeable voice with perfect clarity as he said, "You know how I have been careful to always remind you and Phebe that we must all three remain at all times cautious and inconspicuous in our proceedings—" And here his voice sank to a low undertone, and Nathan could distinguish what he was presently mumbling across to Candy only in vague snatches: "—murders perpetrating—attain the living blood of victims—go undetected by law enforcement."

A longish pause followed, in which Vrancic must have lit a cigarette, for suddenly the air of the early morning twilight straying through the open window brought with it to Nathan's nostrils the faint aroma of smoke from a Marlboro. Then, Vrancic's voice broke out once again, and all the frightening things which he now said or alluded to literally took Nathan's breath away for an instant and made him tremble.

"If any of our crimes should come under the scrutiny of the police, then they must do so as little more than 'mysterious disappearances'. Indeed, it is imperative that these murders continue to baffle all the efforts of law enforcement so that no clues can be uncovered that would eventually connect any of us to so much as a single corpse. And thus far, the two of you have been careful to follow my counsel to the letter." Again a long interval of silence followed Vrancic's words.

By now, stiff and cold, Nathan was stooping forward with his forehead nearly pressed up against the screen of his window so that he could peer down into the yard. He could just distinguish the shadowy forms of both Vrancic and Candy standing directly underneath his window; in fact, he was rather astonished at just how close they actually were. And for an instant Nathan's fingers moved impulsively to the pocket of his jeans for the little glass cruet of holy water: for a strong desire to pour its contents down on Candy's head had suddenly swelled up into his rapidly beating heart.

But just then, that sinister duo moved off together toward the fence of the yard again, where Nathan heard Vrancic, after having lit another cigarette, say to Candy: "The last thing we need now are reports or rumors of vampire activity in town being spread either by word of mouth or the media. I remember just such an incident in the late 1960's, in London's Highgate Cemetery. At first, only rumors circulated about dead animals found inside the cemetery utterly drained of blood and having fang marks in the throat. After that, reports continued to proliferate at a feverish pace. Then, one of the local newspapers quipped about the presence of a vampire, initiating a sensation. As a result, a vampire hunt was organized; and self-proclaimed vampire-hunters descended in droves on Highgate cemetery armed with crucifixes, holy water, and wooden stakes. We don't need such notions here, now, fueling interest among either the curious or the true believers. Should any claims be made, or rumors circulate, about the presence of a vampire in Middle Village now, it could very well expose either you or Phebe (or both) to the peril of discovery. We must proceed carefully in these matters at all times."

"Much the same," (Nathan heard Candy remark) "as the vampire of Highgate Cemetery." But Vrancic countered: "I fear he did not fare so well. There are some who claim he was destroyed." A low, contemptuous snicker followed these words. "No; I happen to know for a fact that *that* vampire fared quite well in his flight from Highgate Cemetery," said Candy, with just a faint hint of sneering amusement in his voice.

"You mean—" Vrancic began, but was suddenly interrupted by Candy, who said, "Yes; I eluded the pursuit of my hunters the night of March 13th, and escaped unseen and unharmed from Highgate. Claims that the vampire there was slain are false, as I can readily attest to the contrary."

After a few more muffled remarks, Nathan, standing numbly motionless at his bedroom window, then heard the cellar door softly opened, followed by the loud miaouing of his cat, Ichabod. Nathan then caught the shuffling sound of Vrancic's and Candy's footsteps as they began to make their way down the shallow cement steps into the basement. Around the last step or two there was a sudden pause, and Nathan heard Vrancic calling up to Ichabod, who must have gone bounding up the steps and into the yard.

"Come, Bram; come back down, Bram!" Apparently (thought Nathan to himself) Vrancic had taken the liberty of renaming his cat. And for an instant or two he stood there musing on the name "Bram", wondering if Vrancic had derived it, by way of a sort of private jest, from that of the author of 'Dracula'. If so, thought Nathan, it was perhaps (given the present circumstances) a far more appropriate name for the beast than Ichabod.

Then, after he heard the cellar door pulled shut and locked, Nathan continued for the next few moments to stand motionless at his bedroom window. And all the while he stood absently staring out into his backyard, he was thinking to, arguing with, and closely questioning himself about the very frightening dialogue he had just overheard between Vrancic and Candy. Had it been *real,* he kept wondering. The whole thing now seemed to him as impossible, unlikely, *untrue* as the things either seen or heard in dream. Even now Nathan was unsure whether he had indeed been wide awake or only dreaming. Perhaps he *had* been asleep the whole time; a victim of nightmare's deceiving nets and veils; and had only imagined all that unpleasant talk with its fearful allusions to 'vampires', 'murders', 'helpless victims', and 'mysterious disappearances'. It couldn't be real, Nathan told himself. It was all too bizarre, too horrifying, too ghoulish to be anything but untruthful.

And yet, and yet, for some moments, Nathan could not help but very seriously consider the *possibility.* For he suddenly found himself powerless to exorcise that disturbing conversation from his mind; the memory of it proved far too potent: and first one unnerving sentence, and then another continued to vividly revive, regardless of every effort he made to repress them.

At length, when Nathan came out of these awful and disconcerting musings, his hands were cold and quivering, and his wide, staring eyes were fixed away in the distance on the faint, trembling line of the sky's hem. Along it he could see the dull grey of a summer dawn just then beginning to slyly grope and stir.

And by the time Nathan had turned away from the window and retreated wearily down the hall to his aunt's bedroom, the grey-shadowed hues of daybreak had already thinned away into the rose-colored and faintly paling blush of early morning.

Then, with something like a groan, Nathan threw himself down across his aunt's bed and shut tight his eyes. But an unendurable fear, an indescribable uneasiness preyed upon his mind, and he simply

could not fall asleep. For amid the many doubts and misgivings
that relentlessly haunted him, certain sentences and singularly
disquieting remarks from that extraordinary conversation he had
overheard would repeat themselves in his memory.

And presently, with eyes wide open, Nathan lay perfectly still,
gazing absently up at the ceiling, as one phrase more than any other
continued to chill his mind and fill him with a profound dismay—
Vrancic's rather casual mention of *her* "birthnight".

With half-glazed eyes still emptily staring up the ceiling, Nathan
sank once more into a dull and heavy muse, as he reflected long
and earnestly on that odd yet curiously *familiar* term—"birthnight".
He was convinced he had heard it before. But where? When? he
kept asking himself. And then, quite suddenly, he recalled having
come across it in a brief passage in that beautifully bound book
here in his aunt's room. And the gathering sense of dread which
only a little while ago had brushed his soul when he had listened
to Vrancic's and Candy's nefarious schemings now deepened into
something very near to actual terror, as Nathan recollected the
unsettling words to the passage in that book:

> '...never does the vampire feed with a more voracious
> appetite and gorge itself more abundantly on the blood
> of the living than on its "birthnight", that accursed
> date on which it passed from the society of the living
> to the abhorred company of the Undead—the night
> when it died to its mortality and was "born" anew
> unto death and darkness without end...'

And almost in the very same instant, the recollection of Phebe's
own words with regard to his (Nathan's) birthday, at Midnight of
the morning of August 26th, flashed across his thoughts—"it's my
birthday, too—in a way". And Nathan felt a deadly chill descend
like a curtain of cold mist upon his mind, and a creeping misgiving
brushed like an icy breath against his heart, as the *meaning* Phebe
had hinted at in those last three words of hers—"*in-a-way*"—swept
with utter clarity now through his brain. The date, then, of August

26th could indeed be designated (in a way!) as Phebe's 'birthday': but Nathan now began to surmise that in all probability it actually signified her *"birth-night",* the moment in time when she passed from the "society of the living to the abhorred company of the Undead"—eternal life in everlasting death, which sums up the accursed existence of the Vampire.

Nathan's own 'birthday' was now only hours away: for according to hospital records and his own birth certificate, exactly at 12:00 a.m., Midnight, of the morning of August 26th, was when his mother (16 years ago) brought him into the world. But it was also Phebe's 'birthnight', when she—how many years, decades, centuries ago Nathan did not even dare to imagine!—died to her mortality, and was "born" anew to "death and darkness without end".

And although every fiber, every axon, every neuron of his being revolted at the mere notion, Nathan was all but convinced now that Phebe *was; had* to be, indeed *must* be—a *vampire!* One thing yet remained to satisfy him beyond any shadow of doubt, any suggestion of denial—when the sun should set, and it had grown dark once more, he must go to the old mausoleum at the hour of midnight. With his own eyes he must *see* Phebe as she gluts herself on the blood of her hapless victims; her teeth fixed in the flesh of their throat; her mouth fastened at the open wound in their neck; her lips stained with the jetting of their blood. Until he should see that for himself, he could not—*would not!*—believe, either willingly or assuredly, any of it.

Now, somewhere around the same time that the chirring of the crickets had given place to the faint piping of the birds, and the sun's pale rays had begun to steal in round the edges of the blinds in his aunt's room, Nathan must have finally dropped off, and slept long and heavily. For when he opened his eyes again, the morning—that of Friday, August 25th, the eve of his birthday—was far advanced. And by the time he had put on a clean shirt, changed into a fresh pair of socks, underwear, and different jeans, then hurried downstairs to the kitchen, and bolted down a late breakfast, he was surprised, when he glanced up at the clock, to see that the noon hour was already upon him.

Be that as it may, the remaining hours of the day seemed to him interminably long, unendurably slow, and excruciatingly dull. Nathan longed now all but achingly for the night, most especially its 'witching hour'—12:00 a.m., midnight. For his resolve to satisfy his curiosity, this gnawing uncertainty regarding Phebe's *actual* nature, by going to see her at the old mausoleum tonight, had taken deeper and deeper root.

To while away the time now, Nathan did anything and everything to keep himself busy. But ever and again he caught himself lapsing into long and somber reveries from which, at the least noise, he would suddenly start. For the strange and growing sense of foreboding with which he had awakened that morning continued steadily to haunt him, blackening his thoughts like the damp clinging mold in some open grave.

And by late afternoon a dark misgiving had begun to stir in his mind that when he should finally arrive tonight at the old mausoleum after midnight, whatever he should happen to see there with regard to Phebe was hardly going to thrill or delight him. In fact, some inexplicable premonition now seemed to warn him that he was going to be a good deal upset, perhaps even—*horrified* by what he should see there.

And yet Nathan would not be intimidated or turned aside from his purpose. He was determined to see the thing through; to at last discover the truth, regardless of its outcome or the shock that might be in store for him.

In spite of this resolve, however, a part of Nathan balked at the mere notion of breaking his promise to Phebe. He had given his word to her that he would not come near the old mausoleum "tomorrow night". But then, the thought occurred to him that *tomorrow night* actually meant *'Friday* night', August 25th; and any time *after* 12:00 a.m.—midnight, the hour when he was born, according to his birth certificate—was, technically speaking, no longer the 'night' of Friday, August 25th, but rather the early *'morning'* of Saturday, August 26th, his and Phebe's birthday. And Phebe had said nothing about the *morning;* he had only promised her not to come to the old mausoleum tomorrow "night", as she had expressly put it.

And so, Nathan thought to himself, as long as he did not go to see Phebe at the old mausoleum until after the stroke of midnight, he would be (once again, "technically speaking") keeping his promise to her by not approaching the tomb until the morning of Saturday, August 26th.

It was on his part a sort of deceitful maneuver, and Nathan knew he was being rather dishonest in doing it; but then, the way Phebe had worded her promise had, in essence, provided him with a convenient loophole by which he would be able to keep his promise to her while, at the same time, breaking it. And so, having in this way somewhat assuaged his guilt, Nathan then began very carefully to plot, and painstakingly devise, even to the smallest detail, just how he was going to accomplish this bold endeavor of arriving at the old mausoleum shortly after midnight. For he now knew that it was Vrancic's intention to prevent him from leaving the house tonight at all costs by (and probably at Phebe's own behest) locking him inside his aunt's bedroom.

But after little more than half an hour of concocting and contemplating first one plan, then another of eluding imprisonment that night without, in the process, alerting his would-be captor to the fact that he had even left the premises, Nathan at last struck upon a course of action which to him seemed the most advantageous. He felt absolute confidence in this plan for three main reasons: a) its simplicity made it the least likely to fail; b) lacking all the complications of the previous strategies he'd devised, he felt it was in all probability the easiest for him to pull off; and, c) it was the one plan which Nathan was convinced would be able to deceive even Vrancic's shrewd and suspicious mind.

Full of mission and purpose now, Nathan diligently set about the preparations to carrying out his scheme. And although he attended to every particular with great care and thoroughness, in the end, these arrangements scarcely occupied more time than it had taken him to dream up his plan.

Having placed a couple of pillows length-wise underneath the bedsheets, Nathan produced, in no time at all, a very convincing representation of what appeared to be his body. Then, by positioning at the top of this, so that it peeped just over the edge of the bedsheets, his aunt's best furred-muff (which Nathan abstracted from the topmost drawer of Amelia's dresser), he managed to improvise a replica of his head, complete with the same dark-colored tousled hair as his own, pressed deep into the pillow. Should Vrancic at some point tonight peep into the room (and Nathan was quite certain that he would) he would see—or, at least *believe* he was seeing—Nathan lying sound asleep on his side, in Aunt Amelia's bed, with his face to the wall.

And Nathan felt no less certain that, without any further ado, Vrancic, having satisfied himself as to the boy's safety and whereabouts, would then shut the door, lock it, and (hopefully) retire to his lair again down in the basement. Should all then proceed as expected, Nathan felt he would have no trouble at all tonight in evading the vigilance of Vrancic, making good his escape from the house, and accomplishing his flight to the old mausoleum shortly after midnight to see Phebe.

With this initial phase of his plan completed, Nathan began presently to consider the things necessary for his clandestine exodus from the house itself. For in his journey in the midnight dark across the uneven ground of the neglected old cemetery to his destination of the old mausoleum, he would need first and foremost *light*. And so his first order of business was to retrieve the flashlight from its place in the cabinet under the kitchen sink.

Having done that, Nathan then slipped his Zippo lighter into the back pocket of his jeans (so that he should not be without any means of producing a light should the batteries in the flashlight suddenly die out on him). He also brought along his old pocket-knife, Arras, as a measure of 'security'; his mother's wedding-ring, "for good luck", he told himself; and finally, he patted and probed the front pockets of his jeans to verify that they still contained (in the one) the little cruet of holy water, and (in the other) the matanie, or Romanian rosary—"just in case". But suddenly there stole across his thoughts a small, secret inner whisper—"Just in case of... *what*?" What indeed!

And for a moment the thought startled him. For the answer that had floated up into his anxious mind, hard upon the heels of this disturbing question, made him shudder, as though a lean hand with long, icy fingers had suddenly clutched his arm... "Just in case Phebe should turn out to be..." But, no! He wouldn't consider *that*; not yet; not *now!*

The afternoon hours seemed now to slip by slower and slower; and Nathan spent them by turns now thinking, now resting. But as late afternoon wore into early evening, bringing the hour of that long anticipated event still nearer, a faint yet disagreeable sensation, which Nathan could not quite identify, steadily grew up in him—something like fear, panic, and a vague sense of dismay all combined into a single vexingly oppressive feeling.

To check or counter, as best he could, this growing unpleasant sensation, Nathan went outside into the backyard, strolled to and fro along its fence, then up and down the narrow alleyway,and finally sat down a while on the loose and crumbling brick steps to the front porch. But it was not until the sun began to decline in the west that a general relief was at last felt by him.

And a little after 7:00 p.m. that evening, as shadows lengthened, and light in the narrowing skies thinned away to the first deepening grey of early dusk, Vrancic came up from the basement for the second time that day. He had already come up to look in on Nathan only an hour before, while Nathan (after having eaten a meager supper which he had hardly tasted) was standing at the kitchen sink washing his plate. Very sternly he told the boy he was not to leave the house tonight; to go to bed early; and be sure to remain indoors! Nathan replied: he had no intention of going out; that he had already promised Phebe that he would stay inside; and that he was too tired to go anywhere. Vrancic stood eyeing the boy severely a moment or two; then, mumbling over something to himself, he returned to the basement.

By 8:00 p.m. Nathan had climbed softly upstairs to his aunt's bedroom to fetch the flashlight from inside the armoire where he had hidden it. Before the nine o' clock hour, he had slipped quickly and quietly out of the room again (intentionally leaving its door half open) and into the hallway. He then hid himself inside the linen closet, which was close beside the door to his own room, and there proceeded to hold a dull and lonely vigil.

In the cramped space of this dark and stagnant retreat, Nathan stood now listening intently, almost breathlessly to the staid old tambour clock in his aunt's bedroom telling off the hour. First ten chimes sounded; then, an hour later, eleven more chimes rang out. And with his heart swiftly drubbing, and clammy perspiration breaking out all over his skin, Nathan kept thinking to himself, only one more hour, only one more hour, and finally... *midnight!*

But then, just a few minutes after the faint, mellow chimes had pealed out the eleven o' clock hour, Nathan stiffened, and caught his breath, as yet another sound from downstairs reached his ears. For all of a sudden the basement door creaked, and after a short pause, slow, heavy steps crossed the dining room floor towards the stairs. By and by, as Nathan anxiously listened, he distinctly heard the stairs themselves groan and creak as someone (whom Nathan knew could only *be* Vrancic) began to ascend them. The creaking of the stairs ceased, then, and Nathan heard Vrancic's heavy step on the stairhead. After yet another brief pause, the footsteps began to advance along the hallway, tramp-tramp-tramp. Nathan heard them go at a slow, measured pace right past his place of concealment inside the linen closet.

Then, at the very end of the hall, before Aunt Amelia's bedroom door, Nathan heard Vrancic's steps come to a sudden halt. Straining his ears now to listen, he heard the door's hinges faintly squeak, as the door itself was pushed slowly inward to its fullest gape. A longish interval of stillness followed, in which Nathan fancied Vrancic stooping his head in over the threshold of the room while peering intently across at the artificial construction of his (Nathan's) body lying in the very center of the bed with a sheet drawn over it. Perhaps even now (thought Nathan) Vrancic's black luminous eyes were regarding that very convincing imitation of his head made out of Amelia's furred-muff.

For the next few moments Nathan held his breath, and the racing of his pulses made a steady, muffled drumming in his ears, as he stood there, behind the linen closet door, utterly still, hoping, praying that Vrancic should not see through this simple yet cunning ploy of his. Then, a moment or two later and Nathan heard the door to his aunt's room pulled softly to, followed by the faint clicking of its lock. Evidently Vrancic had fastened it with the key.

Nathan congratulated himself: his ruse had worked! Vrancic had been deceived. Believing Nathan to be asleep in the room, he had now secured its door on the simulated form in Amelia's bed. All Nathan had to do now was wait.

And presently, advancing up the hallway, the steps approached again, slowly, almost stealthily. Nathan heard them pass the door to the linen closet (tramp-tramp-tramp), continue down the hall to the stairs, which then began once more to creak and groan as Vrancic softly descended them, step by step, to the lower floor. Moments later Nathan heard the low protracted rasping of the basement door hinges as the door itself was first drawn open, then pulled firmly to again. Vrancic (as hoped) had gone down once more into his lair—that netherworld of the basement.

Then, after what had seemed to Nathan the tardy, monotonous passage of several more interminable hours, the wait was at last over: he heard the muffled chimes of the clock in his aunt's bedroom strike midnight.

Upon the twelfth and final stroke, Nathan softly pushed open the door to the linen closet and furtively emerged from his place of concealment. For a moment or two he leant cautiously over the banister in the hallway and listened intently. But not even the tiniest whisper came up from the rooms below. A deathly stillness reigned throughout the house.

Then, with the flashlight in one hand, and his sneakers in the other, Nathan crept slowly down the stairs in his socks, fearful that even the quiet tread of his worn and dirty sneakers might somehow alert the sharp ears of Vrancic to his secret midnight exodus.

Once inside the foyer, Nathan slipped on his sneakers again, quickly tied their laces, and paused once more to listen; and as the pulsing heart behind his breastbone continued its skittery rhythm, its rapid, muffled *tump-thump, tump-thump* seemed instead to articulate, in Nathan's ears, the words, *Be quick: Be quick!*

For even as Nathan soundlessly drew open the front door, and was in the very act of slipping over its threshold, he thought he heard the heavy tread of Vrancic's feet ascending the basement steps. And for a solitary instant Nathan froze where he was, and stood aghast, wondering to himself whether some faint rumor of his flight had been detected by Vrancic after all. Had some creaking tread or riser on the stairs betrayed his stealthy descent, alerting Vrancic to his intended plan? Or, had Vrancic surmised or divined at the last minute some untoward purpose or resolution on the part of Nathan, and was now hastening up the basement stairs to verify his suspicions? Who can say? Certainly, Nathan did not linger another instant in the foyer to find out. In another moment he had quietly stepped across the threshold, shut to the door again, and, by the time Vrancic had opened the door to the basement, Nathan was already stealing, swift as a shadow, up the street to the hole in the cemetery's fence.

As Nathan hurried along, he observed that the night was dark— exceedingly dark; and almost it seemed to him that the heat in its windless, sultry air was as disagreeably close and uncomfortable as that of the day's. Moreover, upon glancing up once or twice into the warm inky darkness, Nathan could not help but note that high overhead neither the moon's expanding crescent, nor a single glittering star were anywhere to be seen.

For on this night the August skies were utterly hidden by towering masses of black and dingy-colored vapors which seemed to stretch away on all sides in a single vast unbroken roof. And away in the distance, on the other side of the cemetery, Nathan caught the frequent gleam and flicker of pale summer lightning, while ever and again there broke out a faint and far-off peal of echoing thunder. And Nathan knew at once that a storm was imminent.

For in the hot, sticky air he could scent the distinct odor of coming rain. And the smell of the clustering leaves and clambering vines along the cemetery fence, as well as the moist earth and mold of the graves was not to be mistaken.

Arrived before the vine- and ivy-veiled slit in the fence's loose mesh, Nathan turned slightly sideways, as though poised to thrust one leg through the shaggy growth to the other side and then slip the rest of himself in after, when all at once he paused. Quite suddenly a curious feeling of heaviness and oppression had whelmed over him; and presently, with his resolve and enthusiasm for the venture swiftly beginning to flag within him, Nathan remained standing where he was in an agony of doubt and indecision. For all at once an acute thrill of guilt, a poignant surge of shame and remorse seemed to flood the very recesses of his heart at the thought of deliberately breaking his promise to Phebe.

And for the breath of an instant, in a hushed and quieting moment of the rain-scented gloom, almost it seemed to Nathan that, as a sudden breeze stole hurrying and whispering through the foliage mantling the cemetery fence, in it, very faintly, he could just distinguish the far-off, barely audible voice of Phebe anxiously appealing to him not to come to the old mausoleum tonight; to keep true to his word; and to return home.

But Nathan's curiosity, his desire to see, to know at last with absolute certainty if Phebe was indeed some monstrous revenant, one of the Undead, a Vampire, was not to be ignored, resisted, or suppressed. He must satisfy this tormenting inquisitiveness once and for all. And so, without another moment's delay, Nathan clicked on his flashlight, plunged through the aperture in the chain-link fence, and sped off along a row of granite tombstones across the tussocky, uneven ground of one neglected grave after another, making for the old mausoleum in as straight a line as he could.

But less than a dozen rows in from a narrow sunken road with shallow banks and broken-up blacktop, Nathan had to slacken his pace. And for a space of some seconds, in the midst of a maze-like cluster of late nineteenth-century family mausoleums and Victorian-era statues, he paused in doubt and confusion about the path. For in the haste and excitement of his flight he had lost in the darkness all sense of direction.

And as Nathan began to glance anxiously about himself, he suddenly observed, by a flash or two of feeble lightning, the figure of a man running in a half-bent posture along a row of graffiti-covered statues and marble spires. It was only the merest glimpse, for the figure quickly slipped behind a nearby mausoleum. But for the solitary instant in which Nathan saw the man, he had noted that his long hair was pulled back in a ponytail and the shirt he wore had gaping rents all in the back.

As to who the man was or what he was doing at that hour inside the cemetery, Nathan had no time to consider. He merely bolted off in the opposite direction to which that mysterious figure had run, and, after one or two wrong turns, eventually regained his bearings.

Hurrying once more over the sunken and half-sunken graves, Nathan rushed almost breathlessly now along huddled row upon huddled row of flat granite markers that were nearly flush with the ground.

Now, about halfway out towards the old mausoleum, as the thunder crashed and rolled in a series of long-drawn, hollow boomings, Nathan felt the first drops of rain begin to fall in a thin warm drizzle on his face and hands. But no sooner had the thunder trembled away again into a hushed and windless quiet, than the rain, too, had all but ceased, and only faint and vaporous gleams of lightning continued to soundlessly flicker away in the distance among the heaped-up clouds darkening the outskirts of the cemetery's old section. And Nathan knew that the storm was merely idling, loitering there; and that the thunder he kept hearing, and the lightning he kept seeing were in truth a kind of prelude, precursors heralding the storm's tardy yet ominous approach.

And presently, as Nathan continued to hasten on his way, he began to notice fireflies, in unusually large numbers, aimlessly flitting, hovering, and revolving here and there, about the graves. Two or three times he darted past large clusters of them thickly studding the parched grass, or the fallen marker of a sunken grave. And several times he was compelled to greatly reduce the speed of his pace and, with his eyes and mouth tightly closed, move on softly through a dense cloud of dozens upon dozens of these insects, so thickly did they swarm in the air among the funereal sculptures and huddling monuments, while the phosphorous glare emitted from their abdomen flashed and gleamed with a curiously bright luminescence.

And suddenly Nathan realized that he was now seeing what he had once heard his father inform him about, but which he himself (until now) had never before witnessed—an assembly, or congregation (as his father had called it) of fireflies. For many years ago Nathan's father had told him that when he was a young man in his late teens, he had once seen these insects mass together one night, shortly after dusk, in his backyard, and there on the leaves and stalks of every plant, shrub, and bush they lingered for long intervals, shimmering and glowing with a strangely intense light. He did not know why they came there, whether for migration, or some other secret purpose, but he was sure, he told Nathan, that it was a great conference; and he had the feeling that something of considerable importance to their community must have been debated there. And it was just such an "assembly" which Nathan felt quite certain he was now witnessing.

But once this still-vivid memory from his early youth had played itself out in his mind, and Nathan's thoughts drew away once more to the old mausoleum, he looked up with a sudden start and, all in an instant, became fully conscious that he had already reached it. For there, all but a dozen paces distant from him, stood the old vine- and ivy-enshrouded edifice itself.

But what had caused Nathan to visibly start, to stand there utterly still now, and gaze on at it in astonishment and wonder, were the myriads upon myriads of fireflies that were thickly distributed in shining motionless clusters all over the aged structure's embowering foliage. Indeed, the shaggy vines and ivy depending over its entrance, clinging to its sloped roof, and clambering about its stone walls, were literally ablaze and coruscating all over with the strange aureate gleam of these insects.

And as Nathan stared with mouth agape and eyes round and wide, he saw that among this assembly of innumerable fireflies there were some that burned with an all but steady and exceptionally brilliant glare, while others glowed with a light which one moment increased and the next decreased in its luminescence. And like tiny constellations in the heavens, multitudes of them revolved and flitted aimlessly with a slow and languid flight now up, now down the broad shallow steps to the old mausoleum.

And Nathan thought to himself, here, then, was that rare sight, that infrequent occasion, of which his father had spoken when these wonderful insects assemble for some unknown purpose in one place to display with unusual splendor their phosphorous lanterns. But why here—why now? he wondered. But just then, Nathan recalled the Star of Bethlehem, whose wondrous fires had blazed across the heavens portending the nativity of the Savior, while at the same time guiding the Three Wise Men to the place of the Holy Infant's birth. And he could not help but compare the mystical radiance of that celestial beacon in some bizarre way to the phosphorescent fires of these insects which seemed now to be shining a guiding light for *him* to the very doors of the old mausoleum; as if illuminating for him the way *to*, as well as the place and hour *of*, Phebe's nativity among the accursed fellowship of the Undead.

And presently, as Nathan continued to stare at the incandescent light emitted by these insects as they flitted and swarmed about, or clung motionless for long intervals to, the mantling foliage of the old mausoleum, he began to experience something like a very strange and singular confusion of mind from its glare. For it seemed to exorcise a powerful and peculiar attraction over him.

And all at once Nathan began to feel not unlike the hapless insect that has been suddenly bewildered and seduced by a brightly burning light. For just like the doomed and unfortunate insect that is unable to avert its eyes from that alluring glow as it rushes through the air, hovering nearer, revolving round and round it, until its wings at last are scorched, so now Nathan drew nearer, still nearer to the old mausoleum, whose exterior, veiled as it was in a thick shroud of ivy and vines, seemed to be refulgent now with its own ghostly incandescence.

Then, having paused for a full minute or two on the structure's bottommost step, Nathan remained standing there motionless, as though lost in a tranced and helpless fascination, merely staring on at the most eerie and enchanting scene he had ever yet beheld. And all the while, that strange and steady glare emitted by the numberless masses of fireflies cast upon his silent face so cadaverous a gleam, that his complexion looked as pale and lifeless now as that of any vampire's.

Slowly, soundlessly, then, one by one, Nathan climbed steadily up the weed-grown steps to the old mausoleum; and, after briefly pausing for the second time, he stole a step or two cautiously nearer to its narrow entrance. Meanwhile, his pondering eyes had become intently fixed on the leaves and stems to the curtaining vines overhanging the mausoleum's doors: so heavily spangled were they, he noted, with such dense clusters of fireflies. And because these huddling insects remained so utterly still, and gave out, individually, a light of all but steadily dazzling brilliance, almost it seemed to Nathan's eyes that the mausoleum's entry was literally screened with a swaying drape of phosphorescent fire.

And as Nathan continued to stand there, very stiff and very still, eyeing this refulgent curtain for a moment or two somewhat doubtfully and uneasily, he suddenly heard behind it an odd supping or slurping sound coming from *inside* the old mausoleum. This was accompanied, ever and again, by a faint shuffling or scrabbling noise, and the low hollow mumbling of a sinister voice.

The muffled beating of Nathan's heart now thumped and jerked with fearful expectation, and an awful and unendurable misgiving began to quicken deep within him. Once or twice he tried to call out Phebe's name, but he found himself unable to produce with his voice even so much as the breath of a whisper, for his dry lips would scarcely stir, and the parched tongue in his mouth lay stiff and useless.

Again Nathan had softly stolen a pace or two forward, and again he stayed his steps to listen intently, his large brown eyes fixed anxiously straight in front of him on the mausoleum's entrance. Then, as the somewhat apprehensive expression that had crept into his features deepened into genuine alarm, "Phebe... Phebe..." his voice, faint and quavering, managed at last to breathe out, "...are you in there?" For nearly a full minute he waited on, listening; his motionless eyes still fastened on the entrance to the mausoleum.

And presently, almost it seemed to Nathan that the very air round about the old mausoleum had suddenly thickened, and the night's darkness had intensified. A peal of thunder, low and hollow, having succeeded a protracted flicker of lightning, again emptied itself into the night's deep stillness; and in the instant before the next flash of lightning and its subsequent growl of thunder, Nathan, saucer-eyed and open-mouthed, prepared once more to utter the sound of Phebe's name.

But even as the first familiar syllable perched itself on the tip of Nathan's tongue, he gulped back his breath with a violent start, for all at once, a vast sheet of intensely brilliant lightning had appeared almost directly overhead. With a ghostly lurid glare it illuminated not only the louring masses of blue-black storm clouds, thick-piled in the thundery heights above him, but every detail of the weed-tousled graves, huddling marble tombstones, and decaying stone monuments round about him for as far as the eye could see.

And Nathan stood there all but cringing with half-shut eyes, bracing himself in anticipation of the ear-splitting crash of thunder he presumed would follow. But neither sharp crackling peal nor low sustained rumble succeeded it: instead, a concentrated hush seemed to have immeasurably deepened over the entire cemetery.

And then, in the same instant that Nathan at last let his breath go, slowly exhaling with a faint sigh, the oppressive silence, thick and heavy and deep as deepest December snow, was suddenly broken by that same voice, low and cold and dreadfully cruel, coming once more from inside the old mausoleum. And Nathan's ears fastened on its every unsettling word, as he distinctly heard it say: "Did I not tell you—promise you!—that in a week's time you and I would meet again? That I would have your blood, and that I would draw the very life from—" But just then, thunder broke out again with a heavy muttering rumble, and the voice was swallowed up in the prolonged reverberation that seemed to continue for at least half a minute.

Notwithstanding this, Nathan felt his flesh crawl and the hair upon his head stir: for that frightful voice, the cruelty of those gloating words, brought with them something utterly chilling to his heart.

All but past the ability to either move or speak, Nathan continued to stand there, shivering now from head to toe, and, in his steadily growing dread, to pray under his breath, "Oh, please, God, please don't let Phebe be a vampire! Please, God, please!" And all the while he repeated those words to himself, his will continued to hover in an anguish of hesitation. He did not know whether to move forward and cross the threshold of those doors, or turn round and flee as fast as his shaky legs would carry him back to the safety of his home.

But after several long, agonizing moments, with an icy sweat beginning to break out all over his face and limbs, Nathan made at last his fateful choice. For upon mustering with an effort what was left of his fast-dwindling courage, he had moved a pace or two cautiously forward toward the living veil of luminous foliage thickly depending over the mausoleum's entrance. There, however, for a moment or two he breathlessly paused to quickly fetch from the pocket of his jeans first the Romanian rosary with its Maltese crucifix of bloodstone, then the little cruet of blessed holy water.

For all at once a tremor of deadly fear had crept softly, coldly over Nathan's quivering heart as the conviction grew very rapidly within him that he was about to look upon something truly appalling, horrific; and for the next few moments Nathan scarcely dared to move or breathe. But then, reaching out his arm, he held his breath, and then slipped the fingers of a cold and trembling hand deep into the tangled, insect-laden vines.

Feeling himself turn cold all over now, Nathan began to softly part the dense growth of this refulgent curtain. As he did so, many of the fireflies rose from the disturbed and trembling leaves, and began to flit aimlessly about his eyes, faintly brushing in their slow flight across his nose, cheeks, brow, and chin. He shuddered at the strange, unpleasant sensation, as the intensely glowing insects rained, light as thistle-down, against the skin of his face, filling his nostrils with the distasteful and (in many ways) repellent phosphorous odor that they emit.

Then, peering anxiously in through the narrow gap he had made in the curtain of vines, Nathan saw that just beyond it one of the doors to the mausoleum was slightly ajar. Softly—slowly—his heart quaking with fear and anticipation, he drew the door open an inch or two still further; edged his way in past the vines; then, over the threshold; and in a moment he was inside, standing just past the doors.

Immediately his nostrils were assailed by a horrid stench of blood so overwhelming to the senses that it choked his breath: it was as though he had crossed the threshold to a slaughterhouse. Revolting nausea instantly rose within him, so that he had to stoop his head and avert his face to refrain from retching.

But upon quickly recovering himself, and his breath, Nathan tightened his grip on the flashlight (which had nearly fallen from his clammy grasp) and, bracing himself with an effort, aimed its cone-shaped beam straight in front of him into the nebulous gloom of the tomb's interior.

And this is what Nathan saw.

Squatting in the very middle of the narrow floor, illuminated quite vividly now by the combined gleam from Nathan's flashlight and the pale steady glare of the lightning that was just then flaring in through the small stained-glass window set high in the rear wall of the mausoleum, was the figure of Phebe. Her pale naked arms were clasped tightly about the recumbent and convulsing half-naked form of Russell Gorman, and, like some carnivorous beast of prey, she had the teeth of her slavering mouth fixed in the flesh of his throat. She kept straining him to her bosom and eagerly sucking the blood from one of several grisly wounds in his neck with long-drawn muffled grunts and sighs. Blood spattered her to the sockets of her eyes, both of which remained fast-shut as she continued, with deep breaths through quivering nostrils, to simultaneously ingest her victim's blood while inhaling its scent as though in a kind of gruesome sanguinary ecstasy.

Moreover, Nathan observed four other prostrate bodies (one or two shoeless and shirtless, and another utterly without clothing) lying sprawled to one side across the floor. Phebe (he conjectured) must have already glutted herself on their blood, for they lay in varying contorted postures and attitudes without the least sign of movement or life.

Quite suddenly, then, Nathan noticed that there was still one other: the figure of a young boy lying slumped in a corner toward the rear of the mausoleum. He was bound with duct tape about the wrists and ankles, and struggling violently to free himself, as he helplessly awaited the same ghastly fate as that of Russell Gorman and the others.

Nathan could not distinguish the child's face clearly, for its lower half was all but wound about with layers of duct tape to prevent any outcries from escaping its lips, but he thought the young features resembled those of the boy Tippy, who he had seen inside Nick and Andy's Stationary store about a week ago.

As if spellbound with horror, Nathan's gaze fixed itself once more on the figure of Russell Gorman. And in the very same instant the shut eyes unsealed themselves a moment, encountered Nathan's pleadingly and, from the pale, dry lips of the straining mouth, a voice, weak and hoarse, faintly issued in a half-choked sob, "Help me... please, Nathan... please... help... me..."

At this horrifying sight, icy shiver upon icy shiver ran frigidly along Nathan's backbone. His jaw dropped again and again, and the lips of his mouth kept vainly working to produce a shriek, a squeal—a gasp!—from his all but paralyzed lungs. But shock and revulsion at what he was now witnessing had virtually asphyxiated him with terror, and he could scarcely catch his breath.

Indeed it was as if dismay and deadly fright had brought upon Nathan a violent illness, for all at once he felt weak and aching and a profound physical nausea. He wanted to turn and flee, but it seemed as if his whole body had become as cold, inert, and heavy as stone. And the surge of numbing horror that now swept through his shuddering heart froze the very blood in his veins. His knees kept shaking uncontrollably beneath him; and he felt the power to stand was fast beginning to leave him, and that he must soon collapse and drop in a quivering heap upon the floor.

Perhaps it was no more than a single minute, perhaps only several seconds that Nathan actually stood there gazing on in horror at this grisly and terrifying scene. Who can say with any certainty? For any and all sense of the passage of time was temporarily suspended, obliterated as far as Nathan was concerned; and he might well have been standing there hours, years, *centuries!* So immense was the sensation of terror he now experienced that it had swept him beyond himself into what seemed an eternal nightmare in some timeless limbo.

At length, however, choking with pure terror, Nathan contrived at last to breathe out in a half-stammered, whispering gasp—"O, Phebe, I know... I know the truth now... you really are a... a Vampire!"

Instantly Phebe's eyes opened, and, weirdly reflecting the beam of Nathan's flashlight with a terrifying beast-like gleam, they fixed themselves fiercely on Nathan's startled face. And Nathan, feeling sick, faint, and deadly frightened, literally quailed before the gaze of those glaring eyes and the dreadful expression of intense hatred that was in them.

Back—back—shrank Nathan, slowly, breathlessly; and as he stumbled, in this awkward, unsteady backward manner of retreat, against the half-open door to the mausoleum's entrance, a furious storm of horror, revulsion, and panic broke out all at once within him. He gave vent, then, to the sudden shriek of unmitigated terror that all the while had been steadily gathering, lost his footing as he staggered out across the threshold, and felt the flashlight slip from the trembling grasp of his chilled and clammy fingers.

At the same time, Phebe straightened herself and let the convulsing body of Russell Gorman drop to the floor. An instant later and she was bounding towards Nathan with her blood-smeared lips drawn back in a hideous snarling grin, revealing to him, in both the upper and lower row of her teeth, a series of large, prominent, gruesome fangs.

But somehow, before she reached him, Nathan, in having stumbled backward over the mausoleum's entrance and beyond its doors again, did something that even astonished himself. Either acting under the merciful guidance of divine providence, or on the last residual impulse of his own swiftly-fading presence of mind, he had unstoppered the cruet of holy water, which was in the same hand whose trembling fingers clutched the rosary, and instantly sprinkled some of its contents in a thin unbroken line along the threshold.

All but in the same instant, Nathan's breath had failed him as, helplessly, motionlessly he watched Phebe rush headlong up to him, her pale blood-splotched arms outstretched before her, and her long, sharp-nailed fingers splayed claw-like for his throat. And for the next few seconds, with every muscle in his body tensed and stiffened, he remained cringing there, anticipating every moment the agonizing torture that would be his when first, those strangling fingers were tightly fastened round his neck, and next, those sharp fanged teeth were greedily fixed in the flesh of his throat.

But to his utter amazement and relief, there had come this strange arrest to Phebe's progress. Quite abruptly she had stayed her rushing steps at the mausoleum's wetted threshold and appeared unable to advance so much as the fraction of an inch past it! The holy water, acting like some invisible Angel's flaming sword, seemed to hold her in check, and impede her forward movement. And suddenly, with a shrill, heart-rending wail, she stood glowering across at Nathan, eyes ablaze in her head in a horrifying look of fiendish malice, her slavering lips frothing, and her long, pointed fangs champing savagely.

For the next instant or two, as Nathan remained standing on the other side of that threshold, limp, helpless, and deadly sick, his only sensations were nausea and vertigo. And with a cold and numbing shock of nightmare-terror, he gazed on stirlessly, out of eyes red-rimmed and weeping, at Phebe striding to and fro along the line of holy water, snarling, raging, glaring at him with a look of diabolic malevolence.

Then, sweat-soaked and trembling, Nathan staggered back yet a pace or two further, and paused with the faintly rustling curtain of foliage pressed up heavily against the back of his neck and head, and hanging in leafy tresses along his shoulders and down his back. With muffled sobs he replaced the stopper on the cruet of holy water, in which less than half of the blessed liquid remained, and slipped it into the pocket of his jeans.

Nathan was about to do the same with the rosary when, for a single solitary instant, his eyes for the first time confronted those of Phebe's steadily, unflinchingly; and horror and fear of so intense and nameless a kind whelmed suddenly over him that he shouted out in terror and hid his face in his hands. And between each half-choked and shuddering sob, he thought he heard his own low sniveling voice whispering wretchedly to himself again and again, "O, God.., it's true, it's all true... Phebe really is a Vam —"

But that last word, only half articulated, died—if indeed he had ever actually uttered it—upon Nathan's lips and was smothered away by a sudden crashing peal of thunder which seemed to shake the entire mausoleum to its very foundations.

And presently, in the succeeding hush and quiet, before the next booming peal, Nathan caught the sound of a voice—Phebe's, whispering softly, soothingly across to him. At first, however, the words, the sense of what she was saying, seemed all but lost on him, for his mind was in a tumult of hysteria and confusion. But then, as her voice continued to penetrate his dulled hearing, and to insinuate itself into the turmoil of his scattered thoughts, their restful, soporific phrases began at last to register: "It's true, Nathan... I can't be, and I'm not a vampire... So you needn't be afraid of me; not you... I promise, all that you desire, all that you lust for, I alone can give you... Only look at me, Nathan; look at me and all will be yours..."

There was an interval of silence; then, once again a heavy rumble of thunder seemed to rock the old mausoleum. Its reverberation continued across the entire cemetery, and before its last faint echo had emptied itself into the stilled and clouded darkness above the graves in the featureless distance, Nathan unwisely peered out between his fingers at Phebe. And the instant his eyes encountered hers, they were caught, ensnared, and immovably held.

Then, with the slowness and leisurely movement of one rapt in an ineffable dream, Nathan drew his fingers from his face, as though in obedience to some silent command—unspoken, yet nonetheless imparted—and continued to gaze straight before him into Phebe's deep, dark, dwelling eyes. Indeed he found himself suddenly powerless to look away or so much as glance at, toward, or into anything but those eyes. Then, all at once, Phebe's face seemed to alter. All its ferocity and fiendishness seemed to melt away, and a beguiling expression of peace and beneficence, more beautiful than in any human countenance, appeared in its bloodless features: an expression that was somehow more dangerous, more devilish than the awful look of venomous hate it had replaced. And very softly, very sweetly, then, in lilting tones, like that of some wonderful song or music, she said, "Draw near to me, Nathan... draw near, that I might take you in my arms."

And in some indescribable way, Phebe's alluring eyes, and the wheedling, seductive tones of her voice seemed to urge Nathan forward—forcibly. For both her voice and her eyes had a numbing effect, like an opiate, upon Nathan's senses, causing his very thoughts—save those of acceptance, compliance, surrender—to sink into a dulled and drowsing stillness. And in spite of all his efforts to resist them, Nathan was aware at the same time that a part of him wanted to yield, to submit with all delight, abandon, and utter willingness to their urging. And suddenly, as though lost in the wonderful ecstasy of some languorous daze, he stood, he stared, and slowly, irresistibly, recklessly began to move forward, step by step, towards Phebe.

No more than half a pace, however, had Nathan advanced when suddenly his foot stepped upon something that unsteadied him. He felt the rigid object uncomfortably through the sole of his sneaker. Was it a pebble, or a twig? he wondered, as he paused a moment to slightly shift his foot and glance down. And for an instant it startled him to discover that the thing upon which he had trod was actually the crucifix to the Romanian matanie, or rosary. Its string, he noted, had been broken, and the strand of beads wound away in an S-like configuration from its pendant with the crucifix to the very threshold of the mausoleum.

And for the brief space of one or two seconds, Nathan stood there thinking to himself that the rosary must have slipped and fallen from his fingers when he had covered his face with his hands. However it may, in actual fact, have come to be there, the mere sight of its crucifix seemed to rouse in him immediate resistance, and to break the awful spell which the potent gaze from Phebe's eyes had cast over him. For all at once the cold, numbing stupor, which seemed to have descended like a heavy, veiling cloud upon his brain, was instantly withdrawn, removed from his senses.

And when once more Nathan had lifted his frightened eyes to meet those of Phebe's, a sudden and horrible nausea again swept over him, for the features of her face had instantly convulsed and hardened into an abominable expression of hostility and cruel malice.

Unspeakably shocked and horrified, Nathan breathlessly, tremblingly stooped to recover the fallen chaplet of beads. But even as his cold, shaking fingers weakly fumbled to take up the crucifix, he heard Phebe's voice bellowing across at him in chilling tones of dreadful command, to let the cross lie where it was; to look again into her eyes; to draw still nearer and give himself into her waiting embrace.

By then, however, Nathan's small fingers were clenched tightly about the rosary's crucifix, and, with its dangling string of faintly fragrant beads, he had at last drawn it up from the floor. In the same instant, Phebe's voice, he noted, had perceptibly altered; a curious tremor had come into it: and, tinged now with a shade of unmistakable alarm, it seemed to have become pleading, almost beseeching.

Paying no heed to either her pleas or demands, Nathan raised and extended his arm, so that he was presently holding the crucifix directly in front of him, on a level with Phebe's eyes. At once he saw that the lips of her mouth began to writhe horribly, while across her face swept one spasm after another of fury, infernal hatred, and lastly, deadly cringing fear. Then, with a sudden convulsive twist of her whole body, Phebe turned to one side with a horrible litheness and recoiled, emitting, as she did so, frightful sounds as of mingled howling and low mournful sobbing.

Having by now fully regained his presence of mind, Nathan, meanwhile, thrust the rosary into the front pocket of his jeans and, struggling to catch his breath, staggered backwards through the curtaining foliage depending over the mausoleum's entrance. The night air, warm and breathless upon his face and limbs, seemed to rouse him to further action; for he turned at once and, in a single leaping stride, he descended the structure's three broad steps.

Then, without the least notion of where he was going, Nathan bolted off as fast as his aching, wobbly legs would carry him, dashing across the uneven ground of grave after grave. Abruptly from behind him, with something between a piercing screech and a long-drawn howl, Phebe's voice, carried shrilly through the windless dark, could be heard calling after him—"Naaathhaann!" Almost instantly, though, it ended in a kind of half-choked shriek as of mingled rage and agony.

Repressing a wild gathering shriek of dismay and terror himself, Nathan's own feeble voice kept emitting short, rapid whimpering breaths as he sped desperately forward, on, on, through the thickening stormy darkness of that August night. And even though his eyes were half blind with his own scalding tears, and his heart and lungs felt as though they must burst at any moment, he continued yet a while to run at full speed for some distance, never once slackening his pace. For a deep and nameless terror for himself, a sudden, nauseating conviction, really, that his very soul lay in danger urged him on.

At length, however, all but dizzy with exhaustion from the frenzied pace of his flight, he ventured at last to pause a few moments and recover his breath. His strength, he felt, was beginning to fail him, and, violently gasping and panting, he caught miserably at a nearby tombstone for support. The cloud-veiled sky above and the darkening, featureless graves of the cemetery seemed to be suddenly revolving around him—dissolving, melting away into the dreadful unreality of nightmare.

Turning his head, Nathan cast a terrified and protracted glance over his shoulder at the old mausoleum. In one and the same instant the night was rent in two by a lightning flash of searing brilliance. For a single solitary moment, that was somehow prolonged and extended, its flickering blaze, of a white-hot incandescence that was dazzling to the eye, seemed to illuminate the sky's thick-piled cloud-masses for miles around. Simultaneously a great and sudden wind swooped down across the graves, thick with dust and the brown parched leaves of forgotten autumns, and, roaring past Nathan with a few heavy, scattered raindrops, swayed to one side the dense foliage that veiled the mausoleum's entrance.

And for that one moment, Nathan, still gazing across, as though caught in some frightful trance, saw that the doors to the mausoleum were now thrust wide open and, poised upon its threshold, stooping slightly forward, was the blood-spattered figure of Phebe! The long black tresses of her hair were uplifted on the wind and floating in writhing coils about her head like the gruesome snaky locks of some horrifying Gorgon. Fireflies, like a shower of glowing sparks scattered from the roaring flames of some outdoor blaze, were ascending into the air, hovering and revolving in slow and languid flight all around her, as she glared furiously across at Nathan, the eyes smoldering wildly from the hollows of her blood-speckled face.

And almost it seemed to Nathan as if all passage of time had gone into complete abeyance, as the gleaming lightning continued to flit dazzlingly all around the plant-enshrouded old mausoleum. But then, all in a moment, the night's inky blackness flowed back again, completely blotting out the least glimpse or hint of Phebe, the old vine-embowered structure, and the cemetery's surrounding graves and monuments. Only swarms of fireflies, like a myriad of glinting sparks afloat in the air, were to be seen.

Notwithstanding this, Nathan remained still as the tombstone to which he yet clung, gazing on over his shoulder toward the old mausoleum. Through his mind rushed one frightening supposition after another—What if Phebe had somehow slipped across the mausoleum's threshold? What if she had made it outside and, even now, was stealing, wolf-like on hands and knees, across the darkened graves towards him? What if this very minute she was lurking, prowling somewhere close by in the fearful gloom, regarding him, preparing to lunge open-mouthed at him, like some ravenous beast upon its prey?

But even as the blood in Nathan's veins ran cold as ice water at these and several other nightmare scenarios produced by his fevered imagination, he suddenly started and caught his breath. For across the gloomy space between himself and the old mausoleum came a solitary blood-curdling wail. In it Nathan detected a distinct note of frustration and seething anger, as if Phebe was in the extremity of a towering rage at finding herself powerless to slip across the decaying tomb's threshold.

And the longer Nathan stood there, the more conscious he became of the fact that Phebe was still confined, restricted to the interior of the old mausoleum. The holy water that he had dashed across its threshold proved to be for her as impassable as a barrier of towering flames, making any pursuit of him impossible.

With this realization Nathan was at last overcome by all that he had witnessed and endured. Revulsion and physical nausea swept up into his throat. And as he was racked with gagging and his belly churned with vileness, he stooped his face past the surface of the marble tombstone's smooth, flat top, and began vomiting what little he had in him into the coarse grass and clumping weeds behind it.

Then, violently shaking in every limb, his face drained of all color, Nathan wearily straightened himself. Once again, from within the old mausoleum, a dreadful howling broke out, but this time it was instantly swallowed up in a clap of thunder that was like the ear-splitting crack of a lash. And scarcely a second had passed when the storm, which for some while now had been crawling at a snail's pace across the old All Faiths cemetery, paused full overhead, and a tumult of lightning, thunder, roaring wind, and sheeted rain surged down without warning from its clamoring heart.

In a blind and heedless panic, Nathan stood for the first instant or two utterly without either thought or motion. So overwhelmed was he by fear, shock, and confusion that he felt as though both his mind and his body had been suddenly converted into lifeless stone. But as his horribly fuddled wits cleared a little, and the power to think and act was restored to him, he turned hastily to bolt off in aimless flight again into the darkness of the storm, or at least scout round for some kind of nearby shelter from its tearing gusts and torrential rain.

Leaning into the wind and lashing rain, then, with his head bent low, Nathan had taken no more than two or three steps forward when, without a moment's heed, he crashed into something rigid and unyielding. That same instant, a quivering stream of bluefork lightning split the darkness between earth and sky like the bright steel blade of a sword. In starkest detail all the surrounding graves and monuments were revealed with a ghostly blue-white glare, and a deafening crash of thunder burst immediately overhead. On and on, with a slow, steady rumble, it rolled away into the distances until every mausoleum in the cemetery seemed to bellow back its echoing peal.

Nathan, meanwhile, had staggered back a pace or two, his senses all but stunned, as he raised his eyes to see what, in his flight, he had collided into. And full in the lightning's quivering flare, illuminating his pallid and partially disfigured face beneath the slanted, dripping brim of his black hat, he stood gazing up into the luminous black eyes of Antal Vrancic.

For a solitary fearful instant he seemed, in Nathan's frightened eyes, anything but human—rather a diabolic creature of some fiendish elemental strain which, by some bizarre kinship of nature, belonged to the tempest itself. For the glare of the levin-bolt seemed to magnify his stature so that he all but loomed, Goliath-like, over Nathan, peering down at him from some lofty height; and the wind, in flapping in and swelling out his dark clothes, made it seem to Nathan as though he were robed about in the gloomy vapors of a bellying storm cloud.

All around Nathan now the large heavy drops of rain, filling the air like innumerable beads of glass-clear crystal agleam with the lightning, fell so fast and so heavily that everything, except the tall, darkly clad menacing figure before him, was hidden from sight. And in the sudden lull of the wind and thunder, Nathan heard Vrancic's deep, astringent voice snarl down at him: "You deceitful little bastard of a fool!" And the cruel, sinister eyes, fixed in a deadening stare upon Nathan's face, glittered with a hatred and malevolence as infernal as that in any vampire's.

A sudden shriek burst, then, from Nathan's lips, but was instantly drowned by a crackling explosion of thunder. And as Nathan abruptly turned in a desperate attempt to flee, a hand, like a vice of steel, caught him by the arm. Before, however, he could so much as yelp, a second hand seized him with violence by the scruff of his neck, and Nathan felt himself dragged forcibly back into, and against, Vrancic's tall stooping frame. Then, leaning his face down low next to Nathan's, Vrancic's dreadful voice cut through the tumult of the storm in a tigerish growl against the boy's ear: "If I could have my way I would drag you right back to the mausoleum and let your lovely Phebe drain every drop of your worthless blood!"

Nathan, meanwhile, frantically squirmed and writhed, struggling, like an animal caught in a snare, wretchedly, hopelessly, uselessly to free himself from the unyielding grasp of those large powerful hands that now clutched both of his arms so fiercely from behind. Again and again Nathan screamed, like a defenseless rabbit trapped by its prey. But Vrancic only bent and twisted his slender arms all the more violently until Nathan wept with the intensity of the pain, and thought that both his arms must any moment now come out of their sockets. "Get off me! Let me go!" he shouted between whimpering, tearful sobs. But the more Nathan pleaded, the louder he sobbed, the more delightedly Vrancic laughed in his ear. "I would gladly let you go;" he cruelly sneered; "and afterwards do a great deal more to you; but I must fulfill a promise, and do as I have been asked."

And suddenly, spasms of pain, one after another, shot convulsing through every nerve and bone in Nathan's body as Vrancic struck him several sharp numbing blows on the back of his head and neck. For a brief time, then, everything was swept from Nathan's sight, and the storm's incessant bellowing seemed to become part of the roaring dizziness within his own throbbing skull. At last, however, the night, with all its shocks and horrors, overcame his senses and exhausted nerves, and from this point on, all the anguish of his experiences seemed to become no more real to him than that endured in an evil dream.

For all at once Nathan had the curious impression that the earth had dropped away from under his feet and pitched itself upward with searing pain into the side of his face. A thousand Perseid-like meteor showers ignited the darkness into which he felt himself plunged; and when once more the lids of his eyes had raised themselves, he found he was no longer standing upright on his feet, but lying stiff and cold upon his back in a miry patch of ground. His clothes were sopping wet, and he was squinting up, through a steady shower of cold spattering rain, at the roiling canopy of storm clouds. A dense moldy smell of the wet grass and sodden earth of the graves reeked up into the air around him, stealing heavily over his senses, and filling him with revolting nausea.

Vaguely, then, Nathan was aware of Vrancic's inhuman face bending over his, the black luminous eyes gloating on at him, the thin pale lips hideously grinning. And Nathan watched, dumb with horror, as those awful sneering lips began slowly to writhe, and their monstrously oversized maw to produce a series of muffled words in an unspeakably dreadful voice. But no matter how intently Nathan listened, or how hard he strove to catch their meaning, for some reason, they conveyed little if any significance to him.

The only thing Nathan knew with any certainty at present was that the booming thunder was fainting further and further into the distance, and the rain, having thinned now to a few scattered drops, fell with scarcely more than a steady quieting hush.

Slowly, painfully, then, Nathan turned his head to peer across at the old mausoleum. But it seemed it had withdrawn itself in that instant to an infinite distance across the cemetery. And as he suddenly recollected just *who,* or *what,* had been confined to its interior, covered in the gore of her victims, pacing savagely to and fro along its threshold with the sole deadly purpose of slipping across to feast on his blood, the terror of his fevered mind renewed itself to its former pitch. He heard his own faint voice contrive to whisper the sound of Phebe's name, only to break suddenly away into sobs of panic and dismay, as he muttered again and again, "She's a vampire... she's a vampire..."

Then, as though obeying a sudden, irresistible impulse, Nathan's trembling hands fumbled desperately at the pockets of his jeans to produce the rosary and little cruet of holy water. But even as he managed at last to feebly draw them out, Vrancic immediately snatched them roughly from his grasp and, with a fierce curse, struck him twice across the mouth. The hand with which he struck him must have had on one of its fingers that strange, diabolical ring, for Nathan felt a sharp, stinging pain in his upper lip and front tooth from its thick metal band.

Very swiftly, then, over Nathan's motionless limbs a horrifying numbness began to spread itself. While, through the stillness that was gathering slowly over his steadily darkening mind, he sensed, rather than felt, somewhere about him, the soft yet icy touch of Phebe's cold, death-like hands, and heard the sound of her voice breathe all but gloatingly into his ear, "I have you, Nathan... I have you."

CHAPTER SEVEN

"...Dreadful is the woe you bid me recall,
For it renews the sad remembrance of my fate:
All that I saw, and part of which I was
...But if your longing is so great to know
how calamity befell me,
Though my spirit shudders at the remembrance
and recoils in pain,
I will tell you of that fatal night..."

—*The Aeneid*

Although Nathan's eyes were fast shut, and he felt himself sinking slowly, irresistibly into a vast and empty darkness, it seemed to him that he never once lost consciousness. For he was distinctly aware that his body had been gently lifted and was being carried through the windy gloom of the cemetery. At one point, he even had the curious impression that the shambling pace of his bearer had broken into a steady run, for he could feel himself borne along now still swiftlier.

But then, quite suddenly, Nathan began to experience a strange, dreadful sense of unreality, so that he could be sure of nothing very clearly anymore. Subsequent to this, a darkness, dense and chill, like the wooliness of a sea-fog, steadily spread itself over his scarcely conscious brain. And presently, out of the stillness and apprehension of an impending swoon, he heard his own anguished voice calling out the familiar sound of a solitary word—"Phebe..."

After that it was some while before Nathan knew or said anything more.

At last, however, with the slow, gradual return to full consciousness, Nathan awoke out of the peace and forgetfulness of a deep and deathlike sleep. And without so much as stirring a finger, he continued to lie for some while yet with his eyes shut, merely listening, in a curiously rapt hush and delicious languor, to the faint gurgling of the rain in the gutters of the house.

For Nathan was all but certain that, every now and again, there came welling up out of the rain's steady cluck and babble, the clear silvery tones of a beguiling voice calling his name. And once or twice he thought he had heard, in a quiet, tranquil whisper breathed against his ear, the familiar sound of *another* name, preceded each time by the words, *"It's me... It's me..."* As though they were the initial phrases to a sweet refrain in some enchanting childhood nursery rhyme.

Then, all at once, Nathan was aware that somewhere about him (or so it seemed) there was a quiet stir of movement: for upon his face and hands he felt the cool gentle touches, faint and refreshing, of small delicate fingers; and a soft yet chill breath fanned his cheek. In almost the same instant, the lips from which that breath had issued pressed his own—lips colder than the deadliest cold in the dark of a winter's night. And yet, how like the heat at the heart of a burning flame the kiss from those lips seemed to kindle his blood.

At once Nathan knew that it was Phebe who was kissing him as though, from some inverted fairy tale, she were the wakeful Beauty rousing him, the Sleeping Prince, from his enchanted slumber with lips bearing the sweetest of magical kisses. Softly, then, those trembling lips withdrew, and the kisser's potent yet tender presence all but distanced itself as his body slightly stirred and his lips strove to utter but one word. For a moment or two they faltered; but then, all at once, he thought they had contrived at last to articulate, in the drowsiest of whispers, the two syllables of that solitary word—"Vampire".

And at the pronunciation of that loathsome term, Nathan felt a sudden, slow protracted shudder pass through his entire body. With a faint groan, he turned his head a little; and for several moments his fingers groped along the side of his face, which ached as from a severe blow. Then, once again, in a solemn, drowsy breath, the two syllables of a solitary word escaped his straining lips: "Phebe." And all at once, that same delightful voice whispered against his ear: "I'm here, Nathan; I'm here."

And presently, Nathan's eyelids lifted, and he found himself gazing intently out of his still brown eyes into the pale, stainless, dreamlike loveliness of Phebe's face, her lips fixed in a languid, pitying, wistful smile. For a fleeting instant Nathan had the dreamlike impression that Phebe was smiling down into his eyes as he reclined on his aunt's best comforter on the floor of the old mausoleum.

"O, Phebe," he began, "I—I was having the weirdest, scariest dream just now" (and his voice slightly trembled as he tried to repress a shudder) "and I think you were in it, and... and there was blood"—a longish pause came, and the look of perplexity that had crept into Nathan's face slowly gave way now to one of alarm—"blood everywhere, be—because you turned into..." But all at once Nathan broke off to catch his breath, and then, half-faintly, half-fearfully whisper, "a vampire."

Quite suddenly then, Nathan's gaze fastened itself in growing apprehension on the deep, dark lustrous eyes in Phebe's face, into whose shadowy depths suddenly appeared a forlorn expression of infinite sorrow. And in the same instant a curtain seemed to raise itself from the arena of his mind—as full remembrance of the night's all too real and terrifying events returned to him in stark flashes of hideously vivid detail.

Shocked and horrified, Nathan sprang to his feet in a single bound of breathless panic and shrank away from Phebe in dread and deadly loathing. For a moment or two he stood aghast in a still and wretched helplessness, all speech smothered by confusion, all sight nearly blinded by fear.

And for a space of some seconds, Nathan continued to gaze across at Phebe with as horrified an expression as when he watched her from the entrance to the old mausoleum greedily supping Russell Gorman's blood from a grisly wound in his throat. At the same time, a very singular point of fact began gradually to dawn upon him. That the four bleak walls about him with their curtained windows, the low ceiling above him of time-yellowed stucco, and the faded sofa off which he had just now leaped, were all familiarly depressing components of the small, drafty living room in his aunt's house. And with that he ultimately came to recognize that he was, at present, standing in that very room together with Phebe, and not (as he had initially thought) inside the old mausoleum.

Nathan realized, too, in all but the same instant, that besides himself and Phebe, there were two other occupants in the room. For only a few paces behind Phebe, standing in the very center of room, loomed the gaunt, forbidding figure of Antal Vrancic in (characteristically) ominous silence. While off to his left, just within the entrance to the room, lurked the diminutive (yet no less menacing) presence of the hermaphrodite child, Candy, with his thin ruddy lips fixed in a peculiarly sinister sneer.

Dumb with horror and revulsion, Nathan continued to stand there glancing very rapidly now from Phebe's face to Vrancic's, then to Candy's and back again to Phebe's. And the whole time he gazed on, speechlessly, at them, he was acutely conscious that he in turn was being closely regarded and steadily watched by those three pairs of shrewd, intently dwelling eyes.

And almost it seemed to Nathan that, for a while, an intenser silence had suddenly fallen between the four of them, broken now and again by the few heavy drops of rain that pattered against the windows, as occasional showers continued to skirt the house. For the most part, however, the storm, he noted, with its clamoring thunder, had drawn away into the distance, and could be heard now as little more than a fainting rumor of sullen rumbles.

Now, for what seemed the slow passage of many dull hours-although in actuality it was scarcely more than half a minute—Nathan neither spoke nor stirred. Indeed, standing there, speechless and in so spellbound a stillness, he was all but certain that Phebe and her two sinister companions must hear not only the thick convulsive beating of his lurching heart, but the desperate to and froing of every fearful thought in his aching head.

But then, Phebe, he thought, with parted lips, suddenly sighed and, watching his face out of mournful eyes that brimmed now with deep anxiety, she moved a step or two nearer to him. In the faintest of whispers, she breathed out to him the sound of his name, and was silent for a little. Then, while she was in the midst of telling him how truly sorry she was for everything he'd seen and undergone earlier this night, quite suddenly, from behind her, there broke out a prolonged miaowing, interrupting her. A moment later, and here was Ichabod, his cat, aka (as Vrancic appropriately enough had renamed him)Bram.

In a slinking, casual strut, with his tail standing straight up in the air, that traitorous feline came sauntering into the room. And as Nathan's startled eyes strayed for a single instant from Phebe to the cat, he saw at once that the scruffy beast's fur was sodden through and through with the rain. Apparently he had been out in the storm for quite some while, much the same as himself (thought Nathan).

And as the faithless brute rubbed its oversized head against the long legs of its new master (Vrancic), Nathan suddenly recollected his own skin and clothing having been no less thoroughly soaked with the rain than the cat's fur. And yet, how was it, he wondered, that he could now feel himself, from top to toe, as dry and warm as the clothes he had on. A swift glance, then, over the shirt and jeans he now wore instantly revealed to him that they were not the same ones he'd been wearing in his flight to the cemetery earlier this night. Evidently, someone had taken the liberty, during the time he had been unconscious, to remove his wet clothes and sneakers, and dress him again in dry ones. Even his hair, he noted, as he drew his fingers through his scattered locks, had been towel-dried, then brushed and combed so that there was scarcely any moisture in it.

But then, at the sudden sound of light steps advancing softly towards him, and the faint touch of a frigid hand, lighter than thistle-down, laid gently upon his arm, Nathan visibly started. Instantly his panic-stricken eyes fixed themselves once more on Phebe's face. To his utter horror, he found her standing quietly close up against him with her lean cold hand clasped tightly in his own. His eyes opened round and wide in deadly fright, and, with something between a low gasp and a shuddering sob, he instinctively recoiled, as if her mere touch were scalding to him.

Then, drawing back a pace or two further from her, "I s-saw you... in-in th-the old mausoleum... t-tonight;" his anguished stammering voice broke out; "and there were bodies in there with you—*dead* bodies!" And for a moment Nathan paused to draw a long tremulous breath into his shivering body. "And it was you, Phebe—wasn't it?—you who killed them—right?" he asked with a low groan, as feelings of trembling dread and revulsion swept steadily over him. "You killed them by biting them in the neck and drinking their blood, didn't you?"

And in the long intense pause that followed Nathan's questions, Phebe never once stirred, never once spoke. She did not seem even to draw so much as a single slow breath into her body. Her dark dwelling eyes, steady in their regard, merely gazed on at Nathan mournfully. "And Russell Gorman—" Nathan managed at last to gasp, after striving to quieten the rapid panting of his breathing: "I saw how you had your teeth in his neck... how you were biting him in the throat... and how you were drinking—O, God!—how you were drinking his blood!"

And for a moment tears gurgled in Nathan's voice before it finally faltered and broke away altogether into a low, steady whimper. Then, brushing the tears from his eyes, "I know what you are now," he moaned. "You're a v—" But before Nathan could articulate so much as its first syllable, the word died with a repressed sob on his quivering lips. Suddenly, inexplicably he found himself utterly unable—perhaps unwilling—to pronounce the reprehensible term; and a dead silence, intensely cold, immeasurably deep, seemed to draw itself over reality.

Phebe, meanwhile, watched Nathan's face with motionless eyes, an expression of unfathomable despair having crept all at once into her pale, lovely features. Then, after a space of some seconds, "Say it, Nathan," she half whispered, "say the word." And so intense was the sorrow, the misery, the hopelessness in her dark luminous eyes that Nathan was compelled to withdraw his own, for at the moment he was finding it nearly impossible to meet them.

"Then I will say it;" went on Phebe; "since you find yourself unable to." She paused an instant, however, as if she suddenly feared to go on; and as Nathan watched the first hint of rising tears gather like a faint mist far down in the depths of her dark eyes, she suddenly breathed across to him with trembling lip, "A vampire..." and she paused again to draw into her body a sharp sudden breath that was like a sob. "Yes... it's true," she said, "I am." And gazing now with utterly miserable, desolate, tragic eyes straight into Nathan's, she added: "And now you know the awful truth."

And then, after a minute or two, as Nathan continued to gaze on almost sightlessly into the mournful loveliness of Phebe's haunted face, almost it seemed to him that something peered wearily, forlornly, sorrowfully out of her eyes directly into his. A phantom image, a fugitive shadowy dweller, just faintly visible behind the features of her face. Whether real or imagined, Nathan could not say, for even as he attempted to fix his eyes on that awful wraithlike presence, it withdrew, faded, dissolved away in the inky midnight darkness of her large-pupilled eyes.

For an instant Nathan heard himself gasp out loud, and a sudden wave of giddiness swept over him as the heart heavily beating within his body gave an abrupt and violent lurch. Cold, awkward, and deadly afraid, Nathan tried hard to think, but his mind was in a whirl of fears, doubts, and confusion. Not knowing what to think, what to say, what to do, he merely stood there, a little stiller, and continued to meet Phebe's dark unstirring eyes.

There was one thought, meanwhile—an impulse, really— which did keep repeating itself in every instant of Nathan's alarm and uncertainty, like a remote, desperately anxious voice. Reach into the pocket of your jeans, it urged, insisted, and quickly take from it the rosary and cruet of holy water; then, drive Phebe back with the crucifix and make good your escape from the house after having dashed the holy water into her face.

But Nathan's trembling hand had scarcely half-groped toward his front pocket, when he paused. For he suddenly realized that in all probability the two religious objects would not be in any pocket of *these* jeans, but rather in the rain-soaked pair that had been removed from him while he lay unconscious.

Once again Nathan's anxious gaze encountered Phebe's, and for an instant he peered into the fathomless depths of the dark eyes with which she so shrewdly regarded him. In them lay such unflinching attention, such corkscrew-like acuity, that, to Nathan, it seemed all but impossible the expression on his face, the apprehension in his eyes had not already betrayed to her his every thought and impulse.

Then, as if it were her intention to prove to him exactly that, Phebe drew a long, slow breath and, gazing steadily across at Nathan with wide, wistful eyes, she said to him in a shaky little voice, "They're not in either pair of jeans, Nathan... the rosary and the holy water. Antal took them from you earlier tonight, in the cemetery."

At Phebe's startling words, Nathan's numbly beating heart sank like lead within him, and he felt his skin chilled with unutterable misery. He realized now that his only hope, his one and only chance of escape lay in a very bold and very desperate course of action. He must dart across the room to the foyer door and quickly bolt over its threshold.

But how was he going to manage that? Nathan kept wondering. Even now Phebe's eyes were studying, searching his face intently, almost suspiciously. Meanwhile, Vrancic, standing vigilantly behind her, never once removed that fixed, stirless, chilling gaze of his from Nathan's face. And from the living room entrance, the piercing eyes of the hermaphrodite child, Candy, continued to glower menacingly across at Nathan with a dead, unwavering glare.

Notwithstanding all of this, Nathan knew he must at least try. And as he mustered the courage to do so, a cold sweat the while beginning to break out all over his shivering body, he heard Phebe's voice, small and faint, as though coming across to him from a vast distance, asking him if he was okay, if he wanted to sit down on the sofa. But Nathan held his breath and did not answer. He only shook his head and, still gazing across at her, began to edge his way towards the foyer door as furtively as he possibly could. He had very nearly reached it, when Vrancic, in two broad strides, had crossed the room and all at once stood with his back to the door, barring Nathan's egress.

Cowed and voiceless, Nathan instantly shrank back from both the foyer door and the dreadful sentinel now stationed, like some earthly Apollyon, in front of it. And for the next few moments he stood perfectly still, not daring to challenge or encounter, even for the breath of an instant, the heavy settled stare which he felt so malevolently bent upon him.

Nathan was fully conscious, too, that other than Vrancic's, eyes no less penetrating—those of Phebe's, gazing pityingly across at him out of the brightness of tears; and Candy's, aglint in the deathly pallor of his face with cruelest disdain—were closely, steadily watching his every movement. Willing to endure the struggle of a brief exchange with either of their eyes, Nathan's glance very slowly moved out, and traveled on from one face to the other, from piercing eye to piercing eye. But the mere intensity of their scrutiny soon dizzied his brain, and in moments his faltered, then fell.

Cold and shivering, Nathan continued to stand there, with tongue silent and lips dry, feeling all but half lifeless with exhaustion. For it seemed his very self had suddenly fainted, withdrawn, and sunk away into the nothing and nebulous chill of a void. And when once more he had recovered as much of himself as he could, he raised his anxious gaze, and stole a long, slow, stealthy glance past Candy's head, away through the dining room to the back door in the kitchen beyond.

And despite the faint, vague foreboding that kept trying to daunt him from risking any further pointless attempts at flight, Nathan's body visibly stiffened as he continued to peer desperately, intently towards the back door, as if in readiness for a mad dash to the freedom awaiting him beyond its narrow threshold.

But again, it seemed, the very thoughts in his mind had been secretly overheard, as it were, by some percipient eavesdropper; for Vrancic's thick, hairy fingers very suddenly fastened themselves tightly round Nathan's slender forearm. "You are to remain here, indoors, with us, Nathan!" he said, in a low, stony voice. "Do you understand?" And thrusting his face down so close to Nathan's that it appeared unspeakably menacing, he added very severely: "I warn you, do not attempt anything foolish!" And before releasing

Nathan's arm, he once more fixed the boy's eyes with an awful, sinister stare. Nathan shivered, and instantly gave up all thought of flight, all hope of escape.

There was dead silence for a while, broken only now and again by the dull, muted sound of Vrancic's hands idly fumbling in his pockets with the ring of skeleton keys. Nathan listened to their clinking, as though Vrancic were some infernal warden to a Circle of Hell which the poet, Dante, in his mystical descent, had neglected to visit, and to which Nathan now felt himself irredeemably consigned.

And presently, there came whelming over Nathan a sudden, indescribable sensation, like a deadly chill. He felt sick, and his body began to shake all over with one cold tremor after another. In a curiously empty stillness, from his chilled toes to the tips of his numb fingers, he continued to stand there as one transfixed, merely listening to the muffled sound of his heart's choked beating. And for an instant, he could not help but wonder whether its dull, lurching pulsations were a sound even faintly audible to the all too heedful ears of Phebe, or those of her two companions.

Then, drawing a deep, shuddering breath into his body, Nathan's glance groped timidly across the room towards Phebe. And for the next few moments, as those dark, anxious, tragic eyes gazed steadily back at him, Nathan's thoughts went winging back to the bodies (some dead, some waiting to die!) which he had seen earlier tonight inside the old mausoleum. What had become of them—in particular, Russell Gorman and poor Tippy—after Phebe had drained them of their blood? Nathan asked himself.

And as he stood there ruminating deeply, uncomfortably on their fate, harrowing images flamed up in Nathan's fevered imagination. He kept seeing the severed heads of Tippy and Russell Gorman, each occupying its own porcelain bowl on either side of the one containing his aunt's head, inside the basement refrigerator. Moreover, he fancied Vrancic cheerfully busying himself with dismembering their corpses, before setting about preparing their flesh for.... But Nathan suddenly refused, for sheer loathing and horror, to speculate, even for another instant, on the ultimate (and undoubtedly evil) fate of either of those unfortunate boys.

And when, at last, Nathan had come out of these morbid reflections, with his hands cold and his startled eyes fixed emptily before him, he discovered Phebe standing next to him. So softly had she stolen over to his side that he never once heard her light steps. And the instant Nathan turned to look into her face, and encountered those eyes so close to his own, a sudden panic leapt up in him, and he stumbled back half a step. For some seconds, tongue-tied and visibly trembling, he continued to eye her cautiously, uneasily.

Then, faintly, softly, Phebe's voice broke the intensely awkward silence between them. "Please don't be afraid of me, Nathan," she whispered out to him. "You have nothing to fear from me." But all at once, a slight yet horrid sensation of vertigo overcame him, and, all but overwhelmed, Nathan quickly sat down on the edge of the dust-veiled coffee table, his downbent gaze fixed on the numbly trembling hands folded in his lap. By now the remnants of the storm had withdrawn themselves into a deep and empty hush. And the night was grown so deathly quiet that, as Vrancic, having drawn his thick-fingered hands out of his pockets, rubbed the side of his face, Nathan could actually hear the rasp of the man's nails against the two days' old stubble of his unshaven jowls.

Phebe, meanwhile, had seated herself on the edge of the coffee table beside Nathan and, with eyes of dusky-darkness that held tears of sympathy, she watched the profile of his face without speaking. After a while, Nathan once more turned his eyes and stole a longish glance at her face. Then, in the faint, quavering breath of a whisper, "Why?" he managed to ask. "Why are you doing this to me?"

There was a silence; Phebe seemed to hesitate; then, "Nathan, I have a chance to be human again," was her low, soft answer. Again there was a long, intense pause; and as Nathan continued to look into Phebe's face, almost it seemed to him that there had come over it a doleful, broken-hearted tranquility. "But," she went on, after taking a slow, deep breath, "I need something... something from you... something of yours that will help me pass from this everlasting horrid existence of the Non-living, the Undead, once more to a natural mortality among the society of the living."

And as the dark lustrous eyes continued to anxiously, almost woefully regard him, Nathan suddenly discovered that he was holding his breath. For a moment or two he felt as though he were steadily shrinking into himself. Instinctively he sidled his faltering gaze away and, closing his eyes, sat there shuddering: for something, like an odd sense or feeling—at once secret, disquieting, and indefinable—seemed to have suddenly chilled his mind.

But then, cold and fretting, Nathan opened his eyes again, stood up, and began walking to and fro, nearly from one side of the room, nine paces to the other. And each time at the fifth pace, he glanced over at Phebe as she gazed on at him out of tortured eyes.

Quite suddenly, then, Nathan stayed his steps and, after steadily meeting Phebe's eyes for what seemed an eon's-long hush of breathless indecision, the faint, anxious question at last slipped off his tongue. "Then, you're not going to do to me what you did to Russell Gorman, or the others in the old mausoleum?" And again, in the tense silence that preceded Phebe's reply, Nathan quietly whispered to her, "You... you don't want to"—he hesitated a moment; then—"to drink my blood?"

A smile, faint and sad, swept over Phebe's face as she stood up and moved slowly towards Nathan. "I would never hurt you, Nathan—never!" she hastened to assure him. And out of troubled eyes, whose dark-lashed lids never once drew down, or whose piercing glance never once strayed a fraction of an inch from his, she gazed on at Nathan. Constraining himself to peer deeply, intently into the depths of those eyes, he suddenly glimpsed his own blanched face reflected in the black, metal-like sheen of their pupils.

At the same time, Nathan felt Phebe's lean, cold hand steal softly into his own, and her narrow-boned fingers twine themselves in his. And when, for a solitary instant, he glanced down at them, he noted the gleaming band of a golden ring encircling one of her fingers. Almost instantly he realized whose ring it was, and his eyes, opening round and wide, swiftly lifted themselves to confront her own. "That ring! It was my mother's," he all but gasped. "It was her wedding ring!" He paused a moment or two and, still and speechless, stared at Phebe with his mouth agape; then, resisting the pressure of her fingers, he suddenly withdrew his hand from hers... "Why are you wearing it?"

Phebe stood in silence a moment; then, in a voice that slightly quavered and suggested tears, she said, "The blood is the life, Nathan... the blood is the life. Do you remember those words? They're from a book your aunt used to force you to read from every Thursday night when she'd come into your room." Phebe was now standing close up against Nathan. "And only a few nights ago," she went on, "I drank some of *your* blood, Nathan. And according to the book which I read to you that very same night, blood and semen are one and the same—linked to each other through symbolism. The one being a figure of speech for the other; and whether I swallowed your blood or your semen that night, your life is now inside me;"—and nestling against him, Phebe put both her arms about his neck—"it flows now through my veins; and the act of drinking it, in the eyes of something higher than ourselves, is seen as a mystical form of matrimony."

Phebe had paused and, for a while, watched Nathan's face without speaking. Then, "Don't you see, Nathan?" she continued. "By the mingling of our blood that night, you and I were married—I am your bride; you are my husband: flesh of my flesh; as I am now blood of your blood." And she held up her hand to exhibit the ring as though it were some private token or unquestionable proof of their secret nuptials.

Nathan, however, eyed her coldly, obstinately; and, after several moments of steadily meeting his gaze, Phebe lowered her own, but not before Nathan had seen the glimmer of tears in her eyes. Without another word, then, Phebe removed the ring from her finger. "But, here," she said in a choked voice, "if you don't think so... take it back." And very softly she placed the ring down on the coffee table.

At first, Nathan remained quite still, and merely gazed down at the ring doubtfully, suspiciously; for he felt a sudden unreasoning disinclination (almost an unendurable aversion) to touch it after Phebe had handled and worn it. But the curious notion, or impression—or whatever it truly was—soon made him feel ashamed and uncomfortable. For another instant he seemed to hesitate, and then, having mastered this bizarre reluctance, he quickly snatched up his mother's ring from the table and slipped it into his pocket.

But then, upon suddenly recalling that he in turn had tasted some of Phebe's blood, Nathan caught his breath and drew sharply away from her. "That night... your blood..." He spoke the words very low, as if to himself. "You made me swallow some of your blood the other night when you read to me from Bram Stoker's 'Dracula'." Then, after another prolonged silence, Nathan asked in a voice-hushed as by a hint of supreme dread, "Will I become a vam—" But Phebe quickly set her mouth to Nathan's lips and kissed him into silence, preventing him from uttering that one solitary execrable word that seemed, even to her own ears, so hateful, so insufferable.

But instantly Nathan drew back his face with a jerk, and stared at her. "Well, Phebe; will I become like—*you?* Tell me!" he persisted.

Out of eyes that seemed still more sorrowful, more tragic, Phebe gazed on a while at Nathan's face in silence. Then, "No, Nathan," was her miserable answer, "you would have to partake of my body *and* my blood in order to be as I am."

Nathan drew back half a step from her and, with pondering eyes, watched her face intently. Then, his own voice caught up her words, and repeated them in a scarcely audible whisper: "Your body and your blood... Almost like receiving communion."

"Yes; only of a most dark and unhappy kind," Phebe remarked, faintly, while in her voice there was again that vague suggestion of tears, almost despair. And suddenly, after a short silence, having gazed long at Nathan with unimaginable entreaty, she asked him: "Will you help me?"

But Nathan stood perfectly still, making no answer; and as he continued to meet Phebe's unswerving gaze, once more into her deep dark eyes there entered the fierce glance of that secret *other*. And for perhaps thirty seconds even the features of her face became less actual, and the *dweller* on the other side of them more sharply defined. And all in a moment, it seemed to Nathan that the visage of something truly monstrous was presently before him, confronting his eyes, glaring into his very soul—the face of the Vampire, which (to Nathan) appeared for all the world like an oversized and misshapen bat. But the image, like some phantom of the mind, that can be seen clearly only in dream, soon grew faint and slowly, steadily melted away.

Before it had entirely vanished, however, Nathan's eyes shut, and for the next few moments, panting, trembling, he hid his face in his hands. And when he had slowly, cautiously removed his hands from before his face and opened his eyes again, he saw only the pale, lovely face of Phebe before him, and the despairing, agonized expression that had now stolen into its features. Then, with his throat seeming to draw itself together, and his parched tongue nearly sticking to the roof of his mouth, he managed to haltingly ask: "You want... me to... help... you?"

"Yes. There's a ritual," Phebe was hastening to explain, when suddenly Nathan interrupted her. "First," he said, "I want you to tell me how you became a—" he hesitated, and seemed to ponder a while in silence, as though searching carefully for the words he wanted; then—"well... I mean," he resumed slowly, "how you became, like, you know."

Phebe's dark eyes gazed steadily into his own. "Like what I am... a—" For an instant Phebe paused; her motionless eyes continued to meet Nathan's, but then looked hastily away; and after a brief silence, she said with a slight shudder: "—a vampire?"

Nathan faintly nodded his head. "Do you remember?"

Once again that strange, peering dark gaze lifted itself to Nathan's face, and became fixed in a mournful, tragic stare. "How could I forget?" she breathed. "The memory has never once ceased to haunt and torture me over the centuries."

That last word caused Nathan to visibly start, and a sudden chill spread itself through his mind. "'Centuries'..." he repeated, uneasily, in a whisper. Then, with eyes fixed anxiously on Phebe's face, he took a deep breath, and asked in a faint, uncertain voice: "How old, Phebe... how old are you—really?"

Phebe stared at Nathan without stirring; then, her glance strayed for an instant or two to the small, battered old book that lay open toward its middle on the coffee table. She reached down, took it up, and handed it without a word to Nathan, all the while her dark, fathomless eyes gazing intently, unswervingly into his. Nathan slowly withdrew his eyes from hers, glanced down at the book she had given him, and saw at once that it was the very one between whose limp, fusty pages Phebe had hidden the thousand dollars and then placed near the pillow on his bed a few mornings ago.

Scarcely above a whisper, then, Nathan read out its title: "'Poems from the time of Galerius.'" And with his brow furrowed in perplexity, he raised his questioning eyes to Phebe's.

"Like the poems in that book, Nathan," said Phebe, in answer to his expression, "I, too, am from that same time—the time of Galerius."

Nathan's voice took up the name in a half-whispered breath, "'Galerius.'" And suddenly he felt as though his heart for a moment stood still in his body as, faintly, almost hesitantly, he asked: "Who was he?"

Phebe gazed on at Nathan in silence a moment, and the dusky eyes of her shone across at him like two small shards of a clouded sky seen in the deepest dark of a winter's midnight. Then, taking a long, slow breath, "As difficult as this may be for you to accept, Nathan," she answered in a shaky little voice, "he was a king, a powerful monarch from very long ago, one of the mighty Caesars of the ancient Roman people who ruled in the latter days of the Empire's fading glory. He was my Emperor; and I lived in the time of his very turbulent and very brutal reign."

A glint of fright sprang into Nathan's eyes. He bit his lip a moment, and, with a dry mouth, managed to murmur, "How long ago was that?"

For some seconds Phebe stared half searchingly, half doubtfully into Nathan's eyes, as if trying to anticipate his reaction to her answer. Then, suddenly she bent her head a little and stood looking for a moment down at the floor. She muttered one or two words which Nathan failed to catch and, in a voice slightly shaking with what just for a minute he thought was sobbing, he distinctly heard her whisper first his name, then the number "seventeen".

And slowly raising her face again, so that presently Nathan saw the forlorn dark eyes regarding him were now glittering with tears, she breathed across to him, "Centuries, Nathan;" and, again, after a long pause; "seventeen long centuries of nights without number... of untold darkness without death."

Still gazing steadily back at Phebe, in a shocked and spell-bound stillness, Nathan felt his whole body shaking now as with a cold and deepening dread. Then, in a voice he hardly recognized as his own, he heard himself whisper, almost incredulously, "One thousand seven hundred years..." but his voice suddenly faltered; and, after a short silence: "You mean," he went on, "you're from the year 300... *three hundred*—A.D.? You're that o—" A protracted shudder through Nathan's body stifled the last word of his sentence.

Phebe, meanwhile, continued to stare at Nathan in silence. And the tranceful gaze within the eyes that dwelt upon his face was so far-off looking, so strangely remote as with some profound reverie, that she seemed scarcely aware of his presence. Then, taking a deep breath, she exhaled a long, trembling sigh, and softly across the silence, "It was very long ago, Nathan," she began slowly, as if she had just come out of a dream. "At the time I was only—" But suddenly she broke off, and for an instant gazed sidelong at Nathan's face; then, "Maybe I should show you, Nathan, rather than merely tell you how it all happened;" she resumed; "I think it would be much easier that way for you to comprehend it all."

And at that precise moment, Nathan happened to notice the face of Vrancic, anxiously peering at him from over Phebe's shoulder. Vrancic coughed, and in a voice that was subdued as by a hint of awe, he offered his opinion to Phebe that he believed it "ill-advised to undertake such a risky procedure. You have considered what the outcome could be for the boy should something untoward arise, have you not?"

Phebe's response was cold, brusque, even a little dismissive; "I have," she said, and from over her shoulder she shot Vrancic a severe look. But Vrancic was not to be so easily daunted. He coughed again, and despite Phebe's stony retort, and the icy glance she had just now cast his way, he said: "And is this pointless endeavor worth jeopardizing all that you seek to accomplish here through this boy? What do you hope to gain from the venture, other than endangering the boy's life?"

Phebe's eyes dwelt on Nathan's face. "It is not what I expect to gain," was the soft reply, "but rather what Nathan stands to comprehend at its conclusion;" she paused a moment to take Nathan's hand in hers, and, leading him over to the sofa, she added: "I owe him that much."

"Little good will the knowledge be to him," Vrancic remarked sardonically, "if it results in his death—a consequence all too possible if something unforeseen should occur." Phebe, however, paid no heed to either his comments or his sarcasm. At which Vrancic coughed yet again and, for a moment or two, swept Nathan's face with a curiously anxious glance. Then, in a language harsh and unfamiliar to Nathan's ears, Vrancic suddenly broke out in a lengthy harangue at Phebe. But after one or two minutes, Phebe, in the same peculiar tongue, interrupted him, and went on a while severely addressing him in a tone which Nathan could not fail to note brought a distinct pallor to Vrancic's face.

"Of course, you must do as you please," Vrancic said to Phebe, submissively, in a half-fearful, half-wheedling voice. "I only meant that you should know I am very near to tracking down the very thing you have so desperately sought and which for so long has eluded you." He paused a moment to fetch out of his pocket the bunch of skeleton keys, which he then jangled uneasily. "It will, however, prove quite worthless to you," he then went on, "if this boy's life is now lost as a result of any mishap here tonight."

There was a longish silence in which, for a moment, Candy could be heard to faintly snigger. He appeared vastly amused by this heated exchange between Phebe and Vrancic; and, with a glint of wicked merriment in his cruel smirking face, he looked first to one, then to the other, and said: "Now, now; if our dear, sweet Nate has already been able to manage a vampire's lust—"

But Phebe's darkly flashing eyes swerved in his direction, and the smoldering glance in their depths instantly silenced him. She turned once more, then, to quietly face Nathan, and, after seating him on the sofa's midmost cushion, she hastened to nimbly seat herself astride him. For the breath of an instant a vague sense of apprehension seemed to gather like a dense, gloomy cloud over Nathan's heart; but Phebe stooped her face close to his ear and all but whispered into it: "There's nothing to be afraid of;" then, pausing a moment to smile down reassuringly into his eyes; "whatever happens, Nathan," she went on, "however strange it may feel to you at first, don't struggle, or fight against it; even if you start to get really frightened. That only makes the feeling worse. Just relax." And without a word, Nathan sat on perfectly still, holding his breath, gazing steadily up into Phebe's face—waiting.

Still smiling, Phebe laid the flat of her palm on the place over Nathan's breastbone. And all the while she kept her hand pressed there, it seemed to Nathan that a strange uncomfortable pressure began steadily to increase around his heart. Very gradually, then, it became more and more difficult for him to catch his breath; and he was soon aware, too, of a deadly chill slowly spreading itself through his body, as though it were flowing into him from the small cold palm and fingers of Phebe's hand. And even after Phebe had removed her hand, that deathly frigid cold continued mounting its way through his limbs: chilling his skin and dizzying his mind. And quite suddenly, for a few brief moments, it seemed to Nathan as if he'd been given the ability to be conscious of thoughts, feelings, impressions, and (stranger still) *memories* that were not his own. One after another, they swept and crowded through his mind, like vivid pictures in a book whose pages were being turned with extraordinary swiftness.

Then, before Nathan knew what was happening, Phebe had raised her small, cold, lank-fingered hands and taken his face between them. Serenely, solemnly she gazed on into his brown, still eyes. And as Nathan continued to regard the faint, tiny reflection of his own pale face in her deep, dwelling eyes, he began, quite suddenly, to have the truly terrifying impression of being drawn slowly out of himself and into their darkness.

Certainly, to Nathan, it was nothing like the darkness of deep, still waters, but rather that of the cold icy shadows in the sunless depths of vast, labyrinthine caves far beneath the earth at the windless roots of mountains. And with each passing moment, he felt as though he were losing himself in that darkness: for almost it seemed to him that veil upon veil of it was parting, letting him through, and quickly closing again behind him.

Softly, heavily, then, Nathan's eyes drew shut, and an instant later he felt the tips of Phebe's cold, lean fingers sweep, light as the settling of dust, across their lids. Then, soft and low, he heard Phebe's voice breathing down into his face a whispered sequence of mysterious, unfamiliar words. It was almost as though she were chanting them to him, over and over: "Ecce enim veritatem... Ecce enim veritatem... Ecce enim veritatem..."

Ever and again these words ran on in a never-varying succession, stealing in through Nathan's ears, filling his thoughts; drugging his senses; causing the very brain in his skull to be steeped in their indelibly potent syllables. And soon Nathan heard his own voice break faintly into speech, repeating to himself slowly, mechanically those same odd, meaningless words, as though his tongue had involuntarily caught them up in obedience to the urgent persuasion of another's whispered will. Then, all at once, the secret of their meaning became, to his astonishment, extraordinarily (and inexplicably) clear—Ecce enim veritatem, Behold then the truth; ecce enim veritatem, behold then the truth... behold... then... the... truth....

And presently (for Nathan), all the world seemed to withdraw itself from him, to grow remote as with the strangeness of a dream. And although he could still feel the cold, soft touch of Phebe's hands on either side of his face, the sound of her voice was gradually hushed away. Then, with a shock, he felt Phebe's lips press themselves suddenly against his own in an icy kiss that seemed to pierce him through to his very bones, like the coldness of death. Moments later Nathan thought Phebe was breathing into his mouth, exhaling in long, slow trembling breaths. Then, all at once, he felt something within him, something more than his mere breath, more vital than his very life's blood, being softly, steadily, irresistibly drawn, siphoned, by Phebe out of his heart, his mind, his very skin, into... he knew not where or what. He was dimly aware, too, after a few black and horrifying moments, that his heart was beating now with a curiously strained effort, and that he was utterly powerless to stir or cry out. Without a solitary breath to breathe, he felt as though he were slowly but surely suffocating.

But in the very instant that he began to feel deadly afraid for himself, he thought he could discern very faintly, as though it were coming to him from across a vast and lightless solitude of untold centuries, Phebe's soothing voice, telling him to be calm; that everything was okay. Then, after what had seemed to Nathan an interminable interval outlasting the still and dawnless dark of a never-ending night, he heard a voice commanding him, "Open your eyes now, Nathan; open your eyes." And he knew at once that it was the voice of Phebe, so near to him now that it sounded as though she had spoken directly into his ear.

And when Nathan opened his eyes, and gazed out before him, he found a change had come to everything around him. The sofa, the living room walls, their curtained windows and the cracked ceiling above, the house, 73rd Place, and Middle Village itself—all had completely disappeared. He was standing with Phebe in the midst of a wide, empty, unfamiliar street, and all about them was utterly windless and still. The street itself, he noted, was enclosed on either hand by stone buildings and structures of a quaint and antiquated style and construction—certainly their design had nothing to do with any modern age.

But what was most curious of all to Nathan, was that everything around him and above him seemed bathed in a grey, nearly colorless half-light. It was as though it all belonged to some image in an old, still black-and-white photograph. And some of the buildings and objects in what he now gazed upon even appeared, in part, fuzzy or a little blurred.

Phebe was now regarding Nathan's face intently. And standing there, for some seconds still and speechless, he continued to meet her dark, unswerving eyes as though he had been suddenly overtaken by the weird, peculiar essence of a dream. Then, "Where am I?" he asked, faintly.

Without moving her head, Phebe's lustrous eyes raised themselves and, as if she had not heard what Nathan had asked her, gazed on fixedly, almost mournfully at one of the buildings before her. Nathan watched her silent face closely, and the expression that had crept into its heart-piercing beauty seemed to suggest to him far more than mere sorrow, regret, or weariness. Then, the pale, narrow face, with its dark, forlorn eyes, turned slowly in Nathan's direction. "This is a street in the city where I was born;" she said, soft and low; "it doesn't exist anymore. But it did—once; more than fifteen hundred years ago."

And across the intense stillness that followed her words, Nathan asked in a halting whisper, "Is... is this... a dream?"

"No. You're not dreaming this," replied Phebe. "When I drew the breath from you, I caused your spirit to come out with it. Your soul is now in here"—she paused to touch her bosom—"in my body;" she went on; "with me."

Nathan slightly started, and gazed a while at Phebe without speaking. "And my body—" he said, then, his voice becoming a little fainter, "—is it..." He suddenly fell silent, and continued to meet Phebe's still, unwavering gaze. Slowly a remote glint of amusement had crept into the darkness of her eyes. "Is it dead?" she all but whispered across to Nathan. "No;" she continued after a long pause; "listen." And for a moment, as Nathan withdrew his eyes from Phebe's, and strained his ears, he suddenly realized that the steady, far-off throbbing sound which he could now detect was actually the slow, faint beating of his heart.

"That is the sound of your heartbeat;" said Phebe, when Nathan's eyes slowly turned and fixed themselves on her face again; "but it will stop, and you will die if I keep your spirit here with me too long."

Nathan stood silently listening to the unceasing pulsation of his heart a few moments longer. "And is that what you and Vrancic were arguing about just before?" he managed at length to ask.

Phebe nodded her head, and answered: "Antal thinks I'm taking too great a risk with your life in having you experience this."

"Why should Vrancic," asked Nathan, "be worried about what happens to me?"

Phebe sighed and shook her head. "He's not;" she replied; "he's concerned that what we've come here to accomplish through you will have been all in vain should you happen to die here tonight because of this little 'escapade'—as he called it—which I'm now letting you undertake." She paused a moment or two; then said, "But never mind about Antal's worries;" and, after glancing round, she said, "what you're now seeing, Nathan, are my thought-memories that have not as yet faded, even after these long past centuries, but which have grown shadowy and blurred in the passage of time. They are all that remain of my former life, when long ago I lived a still-mortal life in the time of the Roman Empire."

For a moment or two Nathan pondered Phebe's words in silence. "Then none of this," he said, "is really here before my eyes. Is it?"

"No;" was the solemn answer; "and you're not seeing any of this with your visual perception. None of this is being realized by the sight of your eyes, but rather by the awareness of your soul, which is now mingling with mine."

Nathan stood motionlessly listening to Phebe's voice, his eyes the while fixed on the curious scene around him, as if he were waiting for something to happen. Then, "Where is this place?" he asked at last.

The dark eyes continued to regard his face steadily. "It was once a mighty city of the ancient world," came the soft answer, "in Macedonia, that long ago had the name of Thessalonica." She paused, and, turning her eyes away, seemed for some seconds to gaze half-pensively at some private or secret mental image. Then, "Here, the Emperor, Galerius," she went on, "had his chief seat of power. There were then two Caesars who ruled the Roman Empire— Constantius in the East, and Galerius in the west."

Then, telling Nathan to close his eyes again, Phebe brushed his lids with the soft tips of her slender fingers. And when he looked again, he found they were now standing in a vast hall, down the length of which, on either hand, uprose massive columns of stone. There were groups of figures, some bent and stooping low, some kneeling with hands upraised in supplication: they were utterly still and silent, like statues, and each one looked cowed and frightened. They were huddled together at the foot of a high, many-staired dais, where a man, occupying a throne, sat like a lord in judgement. Nathan could scarcely see him, he was so shadowy and faint.

"That is Galerius, the Emperor, as best as I can recall him;" said Phebe; "and the people he's glaring down on are Christians." She was silent a moment; then said, "There I am;" and paused once more to point out to Nathan the frightened girl clinging to a tall, dark-haired woman; "with my mother," she added; and Nathan peered intently at the woman, but her face was little more than a faded blur. Phebe sighed, and, with a hint of remorse in her voice, half whispered, "I don't even remember her face anymore, it's so long ago."

And Nathan's eyes, after having studied the scene for nearly a full minute, once more fixed themselves on Phebe's face. "What is happening?" he asked her.

In a low, very solemn voice, Phebe replied, "The year is 305 A.D. The Roman Emperor, Diocletian, has abdicated from his throne and retired into private life, naming Galerius as the ruling Augustus, Emperor of the western half of the empire. It is the time of the Great Persecution of the Christians, Nathan. Two years earlier, in 303 A.D., Galerius himself instigated it out of his zeal and passion for the ancient religion and traditions of early Rome." Phebe paused; and, for a space of some seconds, Nathan gazed at her, speechless and without stirring. For all the while that Nathan had been listening to Phebe's words, almost it seemed to him that her voice was like an echo from the outskirts of another age, an oldlier existence, a long-vanished reality. Then, at last, he managed to ask, "But what does any of this have to do with you, Phebe?"

"In those days, Nathan," was her hushed and half whispered answer, "before I became what I am now, and have been for nearly two millennia—a vampire—I was a young and naive girl of noble Roman ancestry, newly converted to, and baptized in, the Christian faith. A devoted believer in... in..." Her voice had faltered a little, stammered in a faint sob, then trailed away into silence.

Nathan's eyes widened. He stood very still, staring at Phebe. "*You,*" he said, "were a Christian?"

Slowly, mournfully Phebe nodded her head. "Yes... as were all the earliest vampires."

Nathan gazed on a moment in a stunned and awful stillness. "But," he whispered, at last, *"how*—Why?"

Phebe held up her hand, "Listen!" she said, and, slowly ascending the stairs of the dais, she seated herself on its topmost step. "It was because the Christians refused to worship the ancient Gods of Rome—the false deities invented by mortal men and bearing the empty names of Apollo, Jupiter, Venus. And it was also because the Christians would not participate in any of the pagan observances and sacrificial rites at the public altars and shrines of those gods, that our most imperious Augustus here had decided the adherents of the Christian faith were neither to be trusted nor associated with. He believed that rejection of the imperial gods of Rome by the Christians was, in fact, a rejection of the Emperor himself since he ruled over mankind on the earth as the divine representative of those gods. Ultimately it became his aim to eradicate Christianity altogether. For he believed that with the extermination of Christianity, the Roman Empire would be unified again, as of old, in the true faith and sole worship of the old gods, as it had been in the days of Rome's ancient glory."

Phebe paused; and, for a moment or two, her eyes strayed from Nathan's silent face. Then, "And so," she began again, "Christians were therefore forbidden by the Emperor's first edict to assemble for the practice of their religion. Soon other edicts were issued by Galerius. He ordered the demolition of all Christian churches; had all their sacred books confiscated, proclaimed contraband, and destroyed; and eventually revoked their Roman citizenship. Then, with the proclamation of his fourth and final edict, Galerius imposed upon every member of the Christian faith in the empire a requirement of public sacrifice to, and worship of, the Gods of Rome.

Those Christians who rejected this imperial decree, and refused to worship the Gods of the empire—such as my mother, and I, and many other Christians—were placed under arrest for sedition, brought before Galerius, and given the choice to either bow down before the Roman gods, or be put to death by crucifixion." Phebe had paused again, but not as if in wait for any remark or comment from Nathan, for all at once she hastened on to add: "My mother chose martyrdom, as did I, and others." Then, once again Phebe had fallen silent; and, shutting her eyes, she told Nathan to do the same. And when once more he opened them, he found that the scene around him had altered.

He was standing by himself outside the walls of the ancient city, some little distance from its gates, in the middle of a wide, stone-paved road. And rising up on either side of this great thoroughfare, following its every twist and turn for as far as the eye could see, were rough-hewn wooden crosses with the naked bodies of men, women, and children cruelly nailed to them. And Nathan gazed up in horror to see, among that pitiful multitude of the condemned and crucified fringing the road, Phebe herself, hanging naked on the sturdy upright post of her cross, with her arms spread wide and savagely bound to the coarse wooden beam fixed across it. Her hands and feet were pierced with iron nails; and her head was bent forward in anguish and misery.

Nathan slowly drew near, and paused at the foot of the cross. Feeling his heart suddenly swell within him with an unendurable pain, he heard himself faintly breathe, "Oh, Phebe;" and the tears sprang scalding into his eyes, nearly blinding him. For he could see that her face was streaked with streamlets of blood from a wreath of thorns that had been plaited and bound about her brows.

Then, the face slightly lifted, and the eyes slowly opened and looked down steadily into Nathan's. And Nathan continued to meet that dark, peering, mournful gaze all but breathless with astonishment. For some while it seemed Phebe merely stared down at him from the cross; she was very still; and the silence round the two of them lay deep and immeasurable as the sea.

All at once, then, Phebe breathed, and said, "To ridicule me, Nathan, and in mockery of our Savior, a crown of thorns was placed on my head. And my tormentors jeered and said that I should suffer no less than he, since I was so devoted to him. But I could not endure the pain and suffering of crucifixion. After less than an hour I had lapsed from my faith. I begged to be spared, promising, in order to save my life, to worship Apollo."

Phebe's voice had fallen silent a moment; and Nathan, still gazing up at her on the cross, had opened his mouth to speak, but found his voice too choked with tears to utter so much as a single word. Then, once more he heard Phebe speaking to him.

"By the Emperor's own commandment," she continued, "they took me down from the cross, and several others who had also turned apostates." She broke off again, as the lids of her eyes slowly drew down and her head bowed forward. A profound silence ensued, and Nathan, without knowing precisely why, also bent his head low and, for a moment or two, shut tight his tear-filled eyes.

But seconds later, when he looked out again, he saw the body of Phebe lying in the roadside in a crumpled heap at the foot of the cross, bleeding profusely from the grisly wounds in her hands and in her feet. And Nathan was startled by the sound of his own tremulous voice, as he heard himself whisper, "And that's how you got those scars on your hands and feet: you were crucified, just like"—"Yes," Phebe's voice broke in suddenly from behind. Nathan turned at once and, to his wonder and relief, saw Phebe once more standing there, gazing half solemnly down into the slender palms of her hands at the awful reminders left in them by the sharp iron nails.

Nathan took a deep breath and, barely above a whisper, he asked: "What happened to you, Phebe? How did you become—" But Nathan's voice, having grown shaky, suddenly faltered and failed to complete the sentence.

But then, Phebe lifted her eyes on Nathan, long and darkly, and she said, "A vampire? Look!" And when Nathan looked again, the scene around them was utterly transformed. He and Phebe were again standing inside a great hall whose lofty domed vault was upheld by enormous pillars of white marble; but all else round them was shadowy, ill-defined, and obscure.

"As best I can recall," Phebe said at last, "this is the Temple of Apollo, the Sun-god. Those of us Christians who, once taken down from the cross, renounced our faith, had our wounds bound up and on the following day were led here to Apollo's temple. And in the presence of the Emperor himself, we were commanded to now prove our loyalty to Galerius and to the Empire by sacrificing and worshiping at the altar of Apollo, the Sun-god, proclaiming him, in some foul heathen rite, as our Lord and Savior.

"Most did," continued Phebe, after a short pause; "among those, however, who had a sudden change of heart and refused, was I. At this, Galerius became infuriated. I and a number of others were then dragged off to prison, and there we were told a fate worse than crucifixion was now being prepared for us." Phebe stood silent a moment, then said, "Look!" And Nathan, half fearfully, half reluctantly, turned his head and, gazing intently in the direction to which she pointed, saw a gaunt, sinister-looking man robed and hooded in black. He was standing before the narrow, shadowed mouth of a cavern at the bluff-faced base of a dark, steeply sloping ridge of land.

"This is where they led us," said Phebe, walking past the strange, darkly-clad man, and peering a moment or two into the cavernous depths; "here," she went on, "to this evil cavern where the grim, forbidding figure of this man stood, as if awaiting us."

And when Nathan's eyes had come round from surveying the curiously menacing apparition of that man, they fixed themselves once more on Phebe's face. Then, through a half-suppressed shudder, he asked, "Who is he?" And yet the faint, unsteady voice that had inquired after the man's identity seemed not to be in any need of an answer, for somehow (inexplicably) Nathan felt he knew who that cloaked and hooded figure was, as well as the dread infernal reason for his presence there.

Then, "We were told," came Phebe's half whispered answer, "that he was the wisest and most powerful of the Emperor's malefici, or sorcerers, who Galerius kept with him at his royal court. He was a learned Greek, a necromancer, who had dwelt abroad in Babylon, Persia, and Egypt, attaining knowledge in secret rites and the casting of spells, curses, and the evocation of demons." Phebe paused a moment, and her voice sank lower, softlier still as she added: "And it was he, Nathan, who devised for us the curse, that malediction, that divests one of their mortal nature and transforms them into a vampire."

There was a short silence as Phebe continued to regard the darkly-clad figure with a fixed and stony gaze. Then, faintly, almost inaudibly, "The guards brought us before him in the dark;" she went on; "by the red glare of torches they led us out of prison, into the street, and onward through the city's gates. The night was still and moonless and utterly black; and we were driven down a narrow path that wound among the shattered rocks of dense shadowy woods. Far from the city, to the bottom of this remote hill, they brought us. From days agone, the darkness and desolation surrounding the hill's location had attached to it a character of occult sanctity and awe.

"For about the base of this thickly wooded prominence," continued Phebe, "are sheer cliffs whose feet are shagged with huge rocks that are pierced in one place by a deep and sunless cavern. And in its hollow, labyrinthine depths dwell innumerable bats which, when it is dark, emerge and blacken the air in their millions. And for this reason the cave, the hill, and its shadowy woods had among the ancient Greeks, since before the time of the poet Homer, the name of Demos Nukteris, the District of the Bat. And within the tunnels of that cavern were many mysterious sanctuaries that had been polluted of old by human sacrifice. For the blood shed there, as a libation by any man seeking an oracle, would attract the bats, which would then drink the blood and attain the power of human speech to deliver prophecies. It was said that Alexander the Great himself consulted this oracle, and was warned that he was going to die in ancient Babylon within the year. Alexander became so incensed by this divination that he had all the cave-dwelling men who managed the oracle put to the sword; and the practice of seeking oracles there ceased ever after.

But the cavern remained, and the bats still inhabit the darkness of its tunnels in the thousands upon thousands."

Phebe's voice had again fallen silent, and Nathan noted that the beautiful face looked strangely worn and weary, as if it had grown in some degree more aged, more solemn, and paler still in the telling. Her eyes, too, were fixed once again in a dead stare upon the mouth of that cavern, as if in some dread and dour reverie.

Then, in a hushed and quavering voice, Nathan asked: "What happened to you there, Phebe?"

"The guards herded us over to the mouth of the cave," she went on, "where Galerius's sorcerer then drew forth a leaf of parchment or vellum from a fold of his cloak, and he began to recite what was written on it, chanting it, like some incantation, over our heads. I knew at once that it was some kind of evil spell, or curse, that he was putting on us. And he told us that since we refused to worship the Sun-god Apollo, then from sunlight we would be forever banished, and to darkness consigned for evermore."

Phebe's voice at this point had become unmistakably wistful. And, after pausing for a moment or two, she said: "Over our heads with his fingers, he began making strange signs in the air, saying, 'As your savior, the Nazarene and false Jewish prophet, promised you everlasting life so long as you drink his blood, so it shall be! Eternal life you shall have, sustained by the blood of mortal Men, which I now compel you to drink and subsist on through nights, centuries'-long and without number, in a lifetime sunless and unending'. And after he had said this, one of the bats inhabiting the gloomy hollows of that ancient cavern was brought out and offered as a sacrifice to the powers of Darkness. And at the very hour of midnight, I and the others were made to eat of the bat's flesh, and drink of its blood from a rusty old chalice in mockery of our being Christians drinking from the cup of our Savior's blood.

"Then, at the sorcerer's commandment," Phebe went on, after having paused for some seconds to watch Nathan's silent face, "we were driven at sword point by the guards into that cavern; and there, in its cold and fearful darkness, for two days and two nights, we were forced to remain. But then, on the third night we were brought out again; and herded, crying and sobbing, before Galerius's sorcerer. And in the air, over our heads, he made yet again strange signs with his fingers, while chanting these words: 'With the bat you shall now have kinship and community of nature. Of your present shape you shall be dispossessed; and in form and feature you shall become foul as the bat. And like creatures of night and of darkness you shall henceforth shun daylight and the sun, whose rays shall be your destruction and your undoing. And as your so-called Savior said to you, Ask and you will receive, seek and you will find, knock and the door will be open—I now lay this curse upon you. That though you ask, you receive naught; though seek, you never find; and though you knock, all doors be barred against you! Henceforth let neither solace nor safe-haven be given you in the house of any man unless he first invite you in, and is fool enough to let you enter in over his threshold.'"

Phebe was silent for some while, then; and she and Nathan sat down near the mouth of the cavern and stared at one another without either speaking or stirring. After several minutes, Nathan, very faintly, ventured to ask her: "What did they do to you then?"

"We were led away;" came the low, soft answer; "scattered... driven, deported, and dispersed beyond the boundaries of the Empire. Accursed to dwell as the Undead, to live on as the Nonliving, in darkness, like the bat, and sustain our lives by preying upon the living, and drinking the blood of mortal-kind. Among the ancient Greeks we had the name of Nuktipoloi, 'night-wanderers'; and in the Latin tongue of the Romans, Sanguisuga, 'blood-drinkers.'"

Nathan held his breath a moment; then, exhaling a slow, trembling breath, he said, "And that's how vampires came to exist—and how you came to be one yourself."

Phebe faintly nodded her head, and, scarcely above a whisper, "Yes;" she said; then, slowly lowering her face, Nathan saw two or three tears drop from her eyes. And presently there fell between them a long, deep silence. But then, very faintly, indeed more so than ever, the muffled sound of Nathan's heart, pulsating softly in the background, seemed to quieten and dull. And as Nathan listened to it, the even rhythm of its steady beating became distinctly irregular, throbbing now slowlier and slowlier.

Phebe looked up sharply. "Your heart—you must get back into your body, Nathan! Quick. Close your eyes."

Nathan shut his eyes at once. He felt his mouth gently opened. Phebe's breath passed into him; and suddenly, a horrid sensation like suffocation swept through him. Slowly it subsided; then ceased altogether. He felt his lungs fill again with air. He heard himself gasping. He unsealed his eyes and, looking out of them, found Phebe gazing down tenderly into their depths. He was once again on the sofa, in the living room of his aunt's house, and Phebe was still straddling him, in the very same position as when first he had closed his eyes.

Very gently, then, Phebe climbed off of Nathan and sat down on the edge of the coffee table in front of him. And for some time, in a profoundly hushed stillness, the dark lustrous eyes wandered anxiously over his silent face. "And so, Nathan," she said at length, "now that you know the truth —", and pausing suddenly, she looked upon Nathan with such a pitiably beseeching glance, before going on to ask him in a low, faint whisper, "—will you help me?"

At first Nathan did not answer her; indeed he could not, for it seemed he had suddenly lost the power to frame so much as a single word. But then, faintly, slowly, almost dreamily, "Help... you..." His voice had caught up the words, and, sitting perfectly still, he merely gazed long and silently at Phebe's face.

And then, for the first time since awaking again inside his body, Nathan became aware once more of the all-too disquieting presence in the room of those other two, Vrancic and Candy. Slowly, soundlessly they had advanced across the floor and stood now on the other side of the coffee table, behind Phebe: Candy on her left; Vrancic on her right. They were both watching Nathan with unflinching attention. Nathan glanced at either of them for an instant, then refastened his gaze intently, speechlessly on Phebe's face.

At the same time, Nathan was aware that he suddenly felt stiff and cold; and all over his body his chilled skin had gone goosebumps. His knees, too, trembled. For the notion of "helping" Phebe somehow terrified him, although he himself hardly knew why. And for some reason or other his mind became suddenly haunted by an apprehension, a vague foreboding of what that 'help' might, on his part, ultimately require of him! Indeed, what was this desperate need Phebe had for his "help"? What *did* it necessitate—and why *me* to begin with? he kept asking himself.

And yet, a selfish and cowardly fear of discovering (as well as a hideous awe and reluctance to ask) what exactly Phebe wanted from him, kept Nathan for the next few seconds horribly tongue-tied, and all but paralyzed where he sat. But then, an inquisitiveness, a curiosity, at once intractable and irrepressible, overcame his alarm and uneasiness, and that solitary word to the question he had hitherto refrained from articulating slipped in a quavering breath irresistibly from his tongue: "How?"

The intense regard in Phebe's dark luminous eyes, at the pronunciation of that scarcely audible word, suddenly deepened, and a curious glint crept into their depths. In fact, she seemed the whole time to have been waiting anxiously, eagerly for that one word, almost fretful that Nathan would never ask it, as though she were unable to proceed without its vocalization.

"'How', Nathan;" echoed Phebe, still eyeing him with a peculiar intentness; "by freely giving to me something that only you can offer; something that is yours and yours alone. Would you be willing to do that for me?"

Nathan, however, was scarcely able to follow Phebe's words, for all the while she had been speaking to him, his thoughts had gone secretly astray. Back in memory they drifted and ranged to the old mausoleum, where, only one or two hours earlier, he had seen several bodies—Phebe's blood-supplying victims—sprawled about its floor. And where, moreover, he had witnessed Phebe herself feeding, like some ferocious beast, on the next-to last of those victims—Russell Gorman—with her teeth fastened in his throat. Even now, in this dreadful instant of fugitive and nightmare-like reverie, Nathan fancied he was able to hear once more the horrid slurping noise from Phebe's gaping mouth as she greedily supped his blood from the ghastly laceration in his neck.

And Nathan felt an icy shudder sweep violently through his entire body as very coldly, very suddenly he came all but breathlessly out of these frightening musings. At the same instant, he found himself thinking if he had in his hand this very moment—here (*now!*)—that little glass cruet of holy water which he'd taken from Mr Jozsef Szekler's urn, would he have the courage, the daring, the boldness of will to use it? To dash its sanctified liquid squarely into Phebe's face? What *would* happen if he did? Could it truly harm Phebe? Would she really suffer—or (worse still!) *die*—from such a thing so innocuous as that?

Meanwhile, Phebe's dark, motionless eyes continued to peer deeply, steadily into Nathan's, as though she were silently aware of the stir and movement of his every thought. As though, even now, she were intently listening to each and every one of them quietly passing through his mind. For suddenly, drawing a soft, slow breath that was like a sob, the lash-fringed lids descended over her eyes, as if to veil from Nathan the tears then gathering in them. And yet, not before he had seen a look, an expression of unutterable sorrow, disappointment, and regret enter into their shadowy depths, presaging the rise of those tears.

Then, slowly turning her face away from Nathan, Phebe began to speak over her shoulder to Vrancic, addressing him in that harsh, mysterious tongue which she had used several times before. At once, Vrancic's voice and Candy's broke out simultaneously in protest at her speech; but her response, barked across at them in a tone of commandment and authority, instantly silenced them.

Unspeaking, her eyes still shut—although tears were already sparkling along her dark lashes (one or two of which Nathan had seen fall glittering down her cheeks)—Phebe extended her arm to Vrancic. Reluctantly, almost grudgingly he produced from the breast pocket of his jacket some small object, which he then silently placed in the palm of her icy, long-fingered hand.

Turning her head, Phebe softly opened her eyes, fixing once more upon Nathan's face their solemn, mournful gaze, while holding out to him in her upturned palm the very thing that Vrancic had handed her.

"If you still doubt me, Nathan;" she said, gazing with utterly frank, desolate eyes directly into his; "if you still fear me, then maybe this will help change your mind... or," she added, after a long pause, "at least embolden you to do what you feel is the right thing that should now be done." And stooping forward a little, she held the object in her hand out to Nathan, who then looked down at it and saw instantly that it was the glass cruet of holy water. He noted, too, that its stopple, in the shape of the Jerusalem cross, was missing. Nathan stared at it for the next few moments in speechless astonishment, before his eyes fixed themselves on Phebe's face again.

"Take it, Nathan," he heard her voice whisper across to him. Then, in a voice almost as faint as her own, Nathan managed to stammer, "But... it-it's... holy water, Phebe."

Phebe only nodded her head, and, still holding out to Nathan the small glass, unstoppered cruet, she continued to gaze unswervingly out of her dark forlorn eyes at him.

"But isn't—" Nathan's voice suddenly faltered. "I mean, to vampires;" he began again; "isn't holy water d—" He suddenly broke off, and silently continued to meet Phebe's dark, dwelling, mournful eyes. Then, "Deadly," she said, finishing the sentence for Nathan, and, with a slight shudder, she faintly nodded her head, adding, barely above a whisper, "Yes... it inflicts upon them a swift but agonizing death. Which is why I'm now giving it to you."

Still speechless, Nathan hesitated. The knowledge that Phebe must have known what had been passing in his mind only made Nathan all the more averse and ashamed to do now as she was bidding him, and receive from her hand that little glass cruet. And very faintly, then, Nathan shook his head. "But why?" he asked.

"Don't be afraid, Nathan;" came the soft reply; "we had no right to take it from you in the first place. Which is why I want to return it to you. Take it." And the deep dark eyes that remained fastened on his silent face, after the full red lips had drawn together, continued to steadily regard him.

Nathan gazed at her, still hesitating; then, slowly, his trembling hand moved forward and, obeying her, his fingers, almost before he knew it, were tightly clutching the little glass phial of holy water.

Then, with eyes still fixed intently on Phebe's, he asked, "What do you want me to do with it?"

Out of her dark, mournful, tear-moistened eyes, Phebe gazed at Nathan's face long and searchingly. Then, in a voice firm and unfaltering, as if she had reached a momentous decision, she said, "I'm putting my life in your hands now, Nathan. Do with it as you wish." Very suddenly she stood up, and, after Nathan had risen to his feet and she was on her knees before him, she cast up at Nathan a tragic glance of entreaty. Then, with trembling lip, she said: "If you truly love me, Nathan, you'll help me; or, if you don't love me... then end this for me."

There was a long silence, and those dark lustrous eyes, desolate, haunted, and misery-stricken, continued to gaze steadily up at Nathan's pale, anxious face.

Powerless to either speak or stir, Nathan gazed down pityingly into those wide, mournful eyes; then, once again Phebe's voice, small and despairing, broke the tense silence that had fallen between them: "If you wish to be rid of me, Nathan, then go ahead"—and softly withdrawing her dark eyes from Nathan's face—"here it is;" she breathed out to him, after having paused to steal a long and sorrowful look at the little glass cruet in his hand; "I now give you the chance." And in a small tremulous whisper, she added, "Use the holy water: pour it..." But her voice had suddenly become choked with tears, and, quickly bowing her head low, she broke off with a sob.

With extreme caution Nathan held tight the cruet of holy water above Phebe's head. Undecided what to do, he stood there motionless, gazing blankly, almost blindly down at the top of Phebe's head. His heart was drumming now thick and fast; and he kept asking himself, what *should* he do? Should he obey Phebe, and (as she put it) 'end this' for her by pouring the holy water on her; or 'help' her, regardless of what that help might involve or call for?

Nathan's thoughts hovered now between compassion and misgiving, between devotion and distrust; and, like a swarm of agitated bees, they flitted about in his mind, now this way, now that. Within moments his poor wits became desperately confused, and suddenly he was conscious for the first time of a blinding headache. Then, for a moment or two, the room seemed to spin with an odd dizziness of motion before his frightened eyes. And for the space of perhaps ten seconds he shut them tight, in the hope of quieting his mind, of calming his nerves, and as if to breathe out a whispered prayer.

But all in a moment his chilled, faintly trembling hand had become unsteady, and the cramped, clammy fingers clutching the little cruet of holy water above Phebe's head had nearly loosened their grip. And in that instant a solitary drop, not much larger than the head of a pin, spilled over the smooth, curved lip of the cruet's rim, and landed upon a single black slender strand of Phebe's long hair.

Instantly Nathan's eyes re-opened, and he suddenly caught his breath as he saw a thin, faint shadowy frond of grey smoke go wreathing upward from her hair. The strand itself, he noted, began to smolder, and then, in mute horror, he watched as two tiny, fiery-red sparks appeared and began to spread along the fine black strand in opposite directions. One burning its way rapidly up to the hair's root, and the other leaping its way steadily down to the hair's end. And there (at the strand's root and end) either expired, vanishing, along with the wisp of hair, in a thin vaporous reek.

Filled with awe and alarm by what he had just now witnessed, Nathan felt a strange and sudden pang shoot through his heart. For all at once a small, still voice within him, faint, remote, and yet curiously familiar, as from some memoried past now secret and long forgotten, seemed to remind, apprise, *assure* him that this was *her*, the one without equal, beyond compare, and with whom anything and everything in this life was to him as nothing.

And all at once that maddening decision about what he should do—the resolution which he had so desperately sought, and which, until now, had persisted to elude him—became perfectly clear. He debated no more: he could *never* harm Phebe. And suddenly he drew a sharp breath, and, with a violent shake of his head, he said, "I can't... I can't": and he flung the cruet aside. It dashed to the floor, shattering into flinders near the grandfather clock, sprinkling the carved molding of its base with holy water.

Phebe slowly lifted her head, and presently, with her face upturned to Nathan, she once more fixed him with that wistful, forlorn, tragic gaze.

Nathan met her intensely dark eyes, still moist with the rising of her tears, and agleam now with a tenderness of love beyond all human measure, and straight into their depths he peered for some little while without speaking. And making no effort to hide or brush away the tears that had sprung into his own weary, aching eyes, he said, "I could never hurt you."

Phebe stood up, and the next instant Nathan felt her supple, shapely body pressing up against him. Then, the feeling of those slender arms about him dispelled any and all lingering apprehensions, misgivings, and suspicions. And her hair falling forward about his face and mouth seemed to him a consecration; and the burning sensation of her wonderful lips upon his own, a sacrament.

And in a whisper, breathed softly into her little ear, Nathan asked, "Were you testing me, Phebe?"

"Proving your love;" came the whispered reply; "just as I would never hurt you, Nathan, I knew you would never harm me." She paused, and, holding him more tightly to her, she added, in a voice low and soft in his ear: "In my heart, I know you love me—for I belong to you, and you belong to me."

Then, after an interval of some seconds, they drew slightly apart and gazed on a while in silence, steadily, intently, into one another's eyes. And faintly, half solemnly, Phebe asked, "And do you truly love me, Nathan?"

Unflinchingly Nathan met Phebe's eyes, an unmistakable hint of worship in the depths of his own; and without hesitating even for an instant, "I do," came the whispered answer.

Phebe drew half a step nearer, and, with silent, desperate appeal in her deep, dark, luminous eyes, she gazed on into the depths of Nathan's most searchingly. She drew into her body a long, slow, trembling breath, and then, "So you'll help me, Nathan?" she asked almost cautiously, and in a voice that was all but despairing.

Nathan also took a deep breath, and, listening now to his own voice, as if in a dream, he heard himself answer—"Yes."

And all at once, having noted the expression on Phebe's face instantly change to wistful appreciation, she came nestling in close against him, clinging to his body, in a passion of joy and gratitude, with her arms caught about his neck. Nathan felt Phebe's lips slightly quivering, and once or twice, on his cheeks, the wetness of tears, as she kissed his face and mouth many times. Then, burying his face deep into the Elysium, the nirvana of her long black, silky tresses, he asked, "But how, Phebe—how do I help you? What do you need me for?"

Once more, then, they drew slowly apart. Phebe slipped her lean, small hand into Nathan's—cold as glacial ice he felt it clasp his own—and drew him softly down next to her on the sofa.

At the same time, Vrancic and Candy had passed silently round now to their (Nathan's and Phebe's) side of the coffee table, and had taken up positions at either end of the sofa. Candy was perched on the cushioned arm, to Nathan's right, and sat eyeing the boy with a cold, cruel, triumphant leer; while Vrancic remained standing at the opposite end, his small, black, piercing eyes fastened with a peculiar owl-like intensity on Nathan's face.

Nathan glanced a moment at either of them, but neither said a word to him. Then, Phebe spoke:

"For centuries now, Nathan, rumors have circulated among my kind with regard to a spell that can undo the curse that constrains myself and others like me to suffer the blighted nature of a vampire. A spell that can restore to us once more the natural order of our existence—its human condition, its mortal state, of which we were so ruthlessly divested." Phebe paused, and continued to meet Nathan's motionless eyes, all his thoughts, meanwhile, having fallen into a deep and curious stillness.

Then, "At first," Phebe went on, "I could discover little more than hints, vague whispers, and hearsay as to the form this spell was in. But each time I encountered one of my kind, and inquired into the matter, I learned a little more. In the end, what I came to understand was that the spell originally existed on an ancient parchment scroll which became either lost or destroyed at some point over the centuries. Its actual fate is not now known. What *is*, however, known by many of my kind with absolute certainty is that one of the principal requirements needed in the ritual of this spell to reverse the evil malediction we've so long endured, is blood"—once again Phebe paused and, with her eyes fixed unswervingly on Nathan's silent face, her cold, lean hand with its narrow-boned fingers had again stolen into his—"blood from a mortal," she softly continued, "whose month, day, and hour of birth coincides exactly with the month, day, and hour on which the accursed sufferer had their mortality taken from them, and their human nature transformed into that of the monstrous vampire's. Your birth certificate, Nathan, shows that you are that mortal. You were born Tuesday, the 26th day of August, at 12:00 a.m., midnight; and seventeen hundred years ago, on a Tuesday, the 26th day of August, at midnight, the essence of my humanity was cursed; and I was deprived of my mortal nature—changed into a vampire..." Phebe's voice had fallen a little flat, then sank almost to a whisper, as she added: "Reborn, as it were."

Again Phebe was silent; and the eyes that gazed across at Nathan became strangely absent for a moment or two. Meanwhile, Nathan stared at Phebe's face in a dream-like and helpless hush. Then, "All I need from you, Nathan," began Phebe again, as once more the deep, dark, mournful eyes gazed intently, anxiously into his, "is some of your blood. You won't be harmed in any way, I promise. Only a little of your blood, to be applied in conjunction with the spell at a rite to undo this curse. But it cannot be taken from you by force, Nathan; you must offer it to me—freely, willingly."

And presently, a deep silence ensued; not even the ghost of a sound was to be heard in all the house. The moments drew solemnly on. And still no one spoke.

Nathan gazed at Phebe, and, dark as that primordial Night before the world's first morning, the eyes in that pale, narrow, hauntingly beautiful face steadily continued to stare back at Nathan, as though she were hoping, expecting, waiting for him to readily agree, and express his ungrudging consent.

But as under the potent spell of some strange, deep enchantment himself, Nathan could do little more than sit there very still and awkwardly silent, as yet again cold, vague apprehensions began to gather thickly round his rapidly beating heart.

And then, all at once, across the silence, Nathan heard the soft, faint licking sound of his cat, Ichabod—or Bram—diligently washing his face as he lay comfortably stretched out near the bottommost step of the stairs.

But as Nathan withdrew his eyes from those of Phebe's to glance across the room at this less-than loyal feline of his, the cat suddenly paused in its grooming, as though conscious of Nathan's scrutiny. Abruptly it sat up and, for a moment or two, seemed to regard Nathan almost sympathetically with its large greenish eyes. Then, with a blink of one of those emerald-colored eyes, it turned itself away and walked serenely off into the dining room. And after having emitted several long, low mewls, as though it were bidding its new master to come and join it, Nathan heard the cat's heavy paws (and the faint tip-tapping of its untrimmed claws) go retreating down the steep wooden steps to the basement, whose door, apparently, had been left open by Vrancic. Never again after this night would Nathan and Ichabod see one another in Aunt Amelia's house. Only one other time would their paths cross, and that but briefly.

Then, very soft and slow, Nathan took a deep breath, and, when once more his eyes had fixed themselves on Phebe's face, his dry lips managed at length to whisper: "But, Phebe, how can you be sure that this rumor about some spell is anything more than just that?"

Out of her large, dark, lustrous eyes, Phebe gazed for a moment half solemnly, half reflectively at Nathan's face, but before she could answer him, Vrancic said:

"Because over a period of many centuries, this same spell has been mentioned and spoken of by various occult scholars and historians as an absolute fact." He paused a moment or two, and, keeping his eyes firmly on Nathan's, he sat down on the edge of the coffee table. Then, resting his hands on his knees, he said, "And I myself can attest to the veracity of its existence, for I have seen it paraphrased in several Greek, Latin, and Hebrew manuscripts. The history behind it is this:

"In the year 310, the Roman Emperor, Galerius, was stricken by some kind of agonizingly painful and protracted malady. The ancient sources are confused and obscure about the precise nature of this bizarre and terminal illness; but all tend to agree that he began to waste away from it. In some of these sources it is defined as strangely infected wounds or ulcers on his neck, his wrists, feet, and in the genital area. And as the 'disease' he contracted rapidly worsened, and these infected 'wounds' continued to multiply—inexplicably, according to the sources—his flesh began to literally putrefy on his bones, and from his body there arose an unspeakably foul stench.

"And although the learned physicians and healers he kept with him at his royal court were unable to identify his baffling illness, Galerius himself did not hesitate to connect it to the wrath and vengeance of the divinity of the Christians, whose devotees he had ruthlessly persecuted: some by crucifixion, others by way of a malediction that caused them to become vampires." Vrancic was silent a moment. He leaned forward a little, his elbows on his knees, and his black luminous eyes still fastened on Nathan's face. But before he resumed speaking, Candy remarked in a low, rather icy tone of voice, "O, yes; it was certainly vengeance; but it had nothing to do with any 'divinity.'" And as Nathan and Phebe turned to glance over at him, the child deliberately caught Phebe's eye with a look that was full of meaning—a look in which there was concealed some private understanding between the two of them, and which Nathan was unable to share in.

Then, "It was Galerius's firm belief," began Vrancic again, "that the strange infection from which he was slowly dying was therefore a punishment inflicted upon him by the Christian god. And so, in order to appease this god of the Christians, and assuage his wrath, in the year 311, Galerius issued an Edict of Toleration. He called for a cessation to the Persecution of the Christians. He restored to them the places of their worship, and, lastly, ordered the formulation of a spell to undo the vampiric curse and reverse its sorceries that had consigned many Christian devotees to darkness and the drinking of blood, and so restore to them their mortal nature. The crafting of this spell is consistently attributed, in all the oldest sources, to a Syrian Christian of the Gnostic sect who was then living in Serdica, where Galerius contracted his 'illness', and who was said to possess many magical books composed by king Solomon. But shortly after the formulation of this spell, which was inscribed, it is said, with the blood of a lamb upon a sheet of virgin parchment, Galerius died of his infected wounds or ulcers."

In the short pause following these words, Nathan heard Candy emit a low, scornful laugh. And in slightly turning his head to steal a longish glance at him, he noted a malicious smile had spread over the child's death-pale face, and into its brilliant blue eyes had crept a wicked ray of gloating and stony cruelty. But Nathan's gaze immediately settled itself on Vrancic again the moment he heard him speaking.

"A tradition regarding this spell," continued Vrancic, "indeed, a very old one—which harks back at least to the time of the late Roman Empire—maintains that the Roman Emperor himself, Constantine the Great, ordered that a copy of the spell be written down in a vellum manuscript, which was then preserved in the imperial library in Constantinople. And since then, all down through the ages, various authors, historians, and scholars have made mention—in one way or another—of this most extraordinary and unique spell. The earliest known surviving paraphrase of it appears in an obscure work by Michael Psellus, a Greek historian of the eleventh century. In the twelfth century another Greek historian, Michael Glycas, yet again mentions this spell. Nicetas Choniates, a Byzantine historian of the thirteenth century also speaks of it. Paracelsus and the learned monk, Roger Bacon, paraphrase it yet again in their writings; while Petrus Mozellanus, a scholar during the time of the Renaissance, mentions this spell in his works. Moreover, an erudite Friar of Morigny, not far from Etampes in France, cites several Greek manuscripts in the monastic library in which variants of this spell appear.

"Now, the original Byzantine manuscript containing the full copy of this spell, as ordered by the Roman Emperor, in 327 A.D., remained for centuries in Constantinople; and, in the course of time, fresh incantations, curses, and esoteric rites for evoking demons, were added to its pages by various hands. Pope Gregory VI, in the year 1045, makes mention of this manuscript of diabolism under the title of the Arcana Magorum Detestanda, or the Execrated Secrets of the Magicians, stating that at some time in the early part of the century it had passed from the eastern Byzantine world into the Latin west. And by the time of his successor, Pope Clement II, many copies of this occult manuscript were being secretly produced and distributed among the alchemists, sorcerers, and astrologers of the day.

"But then, by the year 1464, Pope Pius II acquired possession of this ancient manuscript. And by means of the relentless persecution and rooting out of all known sorcerers and alchemists in Christian Europe, he managed to confiscate nearly every copy of the Arcana Magorum Detestanda and had them all burned along with the original manuscript. Only two copies are known to have escaped the flames of this biblio-holocaust: a Corvinian manuscript copy of the Arcana, and a very rare incunabulum edition."

Nathan's brow creased with a look of perplexity as, in a low, stammering voice, "Inca... incannabalon..." he attempted (but failed) to pronounce this very curious, unfamiliar term.

"In-kyoo-nab-ya-lum," said Vrancic, slowly sounding the word out. For a moment or two Nathan shyly withdrew his gaze from Vrancic, and his questioning eyes sought Phebe. "Nathan;" she said; "remember how only a few days ago I was telling you that there's a book Antal is trying to find for me, a very old book that may have in it a cure for me?"—Nathan faintly nodded his head—"Well, that's what an incunabulum is—a very old, old book, the first books that were ever printed."

Vrancic's steady regard was still fixed on Nathan as he said, "Precisely;" and then paused, until Nathan's eyes, slowly groping round from those of Phebe's, became intent once more on his own. "Incunabula," he then continued, "are simply the first printed books that were produced in Europe between the years 1450 and 1500. The word itself is from the Latin, and means 'cradle, infancy', and is merely a convenient term applied to the first books that were printed before the end of the year 1500. For among the scholars, historians, and aficionados of old books, any edition printed after the year 1500 is, as a general rule, never regarded as an incunabulum. Today these beautifully bound volumes and editions are collected and valued as works of art and nothing more.

"But in getting back to those two surviving copies of the Arcana Magorum Detestanda;" went on Vrancic, after a short silence; "the Corvinian manuscript—as it has come to be designated—was commissioned in 1458 for King Matthias Corvinus's library in Hungary. As was typical with all the Corvinian manuscripts, this was copied, illuminated, and bound in a workshop in Florence, and then, upon its completion, sent on from Italy to the King's library in Buda. When, however, Hungary was overrun in the year 1526 by invading Ottoman Turks, the book disappeared for centuries, and was presumed to have been either lost or destroyed with the rest of King Matthias's royal library.

"Today there is little doubt among historians that the Turkish Sultan had the bulk of the Hungarian ruler's magnificent library in Buda loaded onto his ships and taken back with him to Constantinople. There, over a period of many years, an illicit trade commenced, and Corvinian manuscripts began to leak into the hands of private collectors, book merchants, and agents working for buyers among the fabulously wealthy and powerful. And it is believed that by this means of felonious trafficking, the Corvinian manuscript copy of the Arcana Magorum Detestanda mysteriously turned up in a bookshop in Dresden toward the end of the nineteenth century. It was instantly identified as one of Corvinus's manuscripts owing to the royal family's armorial bearing on the cover surmounted by a blue raven—one of the chief distinguishing hallmarks of a manuscript commissioned by the Raven King, as Matthias was called.

"The remarkable discovery of this relic from King Matthias's fabled collection of books, however, was all too short-lived. For by the twentieth century this singular volume perished for good, lost forever as a result of the bombing of Dresden during the Second World War. But even if it had survived the devastation unharmed, and we had it here this very instant in our hands, the spell it contains would, in all likelihood, have proven to be of little or no use whatsoever to Phebe. For once the volume surfaced in Dresden, historians and scholars with a profound knowledge of the Arcana Magorum, after having thoroughly examined this Corvinian manuscript, assessed that it was a very poor and hastily executed copy of the Arcana, replete with a number of lacunae in the text, numerous mistakes, and many significant passages in a severely abbreviated form. This assessment alone pronounces the Corvinian copy as worthless to Phebe. No; Phebe's only hope now lies in the Arcana's only extant complete copy, the incunabulum edition; for an unabridged copy of the spell needed by Phebe to undo the vampiric curse and regain her mortality survives somewhere in the pages of that book alone."

Phebe had sat, motionless, with her hands in her lap, listening. Her knees were pressed tight together, and her eyes were still fixed half vacantly on Vrancic's face. Suddenly her hand crept out and had gently stolen into Nathan's. Then, turning tenderly to face him, she squeezed the hand clasped in hers.

And then, after a brief silence, "Today this most rare work of supernatural lore," Vrancic continued almost musingly, "is considered by scholars and historians alike as the most precious book of occultism in existence. Tradition maintains that it was commissioned in Paris in 1462 by Mathurin Chastenet, one of the most remarkable alchemists of the fifteenth century. Chastenet was a seigneur, and a native of Normandy, where it is said he practiced a very dark and dechristianized form of cabbalism; which in his later years degenerated into outright necromancy and satanism. According to one tradition, Chastenet is said to have had the incunabulum bound in the tanned skin of an unbaptized infant who had been strangled by its mother on Walpurgis Night. And emblazoned on its covers—reputedly in the blood of a defrocked priest—are numerous pentacles and other occult, alchemico, and cabbalistic emblems.

"Unfortunately for its owner, this most precious work of occultism did not long remain in his possession. A year later Chastenet was arrested and sent to Rome where he was cast into the dungeons of the Inquisition. After a hasty trial, in which the clergy found him guilty of sorcery and the evocation of demons, he was hanged, decapitated, and then burned. And yet it was never known with absolute certainty whether the Church was able to get their hands on Chastenet's incunabulum edition of the *Arcana Magorum Detestanda*. All that has been recorded in court documents from the time is that the Inquisition burned a number of old 'sorcerous' books found in Chastenet's library. And while some historians maintain that the incunabulum was probably among those books consigned to the flames by the Church, some scholars believe that one of Chastenet's disciples took the incunabulum before his master's arrest. But they have never been able to ascertain the identity of this most loyal devotee. For Chastenet's doctrines were diffused among a very select number of adepts whose names have always been kept in strict secrecy, since some of them were believed to have been among the high clergy and nobility of France. And so, historians and scholars have never been able to discover with any degree of certainty what actually became of the incunabulum. Speculation and debate still continues among scholars and experts in the occult, but its ultimate fate remains a mystery—until now, that is!"

Phebe glanced up sharply. Her deep, dark, large-pupilled eyes opened round and wide, and her body visibly stiffened. "Then you've found it, Antal?" came the almost breathlessly whispered question, and there was an oddly cautious tone, a hint even of incredulity in the tremulous voice. And as Nathan watched her face, he felt the small cold hand clutching his own begin to tremble.

"I believe I have," Vrancic replied. "Through a number of buyers, agents, and other reliable individuals who are knowledgeable in the tracking down of very rare and important books, I have been able to discover thus far that it is in the private library of a wealthy collector on an estate on Long Island. But at the moment I can tell you little more than that, for my chief contact is still in the process of looking more fully into the book's history and how it came to be in the possession of its present owner. Also I have yet to confirm whether the information furnished me is in fact entirely accurate. And it is on these particulars that I am now diligently at work. Before we attempt to make any move, these details must be verified."

And in the deep, concentrated hush that followed these words, Nathan turned his eyes to Phebe. She was sitting very still and silent, looking with the absent gaze of her downbent eyes into her lap, lost seemingly to everyone and everything around her in some dreamlike reverie. And suddenly Nathan observed that the expression on her face had become strangely fixed, as though she were seeing herself already in possession of that fabled, wished-for book containing within its ancient leaves the promise of a life redeemed and an existence uncursed. And for a moment he wondered (somewhat uneasily) to himself if, for one instant, it ever occurred to Phebe that this "spell" might turn out to be no more than a series of weird verses and curiously worded phrases, with no more power to bring her release from her accursed fate than the lyrics to a song by Elvis or The Beatles.

And while in the midst of these rather uncomfortable musings, Nathan's eyes had strayed, without him being in the least aware of it, slowly round from Phebe's silent face to that of Candy's. For some seconds the intensely scornful regard in the eyes of that repellently androgynous face held his own, immovably; and, almost before Nathan realized what he was saying, he heard himself breathe out across to him, "Are you a vampire, too?"

For a moment or two longer, that sinister, chilling gaze continued to dwell on Nathan's face, holding his eyes. Then, "Yes... the offspring of *him*," came the stony reply, "whose legacy in this world are all the forsaken, the accursed, the *Undead*, compelled to dwell in everlasting darkness!"

Nathan stared at Candy in astonishment; and then, as if to himself, he all but whispered, "Galerius... you're his... son..."

"His son, his daughter; his daughter, his son;" said Candy; "both... once; and now—neither." He paused, then, to fetch out of his pocket a golden coin, that ancient Roman aureus, and, exhibiting its obverse to Nathan's eyes, he said, "That is the image of Galerius on this coin. I have carried it with me for nearly two thousand years. And other than this curse, it is the only thing that I now keep in memory of him. A reminder to me of how shallow was the man's love for me, and how deep his malice and cruelty." There was a long, intense pause; and into the features of Candy's face had suddenly crept a cold, inhuman expression as he added: "And with a malice and cruelty no less deep, have I roamed the earth, abiding for centuries in darkness, condemned to drink the blood of your kind in fulfillment of the curse bequeathed by a father to his son!"

Nathan gazed on at Candy without speaking, without stirring; indeed, almost it seemed for the time being that his whole body had stiffened into stone. And yet in the very same instant that he had shut his eyes to hide the aversion that was in them for the malevolent and sadistically ruthless creature they now confronted, he could not help but feel a shade of pity mingle with his repulsion. Some modicum of sympathy for the horrid existence it had been compelled, damned to endure through no fault or choosing of its own.

But suddenly Candy sat glowering fiercely across at Nathan, as if conscious of, and mortally offended by, the boy's heartfelt compassion. For all at once he sprang down from the arm of the sofa with a furious expression, and snarled, "All this talk! Pah! I've had enough!" And away he stalked, with clenched fists, into the sun-room, and drew the doors shut behind him.

For nearly a full minute, neither Nathan or Phebe, nor Vrancic spoke or stirred; each seemed to be deeply engrossed in their own thoughts. But then, quite suddenly, Vrancic gave a slight start, as though he had just recollected something of importance.

"Oh, yes; one more thing," he said, fixing his eyes on Phebe. "You might as well know, I've enlisted the help of a man who has a great many contacts among the top-end dealers in the rare books and antiquities trade, all within the global networks that supply merchants, museums, and the wealthiest private collectors in Europe and the United States. Initially the man showed considerable reluctance in responding to the several emails that I sent him; and when I did receive a reply, he expressed in his email little interest in involving himself in my 'client's' quest to locate Chastenet's incunabulum edition of the Arcana Magorum Detestanda. He seemed to imply that my 'client' might as well seek to discover the whereabouts of the Ark of the Covenant, or the Holy Grail rather than that rarest of books whose ultimate fate remains one of the mysteries of the art world.

"But I would not be so easily put off, and told him that the 'client' that I am representing"—and Vrancic shot Phebe a significant look—"has lived a very long and rich life, traveling a great deal through many parts of the world amassing artifacts, antiquities, rare coins and jewels from divers centuries and periods. Treasures, in fact, beyond compare; many of which would stun the art world were they to mysteriously surface, and, at the same time, make the supplier who should come into their possession a very rich man. Moreover, I told him that my client would be willing to exchange these inestimable pieces for any information leading to the incunabulum's location and the identity of its owner.

"And to clinch his interest and enthusiasm in our cause, I then emailed him several photographs I took of a number of valuable items in your possession. Among them the emperor's Ceylon ruby, the chrysolampis jewel from the Abbey of Egmund, and a dozen or more rare and ancient coins. This instantly caught the man's attention, as I knew it would. And over the next few days, after emailing him numerous photos of the treasures I've already mentioned, I received from him in an email his pledge and promise to assist my client in obtaining Chastenet's incunabulum through all the information he could gather by way of a number of sources among suppliers, merchants, and auctioneers with whom he has long-standing connections. Along with his promise of assistance, however, has come a warning that I should inform my client to be prepared to pay a hefty price for his services."

Vrancic suddenly paused to fix Phebe with a very solemn eye, then said to her: "You may have to part with a great many costly treasures before we get the information we need that will finally reveal to us all the necessary details with regard to the incunabulum's precise location and how it came to be there."

Phebe made a dismissive gesture with her hand. "I don't care, Antal; so long as I obtain the incunabulum," she said, and Nathan noted that the expression of her face was all but forbidding.

Vrancic gave a slight nod of his head, and was about to speak, when Nathan suddenly interrupted him: "Who is this man, Vrancic; what's his name?"

"Among rich collectors of rare books and works of art," said Vrancic, "as well as museums, suppliers of artifacts, and the antiquities markets, his name is well known—to you and Phebe, however, it would be quite meaningless."

But Nathan was insistent. "I know, that's why I'm asking," he said. "Who is he? What's his name? I want to hear it."

Vrancic regarded him steadily for a moment or two in silence, and a sour expression edged its way into his features. Then, his lips parted and he was about to tell Nathan to be quiet. But the moment his glance encountered Phebe's, who he noted fixed on him a vampire's deadpan and ominous eye, he realized instantly he'd better give her mortal lover an answer that was neither sarcastic nor unsatisfying, or the consequences to himself could very well prove quite unpleasant if not fatal.

At once the expression on his face softened. "Well, if you must know," said Vrancic, "the man's name is Walter Farnhill. He is a high-profile London dealer in very old and very rare books and manuscripts, who has run to ground for many of his clients invaluable works, including several priceless incunabula. His underworld sources for ancient manuscripts and artifacts on the antiquities markets are said to be the most reliable. Years ago he made a name for himself in the illicit trade of smuggling antiquities out of Europe and into the United States, and today he is the undisputed lord of dealing in top-end artifacts and the rarest books and manuscripts from the ancient and medieval world.

"And according to what he has been able to gather for me from his sources, the incunabulum had been bought some years ago by a wealthy individual, a 'private collector', who resides in New York, somewhere on Long Island's North Shore. More than that, Mr Farnhill has told me in his most recent email, he has been unable—thus far—to learn. Up until now, Mr Farnhill's preferred means of communication with me has been email. Next week, however, we have arranged to have our first face-to-face meeting in Manhattan, inside the Metropolitan Museum of Art. He says he has some invaluable information on the incunabulum from his European contacts. But again, it must be understood, that the price for this information will be high indeed." He paused and, once more in silence, fixed Phebe with a grave, unwavering eye. Then, "In all probability," he said to her, "you will have to part with no small amount in money, and in valuables such as jewels and rare coins—" But Phebe suddenly broke in: "I care nothing for that, so long as the information you purchase reveals to me the incunabulum's precise location. It must be mine, Antal, at any price! Do you understand?"

"Very well, then," Vrancic quietly replied, and for some while no one spoke another word.

But then, after fidgeting a moment where he sat, Nathan's gaze began to wander slowly, almost doubtfully from Phebe's face to Vrancic's, and back again. For suddenly a very curious and perplexing thought had occurred to him. "There's just one thing I don't understand;" he ventured at last; "how did you know about—me?" And pausing to eye either of them half suspiciously, "I mean," he went on, "how did you know my name; where I live; and about my date of birth?"

"It was Antal," answered Phebe, "who very cleverly managed that. He has a great deal of knowledge in the occult, and is acquainted with many mysterious and mystical rites."

Nathan's questioning gaze slowly withdrew itself from Phebe's face and settled intently on Vrancic's again. For a moment or two he held his breath; and then, "But how?" he half whispered.

Vrancic faintly grinned. "Through a very ancient occult method of divination," he replied, "called 'sortes Biblicae', or Bible sortilege. It involves opening a Bible at random, choosing a word or number randomly from the texts of scripture, and then regarding the choice of that word or numeral upon which the eye, or finger, has first settled, as a divine oracle. The widespread use of this curious system of augury among early Christians was condemned by the Church long ago, for ordinances were soon passed avowing excommunication of any Christian found practicing this forbidden art.

"Now, when I resolved to discover, on behalf of Phebe, the name of the mortal whose date of birth matched the very month, day, and hour of her nativity—so to speak—as a vampire, I commenced this very solemn undertaking with several days of preliminary occult ceremonies and secret rites. I then traced upon my breast, in the blood of a lamb, two triangles united and enjoined, one pointing upward, the other downward, reproducing in this way the grand pentacle, the seal of King Solomon the Wise. Marked with this sacred device, I called three times upon the mystical and ineffable name of God in the Hebrew, the Tetragrammaton, which transliterates in four letters as JHVH, Jehovah, and represents, in the occult, the inscrutable symbol of the Most High's mysterious name.

"Upon completion of this all-powerful invocation, I then consulted a Bible through the forbidden method of sortilege seven individual times. For the number seven in the occult is regarded not only as a divine number, but a number of power, signifying completeness, perfection. There were seven principal luminaries known to the ancients: the sun, moon, and the five planets. The days of the week amount to seven, the seventh of which represents the completion of God's work. And the seventh seal, seventh trumpet, and seventh bowl, in the book of Revelation, symbolize God's plan come to fruition."

Vrancic had paused and, from the breast pocket of his shirt, produced a pack of cigarettes. "And so," he continued, as he casually proceeded to abstract a Marlboro from the open pack, "upon first opening the Bible—I believe at Paul's epistle to the Hebrews, 2:14— and selecting the first word in the text on which my finger settled, I noted that I had randomly chosen the word 'empire'. Randomly opening the Bible and choosing a second time, I had selected— curiously enough! —from John 1 verse 45, the word, or rather the name, 'Nathanael'. The next word that my finger chanced to settle on, somewhere in the book of Genesis, I think, was 'village'. After that, in the 26th chapter of the Acts of the Apostles, verse 28, my finger came to rest on the word 'Christian'. My next seemingly arbitrary choice, I think from the Book of Maccabees, was the word 'state'. Then, from Kings III, chapter 10, verse 1, I had chosen, 'queen'; and lastly, the word 'middle' had been randomly selected from the Book of Judges, I believe.

"And after having written down each of these seven oracular words, 'empire', 'Nathanael', 'village', 'Christian', 'state', 'queen', and 'middle', I came to easily deduce that "Nathanael' was the first name of the person we sought; and then conjectured that the word 'Christian' must therefore be his second name. In this way I arrived at your identity. Then, the words 'state' and 'empire', I came to interpret as 'Empire State', a traditional byword in America for the state of New York, and thus concluded this must be the location in which our 'Nathanael Christian' must presently reside. To narrow it down still further, the word 'queen', I then took for 'Queens', the borough in which the home of our 'mortal of interest' must be situated. And finally, by linking the word 'middle' with that of 'village', I obtained the name of your town, 'Middle Village'."

Once again Vrancic had paused. He lit his cigarette, and took a long draw on it. "After that," he then went on, exhaling a cloud of smoke, "it remained only for Phebe to come to your doorstep and, when the opportunity should arise, introduce herself to you. But somehow, Nathan, you found—her. Whether by fortune's whim, or fate's decree, you found your way inside the mausoleum, that afternoon, and looked straight into the eyes of the one who has been searching for you now for more than a thousand years."

Nathan's eyes fixed themselves almost in awe on Phebe's face, and all at once her lips broke into the most tender smile. "It was no whim of chance, Nathan;" she said; "but fate;" and pausing an instant to peer steadily into his eyes, a light in the intensely dark, unfathomable depths of her own was faintly kindled, as she added: "fate that guided you to me that day, and destiny that led you to the very place in which it was preordained for you to find me—asleep, and yet eagerly awaiting your longed-for approach."

Nathan sat perfectly still, gazing on steadily at the pale beautiful face of Phebe in an intensely curious hush that had suddenly drawn itself over his thoughts. For a space of some seconds not even the tiniest sound was audible; and Nathan and Phebe continued to gaze on into the motionless eyes of one another. But then, the voice of Antal Vrancic broke the silence. "The time;" he muttered anxiously; "the time."

And when Nathan and Phebe glanced up, they saw that Vrancic had risen to his feet, and was staring down gravely at the oval face of the watch on his wrist. Once or twice, on its delicate crystal glass, he lightly tapped with the tip of his finger. "Daybreak is only minutes away," he said, and the eyebrows arched high on his head as he cast a significant glance at Phebe.

Phebe turned to once more fix her eyes on Nathan. Her mouth opened a little, as if to speak; she seemed to hesitate; and then her lips drew tightly together again. She remained coyly watching Nathan's face, the expression in her features a mingled look of acute hope, profound yearning, and grieved expectation. She waited. But Nathan continued to gaze on—still speechless (as of one entranced on the outskirts of a dream)—at the pale lovely features of the beautiful face now confronting his own.

And then, as if in disappointment, Phebe softly hung her head. "I'd better stay in the sun-room," she said, "with Candy; until it's dark again." She was about to withdraw her hand from Nathan's, but he clasped her fingers all the more firmly between his own. And as Phebe lifted her eyes and once more encountered his, Nathan said, "You can stay in my aunt's room... with me."

For a moment or two Phebe's dark lustrous eyes anxiously searched Nathan's face. "Are you sure, Nathan," she asked, faintly, "knowing now what you know about me?"

Without a moment's hesitation, "I'm sure;" Nathan answered; "even though you are a—" But he suddenly choked back the word before even its first syllable had slipped off his tongue. Then, after a long pause, "Even though you're the way you are," he managed at last to breathe, "I want us to be together—forever; no matter what."

And as a smile of relief and joy broke across Phebe's face, displaying to Nathan the small, milk-white teeth in her pink mouth, she lifted his hand and brushed its slender fingers in love and gratitude with her lips. Then, hand in hand, they rose to their feet, and hastened up the stairs to Aunt Amelia's room.

CHAPTER EIGHT

"...Once this face was bright, this brow clear...
And I possessed great wealth...
A manor, with gardens... and many riches...
Now, far from kith and kin, misery is my lot...
It is all but agonizing to tell you of my torments.
I do so that you might understand,
And, upon this, consider well,
You are in grave danger:
If you wish to avoid such woes,
Then learn from my fate..."

—The Awntyrs off Arthure

So at last, Nathan's long-awaited birthday—his sixteenth to be precise (and Phebe's, too, as it were)—had come about. And as Nathan called to mind, on that cloudy Saturday morning of August 26th, all the bizarre and (at times) terrifying incidents which had preceded it (events which he himself had witnessed and been a part of), several rather peculiar notions began to insinuate themselves into his thoughts with regard to his future birthdays.

He wondered to himself what other strange and frightening experiences could he anticipate happening to him due to Phebe's vampiric nature in the days leading up to those birthdays still to come. Moreover, he began to ask himself how many more could he, in fact, look forward to celebrating together with Phebe in time ahead. And suddenly he found himself musing fretfully over just how many more "birthdays" were yet to be his at all before that dire, fateful one, the last, the final, *the only remaining*—in whose company stalks along the dread and shadowy presence which eventually comes to all human beings—drew solemnly near.

And even as Nathan's every thought skimmed and buzzed like a swarm of agitated bees, round this one curiously morbid, and altogether dismaying concept, his lips drew softly together and, scarcely conscious of what he was now saying, they breathed out, "Unless I were to become like Ph—" But no sooner had the words passed his lips, than he caught his breath, and felt his swiftly beating heart for a single solitary instant all but jerk to a standstill within his body. "What am I thinking!" he half whispered in utter repulsion at the thought. "No; no—never!" And he shut his eyes tight, then re-opened them, as one shiver after another crept first up, then slowly down his tingling backbone.

And for some while after this, in the dim and shadowy closeness of his aunt's blind-drawn bedroom, Nathan continued to lie next to Phebe in the bed, restive and wakeful as an insomniac. All the strange notions he had been so intently reflecting on in connection with his 'birthday(s)' (this present one, as well as those yet to come), left him feeling perturbed and distrait.

Like Phebe herself, who lay still as a stone, and seemingly asleep, Nathan had tried, again and again, with tight-shut eyes, to disregard his vexing concerns, refrain from thinking at all, and finally doze off. But it seemed as though a throng of visiting guests and strangers, their faces huddled close together, kept talking, ever and again, in his mind, mouthing at him a multitude of cautioning words that amounted to awful warnings.

And presently, Nathan once more opened his eyes to fix them anxiously on the lovely profile of Phebe's pale, solemn face. Stretched upon her back beside him, she lay now in that eerie, stirless, death-like slumber of hers to which all vampires by day must, without exception, submit themselves. And Nathan sank steadily into a cold, uneasy reverie, as the thought of that fabled 'spell', so long and so eagerly sought after by her, began to haunt his imagination and fill his heart with vague apprehensions over the outcome of its finding.

For Phebe, at least, it caused little or no anxiety whatsoever. She, apparently, looked forward with confidence to the prospect of the spell's success and the promise of release it should bring her. She appeared to exhibit (so far as Nathan could tell) no qualms, no uneasiness about the upshot of all this weird occult business.

But those ominous voices in Nathan's mind kept cautioning him that there was a very distinct possibility the endeavor might fail or, in some unforeseen way, miscarry. What if this supernatural venture, they forewarned him, should in fact come to nothing, the curse itself persist, and Phebe continue as she is—a *vampire?* What then for Phebe? What then for *himself?* Would the two of them be able to remain together under such ill-fated circumstances?

On and on the voices in Nathan's head pricked and prodded him with unpleasant hints, suggestions, and inquiries like these, and others even more alarming. And when, all at once, he came out of these disquieting thoughts, his head was aching, his skin chilled, and his hands slightly trembling. Then, having once again shut his eyes, he turned on his side away from Phebe, making every effort not to think anymore of her curse, the spell, and the likelihood of its failure, while in the same instant trying desperately to fall asleep.

Now, although a sound, unbroken sleep was, for Nathan, all but impossible for the present, there were times when he knew he could no longer be truly awake. For then a deep hush drew itself softly, slowly over his outwearied mind, and those gabbling voices in his head, with all their ominous warnings, were suddenly stilled. But he was also aware at other times, when the voices were again roused to the tiniest of whispers, that he was not altogether truly asleep either, but rather aimlessly adrift in a languid half-drowse somewhere between the two.

And every time Nathan felt himself slip just below the surface of the one, down into a shallow doze, he experienced ugly and uncomfortable dreams. Dreams whose unsettling images would eventually force him helplessly back up again to consciousness and the cold realization of Phebe lying in the bed beside him, utterly motionless, except for those dark, lustrous half-open eyes of hers.

And once, when Nathan was unable to deny, a moment longer, his morbid fascination with regard to those eyes, he turned again to Phebe, lurched onto his elbow, and peered directly into her slightly unsealed eyes. Half in fear, half in astonishment, he noted how they refused to keep still in their sockets. Restlessly, vigilantly—as he now understood to be the habit with all vampires—they kept glancing, now this way, now that. After a space of some seconds, however, Nathan had to quickly avert his face again, and refrain from looking another instant at their weird, disquieting motion for the sheer physical revulsion it caused him.

Still and all, despite this awful and uncanny distraction, somewhere between three and four o' clock that afternoon, Nathan must have slept, and more soundly than he knew. For when once more he had opened his eyes and sat up in bed, he discovered that Phebe was gone, and that the early darkness of night had already begun to deepen on the other side of the window-blinds. He noted, too, that the only light in the room was from the brass candlestick on the dresser, which had barely an inch of wax candle burning in it.

After opening his mouth, then, to emit so vast a yawn it left tears in his eyes, Nathan got stiffly, wearily out of bed, dressed, and went downstairs to the kitchen to eat something. And since he had neither the energy nor the enthusiasm for the tedious process of first cooking, then cleaning up, his supper proved to be a thoroughly simple and hasty meal. Consisting of little more than a slice of bread, peanut butter, grape jam, and chocolate milk, he had prepared and consumed it in less than a quarter of an hour.

Then, only minutes before eight o' clock, Nathan went back upstairs: this time, to his own bedroom. He loitered a while in front of the narrow wooden bookshelf; glanced idly at the book-backs; and randomly selected a volume. Seating himself in the creaky wooden chair by the window, he began to read a little.

But after having browsed through the first few chapters, Nathan gradually lost interest, and his thoughts began hopelessly to wander. He yawned prodigiously; got up; restored the volume to its place on the shelf; and went over to his dresser. Rummaging through its bottommost drawer, he fetched out that worn and battered notebook of his in which he had kept a journal full of entries concerning all the painful, wicked things his aunt had done to him over the years.

For a moment or two, Nathan's eye strayed from the book's faded cover to the few miscellaneous items on the top of the dresser. Slowly, almost vacantly his gaze roved from one article to the next. A stub of wax candle, a book of matches, an old key ring, some paper clips, loose change consisting (for the most part) of nickels, pennies, and dimes, and lastly, a fine point black marker. And there, quite suddenly, it paused to fix itself intently, as some curious and instantaneous resolve came into the pondering, motionless eyes.

Removing the cap from the marker, Nathan raised the cover of the notebook. Then, in large, straddling letters, he began to scrawl over the written entries to each time-foxed page, the following words: 'Phebe and Nathan, Nathan and Phebe—Forever'.

And when he had obscured the writing of the journal's last few entries with the above inscription, Nathan shut up the notebook, set it aside, and walked over to the narrow, familiar window of his room. There, for some little while, he quietly sat down to do and to be—*nothing.* He merely gazed out across the graves and headstones of the old All Faiths cemetery and dreamed of being with *her...* 'forever'.

And once, for no more than an instant, Nathan had glanced over his shoulder. Briefly he scanned the restricted dimensions of the drab, ugly room around him. And almost it seemed to him as bleak, cold, and uninviting as the cemetery's neglected graves over which he now sat peering.

Then, for a full minute or two, Nathan all but sank into a dull and empty daydream. During (and after) it, without stirring so much as a finger, he sat on, listening in a profound and curious hush. Rising up from the dark, vacant, hollow rooms beneath him, he could hear the dreary echoes and faint murmurs of the house.

And with each passing second, as Nathan went on listening, half absently now, he began to feel not only all the more infinitely alone, but unutterably forsaken and friendless as well. Moreover, continuing to sit before the open window, he suddenly caught in the sultry air of that cloudy summer night, a faint scent of coming rain. And in the soft breath of wind that strayed in over the narrow sill, he smelt the dew-damped grass and moist dirt of the ground in his backyard and the cemetery beyond its fence.

Then, raising the screen of his window and leaning his head out over its sill, Nathan's restless thoughts journeyed near and far in search of Phebe. Through darkness and over distance they groped and eagerly ranged. First up, then down the steps of the old mausoleum; then along the skirts of the cemetery's old, old section; and finally beyond the fence of the cemetery itself. Even as far away as the very gates of the Middle Village crematory, where Phebe, in mid-August, had brought Nathan to view the Perseid meteor shower.

There, for some while, Nathan, in his thoughts, paused. And he wondered to himself, could Phebe, at this present hour, be loitering by herself on the rooftop of the crematory, looking out across the way toward his home? Was she, even now, in her solitude, thinking of him, even as he, in an agony of loneliness in the quiet of his room, gazed out across the darkened graves and thought of her?

Nathan softly drew in his head again. And with this one soothing thought he comforted himself that, wherever Phebe might be this night, he felt certain she was spending its dark and lonely hours in longing no less for him than he was for her.

Worn out at length, Nathan drew down the sash of the window and walked down the hall to his aunt's room. He quickly slipped out of his clothes and huddled himself into the sheet of the bed. For some while he lay staring up at the ceiling. He tried hard to stifle one cavernous yawn after another, until all at once his heavy lids drooped down over his tired eyes.

And just as Nathan felt himself poised on the brink of dozing off, dream came stealing softly in to blend and fuse itself with reality. What wonder he was soon fast asleep.

Some while later, though, from out of dreams as curious and bizarre as the actuality into which he had allowed his life to entangle itself, Nathan was roused by a voice, sweet and soft, whispering the sound of his name, faint as a breath, against his ear.

Lying quite still, Nathan blinked open his eyes, and there was Phebe's enchanting face at his shoulder, and he felt her naked little form nestling softly in under the sheet against him. "What time is it?" he asked her, half yawning.

"After one," she sighed.

Nathan's brow creased. "In the morning?" he said, as wakefulness continued to gather into his eyes. Phebe gazed steadily, deeply into them, and, silently smiling, she nodded her head.

For some minutes, in the room's faintly candled dusk, they spoke and laughed in low voices, and Phebe's slim, cold, long-fingered hand clasped Nathan's under the sheet. After a while, the two of them said very little, but continued to gaze steadily into one another's eyes with a kind of strange, close ardor, and they kissed one another lying there together in bed.

The only sound now was that of the rain, a thin, warm drizzle hushing softly down beyond the three narrow bedroom windows. And although the blinds hung slackly down over each one, even to their last slat, the blind to the center window bellied inward as a rain-cooled breath of air came in over its sill. For in climbing into the bedroom through that window, to awaken Nathan, Phebe had left its screen up and its wooden sash raised.

And presently, as Nathan and Phebe lay for a while in one another's arms, without either speaking or stirring, a low peal of distant thunder broke in on their stillness. The two of them listened until its last hollow echo had fainted away into quiet; and apart from the rain gurgling and babbling in the gutters under the edges of the roof, all else around them was utterly still.

Then, twice Phebe kissed Nathan on the cheeks and lips, and between the first and second of those kisses, she asked him, "Are you still tired?"

"No," said Nathan, shaking his head. "What about you?"

Phebe sighed. "I don't sleep at night," she said. "Only in the day—remember?"

And in the long silence that followed Phebe's reply, Nathan found himself staring with unusual concentration into the pale, narrow, and astonishingly beautiful face just opposite his. Then, very faintly, "What's it like?" he asked. "To be—" But his voice suddenly faltered, and, with his eyes fixed half doubtfully, half anxiously on Phebe's silent face, he seemed to hesitate. Then, "To be... you know," he all but whispered across to her. And the face seemed to grow still more beautiful, like a face in dream; and those large, motionless eyes, deep and lustrous and inkly-dark, were for the instant vacant of all thought, meaning, or expression save that of their own seductive beauty.

"You mean," said Phebe, at length, "to be a vampire?"

Nathan took a slow, deep breath and faintly nodded his head. Phebe's eyes regarded Nathan's face steadily. "Do you really want to know?" she asked him. And a silence as vast and fathomless as an abyss seemed to follow such an outlandish question. For an instant Nathan was virtually shocked by it, and he stared incredulously (and yet half fearfully) at Phebe. But then, after hesitating for several moments, he said, "Yeah, I do; tell me."

Phebe smiled faintly. "I can do better than that," she said, meeting Nathan's gaze with the magic of some deep, strange allurement in her eyes; "I can let you *feel* what it's like."

Nathan watched her face in silence a moment. Then, barely above a whisper, he breathed, "How?"

Phebe sat up. "Here," she said, "sit like this, in front of me." And Nathan seated himself (like Phebe) cross-legged on the bed, so that, presently, they were facing one another. Then, taking his hand, she laid the flat of his palm on the place just over her heart, and, fastening her dark, dwelling, deep-memoried eyes unswervingly on Nathan's, she began to speak. Again and again, in a strangely sonorous voice, she repeated the following words, "See as I see; hear as I hear; feel as I feel; know as I know; thirst as I thirst."

And even as Phebe was uttering those same words for the third time, Nathan had the curious impression that the wallpaper and the ceiling of the room were beginning to ripple, and the walls themselves to slowly undulate. Also, he thought that the very bed on which he and Phebe were seated was somehow beginning to revolve; and almost it seemed to him that he was being drawn helplessly, irresistibly forward toward... at... *into* Phebe.

Then, as layer after layer of his consciousness was softly peeled away, a dreadful giddiness began to sweep over him, and a darkness, black as ink, drifted up before his eyes. He was powerless to open his mouth and cry out; to inhale the very air and breathe. He felt every muscle in him slacken, and with that he experienced a motionlessness—horrifying in its initial moments—spread itself throughout his body, as each limb and member of his form went limp. This was succeeded by a deathly chill, and then a sheer and alarming numbness. He could feel nothing.

All at once, though, just before the last thin film of his consciousness was stripped away, the darkness obscuring his eyes lessened and, in smoke-like wisps, cleared away altogether. And quite suddenly, as his vision unclouded, he found himself looking not at Phebe, as he had expected, but at—*himself.*

For minutes together, it seemed, Nathan stared in silent astonishment at himself sitting there, like one fast asleep, with his head stooped forward, his eyes sealed, and his chin sunk upon his breast. Slowly turning his head this way and that, he glanced round the room, but Phebe was nowhere to be seen. And then, as his searching gaze strayed down for a moment, he noted Phebe's shapely legs, and her small, slim hands folded in her lap.

And all in a flash, Nathan realized he was looking at himself— in fact, at everything—through her eyes! His mind, his senses, his very consciousness were all in some kind of mysterious and extraordinary union with hers. He was Phebe, and could now see and *feel* and *know* as she... as a *vampire.*

At first, Nathan's experience of Phebe's supernatural condition was, for the most part, tantamount to a new and unfamiliar heaviness about him. It seemed to perpetually swathe and envelop his senses.

Somehow Nathan came to realize that this curious heaviness was actually the ponderous weight of centuries, enormous periods of time through which Phebe had lived. And the mere thought of reckoning those years, of measuring such a protracted existence seemed to fill Nathan with unspeakable weariness. Moreover, at one and the same time, he felt all mortal concern and apprehension for time's inexorable passage virtually disappear. For a profound awareness, a secret assurance was now his that an endless reservoir of nights, years—nay, centuries!—seemed to lie interminably before him. And from the dark waters of that reservoir he might sip and swill as much, and for as long, as he pleased.

And suddenly, into Nathan's being, there rose up an indescribable satisfaction in the deepening shadows of the dark, coupled with a supreme aversion for sunlight, and a sheer terror of the day itself. And presently, as Nathan paused in his thoughts to listen closely, he had the startling impression that he could distinguish in the night's darkness, the pulsing of many human hearts. Also, like a low, continuous undercurrent in the gloom, he caught the faint lisping sound of far-off voices, and the hum and stir of ceaseless thoughts.

What's more, Nathan knew that were someone near, he need but glance at them, and he could divine their thoughts as easily as someone eavesdropping from behind a door or curtain on another's conversation. And subsequently, he felt his entire being flooded with new and potent forces, many of them violent and disturbing, and some altogether nameless and unknown to him. For some tide of strength and power, utterly beyond the limits and condition of his human frailty, seemed to have rushed all at once from Phebe's *Self* into his own. And the thrill of all these peculiarly alien sensations, the experience of Phebe's vampiric condition, swelled within him, merging into a tremendous sense of wonder and fear.

But then, in the wake of this, Nathan also began to realize (somewhat dimly at first) that there was yet *another* sensation. For somewhere from deep within Phebe's accursed nature, something was gradually creeping over him, obtruding itself into his consciousness as slowly and unavoidably as sleep gathers over the senses. An ominous, troubling feeling: a craving, a desire, a need for blood—a thirst to consume the living blood of another individual. A horrid and irrepressible lust to sink his teeth into the flesh of someone's throat and suck the warm spurting blood from the wound. To drink deep, gorge himself on another's blood until his victim's heart had ceased at last to lurch and flutter.

Steadily this 'thirst' grew sharper, more alarming. Nathan felt it overwhelming him, and a terror, a loathing, a deadly panic swept through every fiber of his being. He heard himself emit a muffled groan; and became conscious that he was struggling desperately to stir his leaden limbs. Then ,with a sharp and sudden pang, and a clamor, like a prolonged shout that had somehow burst from his sealed lips, he withdrew his hand from Phebe's heart as one's fingers will shrink and recoil from the intense heat of a flame. And with that, the link between them, the union of their consciousness was sundered. Gradually the mortal terror in Nathan of the vampire's dreadful 'thirst' lessened, subsided, and thinned away. It was no more to him now than the swiftly fading memory of some vague, elusive nightmare.

And presently, Nathan found himself gazing, safe and sound, from his own shape and appearance into Phebe's large dark eyes. Soon even the faintest remnant of those sensations pertaining to her vampiric condition had been utterly dispelled from his being. And he was left feeling ultimately thankful and relieved that he was nothing more than human, mortal—*Nathan.*

For a long time in silence, Nathan's eyes dwelt on Phebe's face with remorse and pity. Then, "I'm sorry," he said, faintly.

Phebe slipped out of bed and proceeded to get dressed. "So am I," she all but whispered, after she had gone over to the midmost of the bedroom's three windows and raised its blind.

"Where are you going?" Nathan asked her. And in the same instant that he had spoken, there came a fitful gleam of summer lightning at the window, shining pale on Phebe's lovely face. She bent her head low and answered, "I have to feed, Nathan. Didn't you feel my thirst for yourself just now?"

In the hush that preceded Nathan's reply, there sounded, low and hollow out of the east, a faint rumble of thunder, at present no more than a far-off rumor. But the air felt close and heavy with approaching storm. For a moment or two, Nathan stared at Phebe without speaking. Then, "Do you *have* to kill someone?" he half whispered.

With downbent eyes, Phebe remained silent. "What about animals?" Nathan persisted. "Can't you feed off of them?"

Phebe slowly raised her face and her deep, dark, mournful eyes turned themselves full on Nathan. "I have; but it doesn't sustain me like human blood," she answered, in a small, sad voice. "I grow weak and tired soon after I feed on an animal's blood, and in no time I feel hungry again." And in the pause that followed her words, the thunder sounded louder, nearer. "Let's not talk about it anymore," she went on, "this is just the way things are." And without another word, she climbed up onto the narrow window ledge, sprang out into the thundery dark and rising wind, and vanished.

With a startled cry, Nathan dashed over to the open window and thrust his head out. Somewhere in the air above him, he heard the unmistakable sound of great wings flapping heavily. He looked up and glimpsed the large dark shape of some flying creature. For the breath of an instant, Nathan saw it quite plainly, illumined very starkly by a searing-white flash of lightning, beating the air with its huge wings and ascending skyward in its slow, laborious flight.

Nathan strained his eyes to see it more closely and to follow its path of movement. But all at once the lightning's glare had dulled away, and the rain-darkened gloom swiftly closed in again, completely veiling the creature from his sight. And the next instant, the rapid swishing of its great wings was altogether lost in a terrific peal of thunder.

And all in a moment, as Nathan still leaned his head out over the window sill with his face upturned into the stormy dark, he thought to himself that he had at last unraveled the mystery! The very riddle which for so long had baffled and mystified his wits was now finally solved.

For Nathan felt quite confident in the assumption (however bizarre!) that this strange winged creature, which he was now seeing for the third time since making Phebe's acquaintance, was in fact none other than Phebe herself. Phebe, he surmised, in some kind of bat-like semblance; possibly—he further conjectured—her 'true' vampire form.

Moreover, Nathan was now quite convinced that it had been Phebe, in this winged, fiend-like shape, who had crept through the window into this very room nearly three weeks ago. Phebe herself who had slaughtered Aunt Amelia (as he himself had witnessed) in her bed—the very bed which he and her were now sharing. And while Nathan felt all but certain of this awful conviction (as fantastic as it seemed, even to him!), he was anything but satisfied by it. Indeed the mere chilling notion thoroughly horrified him.

Suppressing a faint shudder, Nathan slowly drew his head in and shut the window. Once more he returned to Aunt Amelia's vast colonial-style bed and, quickly huddling himself into the bed-sheet, he shut his eyes. Again and again he tried to clear his mind, compose himself, and fall asleep. But the dreadful reality of Phebe ensnaring some unsuspecting victim, like a spider its fly, and then drinking their blood, haunted his thoughts now like an evil dream.

And so, by the time Nathan had at last managed to nod off into a heavy, but troubled slumber, the storm had subsided. Its hollow thunder and pale lightning had long-since passed out of hearing, and the grey dusk of early daybreak was stealing faintly in round the edges of the window blinds.

Around seven o' clock that same morning, Nathan awoke very suddenly. He had been roused, not by the thick dazzling sunshine streaming in past the blinds, whose narrow slats had been turned open, or the drowsy piping of the birds beyond them, but by the dense smell of cigarette smoke permeating the room.

Turning wearily onto his side, Nathan softly blinked open his sleepy eyes. Squinting them a little against the glare of the pale, slanting sunbeams, his gaze began to stray listlessly along from one narrow window to the next. But in the very instant that his idle glance came to pause for a moment at the third and last of those windows, three things happened at one and the same time to Nathan. His face perceptibly paled; every muscle in his body stiffened; and his eyes opened to their fullest width and roundness in absolute fear.

For sitting next to the window, in his aunt's upholstered armchair, quietly smoking in the sunlight, was the lean, gaunt figure of Antal Vrancic. His long legs were comfortably crossed one over the other, while his large hairy hands rested in his lap with the finger-tips pressed together. About his face and head, a cloud of cigarette smoke, which he had just exhaled, hung in languidly wreathing wisps, like a thin bluish veil.

Horribly startled, Nathan instantly sat up with a sharp gasp, and clutched the bed-sheet to himself with both lean hands. For a moment or two, as he continued to stare at that forbidding black-suited figure in the armchair, questioning himself as to whether the shape he was now seeing were only in nightmare, a curious spellbound look spread itself over his features.

But in the very same instant that the figure uncrossed it legs, and Nathan realized its actuality, the expression on his face changed to one of positive alarm. And for a solitary moment he quickly (and tightly) shut his eyes, in the hope that when he re-opened them, that sinister figure, like some ugly dream or ghastly apparition, should have completely vanished away.

Unfortunately, however, for Nathan, when he had once more lifted his lids and again gazed out of his eyes, there Vrancic still sat. He had once again crossed his legs, he was still quietly smoking his cigarette, and his small, black luminous eyes were looking directly, intently into Nathan's.

Nathan, meanwhile, kept wanting to angrily shout at Vrancic, and demand from him what he wanted. He wished he could scold him severely for coming into the room unasked; and then (without waiting for a single retort or excuse from the man) order him to leave the room at once. But for the life of him, try as he would to stir his parched tongue, he couldn't blurt out a single word. Evidently the sight of Vrancic seated there, only a few feet from the bedside, keenly regarding him with those small black, glinting eyes of his, had so surprised and frightened him.

And so, for the next twenty or thirty seconds, Nathan merely went on sitting there, perfectly still in the bed. Hardly able to manage the sudden lump that had formed in his throat, he continued to gaze on, cowed and speechless, at his unwelcome visitor.

At length, a faint, cold grin of amusement had stolen into Vrancic's disagreeable features. Then, turning his slow, black eyes away from Nathan's face, to fix them for a moment, half musingly, on the glowing tip of his cigarette, his deep, astringent voice suddenly broke the silence.

"Have you ever heard of the author and physician Sir Thomas Browne?" he began; and by no means expecting an answer from Nathan, he hastened on to say: "He was a great stylist and master of English prose. And while he produced a great many philosophical writings that exhibit considerable erudition and psychological insight, he professed himself an earnest believer in the supernatural, and set great store by alchemy, astrology, witchcraft, and demonology. In his 'Religio medici', or A Physician's Religion—if my memory here serves me correctly —he wrote, 'tempt not contagion by proximity, and hazard not thyself in the shadow of corruption.'"

Vrancic had paused momentarily. He smoked on in silence; and his eyes, without stirring by a hair's breadth from Nathan's face, seemed to gather into a concentration still more intense. Nathan, meanwhile, speechless and motionless, had just enough courage to continue (at least for the next ten seconds) to meet the piercing eyes of his uninvited visitant, before he was compelled at last to lower his own in confusion and unease.

Then, quite suddenly, "I mention this to you," went on Vrancic, "simply because you, Nathanael Christian, are now *tempting* 'contagion by proximity', and *hazarding* 'thyself in the shadow of corruption' by being enamored with a vampire, a member of the Undead, one of the Non-living. Love of that kind can be very dangerous—ultimately lethal, if one is not cautious. If you choose to help Phebe, by all means, do so. But do not choose to remain with her. The living cannot love her kind. Those who form a bond of love with the Undead eventually succumb to an evil fate. Be advised: you will lose your soul and come to dwell in the darkness: for in the end she will draw you down into it."

Once again Nathan raised his head and boldly met Vrancic's eye. "But after you get Phebe this incunabulum," he said, "or whatever it's called, and she uses the spell that's in it, she'll be like you and me; she won't be a vampire anymore. The curse'll be lifted." And here Nathan paused, as an awful, irrepressible feeling of disquietude had suddenly stolen over his heart. "I mean," he slowly continued, "she'll be normal again; she'll be human"; and after another longish pause, well under his breath, he added, as if to himself, "won't she?"

Vrancic sat on in the armchair quietly smoking for the next few moments. Then, "If, of course, the outcome is as Phebe hopes it will be," he remarked, gazing at Nathan through the delicately wreathing cigarette smoke he had just then breathed out. "But again, the key word here is, 'if'!"

For a single solitary breath, Nathan felt his heart stand still. "What do you mean?" he asked, faintly.

With those small, black, glinting eyes of his, Vrancic steadily continued to hold Nathan's. "There is no guarantee," he said, gazing an instant sneeringly into the boy's face, "that the spell in the incunabulum will undo Phebe's curse. It is *possible* that it will work; but there is also the very *real* possibility that it will fail." Vrancic had paused again, and Nathan stirred uneasily in the bed where he sat, as those scornful black eyes fixed themselves reflectively for a moment on his silent face.

"For the sake of argument," resumed Vrancic, stubbing out his cigarette on the window sill, "let us assume that the sorceries encompassed within this fabled spell are potent enough to deliver Phebe from the occult bonds of her curse and undo its witchery. Does it necessarily follow, then, that in the twinkling of an eye she will cease to be a vampire, or that her mortality, along with her human nature, will be restored at once? Does the man who suffers from a serious infection, or some awful disease, once a remedy has been found for him, *instantly* recover his health upon taking a medication? No; it may be weeks—months, even!—before he fully regains his vigor, and is completely cured of his affliction.

"And it may very well be that a sorcerer's spells operate under much the same principle as a physician's medicines: needing time to take effect before any results are either seen or felt. Don't forget: for nearly two thousand years Phebe has lived with the condition of a vampire; therefore, we must ask ourselves: can a series of esoteric words in some ancient incantation truly eradicate a centuries'-old curse all in a moment? Or will it take hours... days... years, perhaps, before her vampiric condition is fully removed? Certainly it is something worth thinking about. Something which I have tried on several occasions to convince Phebe at least to consider, but she has refused again and again to pay heed to any such notions."

Once again Vrancic had paused, and, with his steady regard still fixed on Nathan's face, he produced from the breast pocket of his shirt a fresh pack of Lucky Strikes. Nonchalantly he tapped the bottom of the pack before he calmly opened it, abstracted a cigarette, and lit it. Then, "Furthermore," he continued, after slowly inhaling, then softly breathing out a cloud of smoke, "let us just suppose for the moment that the incunabulum's spell does achieve that which Phebe hopes it will—that it removes her curse; that her mortality is restored to her; and she is no longer a vampire. Do you truly suppose that your lovely Phebe will ever again be 'normal', as you put it? If so, then you're a fool! Never lose sight of the fact that this is no ordinary girl, but one from another age, a time long before your own, and a world long-since vanished. She was hung upon a cross, her flesh pierced with iron nails, and after suffering the agony and humiliation of crucifixion, she was then placed under the most inhuman of curses, having her mortality stripped from her, and forced to endure a centuries'-long existence of darkness and damnation as a vampire.

"For seventeen hundred years Phebe has lurked in the shadows, dwelling among the dead; inhabiting cemeteries and abandoned tombs; abiding in crypts and coffins; stalking her fellow man. She has killed men, women, and children when the terrible thirst, the irrepressible craving has come upon her, gorging herself on their blood to fulfill the curse laid upon her and satiate her cruel hunger. Phebe has suffered too much; committed and perpetrated too many horrible acts as a vampire to ever be 'normal' again. Should the spell work, and accomplish what she has so long hoped for—that is, remove this accursed condition of a vampire and restore to her once more her mortal, her *human* nature—the memory of all that she has seen and lived through, the guilt of all the innocent lives she has taken over a span of seventeen centuries as a vampire will be far too great a burden for her to bear. That dreadful legacy will never cease to haunt her mind and plague her thoughts. Indeed, she will be guilt-ridden for the rest of her days, conscience-stricken. And eventually her feelings of regret, remorse, and self-reproach for all her misdeeds as a vampire—the recollection of all her 'sins', if you will—will drive her to despair.

"And just as the scars of her crucifixion will always remain on her flesh as a reminder of her sufferings, so the scars of her heinous acts as a vampire will forever leave their imprint on her memory. So that when—or, if—Phebe should ever become mortal again, those terrible memories of her activity and deeds as a vampire will steadily gnaw away at her very reason, relentlessly enfeebling her mind, until, inevitably, she is driven mad with the horror of it.

"And, alas! how could it be otherwise? For only a madman, only a monster, only a *vampire*"—and here Vrancic looked piercingly at Nathan and his lips faintly curled in a sly grin—"could live under such circumstances, faultless and without guilt; someone who lacks a conscience, who has no soul. Your Phebe, I'm afraid, will never *be* 'normal', even if she should regain her mortality. She is, unfortunately, *doomed,* as are all those accursed and condemned to dwell in darkness."

Nathan sat there in the bed as if transfixed by Vrancic's small, black, glittering eyes. For the life of him, he could neither open his mouth to utter a single word, nor stir his limbs to do a single thing. He merely sat on, breathlessly waiting, listening for what Vrancic would say next.

And for the moment, Vrancic silently watched Nathan doing just that. Then, "My advice to you is this," he began again, after he had risen from the armchair, "enjoy your life; savor its every moment." There was a short pause, as Vrancic sauntered over to the tall curio cabinet behind whose glass doors were those gorgeously bound volumes which comprised the sum total of Aunt Amelia's small library. "Do not entangle yourself," he resumed, "in some mad amour with a creature under some supernatural curse! Find yourself a girl of the common order: enjoy yourself, and enjoy her; otherwise, death may in fact come for you sooner than you know. For when a mortal becomes enamored with a supernatural woman, such a liaison, such a romance, an affaire de coeur can only come to one end—tragic."

For a moment or two, Vrancic stood in front of the curio cabinet with his back to Nathan. He was peering through the glass of the cabinet's long, narrow doors at the book backs. He noted several rather shabby paperbound volumes—Nathan's personal favorites—which the boy had only recently transferred from his room to his aunt's.

Then, quite suddenly, as Vrancic continued passively scanning the titles on each book back, he asked, "Have you ever read 'The Odyssey', by Homer?" And he glanced over his shoulder at Nathan, who, faintly shaking his head, opened his mouth to speak, but before he could articulate a word, Vrancic was already hastening on: "The poet tells us that—much like yourself right now—our hero, Odysseus, became involved with a woman of an otherworldly rank and degree, a goddess, in fact, by the name of Calypso. For seven years she kept Odysseus a captive in her cave, on her island-home in the sea, to be her mate and lover, promising him that, if only he would remain with her, she would bestow upon him immortality and never-fading youth. Odysseus, however, wisely refused such a union. He chose instead to remain human, a Man; to return home to Ithaca, to his ordinary wife, Penelope, and to die as Men die, in old age. You, too, Nathan, should choose as Odysseus: reject this life with the Calypso—the vampire—that now enamors you, and choose instead a mortal, a human, a 'normal' girl. A grievous end awaits you otherwise."

Once again Vrancic had paused. He opened the curio cabinet's glass doors, selected one of the books from the shelf—a thin, worn paperbound volume—and, as he browsed through its pages, he said: "I can see you are well acquainted with 'Undine', by de la Motte Fouque. And by its faded covers, heavily creased spine, and dog-eared pages, it would be my guess that you have read this book several times at least."

Turning round once more to face Nathan, Vrancic glanced up from the pages of the open book and met the boy's wide, unblinking eyes. "No doubt, then, you'll recall," he went on, "the awful fate to which the good and noble knight, Huldbrand, came because of his love, his desire for Undine, a woman who was not of any ordinary or mortal strain." And in the brief pause that followed this ominous hint and reminder, the fixed gaze confronting Nathan from the austere and penetrating deeps of Vrancic's chilling stare seemed to mesmerize the boy, paralyze him. Almost it seemed to Nathan that he could scarcely draw so much as a solitary breath.

"And your life, too, Nathan," continued Vrancic, very solemnly, "is now in the same deadly peril as Huldbrand's, because of your love for Phebe, a vampire, a non-mortal, a being of a supernatural strain. But I must warn you: that divide which exists between what is mortal and *immortal*, or natural and *supernatural*, cannot be bridged. And it is dangerous to try. Those who do, usually perish in the attempt. Do not let your desire for this girl ensnare you. Be warned! For there are some things in this world which have the power to enslave you once tried, tasted, or yielded to: morphine; crack-cocaine in its purest form; *true* love. Believe me, I know whereof I speak. For me, it is human flesh. You look at me as one truly horrified, and yet, it is, nonetheless, true: once consumed, your senses take pleasure in eating no other flesh than that of your own species."

There was a short silence, and Nathan watched (uneasily) as Vrancic calmly restored the book to its place on the cabinet's glass shelf, resumed his seat by the window, and fetched out of his shirt pocket the pack of Lucky Strikes. "Did you know," he said, after first choosing, then lighting, another cigarette, "that little more than a hundred years ago, in the interior of the island of Sumatra, a tribe of hill-people, known as the Battas, not only admitted, with some pride, to eating human flesh, but professed to practice their cannibalism according to a number of very specific regulations. One of these—indeed, the most gruesome—was that any enemy captured in time of war beyond the bounds of their village had to be eaten *alive*.

"Their partiality for cannibalism was so great that every villager kept a private store of human flesh in their home for food. And one Batta chieftain declared that he would eat no other meat, and was very careful to see that he had an abundant supply of it in his house. When asked one time, around the end of the nineteenth century, how they had become addicted to gormandizing thus, they maintained that in time agone they and the other tribes of the island-community lived peacefully together, and the custom of 'man-eating' was unknown to them. But some seven or nine generations ago, a demon appeared among them and taught them this horrific practice of cannibalism.

"I, alas! can make no such claims to some outside party, whether supernatural or common. It was my own ravenous hunger—the will to survive—that would not be ignored, denied which, at one and the same time, introduced and enslaved me to this practice." Vrancic paused, and, for a time, he smoked on in silence. Nathan, meanwhile, never once removed his eyes from the man's partially disfigured face. Vrancic, on the other hand, had fallen into a deep and curious muse, and his abstracted gaze remained downbent, it seemed, in vacant thought. Then, he raised his eyes and fixed them on Nathan's face again.

"Though you may find this hard to believe," he said, "only a few short years ago—it seems so remote to me now—I was a very different man from the one you see here today. Well-respected and highly regarded by no small number of Europe's illuminati, I was then a man of some means, thanks largely to my father, who was a very shrewd and enterprising fellow.

"Since early childhood he had lived in Hungary, in Budapest to be exact, although he had been born in Croatia: and the family name, Vrancic, in Hungarian is actually Verancsics; just as my first name, Antal, in the Croatian tongue is pronounced Antun. Now, before my father had reached his thirtieth year, he had already made his fortune by way of several dubious business ventures and speculative investments. And as a result of his entrepreneurial skills, I—an only child—had the good fortune to be brought up in an atmosphere of the most prosperous conditions.

"As for my mother, she was a dilettante intellectual who dabbled in the occult. And whenever my father was away from the house, she would organize seances, which I always managed to secretly observe either by concealing myself behind one of the drawing room window-curtains, or peering through the keyhole to some closet door. And whenever she was not attempting to contact the dead or conjure up some apparition in our home, she was busy with her Ouija board or tarot cards. And it is chiefly because of her that I developed, at an early age, a fascination for books, and cherished, before I was even ten years old, an enormous interest in the supernatural. In fact, these two things—books and the occult—had become the chief objects of my passion by the time I was a first-year student in high school.

"But there's no need to fret;" Vrancic said, eyeing Nathan's silent face almost archly, as he tapped the lengthening ash of his cigarette onto the window sill; "I'm not about to bore you with a tedious account of my student years, or my scholastic achievements, or the various degrees I earned at this or that university—such information to so young a man as yourself would interest you very little. No. Suffice it to say that though I learned a great deal pursuing my studies in school and in private, and had become, by my mid-twenties, fluent in nearly a dozen languages, I did precious little with the skills and wisdom I attained.

"But then, with only a few months between, I watched as first my mother, then my father sickened and died. Needless to say, I was grief-stricken by their sudden demise. And yet, I knew that it was one of the turning points of my life: for the inheritance I received enabled me to indulge in things which, up until then, I had thought utterly beyond my reach. I began at once to travel widely, for an intense desire for knowledge, a knowledge that cannot be found or taught in either the curriculum or academy of today's schools, led me from city to city across Europe, rooting through the most celebrated libraries and poring over the most renowned book collections. I went wandering from Moscow to Paris: rummaging through libraries and collections now in Amsterdam, now in Toulouse; on to Dresden, Nuremburg, Prague; then to Bucharest; and finally Rome and Florence.

"Around this time, too, I set about seeking and acquiring for myself rare and invaluable works on the occult. And as the yearning grew ever stronger in me for this secret and forbidden learning, it was towards knowledge still more abstruse that I gravitated all the more eagerly. I moved among the illustrious circles of people with the same purpose and interests; and for some while I toyed with the idea of joining one of the Masonic lodges in Budapest. It was then, however, that I discovered a far more secretive and hermetic confraternity known as the Ancient Order of the Forbidden Scroll. And although that name is as meaningless to you as it is strange, I must tell you, young man, that you are among the truly privileged few to hear it spoken and yet come to no harm." And here Vrancic paused an instant to gaze almost forbiddingly at Nathan, who sat there, still and silent in the bed, as if bewitched by those intensely black luminous eyes; "for only future members," Vrancic then resumed, "being sponsored by some long-standing associate of this mysterious organization are permitted to hear or speak its name without suffering the most dire consequences—such is the secrecy that surrounds this very old yet little known society.

"A deep-rooted tradition maintains that soon after Pope Pius II confiscated and burned nearly every copy of the Arcana Magorum Detestanda, along with the original ancient manuscript, several adepts of the celebrated German alchemist, Heinrich Bruhl, of Leipzig, secretly assembled in Augsburg and organized the fraternity around the year 1465. It was these core founding members who made it their goal, by way of sworn oaths, to seek for copies of the Arcana Magorum that may have escaped the flames of intolerance as kindled by an overzealous pontiff.

"At first, membership to this extremely secret association was exclusive to alchemists, sorcerers, astrologers, and physicians. But in only the few short years following its formation, branches of the order began to appear across Europe in cities large and small; then in the Far East; and finally overseas—shortly after the thirteen colonies had won their independence—in the United States. And it is believed that John Adams, Thomas Jefferson, and Alexander Hamilton were among its earliest members in the New World.

"Now, as long ago as 1476, a scribe of the society came to discover, by some happy chance, while rummaging through a number of severely damaged vellum manuscripts housed in the crumbling ruins of a twelfth century Gothic cathedral in northeastern Germany, in the city of Brandenburg, a rare paraphrase of the Arcana Magorum in the form of a parchment scroll. The scroll itself was bound with broad bands of black silk at either end, and secured in the middle by a large seal of wax stamped with a solitary word in the Latin tongue: INTERDICTIO, meaning 'forbidden'. The text of this rare work —whose author very tantalizingly identifies himself at the very end in a brief colophon, dated 1390, as 'an ardent adept of the Cabbala'—is written in Hebrew in a peculiarly exquisite cursive script. And it is from this same remarkable parchment scroll that the learned worthies of the time who founded the order came to adopt the name for their secret fraternity.

"Today, each 'branch' of the Ancient Order of the Forbidden Scroll possesses a copy of this singular paraphrase of the Arcana Magorum, which, like its original, is written in Hebrew in the form of a parchment scroll. And all new members initiated into the Order are sworn without exception on this parchment roll copy. And although the Order had initially been organized in the fifteenth century primarily for the fraternal and clandestine purpose of discovering copies of the Arcana Magorum Detestanda that had not been consigned to the fires as decreed under Papal authority: its many branches these days chiefly assemble for the practice of forbidden rites, and the preservation of ancient and occult knowledge.

"Needless to say, the unique traditions surrounding the Order's origins instantly appealed to me. Moreover, I was fascinated by all of its curious regalia and rites, its strange ceremonies and rules. And so"—he stubbed out his cigarette on the window sill—"a long-standing member of the branch in Budapest, with whom I had become acquainted in my youth through my mother, sponsored me. Through her recommendation, I took initiation into the Ancient Order of the Forbidden Scroll, and swore my oath upon its parchment roll copy.

"As a token of my membership in this secretive association, I was furnished by my sponsor with this ring"—up went his left hand to display, on its annular finger, the heavy gold ring to Nathan, whose gaze instantly fixed itself on the bezel's rather infernal device—"which each member receives and wears on the left hand upon completion of his or her initiation."

Vrancic paused, and after drawing the ring off his finger, he leaned forward in the armchair and held it out, between finger and thumb, before Nathan's eyes. "Some two weeks ago, I believe, while prying into my private affairs in the basement," his thin, colorless lips faintly stirred, almost curling into a smirk, "you took the opportunity to examine this ring very thoroughly; did you not?"

Once more Vrancic paused, and for a moment or two Nathan met the man's chilling gaze, but could do little more than stare blankly in reply. "No doubt you observed," he continued, "the three inscriptions engraved upon it. The first on the bezel, 'meo periculo', 'at my own risk'; the second on the bezel's side, 'sapere aude', 'dare to be wise'; and the third on the hoop of the ring, 'quanti est sapere', 'how desirable is knowledge'. They are the threefold motto of the Order, and only an Artium Magister—that is, a Master of Arts— wears a ring of gold inscribed with the Order's threefold motto."

Vrancic replaced the ring onto the finger of his left hand and leaned back in the armchair. "With that elevated rank and degree in the Order," he went on, "I enjoyed specific powers and privileges which gave me a separate prominence and prestige. And through several members of the Order, who also held the special status of Artium Magister, I first came to hear the name of Darvulia Bethlen, one of the founders and chief luminaries of this branch of the Order in Budapest, which, in its earliest days, she presided over. A protracted illness, however, caused her to relinquish her leadership of the Order, I was told, and she lived now a reclusive and solitary life in a large, baronial manor house, where the wooded hills of Hungary's border marches with that of Romania's. Moreover, when my sponsor informed me of Darvulia's many rare books and manuscripts on the occult, I sought long and eagerly to arrange a meeting with her. But for all my initial efforts, this came to nothing.

"I also came to learn that it had long been the hope and desire of this occult society to at last recover Mathurin Chastenet's unique incunabulum copy of the Arcana Magorum Detestanda. Something which branches of the Order in various parts of the world have been seeking to accomplish for centuries now. And so, when I was initiated into the fraternity, it became my primary goal, my chief ambition to possess this fabled incunabulum copy. My efforts in this undertaking, however, soon roused the envy and enmity of a rival member, Erzsebet Zapolya, the very woman who had been an old acquaintance of my mother, and who had sponsored me at my initiation. It had long been Erzsebet's secret ambition, I learned, to be in control of the Order, and she feared that my finding of the incunabulum would secure for me the incontestable right to preside over the fraternity instead of her. Consequently, she attempted to thwart all my endeavors by launching against me an aggressive series of psychic attacks, or what many scholars and students of occultism more properly refer to as 'psychic vampirism'. Do you know what that is?"

At this inquiry, Nathan, for a moment or two, remained still and voiceless. Then, very faintly, he shook his head, gulped down the lump which had come into his throat, and, barely above a whisper, "No," he breathed out, "what is it?"

"Psychic vampirism," answered Vrancic, "is a steady and vigorous depletion of a person's vital forces by way of magical attack. And Erzsebet Zapolya, being a woman of potent mental capabilities and formidable powers in the occult, had a reputation for being exceptionally adept in this supernatural craft. As she went on to prove very proficiently soon after she and I had had our first quarrel over some trivial matter. For very suddenly I was plagued by a mysterious sluggishness and confusion; and I was beleaguered by troubling dreams. And each night, following this initial phase, whenever I dozed, I suffered nerve-shattering nightmares; while each day, when I was awake, I experienced an inexplicable listlessness and fatigue. And as my health continued to rapidly decline, I would lie for hours, mentally and physically exhausted, in a profound slumber. I soon realized that I was under psychic attack: that Erzsebet was attempting to debilitate me, to weaken and destroy my will, and slake off my vital forces.

"But there she had made her fatal mistake. She had altogether underestimated the extent of my own knowledge and skill in this very risky occult discipline. For I also wield enormous mastery in the supernatural: particularly in psychic vampirism. I soon retaliated with a vigorous salvo of my own psychic attacks on the will and vital energy of Ms Erzsebet Zapolya. My assaults on her life forces were relentless; and in turn her health very quickly deteriorated. She became bedridden in less than a week's time; and, in just a few short days following that, she had to be hospitalized. She accused me openly as the cause of her illness and the reason for her failing health. Her complaints and accusations came to the attention of the leading members in the Order, and many called for my expulsion. The matter, however, went into deliberation, which lasted for several days. During this time, I learned that Ms Zapolya had begun to make a slow but steady recovery, that it was no longer touch and go with her health, and that she was quite out of the woods, so to speak.

"You may well imagine, young man, how I was beside myself with rage, indeed"—Vrancic casually selected, and lit, another cigarette—"I literally seethed at the news! This was something I could neither tolerate nor permit. She must forfeit her wretched life. On that I was adamant. And so, on the very morning that Ms Erzsebet was discharged from the hospital—in a very weakened state and barely able to stand, so I was told —I instantly renewed my psychic attacks against her, and, by day's end I had siphoned off the last feeble remnants of her miserable life force. That same day, I was later informed (much to my satisfaction) that Ms Erzsebet Zapolya had tumbled out of her wheelchair onto her kitchen floor. There, for nearly ten minutes, she lay violently convulsing and gasping for air, before she finally breathed her last and died with the eyes starting from her head and her tongue protruding from her mouth.

"Of course, just about every member in the Ancient Order of the Forbidden Scroll surmised that Erzsebet's sudden demise was the result of my psychic vampirism. Consequently, there was unanimous agreement among those members of the society holding high-ranking grades, degrees, and titles in the Order for the revocation of my membership. I firmly refused, however, to surrender my ring"—Vrancic rested his left hand for a moment on his knee, and Nathan's eyes fixed themselves once more on the heavy gold ring encircling its annular finger—"and dared them to do their worst in taking it from me. In retaliation, I was openly disgraced, designated 'anathema' by the Order and its members, and my dismissal went into effect immediately.

"As you may well imagine, I was infuriated to say the least. I decided to seek the help of Darvulia Bethlen who had founded this branch of the Order in Budapest, hoping that by appealing to her, and obtaining her influence over the Order, I might be reinstated as a member, and the scandal surrounding Ms Zapolya's death— particularly with regard to my *alleged* involvement in it!—hushed up. I therefore wrote to her several times explaining my dilemma, and at last was favored with a response. It was curiously terse: stating simply that she was willing to meet with me, and a day and a time was appointed in which I was to come and visit her at her manor. And in the postscript of a second letter from Darvulia, she informed me that she lived now on the frontier of Romania. Her residence, she told me, was just within view of the shadowy forests of Transylvania, where a tributary to the river Koros flows down from the pine-clad mountain-slopes in a number of white frothing falls. It conjured in my mind truly idyllic scenes; and I was eager for the journey."

Nathan sat intently listening, his eyes fastened on Vrancic's unpleasant face; and all the while the man continued to speak, no sound else reached Nathan's ears than that peculiarly raspy, drawling voice.

"At the time appointed," went on Vrancic, "I departed from Keleti station in Budapest, and traveled by train for the better part of the day to the town of Salonta just over the Romanian border, where the river Koros flows into Hungary. From there, however, I was told there are no modern roadways or transportation by which to come to Darvulia's ancestral estate. Only winding sheep-tracks and narrow mountain-trails over which wood-carts and wagons are drawn by horse and oxen. In this way I traveled through several small rural villages and hamlets on tree-hemmed byways and footpaths until I arrived at last within sight of the extensive landholdings of Darvulia's forebears. It was anything but the idyllic landscape I had imagined: it looked to me more like some half-forgotten corner of the world—lonely, wild, and desolate.

"The manor itself, which I could just descry in the distance, appeared baronial in its picturesqueness and opulence, and stood isolated from any other residence. It had but one neighbor: the crumbling ruins of an abandoned fortress, within whose decaying outer walls stood some twenty or more wretched huts. Occupying these were about a dozen peasant gypsy families cowering in their superstitions, and distrustful in the extreme of all strangers.

"When the men saw me, they stared aghast and made the sign of the cross, while the women caught up their children, hurried indoors, and shuttered their windows. I later discovered why. Though you see me now without much hair on my head, but three short years ago I had a full head of curling brilliant red hair and a bushy red beard. And the redness of my hair and beard filled the superstitious gypsies with fear: for among their many peculiar beliefs is the notion that red hair betokens a demon or a vampire.

"I spent the night in a herder's hut, outside the castle gates where the Romanian shepherd, in whose cart I had journeyed, offered me shelter. From him I heard many shocking tales that were then in circulation among the gypsies in regard to Darvulia. But it would be at least the better part of a month before I was to discover just how true many of these stories actually were.

"Now, just beyond the ruins of the old castle—which I learned had formerly been used by Matthias Corvinus, the Raven-king of Hungary, as a fortification against the Turks—lies an ancient cemetery. Along it, the road, which was little more than a wheel-rutted and well-worn track, winds for one or two miles, then terminates, as my shepherd guide informed me, further on at the gates to Darvulia's manor. The cemetery contains, so I was told, the tombs and crypts of generations of men and women of an ancient Wallachian family dating back before the time of the Crusades, and to whom the castle once belonged. And even though the male and female lines of that ancient family have been extinguished now for more than a century, I was told that there still persists among the local gypsies a very shadowy tradition that Darvulia is the last representative of the family's old line.

"In the morning the shepherd drove me in his cart to the gates of Darvulia's manor house. They were immense wrought-iron gates, rust-caked and rotting with age, and in their very center, the metalwork was shielded with a coat-of-arms, for my Romanian shepherd told me Darvulia's ancestors were the only armigerous family that inhabited that remote region of the country. And ornamenting the gates above this escutcheon was a peculiar device—the crest of Darvulia's very ancient family, I presumed—of a twi-horned crescent moon with its horns pointing downward, surmounted by a bat, with outstretched wings, perched upon the upper edge of the crescent's broad arch. And underneath the moon was a motto, comprised of a solitary word in the Romanian language, 'nemuritor', which means, 'undying, eternal'. I later learned that this motto had only recently been adopted within the last few generations of the family, replacing the much older one—'neomenos', which means, 'inhuman'—and which the family had borne in Wallachia since time immemorial."

Once more, for a moment or two, Vrancic had paused to exhale a cloud of smoke, then to stub out his cigarette. And although Nathan found his mere presence utterly repellent, and he wanted to flee precipitously from the room to get as far from him as he could, the sound of the man's voice, his very words, his story held Nathan virtually spellbound.

Then, choosing another cigarette, Vrancic lit it and, after snapping the lighter shut, drew on it long and slow before resuming his narrative. "Working and living at the manor house in Darvulia's service at the time," he said, almost musingly, as he reclined in the armchair and softly breathed out the wreathing cigarette smoke, "were three very peculiar individuals: two elderly Transylvanian German women, in their late seventies by my estimation, whose people have for the most part disappeared utterly from that region.

Today the Germans of Transylvania are but a fading remnant in that part of the world, which they once knew as Siebenburgen—the seven fortresses. And the third individual, by name, Nadasdy, was a strange middle-aged fellow, a Turk, who claimed to be a Christian convert from the city of Cluj, as it is styled in the Romanian, or Kolozvar, as it is called in the Hungarian tongue.

"And it was this same odd, grim-faced retainer, or footman, or steward of Darvulia's—I never did discover precisely *what* the morose Nadasdy was to his mistress—who met me that bleak, cloudy morning at the front gates of the manor. This rather extraordinary personage stood nearly a foot taller than myself, and had upon his face, hands, and limbs such an abundance of thick, coarse, greying hair that he appeared for all the world more like a werewolf stooping there, peering fiercely at me from the other side of those high iron gates, than a mortal man.

"I handed him Darvulia's letters through the iron bars of the gates, and he read them over, more than once, very carefully and solemnly. Then, without a word to me, he unlocked and drew open the iron gates, and gruffly signed for me to enter. Swiftly and silently in front of me he led the way up to the house, pushed open the door in the low, stone porch, and hurried me inside. From the moment the door shut behind me, I felt as though a still and endless maze had engulfed me, for I followed the dour-faced Nadasdy through what seemed an infinite succession of gloomy passages and rooms. But then, at long last, he ushered me into a narrow antique hall with numerous high-backed chairs ranged round a low, broad trestle table of dark oak-wood that was polished like a mirror. On this was an abundance of food and drink, as if for the provision of a dozen or more guests.

"Here the Turk, Nadasdy, told me I was to refresh myself; after which he urged me to walk about the house and its premises wherever I pleased. By midnight, he told me, Darvulia would be ready to meet with me, for it had become her custom of late to have a little sleep by day and to sup and receive guests at midnight. To pass the time, I nibbled at some of the fruit and bread and meats, and sipped the sweet wine Nadasdy poured out for me before he had vanished, like a ghost, from the room. And soon after I had tasted this dish, and sampled that bottle, I also left the hall and began my exploration of the rooms and rambling passages of that great, seemingly deserted dwelling.

"Although I had been told only one wing was used as a dwelling by Darvulia, the entire house—both what was then being inhabited and that which was not—was lacking in any of the modern conveniences that one expects to find in homes of today. There was no state-of-the-art heating or illumination of any kind as you or I know it today in any of the rooms. All of this came by way of a roaring log-fire on the open hearth of some vast chimney, or innumerable candles and wax tapers placed everywhere in dish-shaped holders and candelabras. And Darvulia herself later told me when we spoke, that neither she nor those in her family who came before her ever had any desire to 'spoil or pollute'—as she put it—the antiquity and atmosphere of the ancient house with any of the contemporary and new-fangled devices of man.

"And so, every hall, chamber, passage, and corridor of the manor which I inspected seemed to be part of an older world; to belong to another time; and to almost resent (very much like its eccentric owner) everything to do with our modern day.

"Not a sound was to be heard, not a footfall detected in any of the chambers and corridors into which I peeped and peered. Indeed, so deep was the hush which lay over the house that it seemed, even to me, unutterably oppressive, for the very air between its walls brooded with an ancient past. And every room through which I wandered seemed haunted by a solitude comparable to that of a graveyard in the night's loneliest hour. I napped a while in one of the large featherbeds; and in the evening, when I woke, wandered on some more through the quaint, high-lintelled doorways and long, candle-lit corridors.

"It proved to be a house as vast, bewildering, and endless as the dreadful Labyrinth constructed by Daedalus for king Minos. And Nadasdy, like the manor's resident Minotaur, came across me at last in some dusty old room whose walls were lined with oaken bookcases containing numerous old manuscripts and moldering leather-bound volumes which I was then idly browsing through. He informed me that it was nearly midnight, and that his mistress would see me now. He then took me to what I presumed must be Darvulia's sitting room—on whose floors were Persian mats, and about whose walls ranged suits of brightly burnished armor, tapestries dimmed and worn by centuries, and scores of gilt-framed portraits representing Darvulia's ancestors.

"Then, a door at the far end of the room opened, and Darvulia Bethlen solemnly entered. The two old Transylvanian German women went before her, each one bearing a candelabra of six wax candles in front of them. These were placed on a low table before which Darvulia seated herself in a deep, upholstered armchair, the wax candles giving only a subdued, almost half-light, like a thin, clear twilight in the room. Neither the two old German women, nor Nadasdy the Turk spoke to Darvulia, unless she first asked them to. Their mistress, I noted, drank little, and ate even less, though the table was spread with a sumptuous quantity of food and drink on which Darvulia urged me to indulge my appetite.

"As I did so, I took the opportunity to survey my hostess very intently. Her long narrow face, I observed, was extremely pale, almost bloodless in color, and she appeared terribly drawn and unhealthy. She had a prominent aquiline nose, thin colorless lips, and large, fiercely-staring green eyes. It is difficult precisely to describe, but she looked old beyond her years, as though Time were aging her at an accelerated pace, beyond what is natural.

"The whole time I sat with her, she seemed steadily engaged in taking me in, and she spoke to me not in her own Romanian, but in excellent Latin. I laid before her my grievances, and explained to her the reason as to why I had come, appealing to her for help. She heard me through in absolute silence, but all the while she appeared to be gazing at me with a suppressed eagerness out of her large green eyes. When I had finished, she advised me to stay on at her estate until I had located Chastenet's incunabulum; she told me that once I had obtained this famed edition, she would return to Budapest with me and the incunabulum, assuring me that with the book and her influence, the Order would be only too willing to admit me once more to the society, and, at her insistence, bestow on me the rank and title of the Supreme Master of Arts." Vrancic's small black eyes dwelt for a moment with a strange, dark intensity on Nathan's face; and a grin, half gloating, half menacing, seemed to linger in their lustrous depths.

"And when I have finally found the incunabulum," he went on, as though he were speaking to himself instead of Nathan, "and Phebe has used the spell in it for regaining her mortality, regardless of the result for her, she has promised that afterward the incunabulum shall be mine, to do with as I please—keep it; destroy it; sell it: whatever I wish."

For some seconds, Vrancic smoked on in silence; and Nathan sat cold and still as a stone in the bed, not venturing to stir, blink, or utter so much as a word.

Then, "As you might expect," Vrancic continued, "Darvulia's encouraging words soothed and appeased me greatly, and we sat on for some hours, speaking together far into the night. She went on to tell me a great deal about her ancestors, particularly those represented in the portraits on the walls, and that not a thing in the house was less than a century old. Her grandfather, Radu Bethlen, she assured me was related by blood to the armigerous and powerful family that had long ago inhabited the now-ruined fortress, and who themselves had been the descendants of a people who originally hailed from a region in Wallachia near the Transylvanian Alps. And she herself claimed that she was the last of that ruling family's direct, or older line; and that in her still ran the old blood of the ancient Vlachs from beyond the Carpathian Mountains, that proud, warlike strain of men from whom the princely line of the historical Dracula, Vlad Tepes, stems. Her ancestors who once inhabited the house and region were of a race and type, she told me, that have now vanished utterly from the land; and never, she affirmed, will there be such a race again.

"Later that night, she escorted me down into the lower regions of the house and allowed me to inspect what had formerly been the extensive vaults of a once magnificent wine cellar, with its great open stone arches and echoing passages and narrow stone steps going up and down to other levels, but which had long ago been converted to a library unlike any I had ever seen. For the walls, from floor to ceiling, were covered with books whose bindings were of leather, silk, and skin: some were duodecimos, fine and large; some folios, stout and squat; and others, quartos of various sizes.

"Many of them, Darvulia assured me, were very, very ancient, having come into the possession of her ancestors from as long ago as the fall of Constantinople. She urged me, then, to remain and indulge myself in these priceless tomes. And for the next few weeks I did just that, rummaging through chest upon chest of ancient scrolls: some of parchment covered in silk with richly worked gilded clasps; and others of papyri encased in crimson velvet with heavily ornate studs of silver gilt. Days wore into weeks, for I virtually lost myself in innumerable codices in Latin, bound in lambskin and embossed in gold with mystical devices; or in literary treasures in Greek and Hebrew bound in gold-embroidered and brightly-colored silk.

"And although I saw Darvulia only during the night hours— usually after midnight—I began to note how the two old Transylvanian German women were regularly sent out by her to the peasant Gypsy families around nightfall, to bring some of the Gypsy children back with them to the manor after promising them food, money, and steady work as servants on the estate of their mistress."

In the brief pause that followed, Nathan hesitated for a breath, then murmured a question or two about why Vrancic was telling him all of this. But Vrancic either deliberately ignored the boy, or had not heard him. For all at once, "About this time, too," he hastened on, "I began to observe that the Gypsy children who had accepted the offers of the two old German women and returned with them to the manor, looked curiously sallow and run down. They became suddenly and mysteriously dazed and listless; and their health began to rapidly decline till they grew seriously ill. And in some of the young girls I noted bruises or red marks on their neck, and, in one or two cases, literal puncture wounds to the throat that bled. I realized at once that the children were being vampirized, both psychically and physically, by Darvulia, for her face suddenly appeared less pale; there was even a ruddiness to her lips and cheeks, and her poorly condition inexplicably improved—she began to look almost *youthful!*

"The Gypsies soon began to speak out against Darvulia, and took their complaints to the provincial authorities in one of the nearest towns. They appealed to the Church and secular courts, accusing Darvulia of practicing sorcery. But the matter was largely ignored by the local officials.

"Then, one evening, only a few days after this, I was in the library alone with Darvulia. I was sitting in an armchair with a gorgeously bound book open on my knees, when a soft, warm drowsiness came stealing over me. My eyelids grew heavy and began to droop, and my head to roll and nod; I strove desperately to lift my head and open my eyes, and when I had, who did I see but Darvulia Bethlen stooping low over me. She had just then withdrawn the moist erotic touch of her lips from my throat and straightened. Her large green eyes dwelt on mine with an intense gaze, and as I continued to meet them, I suddenly realized that she was no longer the aged, sickly-looking woman I had been sitting with in the library. She had undergone some sort of transfiguration, and appeared to me now as a tall, young seductive woman whose beauty and sensuality seemed to intoxicate my senses. I struggled horribly to resist her charms, her bewitching sexual attractiveness; for I knew that if I did not, if even for a moment I submitted to her perilous allure, I would not see another sunrise.

"For although you and others who are not adepts of the occult do not know this, an aura, or invisible energy field, enfolds the body, the physical shape of us all—and I knew that all the while I had been dozing, Darvulia had been steadily attempting to pierce this, to slake off my life-force and vampirize my vitality. But because of the strength and vigor of my own protective energy, I was able to resist her psychic attacks, and maintain the shield to my life-force impenetrable to her vampirism.

"I struggled up, then, from my chair; and several times she sprang at me, open-mouthed and eager to fix her lips in a lethal kiss upon my neck. Each time, however, I repulsed her efforts, and drove her violently back. And then, all at once, the room became filled with a revolting stench. Darvulia, I observed, began to emanate a dreadful aura, and her face and form seemed to waver, shrink, and wither away into a hideous, hook-nosed crone, as shriveled and decrepit as some appalling gnome or troll in Teutonic legend. She turned at once and stalked out of the room in a towering rage, uttering threats and curses against me."

Nathan sat perfectly still in the bed as Vrancic paused yet again, and the pair of them gazed on at one another in silence: Vrancic as though awaiting some word or comment from his young listener. But Nathan sat there holding not only his tongue, but, at the moment, his breath as well: he could do little more than blink. Then, as Vrancic hastened on again with his tale, Nathan breathed and breathed again.

"Now, about the time that I, too, began to fear for my life in Darvulia's manor," resumed Vrancic, "I learned that a party of the fear-stricken Gypsies had secretly gone to a Church in a neighboring village some five miles east of the Romanian border. There they petitioned the bishop for permission to expel the woman, Darvulia Bethlen, from the region. But they were sternly forbidden by him to commit any acts of violence or mischief against her.

"Days later, however, the Gypsies—either unwilling or unable to tolerate another instant what was being done by Darvulia to their children—stormed the house in a great mob in the middle of the night. There were perhaps thirty or forty of them, and they were carrying torches and lanterns, and were armed with knives, pitchforks, mattocks, and scythes. Before I even knew what was happening, half a dozen of them had swarmed into my room and dragged me, half-dressed, from my bed. My captors drove me roughly before them, through the front door, and beyond the stone porch, out into the night where I saw they had already apprehended the two old Transylvanian German women and Darvulia herself. And lying at their feet, prone upon the ground, face down in the dirt, in a welter of his own blood, was the body of Nadasdy. He had already been brutally slaughtered, for I could see that he was covered in ghastly wounds, the Gypsies having. pierced and slashed his body many times with their weapons.

"Commanding this bloodthirsty rabble was the patriarch of the Gypsies, a poor Romanian fiddler by the name of Mikov. He ordered his two sons, Petrov and Radovan, to put the two old German women to death. Struggling in the iron grip of my captors, I watched helplessly as Mikov's sons beheaded the two old women, and then cut out their hearts. Horrified beyond anything that words may express, I watched once again, paralyzed with fear, as Mikov first hammered a large wooden stake into Darvulia's chest, and then took a hatchet and hewed again and again at her neck until he had swept the head from her body. Mikov's sons, and the other Gypsies, then turned their attention on me; but by this time I had become mad with fear.

"A panic terror literally took possession of me, and, witless with horror, I managed to break free of my captors. I fled yelling and screaming back into the house, thinking—however foolishly!—that I could somehow elude my enemies in its labyrinthine halls and corridors. Having no intention of entering the house a second time, the Gypsies set fire to Darvulia's manor, kindling flames around it on every side. They then took Nadasdy's mutilated corpse, as well as the severed heads and decapitated bodies of Darvulia and the two old German women and cast them into the spreading blaze in the porch. In no time at all the ancient house was engulfed in flames. My flesh was badly scorched in my desperate efforts to escape"—for an instant, Vrancic brushed with the tips of his fingers the disfigured side of his face—"and my red hair, for the most part, had been singed away. The billowing smoke was drifting everywhere, choking and blinding me; the suffocating heat of the roaring flames drove me now this way, now that. And yet, and yet, I somehow managed to escape the blaze—although to this day I have no memory as to precisely how.

"Crawling on my hands and knees, as I gasped and choked, I only know that I somehow found my way into the open air again. Mikov must have seen me, for I heard him shouting to his sons, Radovan and Petrov, alerting them with regard to my escape. Blind with terror, I fled for my life, my heart drumming so fast I thought it must burst. I sought refuge in the woods and solitudes of the marshy lands which for many days' journey march with the borders of Hungary and Romania in a wide and trackless wilderness.

"The pursuit of my enemies—Mikov, his two sons, and their murderous throng—was relentless, and for several days, in the wilds and waste of those pathless fens, the Gypsies stalked me mercilessly: for I could hear them hooting and calling to one another far into the night as they scoured the area.

"Hour after hour, for nearly five days, I remained on the run: seldom resting; too afraid to shut my eyes even for a moment. I didn't dare risk falling asleep, lest when I opened my eyes again I should find myself in the hands of Mikov and his two sadistic sons, and so come to the same miserable end as Darvulia and her servants. And then, one night, by starlight and waning moon, I emerged from the wooded marshlands exhausted and faint with hunger, and found that I had wandered, either by some hapless chance or cruel fortune, back to the smoldering ruins of Darvulia's ravaged estate. The great ancient house of her noble ancestors had been reduced to a shattered pile of smoking rubble and blackened timbers. Among the heaps of cinders and ash in what remained of the porch and the scorched timbers of its arched door-frame, I first came across Darvulia's severed head. All of her hair had been burnt off, and the blackened skin about her face was so horribly shriveled that her lips were drawn back, baring her teeth, which were sharp as a beast's. I then discovered her charred and blackened skeleton, along with Nadasdy's and the two old German women. I noted that there were lumps and bits of burned flesh still clinging to their singed bones.

"My limbs and hands were shaking uncontrollably with hunger. I knew that if I did not eat something then and there I would collapse, for my strength was swiftly failing, and I felt faint and unsteady with the terror of the hunted upon me. And then, all at once, the will to survive took control, and without another moment's hesitation I yielded to my ravenous hunger. I sank to my knees in the ashes and began tearing voraciously at the bones with my teeth and broken nails, scraping off bits and chunks of seared flesh, and cracking off bones with joints of roasted gristle.

These I crammed into the pockets of my trousers and my coat, and fled with them into the old cemetery along which the road to Darvulia's estate goes winding. I knew that there I would be safe from my pursuers, for many of the Gypsies regarded that cemetery with a superstitious awe, and, due to their beliefs that its graves and tombs were a refuge for vampires, they seldom if ever entered its precincts.

"And there, for many days and many nights, I hid myself among the Gothic tombs and medieval stone-markers, undisturbed and undiscovered by my hunters; surviving from day to day by greedily devouring the burned pieces of flesh I had pilfered from the bones of Darvulia, Nadasdy, and the two German women. For the first day or two I wept and groaned and violently retched as I champed and chewed on mouthfuls of their burned flesh, and was filled with revulsion by my own behavior. But then, by the morning of the third day, I found myself eating the flesh and sucking on the split bones with a sudden gusto and relish; my senses absolutely delighted in the taste; I began to hum and croon as I eagerly gnawed on now a femur bone, now some portion of a ribcage; and laughed out loud as I licked the grease from the tips of my fingers. And I can assure you that the tears that gathered in my eyes and went streaming down my cheeks that morning were from sheer pleasure and elation instead of repugnance."

For a while Vrancic sat on in the armchair quietly smoking, and his eyes remained fixed on Nathan with a peculiar intensity. And Nathan merely stared and held his breath; his young face all but transfixed in its intermingled expression of horror, pity, and astonishment. Then, "And is that," his dry lips half whispered, "how you became a—" But suddenly he checked himself, and deliberately refrained from uttering that awful word.

In the burned side of Vrancic's face, the left eye, beneath its heavy lid, seemed to fix itself glassily on Nathan's face. "A cannibal?" he drawled, and his lips stirred in a faint smirk. "Yes. And since that day—much like the Batta chieftain on the island of Sumatra—I found that I could eat no other flesh. I craved it, longed for it unlike anything ever before in my life."

Nathan moistened his lips and, very faintly, he asked, "But what happened to Mikov and the gypsies who were hunting you? Did you ever see them again?"

Vrancic leaned forward in the armchair and, for a moment or two, eyed Nathan with an almost roguish grin. Then, "O, yes," he said, "and with the help of Phebe and Candidianus I obtained sweet revenge on Mikov, his two sons, Radovan and Petrov, and all the others who sought to hunt me down and kill me. But that, perhaps, you shall hear about some other day." He paused and, after he had stubbed out his cigarette, rose from his chair. "For now, I have told you all that you needed to hear," he then continued. "Let it be a warning to you, a warning that sometimes we are made slaves to certain things through the senses—whether it be through the channels of the eyes, or by the touch of our hands. Either way they cause our undoing; 'win us to our harm', as Shakespeare warns us, only to betray us 'in deepest consequence'. And you, Nathanael Christian, are now in deadly peril of betraying yourself 'in deepest consequence'. Be wary of vampiric love, for love of that sort is truly fatal; it is insatiable: it will weaken, enamor, entice, and at last waste you to the very dregs of your soul. Do not entangle yourself in it. It may seem, at first, beautiful, passionate, and inexpressibly erotic. In its very nature, however, it is associated with disaster and death, and to be resisted at all costs." Vrancic paused a moment, trod lightly across the floor, and softly drew open the bedroom door. "Tell me;" he said, as he stood in the open doorway, intently scanning Nathan's face; "what have you been experiencing lately whenever you have spent any length of time in Phebe's presence? An inexplicable heaviness? An overwhelming sense of fatigue?"

For an instant, Nathan remained tongue-tied and astonished by Vrancic's shrewd guesses and his acutely discomfiting scrutiny. And he felt his face turn red to the roots of his hair. Then, in a faint and stammering voice, he managed to reply that he had been feeling oddly "tired and sleepy" whenever he spent a long amount of time around Phebe.

"You are being vampirized," said Vrancic. "It happens to all mortals when they are in the presence of a vampire. Phebe, unaware that she is actually doing it, has been steadily draining you, slaking off your vital forces. This will happen inevitably to all who choose (unwisely) to linger in the presence of a vampire. Though they never take so much as a drop of your blood, they nonetheless draw from those around them their life force—psychically. It cannot be helped, for in many cases it is the nature of some vampires, whether they will it or not.

"Have you looked in a mirror lately?" he asked Nathan, after a brief pause. "You are beginning to appear *unnaturally* older: not so much 'mature', as *aged*, so to speak. But then, this is only to be expected. For a mortal cannot remain long in the presence of a vampire without their vitality, their energy, their very *youth* being psychically extracted, sapped, siphoned off." Again Vrancic had paused, and the small black pupils of his eyes continued to peer across at Nathan's silent face piercingly. "Today," he said, "I am but a shadow of my former self, having lost everything I was fond of and took pleasure in. And you, too, Nathanael Christian, will come to the same unhappy end if you do not sever—before it is too late!—this bond of love you have formed with a member of the Undead."

And the next instant, without another word to (or glance at) Nathan, Vrancic had stepped across the threshold and firmly pulled the door shut behind him. Once again Nathan was alone in Aunt Amelia's bedroom. For the next few moments he sat perfectly still in the bed, listening intently, as the sound of Vrancic's footsteps receded down the hall. He then heard the steps faintly creaking, and he knew that Vrancic had gone back downstairs. A moment or two afterwards, Nathan had climbed out of the bed and, with his brown eyes fastened almost uneasily on the sheet-veiled mirror of his aunt's dresser, he moved a pace or two forward. Holding his breath then, as he stood very still and silent before it, he reached out his hand and slowly lifted back a corner of the sheet. For some seconds his eyes fixed themselves on his reflection in the mirror's silvery deeps.

He was startled at the change that was there. He knew how physically exhausted he *felt*, but until now he had been utterly unaware just how much 'older' he actually *looked*. For his pale youthful face seemed to have grown peculiarly thin, careworn, and lined; and the very hollows of his eyes appeared ringed and darkened. And he was all but shocked when he noticed that his hair in places was flecked with grey.

Nathan let the sheet fall from his trembling fingers, and stumbled a step or two backwards. Could it be true? he wondered. Was Phebe 'draining' him? Was she psychically siphoning off his vitality, his very 'life force', as Vrancic contended?

A fit of shuddering came over him, and not wanting to think about it anymore, Nathan climbed back into bed. Huddling himself into its sheet, he laid down again on his side and shut tight his eyes. But the strange potency of Vrancic's words, the tragic and gruesome account of his life, his ominous hints and warnings to Nathan regarding his 'perilous' relationship with Phebe, all had a very telling and awful effect on the boy's nerves. And try as he would, he could neither lie still in the bed, nor go back to sleep. And so, he climbed sullenly out of bed, and began striding up and down the floor of his aunt's bedroom, tired and dispirited, yet never for a moment sorry that Phebe had come into his life.

CHAPTER NINE

*"...You have displayed great zeal... in seeking me out, and
it will not seem surprising if you don't gain a great deal
of good fortune from your encounter with me... I also lay
this curse upon you that these eyes of mine will be always
before your sight... and this will bring you to your death..."*

—*The Saga of Grettir the Strong*

*"...It's my will now that... you have only anguish
from me. And it will come to pass, I assure you.
Moreover, all the miseries that have happened here
were my doing, I'll no longer hide it from you. I'm to
blame. On you, though, I now fix this curse: that my
spell causes you unspeakable woe... Indeed, before
all is over, every person will see and know it..."*

—*Eyrbyggia Saga*

By noon of that same day, Sunday, August 27th—a windless summer
day of slow, sweltering airs—Nathan had got dressed and stolen
downstairs to find something to eat. Anxious to avoid a second
encounter with Vrancic that day, Nathan swiftly bolted the few
morsels of food he was able to snatch from the kitchen closet and
then, soundlessly, hurried back upstairs to the second floor.

And while pausing at the stairhead a while to prick up his ears
for any untoward sound of Vrancic on the floor below, Nathan
suddenly became conscious of the deep and curiously dreamlike

hush which seemed to prevail not only inside his home, but outside as well. It was a peculiarly eerie stillness which (at least to Nathan's mind) soon grew all but unnerving. For there was something about it that was somehow disagreeable, out of the ordinary; some strange indefinable sense, as of expectation, lurking, waiting just within the edges of it—but expectant of... what? he wondered.

For some while Nathan continued to listen intently to it, now at the windows of his aunt's room, then at that of his own. And he could not help but note that while all things beneath the sun's unclouded rays *appeared* for all the world to be stupefied with the blazing heat, not even the sleepy piping of a solitary bird, from drooping tree or wilting bush, came into the weird unnatural quiet on 73rd Place. It was as though life itself on the entire block had mysteriously fled elsewhere, or somehow merely ceased to be at all.

For hours together then, throughout that hushed and stifling afternoon, Nathan continued to linger at the narrow window of his empty and forsaken bedroom. In an endless reverie he stood peering down into the old All Faiths cemetery, as though somewhere in its drowsing graves and decaying headstones lurked some secret and mysterious decoy. And for an instant or two, as he gazed on absently across the neglected graves, almost it seemed to him that the heart within him had suddenly grown as writhen and thrawn as the cemetery's gnarled trees and frowzy grasses. So that no sensation, no feeling whatsoever had any place or privilege to be in it other than his desire to look *upon,* and lose himself eternally *in,* the dark enchanting loveliness of Phebe. A desire which Nathan now realized consumed and devoured him almost beyond what he was able to bear.

And for quite some while now, as Nathan stood idling there at that open window, he could not help ruminating uneasily, and somewhat bitterly, on Vrancic's grave and sobering observations regarding Phebe. Moreover, the man's own cautionary and horribly tragic tale with regard to himself echoed hauntingly on and on in Nathan's brain.

Then, potent word by potent word, Nathan began to sift through and consider more attentively all of Vrancic's dark forebodings and grim warnings. Until, all at once, with a strange, cold misgiving and creeping anxiety gathering heavily round his heart, he began to wonder what would happen if Phebe should never obtain the incunabulum. And as a result, she must remain—one of the nonliving, a member of the Undead, a vampire. Her beauty forever unfading and in check; her youth in eternal suspension, in an everlasting arrest; her life itself endlessly prolonged, without the anxiety of old age, decay—*death*. How, he wondered, could she possibly remain with himself: a mortal, subject to the edicts and decrees of Time, who must inevitably age and (unavoidably) grow old and infirm? A process which (according to Vrancic) had already been hastened simply by his being in Phebe's company. What's more, Vrancic had warned him: to merely linger in her proximity was to have his vitality steadily and inexorably drained by her.

And for a moment or two, Nathan felt himself sink into a chilling motionlessness. Even his thoughts for an instant were stilled and hushed. But then, quite suddenly, they were roused once more to those same perturbing notions, and he could not refrain from asking himself, what, then, must he look like in a week's time? How much "older" should he appear because of Phebe's vampiric condition in another month—or, worse still, by the end of the year? Would his body by then be all bent and decrepit with age; his hair all grey and thinning; and his face creased and seamed and hideously wizened, as a result of his vitality wasted and his youth utterly exhausted? If so, how could Phebe remain with him then? Why would she want to?

And suddenly Nathan held his breath, and the fingers of his trembling hands groped slowly, fretfully along his features, as if to feel for wrinkles and other outward signs of an accelerated senescence. Then, with his heart beating thick and cold, he hurried across the hall to the bathroom mirror.

After a moment's pause, an instant, really, of anguished uncertainty, Nathan slowly, almost stealthily lifted the bottommost corner of the towel that was covering the mirrors of the medicine cabinet. Stooping slightly forward then, he gazed on into the icy stillness of their glass. Astonished by what he saw, he gave a sudden start; and catching his breath a moment, he felt his heart stand still!

For there, instead of his own reflection, Nathan thought, for an instant, another face, faint and shadowy, had been peering back at him, as if in welcome, out of the mirror's silvery deeps, but then, just as swiftly, was gone. At the same time, Nathan was aware that in the very instant in which he had been confronted by that unfamiliar, wraith-like face, across his memory had flashed, inexplicably, that mystifying seven letter word—'prosper'—which had appeared to him in his dream more than a week ago.

Then, as if compelled, Nathan felt his dry lips slowly part, and his tongue softly press against his teeth. And in a low solitary breath, he heard his own faint voice whisper, unaccountably, that other mysterious word which he had traced in the dust on the dining room mirror—"Ichthys."

At the sound of his own voice having uttered that curious word aloud, Nathan's eyes opened wide, and he lowered his gaze. Glancing down for a moment into the basin of the sink, he suddenly realized he had been tracing the while something with his finger in the beads of water that had collected in it from the dripping faucet. He drew a sharp and sudden breath, and he felt the hair rise stiff on his scalp when he saw once again that peculiar sign from his childhood: ⊂×

And a faint cold shiver went stealing up his spine. For a tiny voice from deep within him informed, apprised, assured him, beyond any shadow of doubt, any faintest whisper of uncertainty, that this outwardly trifling fish-like symbol, and that seemingly meaningless word, 'ichthys', were most definitely connected. And somehow, too, they were of tremendous consequence not only to himself, but to Phebe as well.

But how... and (still more baffling) why? Nathan kept asking himself, as he continued to stare down into the sink's basin, with wide, flaming eyes, at that unsophisticated yet inscrutable sign. The answer to this maddening riddle, however, continued (at least for the time being) to elude and bewilder him. And no matter how long he stood there, pondering and puzzling over the mystery—one moment gazing down at the sign he had traced, and the next at his own perplexed reflection—the explanation to it all refused to come clear.

At length, Nathan's aching and outwearied mind was unable to even think about it for another moment. With slow, doubtful steps he turned away from the mirror and, in an all but empty and helpless daze, stole back down the hall, half reluctantly, to Aunt Amelia's bedroom. Once again he was faced with his usual problem: what to do *with* himself when he was by himself—alone, without Phebe near him. For he now dreaded to be in his own company, in the awful solitude and death-like stillness of his home.

And so, with an intensely greedy longing for Phebe's companionship—a longing which to him felt like the anguish of an unendurably grievous wound—Nathan resumed his lonely and idle watch for her. This time at one of the three windows in his aunt's bedroom. He persisted in this vain and drowsy vigil until the last red embers of the setting August sun had faded out of the western hem of the sky, and the twilight's long shadows had fairly deepened into full dusk. For an instant or two he debated whether he should go to meet Phebe in the old mausoleum. But his mind was so weary and his eyes so heavy that he could scarcely keep awake. And just as the first few isolated stars were faintly beginning to shine in the east, and a thin veil of clouds, coming up from the west, had begun to spread itself over the sky, Nathan flung himself down across his aunt's bed and dozed off at once.

His sleep, which lasted little more than a couple of hours, was curiously deep and dreamless, but just along its edges seemed to lurk a haunting echo of thunders. For soon after Nathan had dropped off, a heavy shower or two of thundery rain had swept through the area. And when he had once more opened his eyes, he lay listening a while, as in a kind of trance, to their drowsy waters gently whispering and bubbling in the aluminum gutters under the eaves of the house.

Aching with fatigue and stiff to his bones, Nathan yawned and sat up as his aunt's tambour clock on the night table struck nine. He trod lightly over to the windows and peered out between the slats of one of the blinds. The sky was marvelously clear and starry now, for the clouds, he noted, had withdrawn themselves. And away on his right, a brightening moon, just on its way to becoming a gibbous, was already halfway down the western slope of the sky, silvering in its descent all of 73rd Place.

The scene was so wonderfully serene and dream-like to his eye that, for an instant, Nathan felt his heart all but swell with rapture, and for a moment or two he actually caught his breath. For up and down the length and breadth of 73rd Place, filling every pothole, were little iridescent puddles of rain-water which, like a myriad of silvery mirrors, reflected the white light of the moon, so that the street, from end to end, appeared dotted with a multitude of miniature moons.

And as Nathan continued to gaze on at this surreal and exquisitely delightful scene, he began repeating, almost mechanically, the familiar sound of Phebe's name. Without fail he preceded it each time with the adjective "beautiful", as though he were pronouncing some spell-like verse to a magical song that kept recurring in his mind. But by the sixth or seventh time, roused quite suddenly, as if from the strangeness of a dream, he ceased with a gasp and hurried down the hall to the window in his room.

Leaning out over the wooden, rain-damped sill, Nathan gazed up at the August constellations powdering the night sky with their spangling fires high over the graves and tombstones of the cemetery. By now he knew all of their names, for Phebe had taught them to him, as well as where and how to locate them.

And Nathan's lips broke into a faint smile as there, low in the eastern quarter of the sky and brightly agleam, his wandering gaze encountered the stars of Pegasus. Phebe had taught him to easily recognize this constellation by the 'Great Square' its celestial fires mimicked. Not far to the left of this, he could distinguish what Phebe had described to him as a small cloudy star, faint-hazed and elongated, but which in actuality is what astronomers and stargazers know as the great Andromeda Galaxy. And sweeping upward from the southern horizon, to trail its hazed and heavenly fires across the night sky far into the north, was the Milky Way. Jeweled and bestarred with a myriad of clustering luminaries, Nathan stared at it for some seconds in absolute awe. And clear before him across space, her limpid fires nearly level with his eyes, was the planet Venus, shimmering in the firmament like a large, pale drop of crystallized water. Once more on the eastern half of its orbit, the dazzling light of this celestial body seemed almost to bewitch Nathan as he continued to lean out of his window and confront with his eyes her wondrous radiance.

But then, another glance of anguished longing down into the faint-starred grounds of the old All Faiths cemetery suddenly recalled Nathan to himself. And all in an instant he was persuaded not to linger another moment in the stale, dust-ridden confines of his room, but to go at once and meet Phebe at the old mausoleum.

Now, even as Nathan was preparing to leave his house— having first thrust his old pocket-knife into the back pocket of his jeans, then gone downstairs to retrieve the flashlight from the kitchen cabinet under the sink—unbeknownst to him, he and his home were under a secret and near-continuous surveillance. For Mr Erwin Schiller, in the house diagonally across the street from Nathan's, was standing at his bedroom window with a pair of binoculars, through which he was intently peering across the way at the boy's home.

"But what is the boy up to, Muriel?" said Mr Schiller, suddenly and sharply to his wife, who, sitting up in bed, was on the verge of dozing. Their four year-old Maltese, Blitzen, was lying sound asleep on his side, nestled against her leg. And at the sound of Mr Schiller's voice, the eyes of both Blitzen and Mrs Muriel Schiller softly opened.

"What's that, dear?" Mrs Schiller asked, rather sleepily; then, through a half-suppressed yawn, added: "Did you say something?" Blinking her bleared and tired eyes, she glanced up swiftly. Her hair-netted head, with its grey locks tightly wound in their pink-colored sponge-rollers, had been stooped over an old, shabby, dog-eared pocket-Bible, open at the Book of Wisdom, as she sat nodding there in the bed, several pillows supporting her back.

"Yes, Muriel;" said Mr Schiller, somewhat crossly; "I did say 'something.'" He was evidently annoyed that his wife had not been listening. "I was talking about Amelia Christian's nephew. The boy's behavior is anything but normal. No friends; no activities—he just keeps to himself day in and day out, inside his house! And when he does step outside: off he goes in a hurry up the street and into the cemetery. It just isn't normal behavior for a young boy, Muriel."

Mrs Schiller's gaze returned to her open Bible. "Oh, never mind about Amelia's nephew, Erwin;" she said, after suppressing yet another yawn; "put those binoculars away and come to bed. You've been staring through them out that window for more than an hour now."

There was a lengthy pause.

"It's peculiar, Muriel, very peculiar," Mr Schiller remarked at last, still gazing through his binoculars at Nathan's house. "There's something behind it all; something dishonest, mark my words!"

Mrs Schiller raised her eyes again from the fine black print of her pocket Bible. "So the boy goes into the cemetery, Erwin," she said. "What's so peculiar or dishonest about that?"

"But what does he do there, Muriel?" asked Mr Schiller, setting the binoculars down on the window-sill, and turning round to face his wife. "What is the attraction? And where, I ask you, is Amelia? It's been more than two weeks now since I last saw her. And that tall, thin, odd-looking fellow that comes and goes at all hours of the night—driving off in Amelia's old Grand Marquis, and sometimes not returning until the next night—who is he? Where does he go—and what, I ask you, is he up to? He is certainly no relation of Amelia's, or Nathan's as he claimed to be when he and I spoke: of that much I'm sure. So what is he doing in their house?" Mr Schiller paused a moment and fixed his wife with a significant look. Then, "And once or twice, Muriel," he resumed, slightly lowering his voice, "I've seen a young girl, too, very mysteriously coming from the cemetery to the house, and from the house to the cemetery. Now, *who—is—she*?" Again Mr Schiller had paused to stare across at his wife with his grey bushy eyebrows arched high on his forehead. "And the windows, Muriel," he went on, "day and night they remain shut tight, and the blinds drawn down over them, eh! It just isn't normal, I tell you."

Mrs Schiller had sat, her Bible clutched in her hands, motionlessly listening to her husband, her eyes fixed the while intently on his face. And after pondering on each of the valid points raised by him, she sighed, and said, "Well, then, Erwin, if all of these things are so troubling to you, maybe you should talk to the police about them." She paused a moment, drew a long, slow breath, sighed again, and said, "But if you ask me, I think it's best left alone. Don't involve yourself. That's my advice." She waited some seconds for her husband to agree; but upon observing the strange absent look in his eyes, she frowned, and asked: "Did you hear what I just said, Erwin?"

But Mr Schiller did not at once answer his wife. For several moments more he stood there very still and silent. And all the while his eyes continued to rest on her face, he was deep in thought, reflecting on something of genuine interest. Following up, in fact, some newly developed theory of his with regard to Nathan's unusual behavior which, until now, had not occurred to him. "Wait a minute, Muriel, I just realized something;" he began, in a slow, almost half-whisper, as if he were thinking out loud rather than speaking to his wife; "it may very well be that the boy suffers from a very rare form of psychosis"—there was a short pause, in which Mr Schiller seemed to reflect for some moments: then—"a condition involving perhaps some morbidly repressed sexual desire—a desire which the boy may be hoping to fulfill by going into the cemetery. I can't be sure yet."

For the merest instant Mrs Schiller stared at her husband as if appalled. "With what—or with *whom*—Erwin? One of the dead?"

"Exactly, Muriel, yes!—one of the dead. It's called 'necrophilism'. Freud spoke of this very macabre psychological disorder somewhere in his writings."

"Oh, really, Erwin, please!" said Mrs Schiller, frowning severely at her husband. "You know I don't like it when you bring up things like that. It frightens me!"

"And so it should, Muriel, so it should," said Mr Schiller. "Believe me, my dear, there are many forms of ghoulism in this life practiced in secret by some truly disturbed individuals which, even if you were to hear only so much as the briefest description of them, would cause the hairs on your head to stand straight up. We are touching on truly perverse tendencies here, Muriel. Why, only a few days ago, while I was browsing through several of my books, I remember now coming across an excerpt in one of them regarding a very peculiar form of mental illness—an erratic melancholy, or madness, really, documented by pathologists in numerous case studies under the curious term of 'lycanthropy'."

A faint cynical smile had crept into Mrs Schiller's features. "What on earth are you talking about now, Erwin? Like-a-canopy;" she scoffed, unintentionally mispronouncing the odd, unfamiliar term her husband had just spoken; "you're not making any sense, really! I mean, where do you come up with such gibberish?"

"Lycanthropy, Muriel," said Mr Schiller, peevishly. "The word I used was *lycanthropy*! And if you spent less time ridiculing me, and more time listening to me, you wouldn't have made such a gross blunder in trying to pronounce the term. It's from the Greek word, 'lycanthrope', meaning 'man-wolf'. According to medical literature it's a psychological disorder which modern medicine links to other mental and nervous conditions such as schizophrenia, necrophilia, and bipolar disorder. And the person afflicted with this very bizarre medical condition of lycanthropy actually believes he is undergoing a physical transformation from a human being to a wolf."

For a moment or two, Mrs Schiller stared at her husband with her mouth agape and her eyes round and wide. Then, "Oh, please, Erwin! This is absolutely ridiculous!"

"No, no, Muriel; it's true," Mr Schiller retorted. "And as the condition worsens, and the delusion takes stronger hold on the sufferer's deranged mind, he—or she—begins to act and behave exactly like a beast—running about on all fours; howling; desiring raw flesh; and perpetrating truly aggressive acts or violent crimes against his fellow man. The individual's mental state then very rapidly deteriorates into that of a homicidal lunatic; and in the end, the sufferer himself becomes lost in a twilight-limbo of the psyche, a borderland, as it were, in which he now lives his psychopathological existence as a voracious wolf."

At first Mrs Schiller's eyes merely continued to return her husband's steady and unswerving stare; and she ventured neither the least reply nor the slightest remark. She seemed all but speechless. Then, taking a long, slow breath, "Erwin, are you making this up?" she asked, but without pausing to await her husband's response, she said: "You can't be serious! I find it hard to believe that any of this is true."

"Well, then, if you doubt what I'm telling you, Muriel, perhaps you'll be more willing to believe what's written about it in this book." He crossed the floor of the room in two or three strides to the bookshelves ranged along the wall opposite their bed. From the floor almost to the ceiling, books of various sizes packed these shelves. After fumbling in the breast pocket of his shirt for his reading glasses, Mr Schiller slightly bent, edged his way softly along one or two of the lower shelves, paused an instant, then abstracted a thick, cloth-bound volume.

"And what book is that, Erwin?" asked Mrs Schiller, sardonically. "Another one of your collected works on folktales and myths, I suppose."

"No, Muriel, you're wrong. This," said Mr Schiller, holding the book up to exhibit to his wife the gilt lettering of its title embossed upon the binding, "is an 'A to Z Medical Reference and Dictionary of Medical Terms'. So you will have to refrain from your usual taunts and jeers that my literary diet consists for the most part of fables and fairy stories. We are dealing with medical science here. Unmitigated facts, my dear —and not a trace of fiction or fantasy! Let me hear you scoff at what I'm about to read to you now."

Having adjusted his glasses, Mr Schiller cleared his throat and opened the book. Then, wetting the tip of his finger with his tongue, he began to turn over the pages until he came at last to the one he sought. Slowly, steadily he drew his finger down the page and, stopping towards the middle of it, he said, "Ah, here it is, 'lycanthropy'. Are you listening, Muriel?" He paused to glance up from the page and peer over the rims of his glasses at his wife, to reassure himself that she had not dozed off again, and that he had her undivided attention.

"I'm listening, Erwin. Go on," she answered.

Mr Schiller's eyes fixed themselves once more on the page and, in a deep, forceful voice (a note of eagerness in its tone), he began reading aloud to her from the book:

"Lycanthropy. A severe mental disorder whose central feature is the delusion of undergoing a physical transformation from a human being into that of a wolf.

As the illness progresses behavior becomes distinctly abnormal, and the sufferer may experience bizarre compulsions. There is also increasing alienation, generally leading to complete withdrawal from all social contact. A gross distortion of reality becomes more prevailing, and self-neglect is overwhelmingly evident.

Associated features—"

And for an instant, Mr Schiller glanced up from the page again to make certain of his wife's attention:

"—associated features may include episodes of necrophagia, the practice of eating the flesh of dead bodies; necrophilism, sexual attraction to, and sexual intercourse with, dead bodies; necrosadism, the condition of deriving sexual pleasure from brutalizing dead bodies; bestiality, the practice of copulating with animals; and cannibalism. Any of these conditions may be dominant at a given time, or in some cases aspects of all five of them may be present in the sufferer at one and the same time. Also, symptoms—"

But here Mrs Schiller broke suddenly in: "Erwin! Do you seriously expect me to believe that Amelia's nephew suffers from even so much as one of those terrible disorders of the mind?" She paused a moment to stare incredulously at her husband; but then, without waiting for his reply, hurried on to say: "Erwin! He's a fifteen year-old boy for heaven's sake!" But Mr Schiller merely adjusted his glasses and, ignoring his wife's interruption, continued to read on:

"Also, symptoms of clinical vampirism may accompany the illness in its early stages—"

"'Vampires'!" said Mrs Schiller, interrupting her husband a second time. "Oh, please, Erwin! Are you being serious? Do you really expect me to believe, even for a moment, that Amelia's nephew is a vampire?"

Mr Schiller's bright blue eyes, peering out across at his wife, flashed angrily for an instant from behind the lenses of their bifocals. "I didn't say the boy's a vampire, Muriel;" he replied somewhat testily; "I said he may suffer from vampirism—*clinical* vampirism!"

"And what on earth does that mean?"

Mr Schiller answered: "Another term for it is Renfield's syndrome."

"Renfield... Renfield," repeated Mrs Schiller. "Isn't that the name of some lunatic in one of those old Gothic horror novels you once read to me?"

Mr Schiller gave a faint nod of his head. "'Dracula', Muriel; the name of the novel is 'Dracula,'" he replied. "And, yes, the character in the story is R.M. Renfield. And it is after this deranged character in the 19th century classic novel by Bram Stoker that clinical vampirism has been given the alternate name of Renfield's syndrome, due to the character's morbid delusion that he would perish miserably unless he was permitted to drink the blood of other living creatures. The clinical psychologist Richard Noll coined the term."

"And you honestly believe Nathan is suffering from Renfield's syndrome, Erwin? That this shy, quiet young boy—like the fictional character in Bram Stoker's novel—has some insane craving to drink another person's blood?"

Mr Schiller, by way of answering his wife, merely turned over the page of the medical book he had in his hands, and continued to read on:

"Once some peculiar event has initiated the pathological condition of clinical vampirism (or Renfield's syndrome), the first recognizable symptom, autovampirism—characterized by the sufferer drinking his own blood—swiftly progresses to the next phase of the illness, the consumption of the blood of animals, followed lastly by genuine vampirism: drinking the blood of another living human being.

These three main stages of Renfield's syndrome are generally accompanied by depraved and sexually deviant behavior. Other features are as follows: A profound sense of isolation; detachment from one's family (in some cases from one's own self), and from society in general. A preoccupation with things of the dead, and a fixation with demonic ideas and notions. Making frequent trips to, and spending long periods of time in, cemeteries, as well as—"

But here, once more, Mrs Schiller intervened. "Really, Erwin! Please, I don't want to hear another word about that clinical-Renfield-vampirism-whatever it's called!"

Mr Schiller shut up the book, removed his pair of glasses from the bridge of his nose and, for a moment or two, regarded his wife in silence. Then, "What I can't understand, Erwin," said Mrs Schiller, at length, "is why you would even suspect Amelia's nephew of suffering from any of those horrible mental disorders."

Mr Schiller restored the medical book to its place on the shelf, then drew from the breast pocket of his shirt a small spiral notepad. He opened it, turned several of the narrow pages, then handed the open pad to his wife.

Scrawled on the page were the following dates, times, and days:

(Sunday) August 13th .... 8:21 p.m.
(Monday) August 14th .... 7:53 p.m.
(Tuesday) August 15th .... (time approx.) 8:05 p.m.

(Friday) August 18th .... (afternoon) ?3:00 p.m.?
(Saturday) August 26th .... 12:00 a.m.—Midnight

Mrs Schiller read each of these entries to herself, then glanced up at her husband's face with questioning eyes.

"I've been watching the boy very closely, Muriel," said Mr Schiller, in answer to her perplexed expression. "Oh, yes; watching him for the past two weeks, to be precise. And each night I saw the boy head up the street and enter the cemetery, I marked the date, hour, and the day, and wrote them down. Now what does that tell you, Muriel?"

Mrs Schiller stared at her husband's face in silence for nearly half a minute, then, "It tells me, Erwin, that you are becoming obsessed with this boy!" she answered, giving her husband a severe look.

"No, no, Muriel! Don't you see? All those trips to the cemetery are one of the features of clinical vampirism—as the medical book clearly states—'making frequent trips to, and spending long periods of time in, cemeteries'! And a person suffering from lycanthropy will sometimes exhibit symptoms of clinical vampirism in the early stages of their illness."

"Erwin, you really need to stop obsessing over where this poor young boy goes, or what he does," said Mrs Schiller. "It isn't healthy! Why, ever since his aunt took ill, you've—"

"No, no, Muriel," Mr Schiller suddenly broke in, "Amelia never 'took ill', as you put it. She's been murdered!"

For a full ten seconds Mrs Schiller sat there in the bed staring at her husband in speechless astonishment. Then, "What?" she all but cried.

"Yes, Muriel. I am now absolutely convinced Amelia Christian has been murdered," replied Mr Schiller. "And her nephew, Nathan— if he's not entirely responsible for her murder—has had, at least, some hand in disposing of her corpse. And that may also be one of the reasons why he keeps going into the cemetery. In all likelihood he has helped in secretly burying the body there. And it may be that his guilt now compels him to go to the site where his aunt's remains have been hidden. I can't be sure."

"Erwin, you're talking pure nonsense! Stop it. I don't want to hear another word of this. You sound like, well, to put it mildly, like you're becoming a little unhinged."

Mr Schiller stared back at his wife without stirring so much as an eyelid. "Call it what you will, Muriel," he said. "But I know Amelia has been killed. I can feel it in my bones. For the past couple of days now I've tried again and again calling the home number, but there's nothing. It's as if the line has been disconnected."

Mrs Schiller said: "well, maybe, Amelia is just having some problems with her telephone service."

"And one of your problems, Muriel, is that you're too willing to dismiss the obvious."

"Since when is having a problem with your telephone so impossible, Erwin? These things happen."

"Yes, and so does murder, Muriel. And that's exactly what has happened to Amelia Christian."

"Well, if you're so sure, Erwin, why then don't you call the police?"

An all but sarcastic grin edged its way into the features of Mr Schiller's face as he continued to regard his wife. "And tell them what, Muriel? That I know a murder's been committed because I feel it in my bones?" He paused, and slowly shook his head at his wife. "No, Muriel; when you deal with the authorities in matters such as this, protocol must be followed; and in this case, that means 'evidence'. You must have evidence that a crime has been committed. And I intend to get it."

Mrs Schiller wearily sighed, and the lips of her mouth slightly twisted in a faint grimace. "Oh, never you mind about evidence and crimes, or people turning into wolves and coyotes, Erwin," she said. "Just put your pajamas on and come to bed."

"I have no intention of going to bed, Muriel; not just yet," Mr Schiller retorted. "Like I told you—I need proof, evidence that a crime has been committed: and tonight I intend to get it!"

For a moment or two, Mrs Schiller fixed her husband with a puzzled look. "And what on earth do you mean by that, Erwin?"

Mr Schiller walked round to the night table on his side of the bed. "The moment I see Amelia's nephew leave his house tonight," he answered, "and head up the street to enter the cemetery, I plan to follow him"; and pausing a moment to take up the flashlight he had placed at the ready on the night table, he glanced significantly at his wife, and added: "and I mean to find out exactly what the boy is up to in there!"

"Erwin! At this hour? It's nearly ten o'clock! Have you lost your wits?"

"Yes, Muriel, 'at this hour';" Mr Schiller replied, mimicking his wife's high-pitched voice; "and 'no', Muriel, I have not lost my wits. They are very much intact."

"Erwin, I don't think this is a good idea. Haven't you been listening to all the news reports on TV? Police are investigating a number of mysterious disappearances in the neighborhood; people are reporting their pets found dead in their yards with their blood drained; and now the brutal killing of that poor girl, Lori Carbone, by her own brother! And only a couple of blocks from here. The police still haven't caught him yet, Erwin. I don't think you should—"

But Mr Schiller cut her short: "Please, Muriel! Enough! This is too important to wait on. Another murder may have taken place just across the street from us: and one way or another I'm going to get to the bottom of it—tonight. Now, please, go to bed!" And with that Mr Schiller returned to the bedroom window to continue his vigil: peering diligently through his binoculars at Amelia Christian's house across the street. Watching, waiting for the instant her sixteen year-old nephew should open its front door and slip out over its threshold into the summery night. On his way once more to the old All Faiths cemetery for what (at least to an overly suspicious and heedful Mr Erwin Schiller) seemed secret, perverse—perhaps even ghoulish—activities among the solitudes of its graves and decaying monuments.

As for Mrs Schiller, after shaking her head and glaring indignantly at her husband for another ten seconds, she glanced once more down into her Bible. It still lay open in her lap at the Book of Wisdom; and after her gaze had strayed somewhat absently for several lines down the page, it came to rest a moment or two on the thirteenth verse of the seventeenth chapter. And in the room's deepening quiet, very slowly, almost dreamily, she read, under her breath, the following:

> "But they, being powerless in that night's darkness,
> which swept over them from the deepest, darkest hell"

And at that last, ominous word, Mrs Schiller's heart gave a faint but sudden jump. Then, as a cold tremor ran through her body, her eye, half-reluctantly, strayed on:

> "were beset, there and then, with the terror of monsters"

And she suddenly paused to swallow the lump that had formed in her throat; then,

> "for unto them, sudden and unlooked for, there had
> come a horror...."

But there Mrs Schiller stopped, and her trembling hands quickly shut up her Bible. She simply refused to read another word. For that passage from scripture had seemed—in relation to herself, this night, and how she was presently feeling—all too forbidding, sinister, even somewhat portentous: having, as it were, a peculiarly disquieting influence on her nerves. And as one shiver after another went stealing icily up and down her backbone, she shut tight her eyes and, for several moments held her breath. For she was seized quite suddenly with a strange, vague, unreasoning fear at the thought of her husband venturing out on this night. And her heart misgave her at the mere notion of him following Amelia Christian's nephew into the cemetery, to stalk and shadow him over its lonely graves, and spy upon his doings there. And all in a moment her mind was a whirl of dark forebodings at the outcome of this late-night excursion her husband was so foolishly resolved upon undertaking. But she knew it was no use trying to talk him out of it. His mind was made up: she'd have a better chance at turning lead into gold than convincing her husband to stay indoors and come to bed.

And so, glancing one last time, half ruefully, half anxiously, at her husband, Mrs Schiller lay down and turned on her side to go to sleep. At the same time she tried her best to ignore those alarming feelings of uneasiness and consternation that she found herself utterly powerless to dispel.

Around 10:30 p.m., Nathan had exited his house and dashed a short distance up the street. At the ivy-screened hole in the cemetery fence, he paused and glanced up into the night-sky. High overhead he saw the constellation Cassiopeia. Having come up that night, just after dark, low in the northeastern sky, looking for all the world like the letter 'W' tipped upon its side, it had, in its slow ascension, gradually pivoted, so that its stars at the present moment appeared in every way like a glittering letter 'M', directly above the old All Faiths cemetery.

Nathan continued to stare up at it, and suddenly he murmured, "'M' for 'mausoleum'; and the next instant, he caught his breath and whispered, "Phebe." Then, in the blink of an eye, he had plunged through the hole in the fence, sped as fast as he could over the neglected graves, darted up the steps to the old mausoleum, and slipped quietly between its doors, which he found unlocked and slightly ajar.

But even as Nathan edged softly forward beyond the threshold, and paused to send the slender beam of his flashlight coursing over the mausoleum's walls, he sensed, almost instantly, that tonight he was the tomb's only *breathing* inmate. Phebe herself, he perceived, was not there.

And yet, for the next thirty seconds or so, Nathan must have continued to stand motionless just beyond the entrance, as if in a tranced and dream-like stillness, with his ears intently listening for, and his eyes eagerly to and froing in hopeful search of... *her*, the one, the 'beautiful pale girl' (as Terence Webler had called her). Even though he now knew that she was indeed a vampire, Nathan nevertheless—in the secrecy of his inmost self—worshipped, desired, loved, more than life itself, and without the least doubt or misgiving, his beloved Phebe.

Again and again, under his breath, Nathan kept whispering Phebe's name, as though its mere repetition, like a word of potent sorcery in some magical grimoire, must compel its owner to draw near and reveal herself. But for all that he continued to stand there and breathe out the sound of her familiar name in his unswerving devotion to her, Phebe neither answered his summons nor appeared before his eyes.

And then, as Nathan's mind began to drift on towards the brink of reverie, and Phebe's name for the nineteenth time slipped softly off his tongue in a slow, faint, solitary breath, a curious thought quite suddenly occurred to him. Less than forty-eight hours ago, on his sixteenth birthday, he had come (much the same as now) to the old mausoleum and stood in this exact spot, doing very nearly the same thing, only to discover the horrific truth about Phebe's supernatural condition. What's more, he had witnessed with his own eyes Phebe, squatting only a few feet away, with Russell Gorman's body hideously writhing in her arms, as she greedily supped his blood from the wound in his neck.

But scrutinize that area of the mausoleum floor all he would, Nathan could discern on its smooth glossy surface not a single speck or smudge of blood from the hapless victims provided by Vrancic and Candy for Phebe to feed on. Either she or Vrancic (or the two of them together) had thoroughly washed and wiped away all evidence of that night's grisly banquet. So that, at the moment, almost it seemed to Nathan that the entire terrifying incident had been no more real than if it had taken place within the emptiness of a dream.

And presently, exhaling a long, slow breath, Nathan clicked off his flashlight. Its pale luminous ray, he realized for the first time since he had entered the mausoleum, was hardly necessary. For on the floor at the tomb's further end was a cluster of more than two dozen wax candles whose long, slender flames burned with a clear and steady brightness, illuminating all but its entire interior. Moreover, by their light Nathan could see that Aunt Amelia's best comforter had been very neatly spread out (by Phebe's own hand, no doubt), and half covered the floor. After crossing it soundlessly, he paused once again to listen and look about him.

Near at hand, along the comforter's edge, Nathan observed, with one comprehensive glance, Phebe's hairbrush, comb, headband, hair-ties and clips. And laid out next to them, virtually hobnobbing with the brush and comb, was a familiar pair of small pink Mary Jane watershoes. Also, in the very center of the comforter, Nathan had noticed an open pack of Marlboros, and an ashtray with the stubbed-out remnants of several cigarettes in it. And a little to one side of this, Nathan noted the Zippo lighter Scott Webler had given him; his radio-cassette tape player (from whose speakers a faint, barely-distinguishable drone of music was issuing); and a dozen or more cassette music tapes scattered here and there around it.

One by one over these items, Nathan's eyes traveled, lingered a moment, then traveled on again half absently. Then, in doubt and disappointment, he turned and fixed his gaze on the midmost crypt in the mausoleum's right-hand wall whose long, panel-like door was missing. For although Nathan knew that it was in this crypt that Phebe reposed during the daylight hours, he gazed at its shadowy mouth with an almost certain conviction that he would not find her lying there now.

And so, his lips softly parted; he slowly inhaled: was about to call Phebe's name, when suddenly he froze. Holding his breath, he stood listening intently for an instant. His ears (he was certain!) had caught a mysterious sound, like that of a low, continuous moaning, coming from somewhere near at hand, somewhere *inside* the old mausoleum!

Hardly daring to blink or breathe, Nathan must have stood there a full ten seconds closely listening when, all in a moment, his heart gave a furious lurch in his body and began to jerk and hammer against the small cage of his ribs. For he could hear the unmistakable sound of low, steady groaning, as if one of the mausoleum's long-slumbering inmates had come awake in its crypt and was now trying desperately to get out at him.

Against the paralyzing influence of an overmastering terror, Nathan managed to emit a smothered gasp and half-turned to bolt for the doors. But upon hearing the faint murmuring of a soft voice, he compelled himself to remain standing there perfectly still, attempting to ignore the frantic drubbing of his heart, while at the same time straining his ears to listen on.

And then, all at once, Nathan realized what it was he was actually hearing! It wasn't some wakeful cadaver moaning in its efforts to break out of its crypt, but rather the tail end to a song by 'Black Sabbath' coming from the cassette player whose volume had been turned very low.

Listening carefully, Nathan suddenly recognized the song as 'Children of the Grave': in which a chilling voice towards the end keeps repeating, in a faint whisper, the song's ghoulish title against the sinister background noise of moaning winds just before it fades altogether into silence.

And just as the song began to grow faintlier and die away, Nathan stooped over the cassette player and, with the tip of his finger, pressed the 'stop' button. A dead hush ensued, which Nathan stood listening to with no little relief and satisfaction. Evidently, Phebe (he thought to himself) had turned on the cassette player, inserted a tape (apparently one of Black Sabbath's) and pushed 'play'. And Nathan could not refrain from rolling his eyes, as he thought to himself: of all the songs to catch while standing inside a mausoleum, in the dead of night, in expectation of encountering a vampire—even one so sweet and lovely as Phebe!—why in the world did it have to be 'Children of the Grave'!

Then, stealing over to the mouth of the doorless crypt, and stooping down—although with little hope of discovering Phebe there—Nathan clicked on his flashlight and peered narrowly into its restricted four-sided space. As expected, he neither saw the recumbent form of Phebe slumbering there, nor her dark welcoming eyes unseal themselves (as once they had more than two weeks ago) and look straight into his own.

Deep in thought, Nathan's brow became creased, and a grave, half-absent look spread itself over his features. "So now I know how Saint Peter must have felt," he half-whispered to himself. For it suddenly flashed across his mind how the fisherman of Galilee, upon hearing that the body of Jesus was gone, ran to the burial place only to discover that, except for the shroud which had swathed the

Lord's body, the tomb itself was quite empty—Jesus was indeed not there. Similarly, Nathan now found the crypt in which Phebe routinely took her repose—vacant, unoccupied. Phebe herself was simply not there. But 'where', he asked himself, had she gone to?

And as Nathan continued to peep and peer into the crypt's rectangular space, the slim yellow beam of his flashlight did reveal to him one thing in particular. Stowed away against the back part of the crypt, towards its foot, was what appeared to be a bag, or sack, similar to a kind of duffel bag. And the longer Nathan stooped there, peering in under the upper part of the crypt, with his gaze fixed deep on that mysterious bag, the more it piqued his curiosity to know what was in it.

For a moment or two, Nathan hesitated, biting softly on his lower lip, as if transfixed by some strange, vague disinclination. But then, quite suddenly, acting on some irresistible impulse, he quickly reached his arm into the narrow, four-sided space and drew the bag out. He set it down on the floor in the blaze of the clustering candles and, for the next minute or two, ran his eyes eagerly, almost voraciously over it.

The very first thing Nathan observed about the bag was that it was not of cloth, but of a kind of dull, worn leather, with a single broad shoulder strap. The leather itself, he noticed, was quite faded in places, and bore stains and bruises and marks of long service. And the mouth of the bag, which ran in a long slit from one end to the other, was fastened not by any zipper, but rather a series of shiny gold clasps, exquisitely enriched with little pearl-like gems.

Moreover, Nathan noticed that on one side of the bag appeared a single word of seven letters. The letters were traced in gold, but the word itself he was altogether at a loss to decipher, as the greater part of it had been rendered practically illegible by the action of Time and usage.

But the three letters that Nathan was able to clearly distinguish appeared to resemble in every way the ancient Roman characters. Slowly, half-solemnly, he ran the tip of his finger along each of their faint and faded shapes. As to the remaining four letters that had been all but utterly obliterated, only a solitary stroke here, or a faint, fragmentary curve there remained, so that what he could discern of the word was as follows:

$$ \lceil R \ ` \ S \ ` \ \lceil R $$

And for the next few moments, Nathan's eye continued to scrutinize that half-faded inscription, muttering the while to himself each of those letters he was able to discriminate. The word's initial letter he found impossible to distinguish with any certainty, and so moved on to the second letter. And at the same time as he traced it with his finger, very softly, he breathed, "R". The next, though scarcely legible, he guessed at, and, in a faint questioning voice, he whispered: "Could it be the letter 'O'?" Then, moving on to the fourth letter, he breathed, with utter confidence, "S". But after arduously examining the next two letters, which were so abraded and obscured that he was unable to decipher them, he turned at length to the final letter and said, with absolute certainty, "R".

Still and silent, Nathan continued to gaze on intently at the mysterious word. In a vain and hopeless effort he tried to fathom what it actually spelled, until, all at once, he caught his breath. For suddenly the letters of that inscription looked curiously familiar to him; and he began to wonder if, when the word had still been legible, it had spelled—'PROSPER'.

And Nathan's eyes opened wide with astonishment as he reflected a while on this startling possibility. Could it be true? he asked himself. Was it the very word that he had seen spell itself out inexplicably in his dream?

For the next few minutes, Nathan continued to stand there studying, with a peculiar intensity, the fragmentary letters of that indecipherable word, hoping to finally solve the mystery of its actual spelling. In the end, however, all his efforts were completely frustrated, and he had to concede that it was impossible to be certain whether those four faint and faded letters were in fact a 'P', an 'O', another 'P', and an 'E'. If they were, though, and the inscription did spell 'PROSPER', why (he asked himself) was that word on Phebe's bag? What did it signify? What was its underlying meaning? And in what way was that word relevant to Phebe... or to himself?

With its secret maintained, and its mystery as yet insoluble, Nathan's eyes withdrew themselves from that tantalizing, inscrutable word. Then, stooping once more, over the bag itself, he very gingerly drew it open and peered inside. The interior of the bag, he noted almost at once, was haunted by a delicate odor—by no means unpleasant to him—which had in it the faintest suggestion of the ink and parchment of a centuries'-old book or manuscript.

Nathan appeared to ruminate a while on the curious odor. And for some seconds, a half solemn, half abstracted look spread itself over his face. Then, setting his flashlight down on the floor, he began, with eager eyes and expectant fingers, to explore very softly and carefully the bag's contents.

After having sifted first through Phebe's scanty wardrobe, and put aside her blue Cover-up, denim jeggings, a familiar pair of belted twill shorts, and red tankini, Nathan discovered at the very bottom of the bag what appeared to be a kind of pouch. Fastened securely at its neck by a thick leathery cord, or drawstring, the pouch itself (as far as Nathan could tell) appeared to be made of a rich, costly fabric, a kind of silk, in fact, that was interwoven with threads of gold. And although Nathan was completely unaware of it, in an age long since vanished, this rare, fine cloth was once used for garments by the nobility of the times, and had the name of baudekin.

Whatever unknown items were stored by Phebe in this regal pouch, Nathan saw at once that its neck, sides, and bottom were positively bloated and bulging with their quantity. He also noted, as he lifted the pouch up out of Phebe's bag and set it down again on the edge of Aunt Amelia's comforter, that it was remarkably heavy.

And all at once, a curious thrill of excitement and anticipation ran tingling through Nathan's bones as he proceeded to undo the drawstring of the pouch and part the tautly-drawn folds at its neck. Moreover, in the short pause following these actions, almost it seemed to him that the stillness in the mausoleum had unaccountably and immeasurably deepened. For a moment or two,

Nathan listened to it uneasily. Then, stooping his face low over the yawning mouth of the pouch, he peered down at its contents and was instantly awestruck by what was revealed to him. For the pouch was literally stuffed with a magnificent treasure of assorted coins—coins which, at a mere solitary glance, identified themselves with countries alien to his own, and times now lost in antiquity.

Without hesitating for a moment, Nathan emptied the coins onto the comforter so as to view and examine them all the more easily. And with a sort of faint, half-smothered gasp, he gazed on in silent wonder at how marvelously each coin gleamed and glinted and twinkled in the pale, yellow flare of the candles.

Of course, for Nathan, whose unschooled eyes coursed in astonishment and perplexity over their mysterious inscriptions and devices, the coins were little more than a collection of quaint discs composed of various precious ores. But because some were apparently of gold, and others of silver, he had at least an inkling that the coins must have some measure of considerable value. He had no way of knowing that the hoard he was now examining was in fact of incalculable worth! Had there been present, however, a man or group of men learned and curious in old coins to view such a priceless assortment, they would have seen at once what a truly astounding treasure trove it was.

More than half the coins in the collection were the silver denarius of the Roman Empire, some from the time of Augustus; and others from as far back as the late second century B.C., depicting Licinius Nerva. Some coins which Nathan inspected (though the face depicted on their obverse signified nothing to him) bore the image of Julius Caesar with the legend DICT. PERPETVO, 'perpetual dictator'. And one silver denarius was stamped with the faint image of Brutus on its field, while on the reverse, flanked on either side by daggers, Nathan saw the Cap of Liberty depicted: and in the exergue of the coin he could just faintly discern EID. MAR., words celebrating (unbeknownst to him) the murder of Caesar on the Ides of March.

Other coins in the collection looked over by Nathan were silver shekels of Carthage, and a number of silver tetradrachmae bearing the images of various monarchs of the ancient world from divers centuries. Here were dozens of Perseus, the Macedonian king; then two or three of Rome's mortal enemy, Mithradates VI of Pontus; and then half a dozen of Orodes I of Parthia. Next, he saw several gold staters stamped with the image of Artaxerxes, ruling founder of the Sassanian dynasty in ancient Persia, as well as a number of bronze coins depicting Queen Zenobia of Palmyra from the late third century A.D.

Nathan noticed, too, a number of brass sestertii depicting, in a scattered way, the Roman emperors Hadrian, Trajan, Vespasian, and the young Commodus. And then the odd mixture of several silver drachmae depicting the Persian king, Shapur, a golden aureus of Aurelian, two or three silvered bronze coins of Constantine the Great, and, strangest of all, a Gallic coin depicting Vercingetorix, king of the Gauls. It was a hoard for which the truly fervent, zealous coin collector would have killed to possess, or have gladly sold his soul to purchase. And to the numismatologist, whose passion is the study of ancient coins, it would have been a dream come true and the Holy Grail of findings.

After keenly inspecting the coins for another minute or two, Nathan quickly returned them all to their pouch and fastened the neck again by pulling taut its drawstring. Then, sifting with his hands once more through Phebe's bag, he produced from its depths a longish, slender object, perhaps of the length and slimness of a baton or a police officer's truncheon. It was wrapped up in a very beautiful tissue, or silk-like cloth, unfamiliar to Nathan, but which, in the time of the great Venetian traveler Marco Polo, was known as cramoisy. The cloth was marvelously embroidered with strange occult symbols and the characters of what appeared to be some arcane mode of writing. Also, Nathan noted how it was very securely bound about with numerous leather thongs and sealed over here and there with small wads of yellow wax.

What dark secret was swathed within the folds of that tightly-wound cloth, Nathan could not say. And yet, inexplicably, he felt somehow perturbed, agitated, almost alarmed by the thing. And the longer he held it and gazed on at it, the more the world around him seemed to swim and melt away into a dull and empty dream.

For nearly a full minute Nathan stared at it, wanting desperately to turn back the folds of that strange silky textile and view the thing it contained. But some singularly peculiar misgiving, like that of a sharp pang gathering deep within his heart, prevented him, however, from undoing those binding cords and revealing the mysterious object hidden beneath its wrappage. What's more, a small, remote voice, piping up now as from the mistily far-off confines of some long-forgotten memory, seemed to gravely caution, warn, command him to leave it be. And in deference to the stern bidding of that faint yet all-too ominous voice (be it from his restless conscience or some vague cowardly apprehension) Nathan's curiosity quickly subsided and, averting his face a little, he very carefully and solemnly laid the thing aside.

What Nathan came upon next at the bottom of Phebe's bag was a large manila envelope whose flap was unsealed. Like the pouch before it, the envelope too was heavy and bulging with the bulk of its contents, which, when he drew back its flap and looked inside, turned out to be a literal cache of American dollars in varying amounts and denominations all mixed together.

Breathless with astonishment, and his mouth agape, Nathan realized instantly that what he was now viewing was Phebe's own private treasury, the veritable exchequer of a vampire, as it were, in the form of numerous hundred, fifty, twenty, and ten dollar bills! Straightaway, though, his initial thought was that Phebe must have accumulated the money by way of the foul habit of her nightly vampiric acts: first battening herself on the blood of her hapless victims, then taking from the bloodless corpses their clothes, money, and whatever other spoils she pleased.

It added to the term "blood money", a whole new sinister meaning, thought Nathan. But just then, he remembered Phebe having told him that Vrancic obtained money for her by selling, or pawning, certain curios of value to collectors of such items. And as he continued to peer into that envelope at Phebe's personal hoard of cash, he half-whispered to himself, "There must be hundreds— no! thousands here."

"Almost ten, actually," came a soft, sweet voice out of the stillness behind him.

Nathan started out of the quiet reverie into which he had begun to sink, and swiftly turned. Phebe was standing at a little distance from him, gazing across at him, from the other side of Aunt Amelia's comforter, with all the strange, stirless concentration of a specter or an apparition: her black eyes fixed intently on his silent face.

Nathan instantly felt his heart beat thick with desire, as his eyes strayed eagerly, greedily from head to toe over Phebe's lissome shape. With no little gratification he noted all that she wore: from the pink high-top sneakers on her feet, to the roll-cuff denim shorts hugging her hips, and her snugly-fitting dip-dye tank top.

Gazing tenderly out of the fathomless dark of those large-pupilled eyes, Phebe advanced slowly across to where Nathan was standing, walking so softly that he never once heard her steps.

Then, putting both arms about his neck, she pressed her lips to his. Twice she kissed him, lovingly and passionately; then, from over her shoulders, she drew slowly back her long, black loose-flowing locks as Nathan, continuing to meet her motionless eyes, whispered across to her, "I'm sorry." He paused a moment to steal a sheepish glance down at the unsealed envelope he was still clutching in his hands, and felt his cheeks begin to burn. "I didn't mean to snoop," he added, faintly, feeling extremely embarrassed that he had been caught prying through Phebe's things without first having gained her permission.

Phebe's eyes were keenly searching Nathan's face as he very shyly placed the envelope into her hands. "You're probably wondering," she then said, "how I got all this money."

A faint look of alarm, almost of dread had crept suddenly into Nathan's features. But he softly lowered his gaze, half-fearful that if he continued to encounter Phebe's eyes, he might glimpse in them something truly harrowing with regard to how indeed she had acquired all that money. And there was silence between them for a while.

But then, after Phebe had returned that cash-filled envelope once more to her bag, she said, "Well, in case you *are* wondering—

Antal sometimes takes the rare coins and antique jewels I have, and he finds reputable collectors who are quite eager to part with lots of their money for such trinkets."

On hearing this, Nathan once again raised his eyes and confronted those of Phebe's. In both her explanation and her eyes he perceived nothing false; and he felt reassured that she had given him no perjured account. Phebe (he was now all but certain) had not obtained that money by way of murder.

"Still," said Nathan, exhaling with relief the breath he been holding for the last few seconds, "I had no right to go through your things while you weren't here."

Phebe shrugged her narrow shoulders. "It's alright," she said, faintly smiling. "I don't mind. I was going to show you everything I have in there anyway." And her deep, dark, lustrous eyes strayed from Nathan's and fixed themselves on her leather bag. She squatted down beside it and, gliding the tips of her long, narrow fingers lightly along its smooth side, she seemed to reflect a while.

At length, "This bag is very, very old," said Phebe, almost as though she were thinking out loud, or speaking to herself rather than to Nathan. And raising her intensely dark eyes to once more encounter those of Nathan's, she said: "It's made from the hide of a kind of wild ox that doesn't exist anymore. At one time, long ago, they inhabited a vast extensive woodland in Europe that to the ancient Greeks was known as Orcynia, but, in the time of Julius Caesar, as the Hercynian forest. And just around the time that Constantine the Great was building the city of Byzantium, it was believed that a herd of those oxen still roamed the German forests. But by the time Rome had fallen to Alaric, the king of the Goths, the last surviving remnant of these beasts had been hunted into extinction. Antal told me that he believes they were a kind of bison which he said were called 'aurochs'. I once had part of a pelt and a pair of horns from one of these animals."

And as Phebe stood up again, Nathan asked: "What did you do with them?"

"A couple of years ago Antal took them and showed them to several very wealthy and enthusiastic hunters, one of whom was so eager to possess and add them to his private collection, that he paid more than a hundred thousand dollars for the horns alone. The pelt was bought by another collector for half that amount."

At this startling disclosure of Phebe's finances, and the large sums of money she was obviously in possession of, Nathan's eyes opened wide and he gave a slight start. And as he continued to stare at Phebe with renewed wonder, for a moment or two he reflected on a sudden and curious thought. Did Phebe, he wondered, keep all of that capital here in her bag, crammed into several other large manila envelopes, like the one he'd seen? Or does Vrancic manage those funds for her from secret bank accounts and safe-deposit boxes. But then, with little time to indulge such notions, Nathan's thoughts moved on to other matters, and he said to Phebe: "So where were you all this time?"

In the pallor of her face, Phebe's deep, dark, peering eyes gleamed. "Out;" she answered; and, after a short pause, tersely added: "Getting some food."

Nathan quickly withdrew his eyes from those of Phebe's, and for some seconds the odd uncomfortable quiet that followed her reply seemed to curiously deepen round them and grow still more uncomfortable. But then, not wanting to think about what—or whom!—Phebe had been *feeding on,* Nathan hastened on to quietly stammer out: "I - I thought that when I f-first came in, there was a funny smell in here." He paused a moment to watch her face; then, with a merry gleam in his eye, he quipped, "You don't go to the bathroom in here, do you?"

Out of darkling, motionless eyes, Phebe stared long and solemnly at Nathan. Then, "No," she answered scarcely above a whispered breath.

And at the gravity of Phebe's tone and expression, the mirthful twinkle in Nathan's eyes suddenly fainted, and he continued to gaze steadily, silently back at her. After a while, however, having, it seemed, mulled over something very carefully, there slipped all at once off his tongue that burning question which, in his curiosity, he was unable to refrain a moment longer from asking her: "By the way, where *do* you go?"

"I don't 'go'—period."

"You don't eat; you don't drink; and you don't go to the bathroom."

Phebe's eyes continued to dwell on Nathan's face. "I'm not like you, remember? I'm a vampire;" she said, her voice slightly trembling; "we only drink blood. Sometimes, though, the blood does come out of my nose and mouth—among other places."

"You mean, like, even your rear end?"

Phebe gazed on at Nathan in silence. Then, "I guess," she answered, faintly. "And sometimes I wake—as you yourself witnessed only a few days ago—swimming in blood."

Without either speaking or stirring, Nathan watched Phebe's face for some seconds. Then he said: "So that's like your going to the bathroom, right?"

"Something like that," Phebe answered.

After having reflected a moment, Nathan said: "It must be weird—no eating, no going to the bathroom, like a normal person."

For a moment or two Phebe withdrew her clear, dark eyes from Nathan's face, and her glance vaguely wandered over the walls of the mausoleum with their tiered crypts and inscribed epitaphs. "I'm not a person;" she said, as her eyes, returning once more to Nathan's silent face, half-mournfully, half-intently encountered his own; "I'm a vampire."

And all the while Nathan and Phebe talked together, their voices sounded thin and faint and hollow even in their own ears in that hushed and deeply heedful solitude of the old mausoleum.

"But you like sex, right? I mean, vampires still like sex," Nathan said to her. And the eyes regarding him fixed themselves a shade more intently on his face. "Oh, yes," came the grave, half-whispered reply. Nathan asked her why that was.

"I don't know. I guess since, as vampires, we have been forbidden, disallowed, any spiritual communion with God, we try to fill the void by having carnal unions with men and women. I don't really know for sure."

After quietly mulling over Phebe's answer for several moments, Nathan nodded his head as though satisfied, and remarked: "That makes sense; I guess."

And for the next few moments the two of them remained still and silent. But then, upon noting that the light about them was beginning to steadily dwindle and dim, Nathan said, "The candles are about to go out"; for by now they had burned down to mere guttering stubs, and were on the verge of expiring; "I forgot to go to the store and buy some more," he went on, as the light grew still more faintlier, "and I couldn't find any more in any of the dresser drawers."

"We don't need them," said Phebe. And stooping a little to root through her bag for a moment or two, she suddenly produced from its depths a silver-plated jewelry box exquisitely decorated with floriations of the jeweler's art. Nathan gazed at it eagerly, and together with Phebe stooped his face over its covering. Very softly, then, Phebe raised the lid, and, as she did so, Nathan caught his breath and drew a pace or two back.

For there, upon a bed of black velvet, with which the jewelry box was lined, lay revealed the most marvelous gem, blazing in its luminescence brighter by far than any wandering star or the moon at the fullest of its phases. It was the kind of jewel such as one will only hear of in story, and never gaze upon except maybe in dream.

Nathan saw at once that the jewel was ovoid in shape, and no larger than a plum in size; while in translucence it resembled some kind of crystal rather than a diamond. And yet Nathan knew it was neither. Indeed, almost it seemed to him that Phebe had by some persuading power coaxed down from the constellations one of the incandescent grains of the Perseid meteor shower and imprisoned its celestial fires inside the crystal hollow of this phosphorescent stone. For the whole interior of the mausoleum was awash with its unsurpassable radiance even to its every slant, angle, and corner. And Nathan opened wide his clear brown eyes and stared at it in silent wonder.

Meanwhile, Phebe's eyes were regarding Nathan's silent face. "Why don't you hold it?" she said, presently. Then, picking up the luminous stone, she laid it gently in Nathan's hand. And as he gazed at it on the flat of his palm, it cast a wonderful pallid gleam upon both their faces, so that in each other's eyes they appeared transfigured to that of immortal angels.

With a curious thrill gathering in his heart now, Nathan's fingers slowly closed over the limpid jewel, and for a moment or two his entire hand seemed ignited with its brilliancy. Then, unlatching his fingers again, the lambent gem suffused once more the mausoleum's whole interior with its splendid luminescence.

"Wo! that's so cool!" said Nathan, restoring the jewel very carefully to its bed of velvet lining in the jewelry box. And as Phebe laid the open box upon the narrow shelf-like projection jutting from the rear wall, beneath the stained glass window, questions regarding the jewel's origins rose one after another to Nathan's tongue.

Phebe turned with a sigh to Nathan and gazed at his face out of eyes that had become peculiarly solemn. She seemed for the moment to be thinking very deeply. Then, her eyes, having fixed themselves once more on that magnificent jewel, clouded over with dream, as if up into their lustrous depths had ebbed some wonderful image of reverie. "At one time," she said to Nathan, in a clear-sounding yet almost languid voice, "this stone was housed in an ancient temple where people came to worship the stone idol of some Syrian goddess. And the priests of the sanctuary had crowned this divinity with a diadem in which they set a dazzling gem. They called it 'lychnos', which means 'lamp'. And this"—she pointed with her long finger nail to the radiant jewel before them—"this is that very stone. And such is the brilliant glare emitted by lychnos that the whole temple, just as the tomb in which we're now standing, would be illuminated by it as if with a thousand glowing lanterns."

Nathan's eyes strayed once more from the jewel to the pale profile of Phebe's beautiful face. And very softly then, he asked her: "But how did you get it, Phebe?" She smiled faintly and, looking sidelong at Nathan, replied with the least sigh, "It was given to me"; and pausing a moment, she smiled and said, "as a gift"; and, after yet another pause, she added, "by someone." And she smiled all the more mysteriously at Nathan out of the dark, insoluble riddle of her eyes.

Then, after a moment or two, Phebe said: "I have another luminous stone that's almost just like it. It's called a 'chrysolampis', and it's set, with many other precious gems, in a marvelous tablet of solid gold. It was a gift, from the wife of a noble count of Holland, to the Abbey of Egmund, where the body of some saint was said to repose. And the light of the chrysolampis was so brilliant that when the monks gathered at night in the chapel to recite the Hours, no one carried a candle or a lantern, for they were able to read their prayers by the radiance of that jewel alone."

For some seconds Nathan gazed on at Phebe's beautiful face in a tranced stillness. Then, "Where is it?" he asked.

"I can't fit everything here in my bag," Phebe answered. "So Antal has put it away for me in safekeeping with a number of other things. Although, now that I think of it, it may not be there anymore—it's one of the things Antal promised to his contact, Walter Farnhill, in exchange for information on the incunabulum: so he may have given it away by now."

"But doesn't it bother you, Phebe," said Nathan, as he studied her face, "to sell off all these old treasures just for a few bits and pieces of information about some dusty old book?"

Phebe looked at Nathan steadily for a moment, the black of her large-pupilled eyes suddenly aglint with an infinitely tender smile. "Oh, but you forget that to me the incunabulum is so much more than a 'dusty old book', Nathan," she replied. "If that is the fee to become mortal again, then I'd gladly pay it, and so much more. Besides," she said, with a shrug of her shoulders, "I have lots of other jewels and baubles just as wonderful—like this one." And once more Phebe stooped and, reaching with her slim hands into her bag, she produced from it what seemed at first to Nathan's eyes little more than a burgundy-colored piece of cloth, closely wound up into a shapeless bundle.

But as Phebe began to undo that bundled cloth, turning back its folds, one by one, Nathan's staring eyes, all in an instant, were dazzled by a deep ruddy gleam that fused its brilliance with that of the lychnos-stone's pale effulgence. Shutting his eyes a moment, Nathan blinked them open again, and stood squinnying into the flame-like resplendence whose source, as he now realized, was the fiery-red jewel in Phebe's hand. Lying on its worn cantle of faded cloth, the many-faceted gem was ellipsoidal in shape and as big as a large pine-cone.

"Do you know what kind of jewel this is?" asked Phebe. Withdrawing his gaze from the gemstone, Nathan looked into her eyes and all but whispered, "A ruby?"

With a faint nod of her head, Phebe smiled. "Yes; but not just any ruby," she said. "This ruby was long ago part of the regalia of the kings of Ceylon, until it was purchased by the emperor of China, in whose palace at night its red luster shone so brightly, that it was named 'the Red Palace-Illuminator'. In Chinese it's called 'si-la-ni', meaning 'from Ceylon.'"

Breathless with wonder, Nathan continued to gaze at it. Then, very soft and low, he said: "It's beautiful." Phebe's wide dark eyes were keenly regarding him. "Beautiful," she whispered; and very softly, then, half-reluctantly it seemed, her eyes glanced down at the jewel in her hand. "I don't like looking at it much, though," she said.

"Why not? Don't you think it's beautiful?"

"Oh, yes; it is beautiful—sometimes too beautiful;" and lifting her eyes again, Phebe gazed straight into those of Nathan's; "but the color," she breathed across to him, and paused a moment to lick her lips, "the color," she went on, with her dark eyes fixed intently on Nathan's face, "reminds me too much of blood. And its luster"—and her voice grew slow and faint and velvety soft—"rouses in me a terrible thirst, an unbearable craving when I look at it for too long a time."

For a moment or two an expression of alarm started into Nathan's eyes. But even as he raised them, half doubtfully, to meet Phebe's all-too heedful gaze, she had already drawn the worn folds of cloth once more over that lambent ruby, extinguishing its bright sanguineous gleam. And without another word she restored the jewel to her bag.

Then, "And what's this?" asked Nathan, after having peeped again into Phebe's bag and drawn up out of its depths a small rectangular casket of tooled leather. Its lid, he noted, was secured by clasps and a lock of gold, and studded with so many minute sapphires, rubies, and emeralds that in the clear dazzling glare of the lychnos-stone it appeared to be delicately aflame.

But before Nathan could press the tiny knob that would have caused the lid to yawn open, Phebe suddenly laid her lean, cold hand over his. "Nathan, don't!" she said, in a voice that was at once anxious and afraid. Nathan met her gaze, and instantly noted the expression of alarm in her face. "What's inside?" he asked faintly, as Phebe drew the jeweled casket gently out of his grasp.

Grave and intent, Phebe gazed a while at Nathan's face. Then, "It contains a cross," she said. "But not just any cross. For this one is known as the Templar Cross, and it's one of the oldest and most remarkable jewels of the Christian faith. It was taken by one of the knights Templar during the Fourth Crusade at the capture of the ancient city of Constantinople, and brought back to France where it was donated to a monastery near Lyons and preserved as one of its greatest treasures. There's a very old tradition that maintains it was fashioned in the time of the Roman emperor Tiberius, and that a Christian goldsmith produced it for Mary Magdalen from the very gold offered by the Magi to the Infant Jesus."

And when Nathan had asked her how such a treasure had come into her possession, Phebe raised her narrow black eyebrows and, for the merest instant, a stealthy smile had edged its way into her delicate features. Then, without responding to his question, she carefully returned that ancient relic to its place in her bag.

In silence Nathan watched, then, as Phebe continued to stoop there and quietly rummage through the bag. And when once more she had straightened and brought her hands out again, he saw that in her long narrow fingers a case of crimson velvet was reverently clasped. But his eyes only rested on the thing with a clouded, half-absent look, for his thoughts were still fixed on that ancient cross of gold.

"But I don't understand, Phebe. If the cross is harmful to you, why do you want to keep it?"

"To test myself with it at a date which, hopefully, is not now very far off in my future," she said; and Nathan met her dark dwelling eyes with a perplexed and questioning glance, to which Phebe answered: "When I have finally obtained the incunabulum, and used the spell preserved within its pages that will undo my curse—one of the surest ways I'll know that the spell has truly worked and restored to me my stolen mortality —finally delivering me from this accursed condition of the vampire: is if I can look on that cross, and touch and handle it without the scars on my hands and feet breaking open, or the wounds in my brow, from the crown of thorns they forced me to wear, beginning to bleed. If I can pass that trial and, through the ordeal of holding the cross, suffer no harm, then, and only then, will I know—*truly* know—my curse has at long last been lifted!"

After Phebe had fallen silent, Nathan for some moments continued to speechlessly meet those forlorn dark eyes. Then, "Why does the cross cause vampires such pain?" he all but whispered across to her.

Phebe's intensely dark eyes dwelt a while in silence on Nathan's face. Then, sighing deeply, she said, "The cross represents the crucified Christ, and the potency of his mystical body and blood—in short it symbolizes all that is true and holy and divine."

Then, after a long pause, Nathan asked: "But what's it feel like, Phebe, when you look at one, or touch it?"

Phebe lowered her head a moment; then, raising clear, mournful eyes to Nathan, she gazed long, almost searchingly at him. "Have you ever opened the door to a furnace or an oven," she said, speaking slowly and deliberately, "and the heat was so intense, so unendurable that you had to quickly step away, or suffer your face and eyes to be scorched? Well, it's like that, only a thousand times more severe!"

Nathan was silent. His eyes drifted then once more to the crimson velvet case Phebe held. He observed at a glance that it was fitted with decorative hinge plates of gold and clasps of silver gilt richly ornamented by the goldsmith's art with golden lilies remarkable for their beauty. And he asked, "What's that?"

"It contains a very old book—a manuscript, actually," Phebe replied, "worth quite a lot—to some. Here, I'll show you." She took the case, undid its clasps, and, opening it, drew out a number of very old, time-foxed parchment leaves. Very carefully, then, she put these in Nathan's hands. On the binding leaf, in a thin spidery script, were scrawled words which to Nathan's eyes, unaccustomed as they were to such a hand, were practically illegible.

A fleeting, half-smile passed over Phebe's lips. "Do you know what it says?" she asked. "Can you read it?"

Nathan examined the words with closer scrutiny, but, after more than one or two minutes, finally gave up trying to decipher them, and shook his head. Once more he lifted his eyes and met the luminous dark of Phebe's fixed intently upon himself. And the shadowy twilight shades of the gloaming seemed to deepen in them all the more as she whispered across to him, "It says, 'The Tragedy of Romeo and Juliet.'"

And all at once Nathan felt a curious sense of wonderment stir within him as, stooping his eyes over the manuscript again, he gazed on for the next minute or two at those words as if spellbound.

Phebe pressed her lips together. Then, "You do know who William Shakespeare was, don't you?" she asked.

"Of course, I know," said Nathan, restoring with care that manuscript to Phebe's hands. "I'd have to be from another planet not to."

Phebe was eyeing Nathan almost with merriment, and smiled softly with those dark lustrous eyes fastened on his. "Well, *this* is the working draft of his play," she said. "It has all sorts of deletions and insertions and rejected lines which Shakespeare himself made while he was in the process of composing it." And she paused a moment to exhibit once more the manuscript to Nathan's eyes. "See, it's all in Shakespeare's own handwriting," she said, turning slowly over, one by one, the cockled parchment leaves which Nathan noticed at the very beginning were so mold-stained and injured by damp as to be in great part illegible. He also observed that in many places the once black ink had all but faded out of the parchment, and was very difficult to read.

Phebe looked deep into Nathan's eyes and, leaning a little towards him, she said, "Antal says a private collector would pay millions for it."

Nathan's voice grew all but hushed with awe as he asked, "How'd you get it?"

Phebe was silent a moment. Then, with glinting, dwelling eyes, "I received it as a gift," she answered.

"From who?" Nathan asked her, gazing full into the beauty and mystery of those large dark eyes.

"From Shakespeare," she answered, smiling. "Who else?"

With parted lips, Nathan stood there motionless and in a dreamlike stillness. Bewitched by her faint smile, the pallor of her skin, the slimness of her body, the sweetness of her voice, he could do nothing for the next instant or two but stare at Phebe half-doubtful and astonished. Then, he sat himself down on the comforter, in its very center, next to where Phebe had seated herself with the leaves of that old manuscript in her lap. And while she was slowly turning them over, Nathan again noticed his Zippo lighter lying next to the radio, and casually pocketed it.

Phebe sighed, and the eyes beneath those long black eyebrows withdrew themselves from the manuscript's leaves for a moment to steal a glance at Nathan's face. "Would you like me to read some to you?" she asked him. Nathan met her gaze and, without a word, eagerly nodded his head. Then, after turning over several leaves and arriving at the passage she sought, Phebe began reading to Nathan, her face stooped low over the page:

> "*Juliet.* Thou knowest the mask of night is on my face,
> Else would a maiden blush bepaint my cheek
> For that which thou hast heard me speak to-night..."

And here Phebe raised her face, never ceasing in her recitation even for an instant: her beautiful eyes peering intently into Nathan's all the while. And as he sat listening to her recite the lines—each word beaming into his heart like a piercing ray—Nathan suddenly realized that the entire play was known to Phebe from memory.

And without turning a single parchment leaf, Phebe continued her recital:

> "Fain would I dwell on form, fain, fain deny
> What I have spoke, but farewell compliment!
> Dost thou love me? I know thou wilt say,
> "Ay," And I will take thy word; yet if thou swear'st,
> Thou mayest prove false..."

But here, quite suddenly, Phebe broke off. And her eyes, dark and motionless and steady in their regard, dwelt for some while upon Nathan's face. There was a deep hush. At length, she said, almost inaudibly, "Nathan."

He seemed lost in her eyes. "What?" he breathed.

Phebe sat quite still, her small, beautiful, solemn face full to Nathan's, and her large, dark, penetrating eyes so completely engrossed in gazing at him. "How much do you like me?" she asked.

Nathan stared at her mutely, until it seemed he was sinking, losing himself still further in the fathomless depths of those dark lustrous eyes of hers that were fixed so unswervingly upon his own. "Do you love me, Nathan?"

"Yes," came the scarce audible reply.

"Tell me. Let me hear you say it."

"I love you," Nathan breathed, as though he could say nothing more, but then added instantly: "more than life itself, Phebe, I love you."

"What if I asked you to prove your love for me?"

"How?"

"By killing someone. Would you do that?"

Nathan looked at Phebe, startled, intent. "Why?" he asked, striving in vain to hide his confusion and uneasiness.

Phebe gazed at him deeply; studied his face closely. "Would you do it? Would you kill for me, Nathan, if I asked you to?"

Nathan felt as though he were unable to either breathe or stir, for in the eyes regarding him, deep and dark, there seemed a starless night of endless darkness. Then, "I don't know," he managed at last to whisper across to her.

"Even if my life depended on it?"

"You mean, unless I took someone else's life, you'd lose yours?"

"Yes. Would you kill for me then?" Phebe asked him.

"Yeah... I guess I would. Why are you asking me this?"

Phebe stooped her head and lowered her lash-fringed lids. "Just curious," she replied softly, "that's all." And for a moment she raised stealthy eyes to Nathan's, and smiled faintly.

Then, soon after Phebe had commenced her declamation of the following lines from Shakespeare's immortal play—

"Art thou gone so, love, lord, ay, husband, friend!
I must hear from thee every day in the hour,
For in a minute there are many days.
O, by this count I shall be much in years
Ere I again behold my Romeo..."

—her dark solemn eyes were quite suddenly withdrawn from those of Nathan's, and her sweet, soft voice had abruptly fallen silent.

Nathan sat motionless for some seconds, watching Phebe's face. He observed how her nostrils began to quiver as though they caught the scent of something in the air. And then, at some faint rumor beyond the mausoleum's entrance, on whose doors her eyes had fastened themselves with steady stirless lids, it seemed to him as though every sinew in Phebe's supple body had suddenly stiffened. Instantly Nathan followed the direction of her gaze with his eyes. "Phebe, what is it?" he asked in a low, hushed voice.

And as Phebe placed the manuscript of parchment leaves down on the comforter, "Someone's coming," she said, and rose to her feet.

Nathan stood up beside her, his heart thumping at his ribs. "Who, Phebe; who's coming?" he whispered, his eyes still intent on the doors to the mausoleum's entrance. Beyond them a thin, pale luminous beam of light came stealing inwards, mingling for a moment with that of the lychnos-stone's effulgence. But then, just as suddenly and mysteriously, it withdrew.

Nathan and Phebe stood listening, peering together, as now that same thin beam of mysterious light, and now faint shadows, zig-zagged, alternately, across the narrow rift between the mausoleum's doors which gaped slightly open. And presently there followed the sound of a faint shuffling footfall just beyond their threshold.

Then, breathlessly, Nathan watched as one of the doors opened wider, slowly, cautiously, stealthily wider, until all at once the tall, lean figure of a man was revealed. He paused an instant in the entry, then stepped softly forward a pace or two full into the glare of Phebe's luminous stone. Nathan could see every feature of the man's astonished face with wonderful clarity.

Stooping a little, stiff and motionless, the man's eyes were bolting out of his face as they went restlessly shifting from Nathan's face to Phebe's, and back again.

For the breath of an instant, Nathan froze—aghast—to the tips of his fingers. He felt his heart stand still, and he scarcely dared to blink an eye or draw a breath: for all in a flash he had recognized with absolute certainty who the man was.

Powerless to withdraw his startled eyes from those of the man's, even for an instant, Nathan's lips suddenly parted in a low, small gasp and, faint as a breath, "Mr Schiller!" he said in a half-gulped whisper.

At the sound of Nathan's voice, the white-lashed lids over Mr Erwin Schiller's round wide eyes fluttered, and the outstretched hand, aiming before him the pale yellow beam of the flashlight he was carrying, slowly lowered itself. "Nathan, what are you doing here?" he demanded. "What sort of morbid rendezvous is this?" There was a short pause, and for a moment Nathan stared at Mr Schiller mute as a fish, not knowing what (or even how) to answer such a question. Then, "Does your aunt know you are here?" went on Mr Schiller. "Where is she, Nathan?"

But all of a sudden Phebe went stalking up to Mr Schiller, her gaze fastened upon his in a deadly, menacing glare. "Nathan, what madness is this? Why are you here? And who is this girl?" Mr Schiller continued to demand, as he shrank steadily backward away from Phebe until he was pressed up, skin-close, against the mausoleum wall. Phebe, meanwhile, had followed him and, leaning her up-tilted face in towards him, her lips drew back, with an awful snarl, to reveal a row of sharp, pointed teeth.

Shuddering uncontrollably, Mr Schiller opened his mouth to cry out with a loud scream. But from the instant he had glanced into the luminous, smoldering pupils of Phebe's eyes—which seemed to brim with intense power and darkness—it was as though his very will were caught in a snare. And an appalling helplessness whelmed suddenly over him, both mentally and physically. Moreover, he felt a chill, death-like motionlessness spread itself throughout his limbs, and the heart within him turned cold and leaden.

An instant later, Mr Schiller felt (and heard) the flashlight drop from the loosened grip of his palsied hand. And presently, strive all he would to turn, bend, or flee, he found himself utterly powerless to stir so much as a finger. Unable to do aught else but stand there and continue to gaze deeply, helplessly into the cruel, stony darkness of Phebe's eyes, the expression of Mr Schiller's face became one of unutterable terror. For he now knew, had realized all in an instant, who— and *what*—Phebe was! "The crows; the ravens... the rats!" he said, nearly choking with horror. "It was you... your coming they portended!"

"Yes!" said Phebe, in such a voice that it caused even Nathan to feel a cold terror creeping over his skin. "Ravens, crows, and rats—they are all messengers, harbingers of death. And from of old, were they to be seen gathering in great numbers in or near a town or village, it was always regarded as an ill-omen, and the tell-tale sign that a vampire had arrived, or was about to arrive in the region." And as Phebe drew back her head in preparation to sinking her teeth into the flesh of Mr Schiller's throat, Nathan darted to her side, pleading with her: "No! Please, Phebe... please don't hurt him."

Phebe seemed to hesitate. The eyes in her head rolled furiously. But, after confronting those of Nathan's for the merest instant, she relented and, almost grudgingly, turned her face aside with a dreadful snarl. Mr Schiller's life had been spared—at least for the meantime.

Now, from the moment Phebe had withdrawn her gaze, releasing Mr Schiller from the mastery of her eyes, he began slowly to regain some possession of himself. He tried to speak, but the mere formation of words, even the most elementary sounds of speech, demanded a great effort, for the very wits in his head seemed as yet deadened and benumbed as by some soporific drug.

Nathan stood before his unfortunate old neighbor, and gazed up into his face sorrowfully. "Mr Schiller, why did you come here?" he asked, his voice hushed and faintly unsteady.

Mr Schiller appeared to labor for breath. Once or twice he opened his mouth with a half-choked sob, and almost it seemed to Nathan that the man was struggling to make his tongue form words: for his lips began to writhe and his jaws to move jerkily.

And then, after the sudden intake of a long, shuddering breath, "I... I f-followed... you;" Mr Schiller managed to stammer at last; "I f-feared that you m-might be suffering... afflicted with a certain condition... a disorder of the mind... lycanthropy..."

At this, Phebe suddenly advanced a pace or two towards Mr Schiller, uttering slowly, deliberately, forbiddingly: "As your prying, meddlesome nature has now proven to be your own undoing, so too by your own foolish notions you have proclaimed your own doom!"

"No; please, Phebe—don't!" cried Nathan, attempting to intervene. But Phebe thrust out an arm and stayed him. "Don't try to save him, Nathan;" she said, her voice assuming a tone of awful command; "he forfeited his life from the moment he followed you into the cemetery"—then, fixing her eyes piercingly on Mr Schiller—"You will no longer concern yourself with Nathan: with his aunt: with this place! Do you understand?"

And as Mr Schiller stood there quivering in terror, whimpering like a child, his eyes full of tears, Nathan, for the next moment or two, stood there contemplating the extraordinary change that had come suddenly over Phebe. Almost in the same instant there had drifted up into remembrance the Phebe he had seen that night in the cemetery when Russell Gorman and the other boys had come there to hurt him. And he knew at once that this was again that other Phebe—the very one which had crept in through Aunt Amelia's bedroom window the night of August 11th and slaughtered her in bed! That same cruel, pitiless, bloodthirsty Phebe who had taken Russell Gorman by the throat and throttled him like a stuffed doll. The malevolent, vampiric Phebe whose mere baleful glance and crushing iron grip were enough to cause a man's heart to fall dead-still within his body, and his strength to wither instantly away. And yet, only moments ago, when the two of them had kissed, Nathan thought he had felt Phebe's slender body trembling in his arms.

But then, with a sudden start, Nathan came out of these reflections at the intensely chilling tone in Phebe's voice, as he heard her speaking to Mr Schiller: "Take upon you my curse: a curse as decreed by your own tongue! For it is you who shall now suffer from this disorder; you yourself who shall now be afflicted with the condition of... lycanthropy!"

Nathan wanted once more to intervene on behalf of Mr Schiller, and plead with Phebe to let him go unharmed; but the lips and tongue of his mouth were so dry that he could scarcely utter a single word. Moreover, some strange, opposing influence kept him inexplicably rooted to the spot, cowed and speechless: helplessly looking on—unable to do otherwise.

And so, Nathan watched, almost in some state of morbid fascination, as Phebe stooped to the floor of the mausoleum. Across its stone surface he saw her lightly sweep the long fingers of her hand, to collect on their tips a thin film of dust. Then, mumbling very softly a series of words which Nathan could not hear, she spat into her hand and pressed the dust into her spittle, until she had made of it a fine, greyish-colored paste. This she then smeared on the forehead of Mr Schiller, so that it appeared as though he had been marked with the faint streak of ashes one receives at Mass on Ash Wednesday. And into this ash-like smudge upon his brow,

Phebe traced, in minute letters, with the point of her finger nail, the following word: 'versipellis'.

Then, breathing three times into Mr Schiller's stricken face, Phebe recited as many times a sequence of words which, though utterly unfamiliar to Nathan, he thought sounded like – 'fieri (he missed the next word or two) virlupus...' The meaning of the second element in this last word, Nathan was almost sure he knew. That which preceded it, he did not pretend for a moment to be familiar with: but 'lupus' he was quite certain meant 'wolf'.

In the midst of these very shrewd deductions, Nathan observed that the moment Phebe had ceased to pronounce those mysterious words for the third and final time, Mr Schiller's face instantly contorted, taking on a ghastliness of expression. At the same time, he opened wide his mouth to emit a prolonged and harrowing wail, as if he had been pierced through the heart by the envenomed blade of an invisible knife. And for a moment or two after, his entire body very suddenly and violently convulsed, as though a horrible shivering dread had swept icily through its every fiber.

With tortured mind and aching heart, Nathan continued to gaze on helplessly at Mr Schiller, an agonized look of pity welling into his eyes. He wanted desperately to save him. And yet he dared not challenge Phebe's will in this: that would entail turning against her in order to protect or deliver Mr Schiller from a doom already ordained for him to suffer. Besides, his love for, and his loyalty to, Phebe prevented him from considering even for another moment such a reckless course of action.

It was too late anyway, Nathan realized. Mr Schiller's fate was irrevocably sealed. For Phebe had marked him with some sort of occult symbol or token: and whatever kind of infernal spell, power, or purpose lay couched in its formulation, its sorceries were already in operation.

For even as Nathan continued to look at Mr Schiller, a sort of thin, faint, gauze-like veil seemed to spread itself over his face. And for the merest instant, Nathan thought he could distinguish—cruel, inhuman, and immensely savage—the phantom features of some monstrous fang-toothed beast peering out at him through the quivering, wraith-like transparency of Mr Schiller's countenance. But in the very next moment that Nathan blinked his astonished eyes, that horrifying bestial image had instantly dissolved, and the outlines of Mr Schiller's face had once more assumed their usual distinctness and tangibility.

And then, without realizing it, for the next few moments, Nathan must have slipped into a kind of confused waking dream as he stood there ruminating, in doubt and shock, on the thing he had just seen. For all at once, half-starting out of this trancelike state, he heard once more the sound of Phebe's voice, its tone as yet stern and sinister with fearful command.

Turning his head, Nathan's eyes fixed themselves on Phebe's face as she said to Mr Schiller: "Go now! Go from here, and never return to this place. Remember nothing of this night, or what happened to you here. Do you understand?" And Nathan heard Mr Schiller, in a kind of mesmerized emptiness and obedience, reply: "Yes... I... understand." Nathan noted, too, that Mr Schiller's widely opened eyes stared dazed and glassily before him, as though gazing into the distance at something mistily far-off.

"Now go! Go from here at once!" Phebe commanded, pointing towards the doors. And then, with his shoulders slightly stooped, and both his arms dangling limply at his sides, Mr Schiller advanced, like a sleepwalker, towards the mausoleum's entry. And as he went shambling unsteadily across the threshold of the entrance and disappeared beyond its doors, Nathan thought he heard some senseless gibber that Mr Schiller's lips were faintly babbling: something or other about having to change not only his skin, but his shape as well. It was the last time that he and Mr Schiller would ever meet again.

Nathan continued to stand there still and silent. Then, Phebe's lean, cold hand had stolen into his, and she drew him down beside her on the comforter. And as she proceeded to gather the parchment leaves once again into her lap, Nathan very faintly asked, "What did you do to him?"

"You should have let me drink his blood," answered Phebe, with a little frown, as she continued to turn over the parchment leaves. "It would have been better that way."

For some seconds, Nathan stared at Phebe in startled silence; for her words had in them an undertone that was terribly dark and sinister: something which Nathan was all but certain Phebe had intended. Then, "Why?" he asked, faintly. "What will happen to him? Will he die?"

Phebe lifted her eyes from the manuscript in her lap and, for some while, watched Nathan's face in silence. Then, frowning again, she said, "We all die... someday."

And as Nathan sat there, vaguely listening to Phebe declaim line after line by rote from Shakespeare's tragic romance, he kept wondering to himself about poor old Mr Schiller, and the dark fate he was now bound to endure.

This concludes the second book of the story of Nathan and Phebe.

The third book, **The Incunabulum** part three: *Revelations*, tells of Mr Schiller's gradual transformation into a gruesome "werewolf", and his wife's discovery of his ghoulish activities in the neighboring cemeteries; as well as Nathan's discoveries of Marty Carbone's cursed condition, and the ghastly crimes he has been perpetrating on area residents.

The fourth and last book, **The Incunabulum** part four: *Consummation*, tells of Antal Vrancic's discovery of the incunabulum on the private estate of a wealthy financier on Long Island, and the desperate mission of Nathan and Phebe to steal into the palatial mansion to retrieve the ancient tome and use the spell preserved within its pages to undo Phebe's curse.

CPSIA information can be obtained
at www.ICGtesting.com
Printed in the USA
BVHW070228261218
536360BV00001B/8/P

9 781643 982588